LOVING THE *sinner*

DAISY WREN

Cover design by Brit at The Author Experience

Formatting by Brit at The Author Experience

For rights and permissions, please contact:

daisywren.author@gmail.com

Paperback ISBN: 9798991718912

This book is for all the people who recognize the phrase
"Where will you go?"
The answer to that question is anywhere you want!
There is life after leaving a high demand religion, and it's
beautiful.

AUTHOR'S NOTE

This book discusses topics such as drug use (not on page), religious trauma, death (not on page), mental health and emotional manipulation/abuse. Some of these topics may be triggering for some readers, and reader discretion is advised.

This book also has explicit sex scenes that are not suitable for people under the age of eighteen.

LOVING THE *sinner* PLAYLIST

"Lovebug" by The Jonas Brothers
"Jessie's Girl" by Rick Springfield
"Angel" by Aerosmith
"Hooked On A Feeling" by Blue Swede, Björn Skifs
"But Daddy I Love Him" by Taylor Swift
"Can't Fight The Moonlight" by LeAnn Rimes
"Burnin' for You" by Blue Öyster Cult
"Forever" by Noah Kahan
"Before You" by Benson Boone
"Someone To You" by BANNERS
"Bad Medicine" by Bon Jovi
"I Want You to Want Me" by Cheap Trick
"Ours (Taylor's Version)" by Taylor Swift
"Bad Case of Loving You (Doctor, Doctor)" by Robert Palmer

PROLOGUE

Elli

Hot, fat tears are streaming down my face so quickly I can't keep up with the onslaught.

Packer Boyd Nelson and Tiffany Lorraine Keyes are excited to announce their union for time and all eternity...

I throw the announcement into the trash, where it belongs. The *audacity* of him to send me an invitation to his wedding.

I shouldn't be surprised. Packer never seemed fully invested in our relationship. He wasn't a good boyfriend and he would have been a worse husband. But to see he's getting married *two months* after he broke up with me because he "wasn't ready for a serious relationship" hurts.

A lot.

Never mind the fact we were together for six months. Six months where I tried everything to be the type of girl he wanted. Six months where I was someone I wasn't, all in the name of "following the right path." Six months where I was belittled and told I still wasn't doing enough for him.

I'm twenty-four and unmarried, which is basically spinster age when you're Mormon.

It also feels like a big old slap in the face to my already low self-esteem. *Tiffany* looks as if she's barely graduated from high school. Bleach blonde hair, big blue doe eyes, petite, slim, tan, and with a blinding white smile.

Every man's dream.

I look in the mirror at my shoulder length boring, plain, brown hair, my oval shaped face, dull blue eyes, and my not-so-slim figure.

I'll never compare to her. I wasn't even in the running.

Something I'm sure my mother will use to hurt me as soon as she finds out. I can already hear her now.

"If you would have worked harder to lose weight, maybe you could have kept him."

"If you hadn't focused so much on school, maybe you'd be married by now."

"If you had more faith, maybe he wouldn't have left you."

"Maybe if you weren't so boring..."

The list goes on. I've never been the daughter she wanted. She always wanted a son first, but you can't pick the gender of your first child. She blames me for the fact it took her five years to conceive my little brother, Spencer. She said I "ruined" her womb. She hates the fact that I'm not blonde like her and Izzy. She hates that I take after my dad's German ancestry and have a plus-sized body. She hates that I wanted to go to school instead of immediately getting married and having a baby.

I honestly think she just hates me, but she'd never admit it.

If I'm boring, it's because I was told I was being "too much" as a child. I was to be seen, not heard. When Spencer was born, I was immediately pushed into a caretaker role, so I was never able to actually be a child. I didn't go out and play with my friends all the time. I read in my room alone until I was told I needed to come take care of my siblings.

The itch to up and leave Utah without telling anyone where I'm going is so strong, I almost do it. I eye the duffel bag peeking out from underneath my bed, calculating the best time to sneak out of the house and never return.

I could do it. I have the money. I've been putting every penny I can spare away into savings so I can get the heck out of here someday.

But where will I go?

Emma's in California... Maybe I could go live with her?

No, she's got her own life, she doesn't need her boring cousin bringing her down.

Oregon? No. Too expensive.

Arizona? No, too hot.

Izzy comes barreling through the door, chattering away on her phone, completely unaware of the internal crisis I've got going on. Which isn't her fault, I keep my thoughts to myself for the most part not wanting to be a burden to anyone.

I know instantly she's talking to her long distance boyfriend, Luke. I can practically see the hearts coming out of her eyes.

What a loser you are when even your seventeen year old sister has a boyfriend and you don't.

"I know Lukey." She coos, "I just don't think my parents would ever let me come visit Texas by myself. You know I would come in a heartbeat, but they'd never go for that." She turns her blue eyes on me, and I try not to flinch at how similar she looks to Packer's new child bride. Though Izzy's hair is naturally light blonde, not dyed, and her body is the result of endless theater performances, not a strict workout regimen and diet. They're literally like a year apart though, and that's...disconcerting to say the least.

My stomach turns and I suppress the urge to gag thinking about Izzy marrying someone my age after she graduates.

Thank goodness Luke is the same age as her.

But her conversation gets me thinking. Texas is a good distance from Utah...

What was the name of the city Luke lives in?

San...something.

I pull out my phone and do a quick Google search and find it.

San Marcos, Texas.

It's a quaint little city. A quick rental search shows I can get a one bedroom apartment for a reasonable price.

The gears start turning and a plan starts forming immediately, as if it's been in the back of my head waiting patiently for me to acknowledge it.

If I move to Texas, it gets me away from my overbearing parents, from the toxic Utah culture, and Izzy can come visit her boyfriend more since I'll be there to "supervise."

Maybe I'll even meet a cute cowboy who'll like my curves and extra bits. We'll fall in love and get married and live happily ever after.

Yeah right.

If I wait until Izzy's done with school in June, she can drive out with me and see Luke for a while before she starts her summer activities, plus it gives me about five months to secure a place to live and plan thoroughly, rather than tossing my stuff into a duffle bag and hoping for the best.

Is this idea kind of crazy?

Probably.

But I deserve to live a little crazy.

Looks like I'm going to need a cowboy hat.

CHAPTER I

Wes

T here are only three reasons why someone should be banging on my door at 7:43 on a Saturday morning.

One, Maya Hawke has come to profess her undying love for me and is offering me a spot on her next tour.

Two, I won a lottery I didn't know I entered and someone is bringing me a million dollars.

Three, someone is dying.

Crossing my fingers that it's one of the first two, I begrudgingly roll out of bed, quickly swiping at my phone to see if there are any urgent messages. When I find my notifications empty, I groan as I drag my half-naked ass to the door. Whoever it is better not complain about my lack of clothes, considering *they* are interrupting my beauty rest.

As soon as I open the door I'm greeted by a familiar fidgeting boy with a mass of curly brown hair and big brown eyes.

Luke.

Panic sets in immediately because Luke *always* calls or texts when he comes over, and he's never contacted me before ten o'clock on a Saturday.

"Luke. What's wrong?" I demand as he shoves his way into my apartment, nervously pacing in the small living room.

"I'm sorry it's early and I didn't text or call, but I need a favor." He mutters, looking down at his feet.

My anxiety increases the more I wait for him to explain. "Well? Spit it out, man!"

"Sorry." He clears his throat and finally meets my eyes. "You know my girlfriend, Izzy?" I nod, "Well, her sister is moving to San Marcos and Izzy was able to convince her parents to let her come visit. We have a date tonight."

My panic morphs into relief that no one's dying, then immediately changes to irritation because I realize this isn't a life or death situation. "And what does that have to do with me?" I ask, already skeptical.

"They're Mormon." He says plainly. I give him a questioning look and he rolls his eyes. "Her parents have a rule about dating, and since she's not eighteen, she can't be alone with me." I can hear the exasperation in his tone, this is obviously a sensitive topic for him. "And she doesn't want her sister to be all alone while she chaperones, especially on the first night in a new place, you know? And it would be really good for her to make friends since she'll be living here. I told Iz that I would ask Matt to come, but he has an emergency work thing tonight, so I was hoping that *you* would come?"

I don't know much about Mormons, but the women from the religion sound like prissy, holier-than-thou, entitled brats. I don't know Luke's girlfriend, but I'd assume she's not that way if Luke's dating her.

"You walked your ass all the way here, banging on my door at an ungodly hour on a Saturday, to ask me to help babysit you and your girlfriend? This could have been a text, Lukas." He hates when I use his full name, but I feel the situation warrants it.

"First of all, Mom's not at work yet so I drove. Second, if I had texted you, you would have said no without even hearing me out. Third, I haven't seen Izzy in person in a year, *please* Wes. For me?" Luke pleads, placing his hands together in a prayer motion. It would be funny if he didn't look so damn earnest.

"Luke," I groan, "you know I haven't really gone out with anyone since Shelby. I don't really want to go out with a complete stranger on my first date in over two years. Let alone one who will probably keel over the second she sees me. No way am I her type."

I've had the "bad boy" label for as long as I can remember. I've never so much as littered, let alone anything worse than that- unless you count defending myself when other people start fights- but people take one look at a tattooed, long haired, ripped jeans- metal band tee-wearing guy with a nose ring and ear piercings and automatically assume the worst.

As a kid, that label was given to me because I came to school with unkempt hair, raggedy clothes, and bruises courtesy of Kieth, the asshole my mom was with from ages nine to thirteen. I had to steal lunch because I couldn't afford to pay for it, and we didn't have food at home for me to bring to school. No one bothered to ask about it, they just assumed I was a bad kid who got into fights and had a stealing problem. The other kids would pick on me for being poor, for having a drug addict mom, for not liking sports, or for "smelling weird." Some took it a step further than throwing insults my way and started throwing fists. What was I supposed to do except fight back? Everyone was quick to blame the poor, addict's kid, so I just accepted that that was the way everyone saw me. I kept to myself as best I could, and I didn't have any friends until high school.

When I was in college, I leaned into the bad boy act. I drank a lot, got into a lot of fights, and fucked my way through the student body. I found that a lot of girls wanted to blow off steam with a quick hookup with the bad boy. After a few meaningless hookups though, I felt shitty and unfulfilled. I didn't want to be a check mark on a bucket list anymore, I wanted a connection.

The issue was I had already gained a reputation, and girls thought that it would be a fun challenge to see who could "fix" me. Rarely did any of them want to get to know *me,* they just wanted to be the one to "tame" me. If they weren't trying to fix me, they were too scared to talk to me because of my reputation or my looks.

"I'm not asking you to go steady with her or whatever. I just want you to keep her company so I can spend time with my girlfriend. Please Wes, I'll do anything." Luke literally on his knees begging is something I've never seen. The kid's pride is astronomical, so this must be extremely important for him.

After my mom passed away when I was fourteen, my grandma took me in. Then she died when I was seventeen, and Luke's mom basically adopted me. Jessica and my mom were basically sisters so when my grams passed and I had no one else, Jess didn't hesitate. Luke was ten at the time, and Jess worked a lot, so I spent a lot of time looking after him and he became the little brother I never had. Some of Luke's friends have siblings my age, and somehow we became one big happy mismatched found family. They're the closest thing to an actual family I've got, and I would do anything for them.

I protect the people I love fiercely because I've lost so many people already.

"Fine. But you owe me, big time." I relent, hoping this doesn't go poorly.

"Thank you, thank you, thank you Wes!" Luke tackles me in a hug, and I realize just how tall and strong he's gotten.

Gone is the baby-faced little boy. He's almost a man, and that makes my heart ache a little bit.

"We're picking them up from her place at five so come get me at four forty-five. Don't be late. And try to look less...grumpy. Elliana's not like the girls you're used to." He says.

Elliana.

Even her name sounds prissy.

"Yeah yeah. I'll be there. What exactly do you have planned?"

Luke tells me about his "romantic" date: a night at the arcade. I guess it is romantic for a seventeen year old, but I don't know what *Elliana* and I are going to do. I hate the arcade. It's sticky and loud. I guess loud wouldn't be bad because then I don't have to try to make small talk with *Elliana* as much, but I don't know if that's worth the headache of the crowd.

When Luke leaves just before nine, I really just want to go back to sleep, but I'm too awake now. I sit down on the floor with my trusty acoustic guitar, who I have affectionately named Dolly after the queen herself-Dolly Parton. I tune her, then open my notebook to jot down chords and lyrics as they come, but the same thing that's happened for the last six months happens.

Which is nothing.

No lyrics.

No melodies.

No inspiration.

This is the worst block I've had in a long time, it's like all of my creativity and inspiration is just gone, and with summer gigs starting I really need to get my shit together so I'm not replaying the same covers and old songs over and over.

I used to have music playing in my head constantly. Whether it's a song from my childhood that I used to blast in my headphones, or a new song idea, my head was never empty.

I thought at first it was my anxiety medication dulling my creativity, but I've been on that for years and the music left six months ago. Just vanished one day and hasn't returned.

I let the Instagram notification that pops up distract me, Robin has tagged me in some giveaway for some abstract art piece she wants, so nothing important. I see Luke's story counting down the literal seconds until he sees Izzy again. I roll my eyes at the sappiness. I click on Izzy's profile, curious to see if she has any pictures of *Elliana,* so I know who I'm meeting tonight. I see that Izzy posted a picture yesterday of her at a "Welcome to

Texas" sign, and to my luck, she's tagged none other than *Elliana* herself.

Her profile doesn't have a bio, and a quick scroll through shows there's about a six month gap of posts, which is strange since she posts at least every two weeks before that. Her latest post is of her and her parents, making a joke about moving. They don't look happy, don't look sad, just kind of... annoyed. Or indifferent.

There are hardly any pictures of *her*. It's mostly pictures of family or scenery, the occasional book. The pictures she's in show her in dresses, hair curled to perfection, and meticulously posed for the camera-prissy and stuck up, just like I thought. Although her smile doesn't quite seem to reach her perfectly lined eyes. I'll admit, she is kind of pretty.

But so was Shelby and that didn't make her a good person.

I'm tempted to go to Facebook and look her up, see if there's any information there-just so I'm prepared for tonight- but I get a text before I can do anything.

Robs: Breakfast? Ernie's? 30?

Wes: See you then.

I can't say no to Ernie's. Or Robin.

Thirty minutes later, after a quick shower, I'm in our usual booth at Ernie's- a little cafe that has hosted many study sessions, hangover breakfasts, and celebrations the last few years. It's familiar and cozy and Claudia and Ernie -the owners- are the adoptive grandparents I never knew I needed. They helped me earn money for a guitar and have always supported my music career. They're my first fans, and I owe them everything.

While placing our drink order-coffee, black for me--the only kind I'll drink black is Claudia's--, and an iced vanilla latte with oat milk for Robin- I hear the bell ding at the door and turn in time to see my clumsy, redheaded best friend trip over the welcome mat, a loud squeak coming from her as she lands and the contents of her bag spill all over the floor.

"Christ Robs, are you okay?" I rush over to her, helping grab the random contents strewn all over the floor.

"Other than a bruised ego and possible bruised knees, I'm good." She grumbles as she stands and snatches the tampons and pack of gum from my hands.

Claudia rushes over like a mother hen, "Dang nabbit Red, you gotta be more careful! Are you okay, honey? Do you need any ice for your knees?"

Robin's face flushes at Claudia's attention. "No, thank you Claudia. I'm alright."

"Alrighty then. I'll be at your booth in a minute with your drinks." Claudia shuffles back to the kitchen.

"Well I know how much you love gossip. I have the perfect thing to take your mind off of it." I say as we slide into opposite sides of our booth.

Claudia comes with our drinks giving Robs a gentle squeeze on her shoulder. "The usual for you two?"

"Yes, please." Robs replies sweetly. As soon as Claudia turns away, Robs raises an inquisitive eyebrow in my direction. "Spill, Wessy."

God I hate when she calls me that, but she does, no matter how many times I tell her to stop.

"Luke's girlfriend is visiting for a few days. Her sister is moving here, so they're going on a date toni-"

"The one from summer camp? That's so exciting! He must be thrilled." She cuts in. Robin has this thing where she *has* to say something as soon as she thinks. I'm pretty sure she has undiagnosed ADHD, but she refuses to get tested.

"Yeah, her. That's not even the best part. I'm going with him, on a semi-date thing, with her sister. As a chaperone or something."

"Shut up!" Robs blurts out, then at a more normal volume, she continues, "Isn't-oh, what's her name? Lizzy?- She's Mormon right? So her sister probably is too. What's her sister's name? Why is she moving here? Why didn't he ask Matt?"

"Izzy is her name, yes, they're Mormon. He did ask Matt, but he has a work thing. Her name is Elliana. I don't know why she's moving here, her Instagram doesn't give away much, and Luke didn't provide any additional information."

Robin nods, taking in the information. Then, a knowing smile spreads across her freckled face, her hazel eyes glimmering with mischief. "So, you've already Insta stalked her? Is she pretty?"

I scoff, "It's not stalking if her profile is public. I just wanted to see who I was going out with. You know what's weird, though? She has like a six month gap where there are no posts. Suspicious."

Robs chokes on her drink as she snorts, "Why does that matter? Sometimes people take social media breaks or whatever. You're being awfully judgy, Westley."

"I guess that's true, but she posted pretty regularly before that. I'm not trying to be judgy, I'm just trying to get all the facts."

"Here you go, kids. Belgian waffles with strawberries and whip cream for Red, biscuits and gravy, eggs over-easy for the rockstar." Claudia sets down our plates.

"Thanks Claudia." Robs and I say at the same time.

There's a comfortable silence while we eat, which is both nice and concerning because Robin usually never stops talking. Maybe she knows I need to process everything so she's giving me the space to do that?

When I first met her, it was right before my grams died. We had a ceramics class together junior year, and she was the new kid so she didn't know my reputation. Luckily, she never cared about it when she found out. I immediately fell head over heels for the quirky, boisterous, enthusiastic redhead, and asked her to prom. She said yes, and during the last slow song I asked if she'd go out with me. She laughed in my face, thinking I was joking, but when she saw the confused look on my face she apologized and explained that she's a lesbian. Apparently, she thought I knew.

I had no idea. Which was humiliating. I thought I'd lose her as a friend.

We got over that awkward moment pretty quickly, though and we've been best friends ever since. She's been through some of my lowest of lows with me, and I wouldn't trade our friendship for anything.

Robs is scrolling on her phone while we eat, which would bother me with anyone else, but she's a social media manager for an art gallery in San Antonio, so she's probably just working since there's a big exhibit coming up. When she sighs and puts her phone down, I give her a puzzled look.

"You avoided my question, so I had to answer it myself. She's pretty, though not your usual type. How do you think tonight will go?"

"Okay, fine. She's pretty in a 'goes to church every Sunday and always looks put together' way, I guess. How about I treat you to coffee in the morning and I'll let you know if we even make it through the date?" I mumble as I gulp down my now lukewarm coffee and toss a twenty dollar bill on the table. "I have some errands to run, I'll see you tomorrow."

"Good luck, Wessy boy. Don't do anything I wouldn't do." Robs says, wiggling her eyebrows suggestively.

I flip her off as I walk out of the diner.

Now it's time to mentally prepare for my first date-that-isn't-really-a-date in two years.

CHAPTER 2

Elli

What's that saying about God laughing when you make a plan? Well, that's how my life feels right now- scratch that- the last year. The jury's still out on whether or not God is real, but if He is, He's getting some good laughs in at my expense.

I've had my life mapped out for me ever since I could remember. I've always been told what to do in what order, and they were the only goals I was taught to have.

One: Graduate high school

Two: Go to college, boys like an educated woman. (But not *too* educated. Don't be smarter than the boys.)

Three: Meet a boy and get married in the temple

Four: Start a family ASAP

If I had to drop out of college to be a full-time mom? Well, that was just God's plan.

But when I turned twenty-four and my boyfriend of six months still hadn't proposed, obviously there was something wrong with *me*. It couldn't have been God's plan to be unwed at my age.

I've scrimped and saved every penny I could for the last four years in preparation for a life altering event. I just figured it would be a wedding. So eight months ago when my ex broke things off with me, I decided to take control of my life.

Did I think I'd end up moving to Texas because of my sister? Absolutely not. But the idea stuck with me, and when I mentioned it to Izzy, she was totally on board and helped me plan it all out.

Izzy met Luke last summer at a theater camp in St. George, Utah and it was, according to her, "love at first sight." They've been dating long distance ever since, much to the chagrin of my parents who don't necessarily approve of their relationship. They've made it work with daily FaceTime sessions, late night phone calls, and good old fashioned letters. Luke even sends Izzy flowers randomly.

It's sickly sweet and it makes me want to throw up sometimes, but Izzy is the happiest I've ever seen her. I'd never tell her I'm jealous, but I'd be lying if I said I wasn't. I never had relationships in high school since I spent most of my time doing homework for AP and Concurrent Enrollment classes, as well as taking care of my siblings.

I went on dates, sure, but no one ever saw me as more than a friend. I think most of the time I was just the "in between" date so boys could go on another date with the girl they *actually* liked without it looking too serious.

Let me elaborate. If you grow up Mormon, you're often taught you can't exclusively date someone until you're eighteen and "marriage ready." So you go on a date with the person you *want* to date, but then you go on "filler" dates with friends or people you don't actually like romantically so you can continue to date the other person.

It's stupid, but a rule, nonetheless.

In college, I tried to get through as many credit hours as I could in case I met "the one" and ended up getting married and then pregnant. I graduated with my B.A. in three years in preparation to get married, but it never worked out.

I've only had two serious boyfriends, and they never showed a fraction of the same amount of affection Luke shows Izzy.

San Marcos seems like a nice place to live, though, so I can't be upset at my decision. I found a cute little seven hundred square foot, one bedroom apartment that costs less than a single room goes for in Provo.

The apartment may be small, but it's the first space that'll actually be *mine*.

Izzy and I are currently on our way back from IKEA with the trunk of my 2010 Subaru Forester filled to capacity with shelves, a coffee table, bar stools, a bed frame, a desk, and a nightstand. Before IKEA, we went to a local discount furniture store and bought an L-shaped couch that seats about four people-and pulls out into a bed, a chair for my desk, and a big, oversized reading chair. The store was nice enough to offer free same-day delivery, so my apartment will be fully furnished by the end of next week! The only thing I'm missing is a TV, but considering I have my laptop, I'm willing to survive without it.

Izzy is buzzing with excited energy because tonight is the first real date her and Luke are going on, and the first time they'll see each other in person in almost a year.

"Promise me you'll be nice to Luke. And don't embarrass me. Or act like you're my mom. I'm seventeen, not ten." Izzy says for what feels like the thousandth time today.

I roll my eyes. "I know, Iz. I promise to be nice. I'm not going to follow you the whole time and measure the distance between you two with a Book of Mormon. I'm only going because Mom would kick my butt if I let you go anywhere alone."

"True. She would know, too. She always knows." Izzy gets a distant look in her eyes and shudders, probably thinking about the time Mom found out Izzy kissed Marcus Boller behind the park bathroom when she was fourteen, even though literally no one else knew, and my mom gave her a lecture on being a "proper" lady. Then she turns to me, "You're not going to make me put these together today, are you?"

"No, Izzy. I would never dream of making you do manual labor hours before your date. I know how long it takes you to get ready." I tease, lightly pushing her shoulder. Izzy is one of the only people I feel comfortable teasing and being silly with. Maybe it's because we've shared a room since she was two and it's hard to hide yourself from someone in such close quarters.

Izzy raises her chin proudly and says in a bad British accent, "Beauty takes time, darling."

We giggle, then Izzy jumps right into discussing the plan for tonight. Which she doesn't actually know because Luke wanted it to be a surprise. Unfortunately for me, Luke's friend Matt is joining us. Izzy refused to let me be a "sad third wheel" and insisted I have company.

I had to double check that Matt was indeed an adult and not a teenager, and *then* I had to ask why a twenty-four year old was friends with a seventeen year old. Luckily it's because Luke's friends have siblings that are friends with Matt, so they all hang out sometimes, and it's not a creepy reason.

I would have been fine bringing a book to read and letting them do their thing. The last thing I want right now is a boy to deal with, but Izzy insisted.

If he's a hot cowboy though... maybe I'd be okay with it.

As soon as we get back to the apartment and unload our haul, Izzy immediately dumps her clothes on my floor mattress in search of the perfect outfit. I reassure her that she could wear a burlap sack and Luke would go weak in the knees, but she scoffs and keeps rummaging through her clothes.

"What are *you* going to wear?" Izzy calls over her shoulder.

I glance down at my bike shorts and oversized t-shirt. "Um, this?"

Izzy turns to me and her face twists in disgust as she shakes her head. "No. Absolutely not. You're not about to go on a date looking like you just spent the day running errands." She abandons her own clothes to rifle through mine.

"I *did* spend the day running errands." I grumble. "Besides, it's not really a date. He's only coming because you and Luke didn't want me to be a third wheel."

"That doesn't mean you shouldn't dress to impress. Maybe he'll be *the one*." She wiggles her eyebrows and holds up a blue t-shirt dress. "This is comfy and casual, plus, it'll make your eyes pop."

"Fine. But I'm wearing my converse. Does that suffice, fashion police?"

Izzy rolls her eyes but gives me a nod of approval.

She decides on a sundress that *barely* meets the standard of modesty ingrained in us growing up-not that I'm going to, or *could* enforce it. It's cap sleeve, flowy, and comes barely two inches above her knee. It's a light sage that makes her already tan skin look even more tan, and surprisingly makes her electric blue eyes pop. She spends an hour curling her bright blonde locks to perfection and making sure her makeup is flawless.

Me? I toss my hair into two Dutch braids, throw on a coat of mascara, and call it a day. I spent too much time growing up trying to fit in with everyone else in my community by spending hours getting ready, just to feel inferior anyway. Plus, we've been traveling for two days and I'm exhausted.

And it's not a real date.

The differences between me and Izzy could not be more apparent. Izzy is all blonde and bubbly and I'm brunette and... boring. My mother has never explicitly said she's disappointed in how I look or who I am, but it's always been implied.

Glancing at the clock, it reads **5:05** and I scoff, irritated that the boys are running late because Izzy's about to wear a hole in my carpet from all of her pacing. She's chewing her lip anxiously, but right as I'm about to suggest she give Luke a call, there's a knock at the door.

Izzy's eyes light up as she rushes to the door and flings it open.

"Izzy-kins!" Luke shouts, holding his arms open for her.

"Lukey-poo!" Izzy squeals, jumping into him.

"I missed you so much. I'm so happy you're here." Luke rubs his nose against Izzy's––*gross*–– and I clear my throat, hoping to stop this PDA train before it runs further. "Hi Elliana. Nice to finally meet you in person." He extends his hand to me, looking completely unapologetic at their display of affection.

"Please, call me Elli. It's nice to meet you too, Luke." I shake his hand with a smile. "You two head to the car, I'm just going to make sure everything is locked up and I'll meet you out there."

They don't answer verbally, too busy making heart eyes at each other.

Izzy pulls Luke from the apartment while I take a few breaths to gain my composure.

I hate dating. I hate first dates. I hate meeting strangers. I don't know what Matt knows about me already, but I'm always afraid I won't live up to other people's expectations. I'm not thin, I'm not outrageously smart or witty, and I don't have a lot of romantic experience.

Once I turn from locking my front door, I stop in my tracks as I take in the man leaning against the black Honda Civic Luke and Elli are sitting in, chattering away with each other. He's looking down at his phone, so his long, wavy, jet black hair falls in front of his face. He's tall, probably six feet, and lean. He's dressed all in black.

Black t-shirt with some band on it, black jeans with rips in the knees, and black boots.

In this Texas heat? Bold.

His left arm is covered in intricate tattoos. His hands are adorned in chunky silver rings, as well as a thick silver chain bracelet on his wrist. A red guitar pick hangs around his neck on a silver chain.

As I get closer, he looks up and my breath hitches when I'm met with coffee brown eyes so dark they're almost black, framed by thick, dark lashes that any girl would kill to have. He tucks one side of his hair behind his ear and pockets his phone.

This man has a nose ring *and* two piercings in his ear. The silver jewelry in his nose glints in the sunlight, drawing attention to it. The silver hoops in the first piercing on his lobes contrast his dark hair.

I wonder if they match the other side.

He looks like every girl's bad boy dream, and he is most definitely *not* my cowboy fantasy. His facial expression remains impassive as I approach, and I can almost *feel* the broodiness and angst rolling off of him. I get the distinct impression he doesn't want to be here.

Looks like it's going to be a long night.

Chapter 3

Wes

Luke insisted it was the *gentlemanly* thing to do to wait outside of the car so I could open the door for *Elliana,* so that's where I am when he comes walking down the pathway holding hands with a giggly blonde, but no one else.

I'm going to be really fucking mad if she's standing me up.

"Wes, Izzy. Izzy, Wes." Luke says as soon as they make it to the car.

"Nice to meet you, Izzy." I shake her hand and she gives me a confused look.

"Wait, I thought your name was Matt?" She looks between me and Luke.

"Luke! You didn't tell them Matt isn't coming?" I lightly slap his arm.

"Sorry! I was preoccupied." Luke shrugs and opens the door for Izzy, still giving each other gooey smiles as they climb into the back seat and start nuzzling each other like puppies.

Ugh. Young love is so gross.

"Ooo Elli's going to lose her freaking mind." I hear Izzy not-so-quietly whisper before the door closes.

After two minutes, I think she's standing me up, which would be awkward as hell, but then I hear footsteps growing closer so I glance up from my phone and there she is.

She's shorter than me, hell, she's shorter than her own sister. Even in the oversized shirt dress thing she's wearing I can see she's curvy as hell. Her chocolate brown hair is pulled into two long braids, and she's got barely any makeup on. The total opposite of her little sister.

The thing that surprises me the most is the beat up black converse that look like they've seen better days. A prissy, stuck up girl like *Elliana* should be wearing sandals or heels or whatever the fuck, right? Anything but beat up sneakers. She has a bored expression on her face which makes me think she matches my level of enthusiasm about all of this.

"Hey, Matt?" She asks quietly.

I try to contain my eye roll since it's not her I'm upset with, it's Luke. "Wes, actually. There was a bit of a mix up- Matt had a prior engagement. Luke forgot to relay that information." I say brusquely.

"Oh. Well, nice to meet you, Wes, I'm-"

"Elliana. Nice to meet you too." I grab her extended hand and give it a quick shake, noting the size difference of our hands. Her hands are so tiny I could probably fit both of them in one of my own. I'm a good foot taller than she is, so I can see the way her eyelashes cast a shadow on her cheeks when she blinks.

"Elli." She says, then clears her throat. "I prefer Elli." *Elli* says timidly.

"Elli." I open the door for her and motion to the seat. "Your chariot awaits."

She gives me a small, forced smile and a nod in return as she climbs in.

We don't get a chance to talk at all on the way to the mall since Luke and Izzy barely stop talking to take a breath. It makes sense, considering they haven't seen each other in almost a year, but I *know* they talk every day so what on earth could they possibly have to talk about?

Elli keeps her hands folded primly in her lap, gently twisting the ring around her left middle finger every so often. She's got gold rings on her middle fingers, left thumb, and right pointer finger. She's got her legs pressed together and her shoulders hunched like she's trying to make herself as small as possible.

Sometimes I'll see her knee bounce as she taps her foot to the beat of whatever song is quietly playing, but she usually stops it as quickly as it starts. I look over at her more than I probably should, but I can't really help it. I can't stop thinking about how different she seems from her sister.

Izzy exudes confidence, is boisterous, open, and talkative with her vanilla blonde hair curled and meticulous makeup. Elli, with her cocoa brown hair and understated outfit and makeup, seems reserved, quiet, maybe a little judgmental.

God, I hope she isn't judgy.

As we park, Elli turns to Izzy and Luke and says, "I have three rules. Number one, you text me if you want to leave the arcade so I know where you are. Number two, keep the PDA PG; there are families here and I don't need anyone arrested for public indecency. Number three, have a good time. You two deserve it." She gives them a soft smile.

Maybe she's not boring. Just nervous?

Once Izzy and Luke give some sort of vague affirmation to what Elli said, they're getting out of the car and sprinting to the entrance hand in hand. Elli sighs before getting out, folding her arms across her chest as we start to trail behind.

The arcade is, unfortunately, in the mall, which means everyone in San Marcos is here this fine Saturday evening.

"So," I clear my throat, "do you want to go to the arcade?" I question, attempting to break the ice.

Elli slows a bit and scrunches her nose. "Not particularly. You?"

I shake my head. "Too many people. How about some snacks and we find a place to... hang out, I guess? Unless you want to go shopping?"

Elli nods. "Snacks sound good."

"Cool." I open the doors with another dramatic sweep of my arm, bowing as Elli walks past. "After you, m'lady."

She gives me another tense smile and ducks her head as she walks past.

Tonight's going to be a long night.

Especially if she only speaks in three word sentences and doesn't fucking smile.

Okay, she doesn't smile at *me*.

The food court seems to be the hub for everyone's outings, so as we make our way to the line for the pretzel booth, the minimal conversation we were having is put on hold. I'm forced to stand slightly behind Elli in line, so when a kid bolts past and she stumbles into me, my arms instinctively go around her waist to keep her upright. The position makes it so I have to bend slightly, meaning my mouth is close to her ear. I can see her ears turn red in embarrassment as she squeaks out something that sounds like "thank you."

"Falling for me already, Elli? I told Luke that wouldn't happen, and I'm a man of my word." I say in her ear, nudging her shoulder playfully.

Her face burns even brighter red at my comment, but she just mutters "sorry" and curls back in on herself.

When I refuse to let Elli pay for our food, she protests and scowls at me, which is honestly just funny because I don't think she has a mean bone in her body.

We make our way to a bench in a quieter part of the mall, and just silently eat our pretzel bites for who knows how long. Neither of us seems keen on making small talk, but the awkward silence is killing me.

I notice that she keeps looking at me with an assessing look, like she's trying to figure out all my secrets. We make awkward eye contact a few times when I do the same thing, and the first time it happens I notice how pretty her eyes are. I don't know how I didn't notice the cornflower blue orbs with a sapphire ring on the outer edge before this. They're intense and beautiful, and the blue of her dress and the black of her lashes makes them pop even more.

I look away, not wanting to make her uncomfortable, and notice a penny on the ground beneath the bench. I pick it up, flip it once, and hand it over to her. "Penny for your thoughts?"

She gives me an assessing look as she takes the penny and inspects it. Her eyes roam over my body quickly before they land back on mine. She nods in the direction of my left arm, which is covered from shoulder to wrist in flowers. "Is there a meaning behind all the flowers?"

Oh great. As soon as I tell her, she's going to give me the look people always give me. *Poor, broken, orphaned Wes.* Then the night will be spent with her dancing around conversation because she doesn't want to upset me and it'll just be awkward. I won't lie about this, though. It's too important to me.

"They're um. They're flowers that represent signifi-cant months." I point to each black, white, and gray shaded bloom, "A violet for my mom's birthday month, a rose for my grandma's, a poppy for mine, two daffodils for my dad and Luke, a chrysanthemum for Jess. A daisy for the month my mom passed, and a cosmos for the month my grandma passed, and an aster for the month my dad passed. The bluebell is native to Texas and my gram's favorite flower, and the buttercup is my mom's favorite."

When I meet Elli's gaze again, I expect to see pity, sad-ness, maybe even apprehension. But I don't find those things. Her eyes are soft, something akin to affection in them, and she has a sad smile on her face.

She says in an almost reverent way, "It's beautiful. The artwork is stunning. I'm sure your mom and grandma would love it." Then, her eyes widen in shock like she's surprised she said that. "I'm so sorry. I shouldn't have assumed anything. I mean, *my* mom and grandma would rather me chop my own arm off before I get a tattoo so if someone said that to me I'd laugh in their face. I'm sorry if I overstepped-"

I can't help the smirk that pulls at my lips as I cut off her rambling. "Elli, it's okay." I give her elbow a gentle squeeze. "I appreciate the sincerity. I'm sure they'd like it, too. I'm just not used to telling people I just met about my dead family, you know?"

Elli nods, and then it's silent again.

I don't like it. I liked her rambling. It was the most animated I saw her, and I find myself wanting more.

I don't know how long we sit there; it could have been five minutes, it could have been an hour. It was long enough for us to finish our respective pretzel bites, and long enough for me to notice that Elli has a few smatterings of freckles on her cheeks that look like little constellations.

"So," I start, wanting to break the silence, "what brings you to good ol' San Marcos, Texas?"

"Oh, um, I needed out of Utah, and Izzy needed a reason to visit Luke more. San Antonio and Austin are close enough for a day trip, and San Marcos is cute." She shrugs. "My job is remote, so I could go anywhere, and here seemed like a good place."

"Won't you miss your family? Friends? Partner?"

Elli shrugs again. "I mean, of course I will. I'll miss my siblings, but they're all growing up and finding themselves, so I don't have to take care of them anymore. Most of my friends are married and starting families so I don't see them anyway. My parents are... a lot. I need space from them to figure some things out. I don't have a partner to miss, so no worries there."

I'm ignoring the flutter in my chest at the revelation that she's single.

What the fuck is that?

Before I can open my mouth to respond, a giggly voice calls out to us.

"Hey you two!" Izzy calls, her smile a mile wide, dragging Luke with their fingers firmly interlocked.

Luke's got two matching stuffed dinosaurs in one arm, and the dopiest grin on his face.

He looks so happy my heart squeezes. As cringy as they are, he's happy, and that makes me happy.

"Hey kids, done already?" Elli asks.

Izzy gives a confused look. "It's been two hours, Els."

Elli and I simultaneously look at our phones and find that it has indeed been two hours. It feels like we've only been here for twenty minutes.

"Anyway...We want to order pizza and then watch a movie at your apartment." She bats her lashes at Elli.

"Iz, that's the one thing we didn't get today." Elli sounds exasperated.

Izzy turns to me with a saccharine smile, "Wes, would you mind stopping by Target so we can get a TV?"

"Isabelle!" Elli chides in a stage-whisper. "You cannot just ask someone you just met for a favor that big."

"I don't mind." I want to put Elli out of her misery. Though, her cheeks have turned a delightful shade of pink and I think I want to see them that color again.

I regret offering as soon as we enter Target and Izzy and Luke saunter off to god knows where. We've been walking around aimlessly for half an hour to find them with no luck. Elli seems just as frustrated as I am.

I will admit it hasn't been all bad talking more with Elli. It seems that the more we walk, the more we talk, the less closed in on herself she becomes. I've learned that she has a thing for bees, butterflies, and mushrooms. Anything with those things on it draws her attention and she gives a wistful, longing sigh before she puts it back. She graduated from Utah Valley University with a degree in Human Resources and got her B.S. in just three years. She works from home as the assistant HR representative for a law firm.

I tell her that I work as a music teacher at the private school here, but that I ideally want to get out of teaching and write music and perform full time. Usually, people are quite condescending or judgmental when I tell them I want to quit my steady income for something so unpredictable, but she is neither condescending nor judgy. Instead, Elli asks me about how long I've been writing, and what inspires me.

"I haven't had a lot of inspiration lately, I've kind of hit writer's block." I shrug. I wish I had something, but

I've written so many songs about my dead family and my ex-girlfriend, there's nothing else to say.

She hums in understanding. "I'm sure you'll find some inspiration soon, and you'll write something amazing."

"Thank you, Elli." She's not the first person who's said that to me, but she's the first person who isn't in my close circle of friends. She's so genuinely good, I almost feel like I can write a song about her.

Nope. Chillax Wes. You're way ahead of yourself, man.

Elli isn't what I judged her to be. She's not vain, or prissy. She's not a know-it-all with a holier than thou attitude. She's not judgmental. She may be a goody-two-shoes, but not in a way that I dislike.

I'm not someone who enjoys being wrong, but I'm glad I was about her.

"Elli! Wes! Where have you two been?" Luke calls from behind us.

Elli and I trade annoyed looks and she rolls her eyes, making me bite back a laugh.

"We've been looking for you! We were supposed to get the TV and get out of here. This was your idea." Elli points at Izzy. Izzy, who is sporting flushed cheeks and swollen lips.

Someone's been making out in the aisles.

"We went to look for snacks." Izzy says innocently as she holds up a pack of gummy worms and some popcorn.

"Right, well, if you're done, I'm ready to go." Elli grumbles.

"Is now a bad time to ask about the pool party tomorrow at Matt's? I know it's Sunday but Luke wants me to meet everyone before I leave Wednesday." Izzy rocks back on her heels anxiously.

Why would it being a Sunday matter?

"Of course we can go, Iz. I'm not going to make you go to church." Elli says as we approach the checkout.

Oh, right.

Izzy squeals loudly, hugs Elli, then goes with Luke to pay for their snacks.

As Elli is scanning the TV, I lean down and whisper in her ear. "You know what they were doing, right?"

"Of course I know what they were doing." She hisses. "But it's not like much can happen beyond kissing in a public store. They haven't seen each other in a year. I'm letting them make up for lost time."

"You're a terrible chaperone." I tsk.

She gasps in offense, swatting my arm. "I am not! You take that back."

"What kind of chaperone loses the person they're in charge of for half an hour and lets them get away with locking lips in the candy aisle?"

"The kind that wants their little sister to be happy and experience being a teenager in love. And besides, *you're* just as much to blame." She pokes my chest.

"Touche. Alright, you're not a bad chaperone."

"Thank you." She lifts her chin smugly.

CHAPTER 4

Back at my apartment, Wes is gracious enough to set the TV up on a stack of unpacked boxes while we chow down on pizza. I definitely do *not* admire the way those black jeans hug his cute butt as he's bending over to plug it in.

Nope, not at all.

I sign into Netflix and let Izzy pick some trashy teen romance movie that I'm not super excited to watch, but I'll suffer through for her. I panic internally when I realize how small my couch actually is. How are we all supposed to fit? Especially with Wes's six foot frame?

As if he can read my thoughts, Wes says, "I can sit on the floor."

Izzy and Luke have taken the lounge part of the couch, sitting with Iz's back to Luke's chest, so there's two more cushions that can comfortably, albeit a bit snuggly, fit me and Wes.

"Nonsense. Since the lovebirds are trying to melt into one person, there's plenty of space. I'll sit by them so you don't have to catch the love bug." I plop down in the middle and pat the cushion next to me.

"What if *you* catch the love bug?" Wes asks as he sits as close to the arm of the couch as possible, crossing his long legs.

"I'll survive. I've already had it, and I'm immune." I give him an exaggerated wink.

Who am *I? Am I really* flirting *right now?*

"I appreciate you sacrificing yourself to protect me. What are the symptoms? You know, so I know what to look for."

"Oh boy," I let out an exaggerated exhale, "Sweaty palms, flushed cheeks, chapped and swollen lips, butterflies in your stomach, a rapid heartbeat. Perhaps the most dangerous symptom is thinking about the person all day every day, sometimes even dreaming about them." I keep my face as serious as possible.

Wes lets out a low whistle. "Wow, sounds very serious. You let me know if you have any of those symptoms. Wouldn't want you to suffer alone."

Is... is he flirting with me?

He can't be.

"Will you two shush so we can start the movie?" Izzy whines.

Wes and I share a knowing look, and I can't help the small flutter in my belly when he looks at me.

I try my hardest to watch the movie, I really do, but Wes is so close and I can smell him and he smells woodsy and earthy and so *good.* In the blue light of the TV, his features are highlighted. The softness of his cheeks, defined jaw, the long slope of his nose, and the faint indent of dimples bracketing his soft, pillowy lips.

He's outrageously gorgeous. Probably the prettiest man I've ever seen.

Halfway through the movie, Wes has shifted from the edge of the couch, closer to me, and now his denim-clad thigh is pressed up against my dress-covered one. I'm trying not to focus too much on that, or on the fluttering in my stomach at the contact. I've only known him for a few hours, way too soon for any sort of feeling other than friendship.

At least, that's what I'm trying to believe.

Maybe it's the appeal of someone who's so different from the boys I've dated before. He's not a white shirt and tie, cropped hair, strait-laced Mormon boy who is looking for a wife above all else. Wes's goals in life aren't to become the next best Vivint Sales rep or trade stocks for a living. He's so passionate about music, and obviously about his late mom and grandma. He clearly adores Luke, and he's *so* kind. He could have easily just sat on his phone and ignored me the whole night, but he didn't. He made an effort to get to know me, and let me see a little bit of him. I haven't felt uncomfortable in any of our silences other than the initial one.

I have a feeling the bad boy act is just that, an act. He looks the part, but I think my assessment of him being a bad boy was wrong.

Wes stands, bringing me back to reality as he turns the lights on. Izzy pouts when Wes reminds Luke of his curfew, and I can't help but share the feeling.

"I know, Izzy-boo. But I'll see you tomorrow, and I'll make sure to text you when I get back and we can do our goodnight routine." Luke coos as he and Izzy make their way to the front door.

Wes and I make eye-contact and he gives me a puzzled look, arching his eyebrow as if I have the answer to what Luke's talking about.

I do. I know exactly what their "goodnight routine" entails, and because I do, I have to cover my mouth to stifle a laugh.

"See you tomorrow, Luke." I say as Luke and Izzy head to the car for their goodnight kiss in private.

"Thank you for chaperoning with me tonight. It was really good to meet you." I say to Wes as he stands in the doorway.

"No thanks necessary," he gives me a small smile and his dimple is *almost* visible, "I had a good time too. I'll see you tomorrow, right? At Matt's?"

Right. Tomorrow.

"Yeah, I'll see you tomorrow."

"Night, Elli." He dips his head in a nod before turning to the car.

"Goodnight Wes."

Izzy and Wes trade fist bumps and goodbyes as they pass each other, and Wes turns to smile when he hears me giggle at the interaction.

Izzy wiggles her eyebrows at me as I shut and lock the door.

"You *like* him." She says smugly.

I glare at her and scoff. "I don't know what you're talking about."

Izzy groans. "Els bells don't do this! You haven't even *looked* at another man in eight months. You can't let Packer win."

"Packer won when he married Tiffany." The familiar, bitter taste of rejection sits on my tongue. It's not as prominent as it once was, but it's definitely still there. .

Izzy rolls her eyes, "I *mean* you can't let him keep you from finding your happiness. If you like Wes, you should go for it."

I let out an exasperated sigh, wanting to be done with this conversation, "We should get some rest. Long day tomorrow. I'll make up the bed for you."

Izzy grumbles something I don't understand under her breath, and stalks off to the bathroom to get ready for bed while I make up the sofa bed and retreat to my room.

As I'm getting myself ready for bed, I can faintly hear Izzy and Luke on FaceTime gushing to each other about how excited they are that she's here, that she's meeting his friends in person tomorrow. They listen to their song, *Something to Believe In* from *Newsies*, and tell each other one thing they love about the other.

I've heard them do this almost every night for the past year, and usually it gets on my nerves, but tonight it brings tears to my eyes and makes me yearn. It makes me want to be blissfully in love like that.

If I cry myself to sleep thinking that love is just not something I'll have, no one will ever know.

CHAPTER 5

Wes

I woke up with the memories of last night replaying over in my head, my conversation with Luke at the forefront.

Luke is waiting for me to unlock the car, eyebrows raised in suspicion as I approach. He looks at me expectantly as we get in, like we're about to trade notes on how our dates went. I give him my best "what do you want?" face and he just chuckles and shakes his head.

We last approximately five minutes in silence before he says what he wants to say. "You like her."

"No I don't."

"Then why were you staring at her all night?"

"D'know what you're talkin' 'bout." I mumble.

"Right." He drags out the word, clearly being sarcastic. "I'm going to be honest, Wes. She's not exactly your speed. Mormons have very high dating standards and expectations. Not even just about the person they're dating-about relationships in general. Izzy's considered rebellious because of our relationship. From what she's told me about

Elli, Elli is a stickler for the rules. I don't want to see you get hurt."

I know he's just looking out for me, and he has the best intentions. But damn it if that didn't hurt a little bit. Of course the first girl I've been vaguely attracted to in almost two years has to be super religious and have high standards and expectations. Standards and expectations I most definitely couldn't meet. It'll be fine. After tomorrow, I probably won't see her again and the feeling of wanting to be near her and learn everything about her will go away.

Right?

Then, I went down a deep rabbit hole of information about Mormons as soon as I got home, and didn't fall asleep until around 2 AM.

I found out that they have their own religious texts-*The Book of Mormon, The Doctrine and Covenants,* and *The Pearl of Great Price*- that they read along with The King James version of *The Bible.* The leaders, "prophets" are these old men who stay as the leader until they die-their current one is ninety-nine years old! Their founder was fourteen when he started the church, and I pictured Luke, Ethan, Jack, or Dallin coming and telling me they saw God and they're starting a religion. I would smack them upside the head and tell them they were out of their minds! That information alone was enough to make me shut my laptop before I got sucked in deeper.

So this morning, I'm standing at Luke's door to ask him to give me the basics. When Luke answers, I don't give him a chance to ask why I'm there. "I need you to tell me everything you know about Mormons."

"Woah, okay. What do you want to know?" He holds up his hands in surrender.

"Everything you know." I shrug.

"Okay... From what Izzy's told me, they have a lot of rules they have to follow like no swearing, no smoking, no drugs, no drinking, no coffee, no tea, no tattoos, no piercings other than two in the ears, no dating until they're sixteen-Izzy's parents are more lenient on this with her because we're long distance. They have to always wear long shorts, crew neck t-shirts, and no tank tops because of 'modesty' or whatever-they can't even wear bikinis! Anything that has to do with sex-masturbating included-is considered really, really bad, unless you're married. They aren't even supposed to make out. When you're eight, or if you join later, you get baptized, and then you get what they call 'The Holy Ghost' but I don't really understand that.

"When boys turn eighteen they go on mandatory service missions for two years. Girls can go for eighteen months when they turn nineteen, but it's not mandatory for them. They usually only date and marry other Mormons because they believe in order to get into Heaven you have to marry in their temple and you can only go in the temple if you're a member. When you go to the temple you get this special underwear you have to wear all the time, which is another reason they dress the way they do. They get married super young, and super-fast usually. Like, less than six months from meeting to marriage fast. They used to have to go to church for three hours every Sunday, but they switched it to two hours in 2020, and every six months they have this big conference thing. That's all I know."

"That is… A lot. And Elli's a stickler for these *rules*?"

Luke shrugs, "According to Izzy. Elli's ex is the grand-son of one of their leaders. Trust Fund kid, lots of power. He didn't propose after six months of dating, so they broke up. According to Izzy, he got married two months after he and Elli broke up."

Well *that* doesn't make any sense. Why would they break up if he wanted to get married so badly? Did Elli break up with him? Or did he break up with her? He'd be an idiot if he was the one who broke up with her.

"I've got to go meet Robs for coffee. I'll see you at Matts." I say as I clap him on the shoulder and make my way to the door.

He yells out, "I knew you liked her!" But I'm gone before I can reply.

Robin is already there with our drinks when I come sulking into the Toasted Bean. I get there just in time to see her almost knock over her own latte, spilling a bit on the table and mumbling under her breath. She perks up when she sees me.

"Date didn't go well?" She gives me a curious look.

"It was fine." I know that answer isn't enough for her, she's just going to keep asking me questions until she's satisfied, so I figure I might as well save us both the time. "I told her about my mom and grandma. She asked about my tattoo, so I told her the meaning. I just didn't mention *how* Mom died."

"No shit. What did she say?" Robin's cup stops halfway to her mouth in surprise.

"She just said that she's sure my mom and grandma would have thought it was beautiful."

Robin's eyebrows raise as if to say *"and?"*

"And..." I sigh. "That's it. That's all she said about it. She tried to apologize, thinking she overstepped, but I told her it was okay. She didn't give me the usual 'oh poor broken Wes' pitying look people have when I tell them. She just looked...understanding? I don't know. I told her about wanting to be a musician, write songs, ya know? And she didn't judge me *at all* for it. I thought she was going to be this uptight, prissy snob, but she's so selfless and kind, and actually funny when she lets herself go a little bit..."

"But?" Robin prompts, and I hate and love that she knows me so well sometimes.

"But Mormons have a lot of fucking rules that don't make any goddamn sense. I could never meet the stupid standards that they have, that *she* has. I don't even-"

"Pause. Did she actually tell you that?"

"Well, no, but-"

"Then you don't know if you can't meet them. It sounds like you might be trying to self-sabotage because you're scared of getting hurt. You're also making snap judgments about her, like people do to you." Robin chides, giving me a smug look.

"I don't like you." I don't like that she's making sense. I don't like that she's probably right.

"You love me. Matt gave everyone the heads up that she would be there today. Maybe I can see where she stands?"

"No, just..." I run my hand over my face in exasperation. "Just get to know her. I think you and her could be really good friends. Sav too. If you don't like her, fine, you don't have to be friends with her, but don't try to pry information out of her for my sake."

Robin grabs my hand from across the table. "Okay. I'll get to know her. But you shouldn't count yourself out before you've even tried."

I don't know if I have it in me to try again, though.

CHAPTER 6

Elli

I should be unpacking a little before we go to the party, but instead, I find myself scrolling through Wes's Instagram. His profile has mostly pictures of his guitar, some of which he's in. He's also got a few pictures of him and Luke.

He looks *very* good holding a guitar. Who knew arms could be so sexy?

There are a lot of reels of him playing songs, covers and originals. He's incredible. Better than I had even imagined. There are a few pictures of him and Luke with a bunch of other teenagers and people our age. In his tagged photos, he's tagged a lot with a pretty redheaded girl.

He wouldn't have come yesterday if he had a girlfriend, right?

Before I get too deep into a spiral, I decide to put my phone down and start unpacking the kitchen. Izzy comes out of the bathroom and stands across from me at the other side of the counter with her "spill the beans" look.

"Are you excited to meet Luke's friends today?" I know the best way to avoid talking about myself is to distract her. Luckily, it works.

"I'm so excited! I've talked with some of them over FaceTime, but it will be nice to actually talk to them in person." Her usual bright smile falters to a half frown. "Do you think they'll like me?"

Izzy is one of the most social people I've ever met. Her bubbly personality and ability to talk to anyone about anything makes it easy for people to fall in love with her, and her generous heart helps keep people close. She has friends all the way in Rhode Island that she met at summer camp, that she still talks to on a weekly basis. The fact that she doubts herself makes my heart hurt.

"Iz, they're going to love you." I circle the counter to wrap her in a hug and stroke her hair. "If you want to leave at any point, you just say the word and I'll fake period cramps or something and we can go, okay?"

"Yeah, okay. Thanks, Els. I'm going to go get ready. We have to leave in half an hour." She gives me a quick squeeze before she skips off.

Forty-five minutes later we pull up to a house - no - a *mansion* and I have half a mind to call Luke and make sure he's not playing a prank on us. Izzy wastes no time getting out and bouncing up the front steps, knocking on the door before I can even catch up to her.

Wowza.

The shirtless man who opens the door looks like he belongs on the cover of *GQ* or some other magazine that features hot men. Shaggy light brown hair effortlessly falls across his forehead, golden brown eyes, tan skin, muscles for days.

He's not even flexing and you can see the definition in his biceps.

He's probably around six feet tall, a bit taller than Wes, and his smile is bright and warm. Bulging arms and shoulders, washboard abs right above a V that dips down into his swim trunks.

"I'd recognize Luke's girl anywhere. Nice to finally meet you, Izzy. I'm Matt." He says with a slight southern drawl, extending his hand to Izzy.

Izzy, uncharacteristically speechless, takes his hand like she's in a trance. "Hi. That's Elli." She motions towards me, and I give an awkward half wave.

Luke pulls Izzy inside, leaving me alone on the porch with Matt. He motions for me to follow him inside, and once we're through the door, he turns to me and I see his eyes do a quick once-over before clearing his throat.

"Elli, I'm sorry about last night. I hope Luke didn't give you too much trouble. I know how he can be."

I wave my hand dismissively. "No worries. Wes came along to keep me company. Besides, Izzy's the trouble-maker in that duo."

He looks a little surprised when I mention Wes, but he quickly covers whatever emotion flashed across his face with a megawatt smile and a charming chuckle. "Luke needs someone to keep him on his toes. C'mon, let me introduce you to the rest of the group." He places his hand gingerly on the small of my back and leads me through the entryway, through a pristine living room and huge kitchen, and to the back yard.

As Matt leads us outside, I immediately recognize the redheaded girl, *Robin,* from Wes's many tagged pictures on Instagram. She's sitting with a Latin girl with darker skin and curly black hair that goes just past her shoulders, and a white guy with cropped black hair. A man with short brown hair comes and wraps his arms around the curly haired girl's waist and gives her a quick peck on the cheek before settling in behind her.

Apparently, having the ability to be on the cover of a magazine is a requirement in this friend group.

"Hey guys, this is Elli. Elli, this is Robin, Sean, Savannah, and Drew." They give a small wave when he says their name. "And over there," he points over to the pool where Izzy and Luke are, "Jack, Samantha-but don't call her that, call her Sam or she'll probably punch you, Ethan, Lexi, and Dallin. Sav is Jack's sister, Drew is Ethan's brother, and Sean is Sam's."

Izzy is, of course, already in a giggly discussion with Sam and Lexi, and it warms my heart at the same time it makes me jealous. I've never been great at making friends-I'm not confident, or outgoing. Growing up, most of my friendships came from being forced into closeness by church or school. Almost like she can sense me watching her, she turns to look at me and gives me a sassy, twinkly fingered wave. I mimic the wave and dramatically blow her a kiss, which she pretends to catch and throw in the pool. The little sisterly interaction helps ease my nerves a little bit, but they quickly come back when my attention is drawn back to the group.

"So, Elli, how was your date with Wes?" Drew asks with a teasing tone and a wiggle of his eyebrows. Savannah slaps his leg and gives him a look that seems to mean *shut up.*

"It-it wasn't a *date*. Not really. He was just keeping me company while I played chaperone." I raise one shoulder, trying to hide the way my belly flutters thinking about Wes. I can tell that answer isn't going to be enough for this nosy group of friends. Especially when Matt sits on an empty bench and motions for me to come sit by him. Robin leans forward, placing her chin in her hands with a wide, expectant smile.

I continue on, trying not to sound like a kid with a crush. "He was a gentleman, very kind. Izzy's good at imposing things on people so he was sort of forced to help us haul a TV back to my place so we could watch a movie and he didn't complain. He even helped set it up." I watch Robin's face beam with a smile, and she exchanges a look with Sean.

"Well, we're glad to know Wes has still got game. He hasn't been on a date in a loooong time. Not since Shelby che- OW." Drew is cut off by Savannah elbowing him in the ribs. She whispers something to him in Spanish that I don't understand and he looks apologetically at me.

Robin draws my attention with a chipper "Elli! Do you want me to show you where to change into your swimsuit?"

I nod, following her as she stands and walks inside, even though the prospect of being alone with Wes's lover, or ex-lover, or whatever she is, makes me want to jump in the pool fully clothed.

Once inside, Robin leans against the counter and just stands there, head tilted, eyes squinted like she's trying to see through my skull.

Finally, she breaks into a smile. "I'm glad Wes went last night. I know his exterior can sometimes scare people off, and he's not exactly the most talkative or forthcoming. But I'll tell you a secret-" she leans in and whispers, "he's a big ol' softy on the inside."

"Oh." My shoulders relax, I didn't even realize they were tense to begin with. "I can see how people could find him scary, but-"

"Who's scary?" Wes's voice cuts me off and startles Robin and me as he enters the kitchen.

"Holy shit Westley! You can't just sneak up on people like that!" Robin yells as she swats his arm.

"Oh, toughen up Robs." He ruffles her hair. "Sorry if I scared you Elli." He turns and looks at me, his expression playful.

"Why didn't you tell her to toughen up?" Robin grumbles.

"Because I actually like *her*."

"You love me and you know it." She chides.

"Yeah, I do." He sighs as he places a dramatically loud kiss on her cheek, making Robin gag in faux disgust.

There's definitely something more than friendship there, right?

But I'm not jealous.

I clear my throat, "I think I'm going to go change, where's the bathroom?"

"Oh! Sorry about that, second door on the right, down that hall." Robin says cheerfully.

I nod in thanks, and quickly find the bathroom and take some deep breaths. As I put on my plain black one piece, I can't help but compare myself to Savannah, who is all curves for days, and Robin., who looks like a Victoria's Secret Model.

I look...not like that.

I've got a 'B' belly that pokes out a bit in the tight polyester, cellulite all up my thighs that have *never* had a thigh gap. My arms jiggle, my boobs are weighed down by gravity, and my back has rolls.

"You are more than what you weigh." I tell myself in the mirror. This day is about making new friends and letting Izzy have fun. I can't be a downer because I'm having a bad body day.

Steeling my nerves, I walk through the now empty kitchen, out the back door, and over to where my bag is -right by Wes and Matt- to drop off my clothes.

"Izzy! Sunscreen!" I yell, holding up the yellow bottle.

"I already put it on!" She yells back, rolling her eyes.

"If you burn, I'm not going to feel sorry for you." I chirp. I know she didn't apply sunscreen, and I will not be listening to her complain about it later.

Izzy stomps her way over to me like a petulant child, but lets me lather it on her back where her tankini top dips low. She applies it to her arms and face while I do her back.

"Happy now?" She grumbles.

"Much." I say with an exaggerated kiss on her cheek.

"Ewww." She pretends to wipe it off, then leans closer to me and whispers, "Go kiss Matt or Wes on the cheek.

They're the ones who can't stop staring at you." Then she saunters off like she didn't say anything.

I pretend that she didn't say anything. I pretend I don't feel the gazes of two of the hottest guys I've ever seen staring at me while I apply sunscreen on my arms. I can't fathom why either of them would be interested in *me,* so it's better to pretend they don't. Then I don't get my hopes up.

I feel the presence of someone at my back and look up to see Matt standing over me.

"Do you need any help putting sunscreen on?" Matt asks me, his tongue swiping his bottom lip.

"Oh, um. I can get everywhere but my back, so I would appreciate the help actually." I say pulling the bottle from my bag.

"I'll help you with that." Robin plucks the bottle from my hands and waves Wes and Matt off, the two of them rolling their eyes and grumbling.

"Thank you." I say over my shoulder as she starts to rub the sunscreen gently onto my back.

"Don't mention it, it's what friends are for. Besides, I don't think Wes would let Matt do this without someone getting a right hook to the jaw." Robin mumbles.

What does that mean? I want to ask her, but I'm momentarily distracted by Wes taking off his shirt and... *ooooh boy.*

Wes's fair skin tone is deliciously contrasted by dark lines of tattoos littering his body. I thought he just had some on his left arm, but he has some type of script over his left peck, some type of potion looking bottle that I can't make out on his right side, and something else that's peeking up right above his swim trunks on his right hip next to a dark happy trail. He's all lean muscle, trim waist, and strong thighs. When he turns around to say something to the kids, I take in his perky butt that looks so squeezable. I avert my gaze, embarrassed, as soon as Wes's eyes lock on mine.

Just because I think he's probably the most attractive man I've ever talked to in my life, and he makes my belly flutter, doesn't mean he reciprocates the feelings.

CHAPTER 7

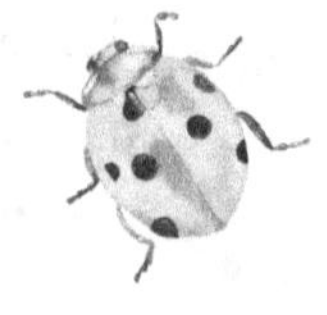

Wes

Holy curves.

Elli's body is fucking immaculate. Her ample breasts are nearly spilling out of the top of her swimsuit, and the bottom of her ass is peeking out the bottom. Her hips are wide and look like the perfect place to hold on to. Don't even get me started on the way her thighs squish together. I can see the cute little pouch of her tummy too.

She's fucking perfect.

Robin pulls me away from gawking at Elli in that sinfully tight garment to grab the party trays in the kitchen. As soon as we're alone I ask, "So, what do you think of her?"

"First impression: she's a sweetheart. Shy, but I think anyone would be in her situation. She's very pretty." Robin sighs.

"I know." I narrow my eyes at her and bump her with my hip. "I saw her first."

"I don't think it's me you have to worry about. Matt seems pretty interested too."

I try to ignore the pit that forms in my stomach when I think of Matt and Elli together. Matt and I met through Robin. They were in the same ethics class during their sophomore year of college, and started to get along really well. Robin ended up trying to set him up with Savannah, so she made all of us come over for a game night to get to know Matt. Robin didn't know that Savannah and Drew were already hooking up at the time, so when Matt tried to ask Savannah out, they had to come clean about their relationship-which made things a little awkward. Even though the set up didn't work, Matt fit in pretty seamlessly with our group so we kept inviting him to stuff. Almost four years later, he and I have become good friends- he's like a brother to me. He and I used to play wingman for each other when we would go out, and it worked pretty well for us since our taste in women never seemed to overlap.

Apparently, it overlaps now. I don't think either of us will be playing wingman when it comes to Elli.

In all honesty, Matt is probably better for Elli. He's the type of guy you take home to your parents. He's got a trust fund, his master's degree in business, a 401k, life insurance, and a comfy corporate job. Sure, he lives at his parents' place, but that's because they travel most of the time, so he takes care of the house. He's the kind of guy who you have the white picket fence, a few kids, a minivan, and a dog with- and he's ready to settle down and have all of that in the next few years.

Me? I'm scraping by on a teacher's salary while trying to be a musician. I don't have a 401k, nor could I even begin to tell you what it is. I don't want kids, or a white picket fence. I've got so much baggage I could fill a whole damn airplane.

I'm not the settling down type.

At least, that's what I've been told.

I take the party trays out to the tables outside and I'm immediately swarmed by the teens. In a few minutes of shoving, grabbing, and shouting, they've managed to clear off a tray and a half. When the swarm finally dissipates, my attention is drawn to Elli and Matt sharing the patio bench, facing each other.

"Looks like Matty's tryin' ta steal your girl, Wes." Drew taunts as he approaches the table with Sav and Sean in tow.

Elli's facing Matt completely on the bench, one leg pulled up underneath her, listening intently on whatever Matt's saying. He apparently says something funny that makes her giggle and shake her head, causing a loose strand of hair to fall in front of her face. Matt wastes no time gently tucking the strand behind her ear, leaving Elli's face flushed at the contact.

"She's not my girl," I mumble.

"Yeah? Then why do you look like you're trying to make his head explode with your mind?" Sean interjects.

"Sun's in my eyes." I grunt as I take a tray over to Matt and Elli. "Snacks?" I offer them with a forced smile.

"Oh, thank you." Elli takes a strawberry and a cookie with an appreciative smile that makes my jealousy melt just a little.

"Thanks Wes. Glad you could make it." Matt says as he takes a few grapes.

I don't reply, instead, I watch in fascination as Elli eats her strawberry-her perfect pink lips wrap around it seductively. When she pulls it away, a bit of juice drips down her chin and she quickly wipes it with her thumb and sucks it off, humming in delight. She notices me- and apparently Matt- watching her as she pulls the thumb from her mouth.

"Do I have something on my face?" She questions timidly.

"No." Matt and I say in unison, glancing at each other quickly before staring back at Elli.

Elli's eyes dart between the two of us, confusion evident on her face as she finishes the strawberry.

Robin bounds over "How about a game of volleyball? Will you two go set up the net please?" She gives me a pointed look.

Matt stands and we make our way over to the small shed to grab the net and poles. "So," Matt clears his throat once we're out of earshot, "it sounds like you guys had a good time last night."

"Yeah, Izzy and Elli are really cool." Do I ask him to back off? I have no right to do that, I can't say *dibs, I saw her first* when it could have been Matt that saw her first. If he hadn't been unavailable, I might have only just met Elli today.

"Yeah, she, I mean, they seem really great. I wanted to-" Matt's cut off by the sound of squealing as Izzy tackles Elli into the pool. As they resurface, they're both laughing hysterically and splashing each other. Elli looks so happy it makes my heart swell.

Robin is calling everyone over to separate into teams just as Matt and I finish setting up the net. "Alright, girls against boys?" She suggests.

"That's not fair! Sav, Sam, and Lexi have all played volleyball in school." Luke outrages.

Robin rolls her eyes, "Fine, we'll split up. Sam, Izzy, Sav, Jack, Drew, Wes, and Luke on one team, everyone else on the other."

"Sean and Matt can't be on the same team, they're the most athletic ones." Luke says, "No offense, Wes and Drew." I wave him off. He's not wrong, I am *not* the most athletic.

"This isn't the Olympics, Jesus. Fine. Wes and Sean switch teams. Let's play!"

After an intense afternoon of volleyball, chicken fights- Robin and I lost many rounds because her clumsy ass can't stay balanced for shit, marco polo, and races, we're all ready to relax and watch whatever movie Luke's picked out while we chow down on pizza. Robin and I are tasked with picking up the pizzas, which would usually be fine, but I know she wants to ask me about Elli and I don't know what I'm supposed to say.

And if I'm not there, Matt has Elli all to himself and I don't like that.

"Are we not going to talk about the fact that you and Matt have been throwing yourselves at Elli all day?" Robin asks as soon as we pull out of the driveway.

"I don't know what you're talking about." I mumble.

"Elli, be on my team. Elli, here's some water, you look thirsty. Elli, be my partner in chicken so I can have your gorgeous thighs wrapped around my head. Do you need any more sunscreen applied? I want to kiss you, Elli." She's pitched her voice low to mimic a man's voice.

"I know *I* didn't say the thigh or kissing thing, did Matt?" Damn, I sound defensive.

"No, he didn't, but I can tell you were both thinking it. So you're not denying the rest?"

"Okay maybe we were being a bit... over the top. I just wanted to make her feel welcome is all."

"See, I would believe you if you hadn't told me you took a deep dive into her religious beliefs, or thought about if you were good enough to date her. Or if you and Matt weren't having a pissing contest. Or, you know, didn't have a semi all day." Robin playfully pokes my arm.

"Jesus, Robin, what the hell? Why were you even looking? God, that's embarrassing." I'm half tempted to not even go back to Matt's. I'll just send Robin in my car and spend the rest of the day packing to move to a different country so I never have to hear my best friend talk about my dick ever again.

"Your swim trunks are *real* thin, Wessy. If it makes you feel any better Matt and Drew had one too, but we all know that Drew's was because of Sav."

"That doesn't make me feel better." I grit out through clenched teeth. "And we weren't having a pissing contest. We're just competitive." Robin snorts in disbelief because she knows I'm full of shit, but she lets the conversation die there.

Okay, fine. Maybe Matt and I cost our team some points because we were acting like goddamn teenagers instead of grown ass men. Maybe I *was* wishing Elli would wrap her thighs around my head, though in a completely different scenario. Sue me.

I wish I could explain this attraction to Elli. Sure, I've seen women and thought "she's pretty," but I haven't felt *attracted* to anyone in two years. It's getting a little out of hand, to be honest. My thoughts should not be so consumed with a girl I met only yesterday.

After we've eaten our weight in greasy, cheesy goodness, everyone starts lounging around in the movie room, paired off into romantic- and platonic, in Robin and Sean's case- couplings. Jack and Sam on one beanbag, Luke and Izzy on another, Lexi and Dallin on the floor, Drew and Sav on the oversized armchair. Robin and Sean are sharing the loveseat, and Ethan is occupying the hammock chair in the corner. My eyes roam over to Elli sitting alone in the middle of the three seater sofa, tapping away on her phone. Her hair is in a messy braid over one shoulder, a few stray hairs framing her face, and her cheeks are rosy and sun kissed.

She looks so damn pretty.

Elli glances up from her phone and smiles when she sees me, patting the cushion next to her in an invitation for me to sit down. I don't know how I'm supposed to sit that close to her for an entire movie and not try to hold her hand. Maybe I can convince her to scoot over to one end and I'll sit on the other and-

And then Matt pushes past me with a slight slap on the back before taking a seat to Elli's right.

Damn it.

Swallowing down the groan that wants to surface, I take the seat on Elli's left and scoot as close to the arm of the couch as I can. Elli's in an animated conversation with Matt, but it halts as soon as the lights turn off and Sav starts the movie.

Luke decided on *The Princess Bride* for some reason-he usually opts for a sci fi or horror movie. This movie brings me a mix of emotions since it was my mom's favorite and I was named after one of the main characters. Apparently, my confusion is evident because Elli leans over to me.

"This is the movie they watched at camp the first night they held hands." She whispers.

As I turn to respond, our faces end up only inches apart. I could close the gap so easily and kiss her cupid's bow...

"I was wondering why Luke picked something so...cheesy." I whisper back.

That earns me a light slap to the arm. "It's not cheesy. It's romantic. Have you ever seen it?" She cocks an eyebrow at me.

I don't answer, just give her a playful shrug.

I can just make out an eye roll and hear her mumble "insufferable" through a deep exhale. Then, her head whips back to me, wide eyed in realization. "Wait a minute. Robin called you Westley earlier..."

She remembered?

"My mom was a big fan of the movie. If I were a girl, you'd be calling me Buttercup, guaranteed." I laugh.

Elli giggles, and the sound is music to my ears. "So you *have* seen it. That's amazing. Your mom had great taste."

We're promptly shushed as the grandpa begins reading the story, and Elli settles more comfortably into the couch by bringing her left leg up to fold slightly underneath her, which causes her thigh to be less than three inches from mine. Her *bare* thigh because of the length of her shorts and *damn it* if I don't want to squeeze the softness, trace my fingers along the smooth skin. Trace the curves of her body up her thighs, her sides, up her arms, across her shoulders, and loop my arm around her waist to pull her closer to me so I can place a kiss on the crown of her head before resting my head on hers...

I glance over at Matt, who looks like he's thinking the same thing as me as his eyes scan her from her legs all the way up, up, up-then his eyes meet mine. He looks embarrassed for all of two seconds before he gives me a smug grin.

The thought of fighting with Matt over a girl makes me queasy. We're adults, and Elli can make her own choices. If Elli were to decide she wanted to date Matt instead of me, I would back off. I just want them to be happy. All I ever want for the people I care about is to be happy.

Even if it would hurt me in the process.

Elli's reactions to the movie are so genuine and adorable, I'm having a better time watching her than the actual movie. She sighs dreamily at Buttercup and Westley's first scene together, gasps at the eels, tenses at the sword fight between Inigo and Westley, and scowls at Prince Humperdink.

I don't know when she scooted closer to me- okay *maybe* I scooted closer to her- but now the few inches between our thighs are non-existent. She's sitting with both legs crossed underneath her, her chin resting in her right hand. My hand has been resting on my right thigh, so when Elli's hand comes down to rest on her left one, our pinkies brush slightly and it sends a wave of tingles up my hand. Except for a sharp intake of breath, which could have been a reaction to the movie, there's no indication that she notices, so I tell myself it's an accident.

"I'm going to go get a drink, do you want anything?" Elli leans over and whispers right as Miracle Max says, "have fun storming the castle!"

"I'm okay, thank you."

She gives me a small nod, then leans over to whisper presumably the same thing to Matt. Matt shakes his head, so she stands and walks out of the room. Matt waits maybe thirty seconds before he stands up and follows her. I try to convince myself that I don't care. That whatever happens, happens and I can't do anything about it.

After five minutes I can't take it anymore and I follow them too. I second guess myself right before I turn the corner, but I can't stop myself from listening to their conversation.

"Are you busy tomorrow?" Matt asks.

"Seeing as I have a mountain of IKEA furniture to put together and another mountain of boxes to unpack, I think I'll probably be busy for the next week. Plus, Izzy leaves Wednesday so she and Luke have a big romantic date planned for Tuesday, so she wants to help me get it all unpacked tomorrow." Elli says.

"I see. And you have to go with them? On this big romantic date?"

"To chaperone, yes, unfortunately."

"Is anyone else going with you?"

"Nope. Luke has this picnic planned so I'm going to find a nice shady tree to read under while they make out or stare at each other or whatever they do." She giggles.

I know exactly where this is going, so I save myself the trouble of hearing Matt get the girl. When I get back into the movie room, I lean over the couch and ask Sean for a favor.

Chapter 8

Elli

I'm not the girl that guys want to date.

I don't mean that in a self-deprecating way, I mean it in a "this is how it's always been and I've come to terms with it" kind of way. I don't get hit on, and I *definitely* don't attract guys that look like *GQ* models. So when Matt asks if he can take me out on Saturday, I don't think I heard him right.

"Wait. What?" I shake my head, trying to get my thoughts to be coherent again.

Matt steps closer, chuckling a little bit as he tucks a stray hair behind my ear just like earlier, then slides his hand down my arm and grabs my hand. "I think you're smart, funny, and beautiful, Elli. I want to get to know you better. I'd like to take you out on Saturday. That way we can get to know each other without twelve other people around."

Oh.

Oh my goodness.

"Okay." It comes out as a squeak. So quiet, I'm pretty sure he didn't even hear it.

Apparently he does because he smiles, winks, and kisses the back of my hand. "Great. Can I get your number, so we can work out the details?"

As I put my number into his phone, my mind wanders to Wes, and how *he* didn't ask for my number. Maybe Robin *is* his girlfriend, and it really was just a friendly favor to Luke. Maybe he didn't feel the same things I felt.

Then why wasn't he sitting by Robin tonight? Why didn't he scoot away when our pinkies touched? What if he-

"You okay, Elli?" Matt gently touches my arm, startling me and bringing me back from the barrage of questions in my head.

"Oh, yeah. Sorry. I spaced out for a second." I force an awkward laugh as I hand him back his phone.

"No worries. Come on, gorgeous, we don't want to miss the big fight scene." Matt loops an arm around my shoulders and guides me back to the movie room.

When we walk in, I notice that Sean is sitting in Wes's spot, and Wes is sitting next to Robin, whispering with their heads bent together. *Sure looks like they're together.* A sudden wave of jealousy crashes over me at the same time Wes looks up and sees Matt's arm around my shoulders. He quickly averts his eyes, but I see his jaw tense and his fists clench on his knees.

Weird.

Matt leads us over to the couch, switching us so I'm not sitting between him and Sean. He removes his arm from my shoulder, but quickly places his hand on my knee as we settle in.

When Wes's pinky met mine it sent a million little bolts of lightning through my entire body.

All I feel with Matt's hand on my knee is slight heat where his skin meets mine.

I try to focus on the movie, instead of the war of emotions going on inside of me.

That doesn't last very long.

I feel like the walls are too close and I'm too hot and my stomach is turning like I've been going around the loops on the *Colossus: The Fire Dragon* at Lagoon for hours.

"I'm going to go get some fresh air, I'm feeling a little nauseated." I tell Matt. Without waiting to hear his reply, I walk out of the room and head to the backyard.

The moon is a bright waxing gibbous that reflects off of the pool, making the water look like it's glowing and as I take deep breaths to calm myself, I try to name my emotions.

I'm not exactly *nauseated*, more like my stomach feels like it has a fifty pound bowling ball sitting in it. I can't tell if it's jealousy, anxiety, or... regret? Part of it is definitely confusion. Should I have said yes to Matt when I clearly feel *something* for Wes? Am I interested in Matt? Matt is really attractive and really nice and interested in *me*- why wouldn't I be interested in him? But there's something about Wes. Conversation flowed so easily with us. I felt so comfortable to be myself, not a version of myself I thought Wes would like better, but *me*. Matt and I haven't really had the chance to have a conversation without being interrupted, let alone spend any time together. Maybe I just need to give Matt a chance. If Wes were interested in me he would have at least gotten my number, right? Plus there's Robin and I don't know where she fits in to all of this.

The last thing I expected when I moved here was to be confused over dating *a day* after moving here. Heck, I wasn't even going to try to date for at least a few months. Now I'm worried about which hot guy I like?

Pull yourself together, girl.

I hear the backdoor open and close, figuring it's probably Matt or Izzy coming to check on me. But it's neither of them, it's Robin.

"Hey, are you okay? You got out of there pretty fast, and right at the good part too." She asks as she sits down next to me.

I run a hand down my face and put on a fake smile. "Thank you for checking on me, I'm okay though."

She nods and then we sit there in silence. I figure I might as well just ask what I want to know and rip off the Band-Aid.

"Look, I'm just going to ask. Are you and Wes together?"

Robin scrunches her nose like she smelled something bad and then bursts out laughing. "Oh my god you're so funny."

I toss her a look of confusion and indignation because honestly, I'm a little upset. I don't think the thought of dating Wes deserves to be *laughed* at.

Robin stops laughing when she sees my face, "Oh, no. It's not- I'm a lesbian."

Ah. Way to go, Elli.

"Oh wow. Now I feel really stupid for assuming." I grumble, hiding my face in my hands. "I'm so sorry."

"Elli, you have nothing to be sorry for. You obviously didn't know, and I know Wes and I have a very close relationship. But he is *definitely* not my type." She pulls my hands from my face. "I, uh, was actually wondering if you wanted to go to lunch or something sometime? I would really like to be friends, if it's something you want."

"I would really like to be friends, too." I take out my phone and hand it to her, "Izzy leaves on Wednesday so I'll text you and we can set up a time to hang out after that."

Robin smiles and shimmies back and forth as she puts her number in my phone.

Is making friends really this easy?

We hear a chorus of voices drift out through the back door, and we turn towards the noise to find everyone filtering into the kitchen.

"Before we head back can I ask you something random and personal?" She says as she gives me my phone.

"Sure."

"What are you looking for in a romantic relationship?"

"Why do you want to know?"

She shrugs. "Matt's one of my best friends, I just want to make sure neither of you are wasting your time."

I nod, that makes sense. "I don't know, honestly. I've only had two serious relationships and they weren't good. They ended even worse."

She nudges me with her shoulder, "Ideally, then?"

Honesty is the best policy, right? It's not like I haven't given this a lot of thought. Growing up Mormon, as soon as I turned twelve a lot of lessons were about dating

standards, how to be a wife and mom, and all the quali-
ties you should look for in a future husband. The number of activities I spent looking through bridal magazines
to plan my ideal wedding is disturbing. The amount of
lists I was forced to make on my "perfect husband" is
equally as disturbing.

"I'm definitely a romantic, but with what I consider
realistic expectations. I guess ideally, I'd like to be with
someone who helps make the mundane tasks like gro-
cery shopping or cleaning fun. I'd rather be with someone who can say 'hey, I planned this date for us. Be ready
at 7' or 'I saw this flower at the park and thought of you'
than someone who tells me all the things they *want* to
do, but never act on it, or make me figure out every date.
I used to leave my ex little notes around his apartment,
or in his car while he was at work and he would get so
mad and tell me it was embarrassing and clingy, so I want
someone who likes the little gestures I do, and hopefully
they'll return them... Actions over words, you know?
Maybe I'm asking for too much and that's why I'm still
single." I say with a self-deprecating laugh.

"I think those are realistic and attainable. How important is religion?" Robin studies my face as she asks.

"That's complicated. I'm kind of in the middle of-"

"Robin! Come on! I have to be home soon and you're
our ride!" Lexi yells from the back door.

"Ugh. Kids. That's my queue. It was really nice to
meet you, Elli. I look forward to getting to know you
better." Robin and I both stand, and she brings me in for
a bone-crushing hug. She's surprisingly strong for such
a petite woman.

"It was nice to meet you too."

As soon as Izzy and I get in the car, she's bursting at the seams for me to tell her about what's going on with Matt. I casually tell her about how he wants to take me out on Saturday, and from her reaction, you'd think I'd just told her that I won a trip to Italy or something.

"This. is. AMAZING. Ugh. Matt is *so* hot." She gasps. "Don't tell Luke I said that."

"I won't tell Luke." I chuckle.

"I think dating him will be good for you. Maybe he's the one! You can get married, and then you guys can move back to Utah to have babies and I can be the super fun and cool aunt that spoils your kids!"

"Woah, Iz. Pump the brakes. I *just* met him. We haven't even been on a date yet! Besides, I can't plan a future with a guy without talking to him. Not that there's a future to plan, because we JUST MET." My voice is raised on the last two words for emphasis, and I think it's gotten through to Izzy.

She sighs and waves her hand dismissively. "Whatever you say. But if things don't work out with Matt, I'll probably end up married before you." She gives me a grin that can only be described as devilish.

Yeah, at the rate things are going with my love life, she's probably right.

CHAPTER 9

Wes

Did I stay up too late last night thinking about Elli? No.

Maybe.

Fine, yes.

As a creative, you've gotta create when inspiration hits you, and inspiration hit me at midnight last night as I was lying in bed.

Apparently, all my inspiration needed was a beautiful, curvy girl in a swimsuit to agree to go on a date with my best friend, who is a really great guy. I can't be mad at either of them.

I'd probably never perform this song live because anyone who knows me would know who I'm talking about and Robin would one hundred percent give me shit on it. And if Elli starts dating Matt seriously, that means she's going to be part of our group for a long time- possibly permanently- and that would be embarrassing for me to have written a song about another man's woman.

Although *Jessie's Girl* is quite the popular song, I don't see myself as the next Rick Springfield.

I finally put my guitar and notebook down and went to sleep at two a.m. and woke up to my phone buzzing at seven-thirty.

Luke: Mornin Wes! :) I need your help :D

Wes: No. You've run out of favors for this decade.

Luke: I'm calling you.

Wes: Please don't

But the phone rings anyway because of course Luke doesn't listen.

"What, Luke?" I groan into the phone.

"Well good morning to you too, Wes."

"Cut to the chase please." I lean back against my pillows, ready to deny him his favor and go the fuck back to sleep.

"Fine. Izzy and Elli are unpacking all day today…"

I sit upright at the mention of Elli, not hearing anything else Luke is saying. I already know I'll agree, even if I told myself no.

"...sooooooo... will you drive me? You don't have to stay, you can just drop me off and leave but I-"

"I'll be there at nine to pick you up." I hang up before he can answer.

I'll just take Luke and drop him. I won't have to see Elli- maybe just a glimpse.

If I don't see her, I won't have to think about Matt's arm around her shoulder, or his hand on her knee, or how I missed my chance to ask her out because I was too worried about not being good enough.

Last night after the party, Robin told me that she asked Elli what she wanted in a partner-even though I *specifically* asked her not to pry-and Elli's wants were so simple. Romantic gestures? I can do that. Making mundane tasks fun? Hell yeah I can! She said the religion thing was "complicated." "Complicated" is good, right? I can work with "complicated."

I spent all of last night thinking about dates I want to take her on, all the things I want to do with her. I would take her to a bookstore and give her five minutes to pick out whatever books she wanted, and I'd buy all of them. I'd take her to Robin's gallery in San Antonio and then get churros at my favorite churro stand.

I dreamt of the domestic tasks being with a partner would bring. Making dinner side by side, stealing kisses every few minutes. Blasting music and cleaning the house together. I thought of waking her up with breakfast in bed, lazing around together all day, playing guitar for her while she lays next to me on the couch. I thought about asking her to braid my hair, just to feel her hands on me.

And then I remembered that Matt already asked her out.

And she said yes.

It was like someone lit a match and burned up my fantasy.

Drop Luke off at the curb, wait until he's inside, then leave. I repeat to myself the whole drive to Luke's, to the donut shop, and the whole way to Elli's.

"You can just drop me off here, unless you want to come in with me?" Luke asks as we pull into the complex.

"Seeing as I have a mountain of IKEA furniture and another mountain of boxes to unpack..." Elli's words from last night pop into my head. IKEA furniture isn't easy to put together, and, knowing Luke and Izzy, they won't be much help. *Actions over words.*

"Maybe I'll come in for a minute and see if Elli needs any help." Luke gives me a tired look and rolls his eyes, but ultimately keeps his mouth shut, thank god. I don't need another lecture from him.

The closer we get to the door, the more my heart starts to race. Maybe Elli won't want to see me, and she'll ask me to leave.

Izzy answers the door with a squeal, jumping into Luke's arms as he hurriedly shoves the box of donuts into my arms. "Hi Wes." She smirks over his shoulder.

"Izzy." I nod.

"Elli's in her room. Go on in."

I was going to protest, pretend I wasn't here to see Elli, but no one would have believed that, and apparently they don't really care. So instead, I take the box of donuts and place them on the kitchen counter before going down the hall to her room. Elli is clad in tight biker shorts that hug her delicious thighs, a light pink t-shirt, with her hair piled messily on top of her. She has on big purple headphones and is swaying her hips to whatever she's listening to. I lean against the doorframe, feeling a little bad about creeping, but I can't help it. She's so fucking cute.

When Elli turns and sees me, she freezes. She's not wearing any makeup today, not that she wears much anyway, but she looks so stunning, I can't help but stare. Her cheeks are sun kissed and pink, and the pink color deepens as she slowly removes her headphones, her surprised, wide-eyed gaze never leaving mine.

Chapter 10

Elli

"**G**ood morning, Elli." Wes smirks, brown eyes lit up with amusement. He looks good today. *Obviously.* He has his hair pulled back into a bun, which is something I didn't realize could be so attractive, but *damn.*

"What are you doing here?"

"Luke needed a ride to deliver donuts." He nods towards the kitchen.

He's not here because he wants to see you. The mean girl voice in my head unhelpfully supplies.

"Oh. That's nice of you." I turn back to the shelf I was putting together, hoping to hide the disappointment on my face.

"I also came to help you, if you don't mind an interruption to your dance party."

I whip around so fast that I lose my balance and crash into the shelf, causing it to topple over. Wes, apparently blessed with superhuman speed, is in front of me, grabbing the shelf on either side to stop it from crushing me and crashing to the floor. His chest is an inch from my face and it's taking all my willpower not to lean in and take a big sniff of him. He smells like coffee and something woodsy and ohhhh my goodness does he smell good.

Once the shelf is stabilized, he steps back a bit, spinning around and surveying the room.

Izzy pops her head into the door, a mischievous grin on her face as she says. "Now, remember, Elli. The door stays open and no boys on the bed. Luke and I will be in the living room, so no funny business." Just as quickly as she came, she's gone.

"You have a habit of bringing boys into your room?" Wes teases.

I give an awkward half laugh, half sigh. "Not really. You're kind of the first non-related boy I've ever had in my bedroom- here or in Utah."

His mouth hangs open in shock and disbelief. "Didn't you go to college? You never had a date in your dorm room? Make out session, study session, anything?"

I shake my head. "I lived at home in college to save money, so I never got the chance."

He has a smug grin on his face as he closes the door and walks over to the stack of boxes.

"Where should we start?"

After a few hours we've managed to put together the two bookshelves, the nightstand, and the dresser. Izzy and I put together the bedframe Saturday night, so we're making good progress. Wes put on some music before we got started, so we worked in comfortable silence listening to a lot of Indie artists I'd never heard of. Wes would occasionally pipe up to give some backstory on some of the artists or want me to listen to a specific guitar part. His eyes lit up when he would talk, and I always made sure to give my full attention.

Once we had the shelves where I wanted them placed on either side of my desk, I gave Wes the go ahead to start unpacking my books.

"Any specific way you want them organized?" He asks, plopping on the floor and opening the first box.

"I usually do it alphabetically, with all the series staying together. You can do it however you'd like, though. If I don't like it, I'll just rearrange them later." I say playfully, earning an eye roll from Wes.

Wes makes a lot of comments about my choice in reading material, but not in a negative way. He comments on what he's read, praising my choices and we talk about our favorite parts of the books.

He's a big *Lord of the Rings* fan, apparently. He even had "the ring" that he wore on a chain around his neck in elementary school.

I have a lot of classics- *The Lord of the Rings, Jane Eyre, Sherlock Holmes, The Great Gatsby*- along with more mainstream books- *Twilight, The Hunger Games, Pretty Little Liars, Divergent*. He wastes no time making fun of me for liking a "sparkly vampire and werewolf love triangle disaster."

I make sure to tease him about the fact he knows what it's about.

"Did you know that Stephanie Meyer is Mormon? The vampires are basically described how angels are described in some parts of Mormon doctrine." This fact is wild to me. It makes me laugh every time I remember it.

"I didn't know that. Wait, isn't *50 Shades of Grey* based off of *Twilight?*"

"Oh yeah. It was a big craze with a lot of Mormon women when it came out." I remember the craze and how my mother freaked out and told me I was never allowed to even touch one of those books. She was appalled that our bishop's wife read it.

"Interesting. It's a terrible book, and doesn't represent the BDSM community or sex for that matter in a positive way *at all.* But it's still basically porn, so I figured they'd want to burn the books."

The word "sex" coming from Wes's mouth, especially in such a nonchalant way, sends chills down my arms. I've never been in a situation where sex is openly talked about, or discussed as a normal thing, so I'm not sure how to respond.

Luckily, I don't have to, because Wes asks, "Have you really read all of these?" Partially skeptical, partially in awe.

"I think there are a few I bought right before the move that I haven't read, but other than that, yes. I've read them all." I don't know what makes me keep rambling, but I can't stop the words from coming out.

"We weren't allowed to watch TV on Sundays in my house, and rarely would we be able to during the week unless my dad wasn't home, and even then, the younger kids usually took priority so they'd be occupied. So I read a lot. We would go to the thrift store one Saturday a month, and I would spend the whole time combing through books to find ones I was interested in, and I would read all of them by the next time we went."

He hums in acknowledgement, breaking down the box he was working on, and grabbing the last box in the stack. "What... is this stuff?"

I turn to see that he's opened up the box with a giant 'X' on it, and my face pales. "Oh, um. That's. Uhhhh" *smutty romance novels, the lingerie I've never worn, anti-Mormon literature, my faith crisis journal...*

Apparently I stand there frozen for too long because before I know it, Wes is standing in front of me, guiding me to sit on the bed. "Elli, I'm sorry. I didn't mean to pry. I'm not going to make you explain anything you don't want to. Just know, I'm not going to judge you."

"That stuff shouldn't be a big deal, you know? Not for a normal adult. But if my parents knew that I had that stuff when I was at home, they would have made me throw it away and talk to the bishop to 'repent'." I huff, throwing myself back onto the bed.

"That seems like an overreaction." Wes mumbles.

I bark out a humorless laugh. "You're not wrong."

Wes chews on his bottom lip, his eyes darting between me and the box. I can tell he's extremely curious, but I haven't said anything about that stuff to anyone. I *just* met Wes, and yet...

I slide myself down so my back is leaning against the bed, slide the box in front of me, and motion for Wes to sit on the other side of the box.

"Before I show you what's in here, I want to know what, if anything, you know about Mormons."

"Oh," his eyebrows raise in surprise, "Uh, Luke explained some rules like no swearing, no smoking, no drugs, no alcohol, no coffee, no tea, no tattoos, no piercings other than ears, no dating until you're sixteen, only dating other members. Something about missionaries, getting married young, giving ten percent of your income, and something about a temple and special underwear." He clears his throat like he wants to say more. "He also said sex before marriage, and you know, touching yourself and making out is considered really bad."

I can't help but laugh, because what he said sounds absolutely ridiculous, but he's not wrong. Wes looks confused that I'm laughing, so I try to compose myself.

"I'm sorry, it's not funny. Well, it's kind of funny. All of that stuff is right, but sexual sins- masturbating, porn, anything that intentionally arouses-aren't just 'really bad.' They teach us that they're the worst sin, second only to murder. Specifically sex before marriage is second only to murder, but the other stuff is considered just as grievous. Which is why these," I pull out the spicy romance novels, "are in here. My mom would die if she knew I was reading explicit sex scenes."

Wes looks horrified, then he shakes his head like he's trying to clear up his thoughts and he says, "Wait a minute. You're telling me masturbating is compared to murder?"

"Yep." I pop the "p" for emphasis. "Making out leads to temptation, so we're strongly advised against it. Some people don't even kiss until their wedding day."

Wes's facial expressions go through disgust, awe, confusion, and finally lands on curiosity. "Well now I'm curious about the other stuff, if you're willing to share?"

I nod, pulling out the bag of lingerie. "Modesty is one of the most important things taught, especially to girls because obviously we control the sexual purity of men." I roll my eyes. "Anyway, I was forbidden from wearing anything other than white or nude bras or underwear, because anything else is 'impure.' My mom used to ask who I was showing my bras to if I wanted a cute patterned one, so I just stopped asking. This bag is lingerie and fancy underwear I've been saving for when I moved out."

Wes's face is very flushed as he stares at the bag of lingerie. A small, vain part of me hopes he might be picturing me in them. His voice is low and strained when he finally speaks again, "Anything else?"

I pull out my journal and three books: *The CES Letter, Leaving the Saints: How I Lost the Mormons and Found My Faith,* and *The Pattern of the Double-Bind in Mormonism.* I hand them to Wes so he can read the titles and skim the back cover, and when he sets them down, he looks even more confused.

"This is my faith crisis journal. I started it 2.5 years ago, and have documented pretty much every thought, question, or concern I've had. Six months after I started the journal, I found *Leaving the Saints,* which led me to reading the other two. They validated my questions and made me realize I wasn't just a bad member who lacked faith. A year after I started the journal, I knew. I knew that I didn't believe anymore. I knew an organization who hides so much of the truth *can't* be true. For the last 1.5 years this journal has been the only safe place to express everything I've been feeling. If I left the church before I moved out, I would have been kicked out and disowned. I wanted to believe *so* badly. It's the only life I've ever known, and so much of my identity is tied into it so now I have to learn who I am outside of the church. I'm not sure I want to leave, though, because what if I'm wrong and I'll go to hell if I do? But it feels wrong to go through the motions of being a devout member if I don't really believe it, you know? And I'm not happy in the church, but what if I'm even more miserable outside of it, because I'm not 'doing what I'm supposed to be doing?'"

I don't realize tears are streaming down my face until Wes gently wipes them away whispering, "That sounds so hard, Elli. Especially to deal with it all on your own. I'm not going to even pretend I know what you're going through, but just know I think you're pretty damn strong."

"It feels really good to get it out there. Thank you for listening, and for thinking I'm pretty damn strong." I grin through the tears, and he gives me a small chuckle. "That's the first curse word I've ever said out loud."

"Have you been saying them in your head?"

"Yeah..."

"Well that's a start."

Izzy walks into the room, saying something about going to get something to eat, but she halts when she sees me crying. "What did you do to her?" She points an accusing finger at Wes.

"Calm down, Iz. He didn't do anything. I'm just emotional today." I say, wiping the rest of my tears.

"If you say so." She narrows her eyes in suspicion, "I'm starving. Come on, Mom sent money for lunch." She walks to the doorway, stopping to glance over her shoulder and say, "Wes can come too as long as he doesn't make you cry again."

Chapter II

Wes

I check with Elli to make sure she's comfortable with me joining them for lunch, because I don't want to impose on them. She assures me that it's fine, so we jump in her car and head to Schneider's, a little German restaurant downtown that has the best food.

I'm still trying to wrap my head around the information Elli gave as we pull in, order our food, and sit at a little table on the outside patio.

I order a reuben sandwich with a bag of chips, and Luke and Izzy are splitting the Weiner schnitzel plate with fried potatoes and a salad, and they each got a different flavor of cake slice to try. I think one was marzipan and one was napoleon cake, but I wasn't paying that much attention.

Elli orders a bratwurst sandwich with a side of fries and I can't help but smile when I see she has two desserts on her tray. An eclair, and another cake that has caramelized almonds on top. She has a sweet tooth, I've noticed.

She probably tastes sweet too.

No! Bad brain. She shared something very vulnerable with me today and she's going on a date with my best friend. I can't be thinking about how sweet she'd taste.

I clear my throat and point towards the cake on her tray, "What's that?"

"It's called 'Bieninstich' which means 'bee sting cake.' It's a really old German and Swiss recipe that dates back to the twentieth century. It's got custard in the middle and caramelized almonds on top and it's delicious. My grandma made it once when we visited and I've never seen it anywhere else so I had to try it." Her eyes light up when she talks and I can't help but smile.

Elli seems lighter now that she's gotten her secret off her chest. I can't even imagine holding all of that in for almost two years, with no one to talk to or a way to process and work through it.

Jess made me see a therapist when she took over guardianship of me. I tried to fight it, tried to say nothing was wrong with me. She told me that anyone who has gone through as much as I have in my lifetime needs to hash it out with an impartial third party.

I refused to talk to my therapist, Roy, at first, thinking it was a waste of time, but one day, he asked me about my mom and the flood gates opened.

I never hated my mom, I think she was broken and lost, but she tried her best given the fact that she was also traumatized. I told him how I was worried I would turn to drugs in my low times and that I would end up in a shitty relationship like she did.

I didn't have much of a plan after high school. I had applied to schools because everyone else was, but I didn't know what to major in or what field to go into. When

I told Roy that I wanted to be a musician, we talked through how to make that happen, while still being able to support myself.

Roy referred me to a psychiatrist when I told him about the panic attacks I was having almost daily, and that's when I was prescribed my first anti-anxiety medicine. It was eye-opening to see how different I felt when the chemicals in my brain were balanced.

I wonder if she would benefit from therapy. I don't know much about religious trauma, but I'm almost positive that anyone who walks away from a religion like hers would have some.

"Wes, you went to UTSA, right?" Izzy asks halfway through lunch.

"I sure did." All of the adults, besides Sean, went to UTSA for school.

"What was the commute from here like? Was it bad?"

"Depends on your schedule. It's about an hour drive on a good day, so two hours travel time. I would make sure all my classes were scheduled for two days a week or online so I didn't have to travel every day. It helped that Sav, Drew, and Robs went too, so we could carpool."

"Are you considering moving here for college?" Elli asks Izzy.

Izzy shrugs. "Maybe. It's an option for sure."

"I told her I'd be willing to move to Utah for school." Luke chimes in.

"Yes, but Elli lives here now, so it would make more sense for me to move in with her and go to school here than for you to have to move and find housing in Utah." Izzy boops Luke's nose like he's a silly little kid, and he preens at her attention.

He really is like a touch starved cat with her. I haven't seen him _not_ touch her since that first night we were here. Right now, he's got his arm wrapped around her waist while he eats with one hand.

I still think their love is sickly sweet, but I know if I were able to touch Elli like that, I'd never let my hand leave her either.

"Izzy, I love you with all my heart, but I *just* moved out and got into my own space. I've shared a room with you for sixteen years, I don't want to share with you anymore." Elli says.

Elli takes a bite out of the eclair after she's finished talking and the cream filling spills out all over her lips, and there's a chocolate streak on her top lip when she pulls away. She uses her tongue to swipe at the cream and chocolate and makes a little humming noise, just like when she bit the strawberry, and my pants get a little bit tighter.

Fuck, why does her eating make me so hot and bothered?

"Oh wow, this is really good. Does anyone want to try it?" She offers the pastry around.

Izzy and Luke say no, and I *should* say no, I'm not a sweets guy. But I want to taste what she's tasting. I want to put my mouth where hers has been, so I say yes. She brings the eclair to my lips and I take a bite, never breaking the eye contact we've locked ourselves into. The sweetness explodes on my tongue and it's not my favorite flavor, but I imagine this is what Elli's lips would taste like if I were to kiss her right now and I stifle a groan.

"So?" Elli asks, her cheeks pink. Though I can't tell if it's from the humid Texas heat or watching me eat the pastry.

"Delicious." But I'm looking at her lips. Her eyes dart down to my own, like she's thinking the same thing I am.

Like she wants to taste me as much as I want to taste her.

"I think if we can share a room for sixteen years, we can share an entire apartment." Izzy breaks whatever trance Elli and I were under.

Elli doesn't miss a beat. "I know we *can* but I don't *want* to."

Izzy huffs. "I'll convince you in the next year. Don't you worry."

Elli shakes her head. "No, you won't. But you're welcome to try. I'm not opposed to accepting bribes."

Izzy sticks her tongue out at Elli and pretends to pout, but Luke says something in her ear that makes her giggle. Once again, they're in their own little bubble. The rest of the world doesn't exist to these two kids who have found their person at such a young age.

A pang of yearning shoots through me and the dread I've kept buried deep down starts to creep into my mind like a dark cloud, making me wonder if I'll ever have love again. It makes me wonder if I'll ever be enough for someone, if I even have enough to offer someone.

Will I ever find someone who fully gets me, and wants me with all my dark parts? Will I ever find someone who'll be supportive of my dreams and not just entertain them as some unachievable thing? Will I ever gross out my friends with how in love I am?

The clouds in my head start getting darker, and I think back to if I've been taking my meds the way I'm supposed to. I may have skipped a day or two. I need to get back on track.

"Good thing I've finished eating or I would lose my appetite." Elli mumbles at my side.

When I focus on her, the clouds don't seem so dark. The dread doesn't seem so heavy. I feel a little bit of hope, that even if we'll never have a romantic relationship, maybe this is the start of a beautiful friendship.

Chapter 12

Elli

I barely slept last night; my mind was racing in a million different directions. Izzy asked what happened with Wes when they dropped us off after lunch, so I told her about the box and about wanting to leave the religion we grew up in. She was understandably shocked and full of questions, but she wasn't mad and she promised not to tell our parents. What I didn't expect is for her to want to know everything that I disagreed with. I didn't want to sway her in a specific direction, so I told her if she wants to research things herself, I will be happy to discuss it with her.

Izzy didn't like that answer. But if I know her, she'll go research things herself. I think she's always had a few doubts, just like me, but I don't want to push her to follow my example.

She asked if it meant that I was going to "dress cool" now that I didn't have to follow modesty standards.

I told her I haven't made a decision on that yet.

She said I should try out an immodest dress on my date with Matt.

The date with Matt was another reason for my sleepless night.

Matt seems like a really great guy, extremely good looking, strong work ethic, so kind. The "settling down with a white picket fence, two-point-five kids, a dog, and a minivan" type.

I know, I know, we haven't even gone on *one* date and I'm already talking about kids, but that's the kind of mindset I was taught to have growing up. You date to marry, or you're wasting your time. You marry quickly so you're not tempted to have sex, but as soon as you get married, you start trying to pop babies.

The point is, Matt is great. And he wants to go out with *me*. So why don't I feel more excited?

I don't want to admit it's because of Wes. Even though I know in my heart that's why.

He's another reason I didn't get much sleep. At first I chalked my attraction to Wes up to him being the complete opposite of the guys I dated in Utah.

That's not the case, though. It would be much easier if it were though.

Yes, he is the total opposite of them, but not just in how he looks. My first boyfriend, Brigham, would have thought that helping me unpack furniture in my bedroom was a ploy to seduce him and make him "unworthy of a temple marriage."

My most recent ex, Packer, would have never shown up to help put together furniture and unpack books without me begging him. It took me two weeks of pleading for him to agree to come to my birthday dinner and we had been dating for almost four months. Other guys I've gone on dates with would take any opportunity to stick their tongue down my throat and dry hump on the first date, or they would refuse to touch me at all. Wes is so easy to talk to and be open with, too. If it would have been anyone else who found the box, I don't think I'd have gone into detail about it.

So, yeah. Wes is completely different.

Around midnight last night, my phone lit up with a text from an unknown number.

Unknown: Hey it's Wes. I hope this is okay, I asked Luke for your number. I wanted you to have mine in case you need anything.

Elli: You could have just asked me, silly. But it's okay. Thank you, I appreciate it, and now you have my number in case there's something I can do for you. Thanks again for your help today, you have no idea how much it means to me. <3

Wes: Yeah, I know I could have asked you, but it slipped my mind lol. No need to thank me though, I had a lot of fun.

Wes: Shouldn't you be asleep?

Elli: I had fun too.

Elli: I was about to go to sleep when some guy texted me and interrupted my beauty sleep ;)

Wes: what an asshole…

Elli: I can forgive him. He did help put together furniture all day :)

Wes: you don't need beauty sleep anyway

Elli: Are you saying I'm too far gone to be saved? :O

Wes: Never. I'm saying you're beautiful anyway. But you still need sleep. I won't bother you anymore tonight. Goodnight, Elli. Sweet dreams <3

If Wes calling me beautiful made me fall asleep with a ridiculously dopey grin on my face and made my stomach flutter, no one will ever know.

When Matt called me beautiful, it felt nice, but it didn't have the same effect, and he said it to my face and not over text.

I groan and flop back onto the bed, throwing my arms over my face. The mattress dips as Izzy lays next to me and I hear her dramatic sigh.

I move my arms enough to peek at her, "Can I help you?"

She turns and props herself on her elbow. "No, but I can help you!"

"What are you talking about?"

She gives me a pointed look. "I know you're nervous about this date with Matt. Who wouldn't be? He's a total dreamboat. But Els, you're *so* pretty. You don't need to worry that this is a pity date. Luke didn't ask him to ask you."

"Gee thanks." I say sarcastically.

"Come on, grumpy gills. Help me get ready for *my* date!"

At the park, I give Izzy and Luke enough space where they don't have to worry about me staring at them all night by finding a shady tree to read one of my smutty romance novels underneath. I'm just about to get to the part where Miles and Taylor are *finally* about to have sex when my phone vibrates.

Wes: Hey, did you know that nut-meg is a hallucinogen?

Elli: OMG really?

Wes: Really. You have to ingest a LOT, but next time you have pumpkin pie, you'll be wondering if you're seeing things.

Elli: At least that would SPICE up Thanksgiving :P

Wes: that was very punny ;)

Elli: Wait.

Elli: Wes, did you ingest copious amounts of nutmeg? Is that why you know this????

Wes: pshhhhhh

Wes: no ;p

Elli: Riiiiight. What if I'M a halluci-nation? ;)

WES: I don't think my sub-conscious could even hallucinate someone as beautiful as you

WES: Shit, sorry if I'm interrupting. I forgot it's Izzy and Luke's picnic date.

I'm really glad he can't see me right now because I know my face is bright red and it isn't from the June heat. It doesn't help that my book has me flustered and a little aroused, now Wes has me flustered too.

ELLI: You're not interrupting. I'm just reading while they do whatever it is they do.

WES: Ah, Elli. You know EXACTLY what they're doing. ;P Don't let me interrupt your reading. I just wanted you to know about the nutmeg.

WES: Just in case you were worried.

ELLI: They're just having a picnic! And thank you, I'll be sure to watch out for nutmeg overdose ;)

WES: Anytime. Hey, what time is Izzy's flight tomorrow?

ELLI: We're headed to the airport at 2 since her flight is at 4

WES: Gotcha. You going to be okay?

ELLI: Yeah, it'll be tough, but I know she can't stay forever.

WES: You'll let me know if you need anything?

ELLI: Will do, Wes. Thank you <3

WES: Anytime <3 Talk to you later, Elli

My heart is racing with the hearts and the compliments and the flirty banter. Is it flirty? Or is he just being friendly? I genuinely can't tell. I groan inwardly and try to focus on my book again.

Izzy and Luke approach an hour later, looking forlorn and I can tell Izzy's been crying.

"My curfew is earlier tonight, so it's time for us to head out." Luke says quietly while rubbing Izzy's back soothingly.

I nod and we make our way to the car.

Izzy is quiet when we get to the apartment, giving me the excuse that she's just tired, but I can see how sad she is. She doesn't even gush to me about her new necklace promise ring. We barely talk as we get ready for bed, and when I come out of the shower, she's already asleep on the pull out couch.

I head to my room, and see there's a new text when I pick up my phone to plug it in.

Matt: Hey gorgeous, it's Matt. just wanted to make sure Saturday is still good for you? :)

Elli: Hi Matt! That sounds great :)

Matt: Yes! :D I'll come get you at 6? Dress code is cocktail. <3

Elli: Perfect. :) I'll see you then.

Matt: I'll be counting down the minutes ;)

I wait for the flutters to come at Matt's blatant flirting, but nothing comes.

I go to turn off the lamp on my nightstand, and see Izzy standing in my doorway, tears streaming down her face. I pat the bed next to where I'm sitting and she crawls over and lays her head in my lap while she continues to sob.

"Iz, I'm so sorry. This really sucks. But I promise I'll keep an eye on Luke and you can come visit me anytime Mom and Dad let you." I whisper as I stroke her hair.

Izzy looks at me, wiping away the tears on her cheeks and shakes her head. "It's not that. I'll miss Luke, of course, but I'm used to long distance with him. I don't want to leave *you*. I have a lot of friends, but you're my best friend, Els."

My heart warms at Izzy's confession, and now I'm trying not to cry too. Damn her for being so sweet. "You're my best friend too, Iz. I'm always just a phone call or text away, okay?"

"You better keep me updated on this whole Wes and Matt situation. I'm bummed I won't be here to watch it play out." She sighs, sitting against the headboard, and interlacing her fingers with mine.

"What situation?"

Izzy sighs in exasperation, as if I should know exactly what she's talking about. "How you like both of them, how they both like *you*. Did you know Wes went over and interrogated Luke about Mormonism Sunday morning? Luke told me he hasn't dated anyone in almost two years, so he's probably just really scared to ask you out, but he obviously likes you. Or Matt beat him to it and he doesn't want to step on his toes."

My mind flashes back to Sunday, how Wes and Matt were always next to me. How after Matt asked me out, Wes traded spots with Sean- had he heard Matt ask me out? Then there was Robin's question about what I want in a partner. Did she ask for Wes? She said she asked because of Matt. Then he showed up and helped put together furniture and let me share something extremely personal with him without judging or getting scared off. The random, lengthy text conversations.

"I knew that Luke told him about it, but he didn't tell me he *asked.* I assumed Luke had told him because of you."

Izzy shrugs, "Nope. Luke said he was disappointed to learn some of the stuff, but I don't know what."

"*...only dating other members.*" Wes had said that's what Luke told him. Did he think I wouldn't agree to go out with him because he's not a member?

"Anyway, I'm going to go to sleep, love you sis." Izzy gives me a kiss on the cheek before she stands and walks out of the room.

"Love you too!" I call out after her.

All this new information is making my head spin, and now I'm even more confused than before. Is Wes playing some kind of game? The idea that Matt and Wes had a competition to see who could ask me out first crosses my mind for a fraction of a second, but I quickly swipe that away because that doesn't sound like them, and I don't think Robin would let them do that.

Robin. I should ask her what the hell is going on.

Maybe she doesn't know.

Nothing is going to get sorted tonight, and I have to drive Izzy to the airport tomorrow so I need to sleep.

As I close my eyes, my mind drifts and before I know it, I'm lost in pools of dark chocolate that look a lot like Wes's eyes.

Chapter 13

Wes

I haven't stopped thinking about Elli since Monday.

Okay, she's been on my mind constantly since I met her, but I've had her number for two days and I have to use all of my willpower not to text her constantly. I was so tempted to call her last night when I couldn't sleep just because I wanted to hear her voice all sleepy and sweet.

And because I'm a pathetic sap who is falling hard for a girl he's only known for four days, I'm driving to her house to take her and Izzy to the airport. Luke's too sad to be suspicious about the fact that I offered to drive him, thank god, because I don't know how I would spin this in a way that doesn't sound like a romantic gesture.

It's totally *not* romantic. Just a...friendly gesture. And I have a proposal for her afterwards. One I've been planning for the last twenty-four hours.

Elli answers the door and her expression softens when she sees it's Luke, and quickly ushers him inside. Then her attention is drawn to me and she tilts her head in confusion. "Wes? What are you doing here?" She leans against the doorframe, looking fucking adorable in black overalls with a white t-shirt underneath. The overalls accentuate every curve on her body and it's taking all of my dwindling willpower not to blatantly stare at her.

"I wanted to offer my chauffeur services to the airport. You know, so you don't have to spend the whole ride back with a mopey Luke."

She sighs dramatically, "I mean, I guess I did save you from catching the 'love bug' so I guess it's only fair you save me from catching the grumps."

I want to say *"Actually, you didn't save me from it. I caught it, and the only cure is you."* and wrap my arms around her waist and kiss her plush pink lips.

But I settle on shrugging and a simple, "Fair is fair."

"Let me just grab Izzy's luggage and let them know it's time to leave. It'll take at least ten minutes for them to let go of each other long enough to make it to the car."

And she was right.

Izzy and Luke cling to each other the entire ride to the airport while Izzy sniffles and Luke makes reassuring predictions for their future. In eleven months they'll graduate high school, and Luke will go to Utah for her graduation. They're going to apply to the same colleges and see where they both get in, and they'll figure out where they want to go together. Luke gave Izzy a promise ring yesterday, and he reminds her that they are going to be together forever, they just have to be apart for a little while longer.

And damn it if I'm not jealous of seventeen year olds.

I don't think all teenage romances last, but if anyone's going to last, it's going to be Luke and Izzy. They've already made long distance work for a year, there's no reason to believe they can't last another.

I couldn't even make it work with a girl I lived two blocks away from.

I stay in the car as Luke and Elli help Izzy get her luggage and they say a tearful goodbye. When Elli gets back in the car, her blue eyes are made even brighter by the tears welling in them, and it's unfair how gorgeous she looks, even when she's crying. I want to kiss the tears off of her face. Without thinking, I reach over and squeeze her thigh just above her knee in a comforting gesture. I can hear her little gasp, and immediately pull my hand away, an apology on the tip of my tongue, but she reaches over and squeezes my hand instead. I look over at her and she gives me an appreciative, watery smile that makes my heart flip flop.

To break the tension on the way back, I ask Elli what her weekend plans are.

"Um Matt's taking me out Saturday. No other plans." She says sheepishly.

"Oh," I grip the steering wheel so hard my knuckles start to turn white "that's cool. What are you guys doing?" I don't really want to know. In fact, I would rather hear about someone's colonoscopy than listen to Elli talk about a date. Luke's eyes meet mine in the rearview mirror, a confounded expression on his face. He's probably wondering why I'm putting myself through the torture of hearing about it.

I am too.

Although, I did tell myself if Elli wants to date Matt I would back off. Elli and I can be just friends. I can get past this little crush.

Ha ha, right.

Elli's shoulders slump slightly and her brows furrow, "I don't know yet, he didn't say. He just said the dress code is 'cocktail.'"

"I'm sure it'll be something great, Matt goes all out for dates."

Elli hums in response, and I see Luke roll his eyes in the back seat.

When we pull up to Luke's, Elli turns around and puts a hand on his knee with a sincere smile. "I want you to know that I'm here if you ever need anything. You're family now. I'm already trying to figure out how to get Iz here for fall break or over Christmas break, so it won't be an entire year again. Thank you for being so good to my sister, Luke. She's lucky to have you."

"Thank you Elli, I appreciate that. I have to amend the last part though, I'm definitely the lucky one." Elli gives his knee a final squeeze before he gets out of the car.

I may be overstepping by trying to insert myself into Elli's life. She might not even want to keep spending time with me. Still, that doesn't stop me from asking, "Do you want help picking something to wear for Saturday? I've gone to enough events to know what cocktail attire means."

She hesitates and just stares at me, and I immediately regret asking. I overstepped, she's going to think it was weird-

"I'd actually really appreciate that, thank you." She finally says, and I almost sigh in relief. "I don't have any options at my place, would you mind coming to the mall with me?" She asks shyly.

"Of course not, do you want to head there right now?"

At her nod, I take off in the direction of the mall. While we're driving, I replay the plan I've come up with in my head to psych myself up to ask her. When I finally feel confident enough, I clear my throat.

"So, I've been thinking about what you said on Monday." I start, "And I have an idea I want to run by you." She nods, so I continue. "I know you're worried about being happy outside of the church. I can see how the unknown can be scary, and going through that big of a change by yourself would be extremely overwhelming, so I have a proposition for you."

"I'm listening..." She says carefully.

"I propose that for one month, you try all the things that go against the rules you grew up with, and at the end, you can decide if you're happier with or without them."

"Okay... so like, try coffee and alcohol and dressing immodestly?"

I nod, "Exactly. For one month, you live like any other twenty-four year old would. You skip church on Sundays to go out for coffee with your friends, you go to a club in a strapless dress, you go out for drinks on a Friday after work..."

"I try masturbating for the first time." She says quietly, then covers her mouth. "Sorry. That was awkward. That was supposed to be an inside thought."

"Right. That too."

Fuck.

Visions of Elli sweaty, writhing on the bed with her hand between those thick thighs flash through my head.

I clear my throat to try and get them away, and continue my pitch.

"Today is a good start with this experiment. We'll find you a suitable cocktail dress that's 'immodest' to wear out with Matt. Maybe we can find some summer clothes that you wouldn't have worn before too?" The imagery of her in a pair of short shorts and tank tops doesn't quell my arousal, but the thought of her on a date with Matt definitely dampens it a bit.

I glance over at Elli who's biting her bottom lip while she mulls over my offer.

"You'd help me experience all of these things?"

"Well, *almost* all of them." Although the thought of helping Elli figure out how she likes to be touched is so fucking appealing, that's the line in the sand. "I'll help with the coffee, alcohol, and immodest clothes. If you want to get more piercings, I can take you to my person. If you want to try weed or something, I can help with that too."

I pull us into a parking spot and wait for her to answer. I could have totally just overstepped and made everything super awkward between us. That would suck, but overall, I'd respect whatever decision she makes.

"I'm in." She says firmly, and the relief is instantaneous. "If you're sure you want to do this with a girl you only met a few days ago." She adds.

I turn to look at her and see the trepidation in her eyes. "I'm positive, Elli. I've been thinking about a way to help for the last two days. I know we're practically strangers, but if you put your trust in me, I won't let you down."

"Thank you, Wes." She sucks in a deep breath and with a determined nod says, "Let's do this."

An hour later, I'm sitting in the dressing room of the third store we've been in. Apparently a lot of stores don't carry clothes for plus size women and that makes me irrationally angry. Why don't companies make clothes bigger? Don't they know the profit they'd make if they extended their sizing?

We went into Torrid, where it's a bit pricey, but she was able to find some cute shorts and some casual dresses on their clearance rack. Then, we went to H&M where Elli says she can usually fit into their largest standard size for tops, so she got some tank tops. Now, we're in Forever 21 because it's relatively cheap, and they have a decent plus size section. Elli's got two dresses and some skirts she's trying on.

We weren't able to find any cocktail dresses that Elli liked at the other two stores, and if these don't work, I guess we'll have to try another store.

"Alright. Are you ready for option number one?" Elli calls out from behind the door. This is the first dress she's trying on, she's already tried on the skirts but she didn't show those to me.

"Bring it on." I sit up straighter as Elli opens the door and steps out.

I clench my jaw to stop it from dropping when she walks out in a sleek, black satin dress. It's got spaghetti straps and a sweetheart neckline that sits just above her cleavage, hits her mid-calf, and has a slit that runs up one side to her thigh. She spins, showing me the whole thing. It crisscrosses in the back and it shows her lack of bra, and the sexy little rolls on her back. I *barely* suppress a groan of appreciation.

"What do you think?" She asks when she stops spinning.

I think that dress would look much better on the floor, and you naked.

But I don't say that, of course. I say instead, "It's the perfect cocktail dress. Simple and classy. Let's see the other one and then we'll decide."

"Okay. Thank you, this is really comfy so I think it'd be good for my date." She turns back into the dressing room shutting the door.

I take some deep breaths, willing myself to calm the fuck down because if she chooses not to go with any of these dresses, then I'm going to have to watch her twirl and pose in even more of them and I'm not going to be able to keep my dick soft no matter how much I try.

I hear the click of the door open and my heart starts beating in my ears as I take in the goddess before me.

This dress looks like it was made for Elli. The light blue satin fabric makes her skin glow and her eyes pop. The cowl neckline dips just below the valley of her breasts, giving a peek at the top of her glorious tits. The top is tight against her belly and the skirt flows down just above her knees. When she spins, I see it's an open back with a crisscross tie that she's knotted, and the skirt sits just above the swell of her ass.

My dick is rock hard in my pants now and I'm so glad I wore dark jeans so hopefully she can't see how much this is affecting me.

"So? What do you think?" She asks, nervously chewing on her bottom lip.

"I think you look ethereal," I whisper.

"Thank you." She blushes, and I see it travel down her chest. "So, which dress should I wear?"

I pretend to think about it for a minute, but I know my answer immediately. And it makes me feel like an asshole. "This dress is less cocktail, and more 'club'. I think you should wear the black one for your date."

The word "date" is sour on my tongue, but no way in hell is she wearing this on a date with Matt. Some caveman part of my brain never wants her to wear this for anyone else but me. Unfair? Probably. But I'm just going to go with it.

"Yeah, I thought so too. Plus, I don't want to embarrass anyone."

"You could never embarrass anyone in that dress, Elli. I promise. I just know Matt, and I think you'll feel more comfortable wherever he takes you in the black one."

She nods, "I'm going to go change, then we can head out."

The door closes with a soft click and I scrub my face and try not to groan. I hear some shuffling in the room and Elli mutters something I can't understand.

"Wes? Can you, uh, help me? I think I tied the knot too tight and I can't get it undone to take the dress off."

Fuck me sideways.

"Yeah, of course." I stand, try to subtly adjust myself in my jeans, and wait for her to open the door.

Untie the knot then leave. It's not difficult. She's your friend. You're just helping her out.

Elli opens the door and ushers me in. It's more cramped in here than I thought it'd be, which does nothing for my aroused state. Elli's facing the mirror and gives me an embarrassed, appreciative smile.

My calloused fingers gently grab the thin silky material tied in a knot in the middle of her back, and as hard as I try not to, I graze her skin as I work the knot loose. I hear Elli's sharp intake of breath and look up to make sure I didn't hurt her, but she's not looking at me.

Her face is flushed as she stares down at her toes, and as my eyes snag on her taut nipples pressing against the fabric of the dress. They're just *begging* to be licked and nibbled on.

It makes me feel a tiny bit better that I'm not the only one feeling hot and bothered in this cramped dressing room.

I take my time working the knot loose, teasing my fingertips against her soft skin. I want to kiss the exposed skin of her shoulder and up her neck, pull her closer so she can grind her ass against me. I want to drop this dress to the ground and make a meal out of her.

"There you go." I rasp as the strings come loose and I step back away from Elli.

"Thank you." Her voice is breathy as she responds.

I step out of the dressing room and immediately miss the closeness to Elli's body. This next month is going to be difficult if I can't get my feelings in check.

Once Elli's paid for the clothes, we head back to my car and drive silently back to her apartment. Like the gentleman I try to be, I help her take her new wardrobe in and drop the bags in the living room.

"Thank you for taking me shopping. And for taking Izzy to the airport with me. I really appreciate it. Although I'm sure you had other plans that would have been more fun." Elli and I are standing at the threshold of her apartment saying goodbye.

"I wouldn't have wanted to be anywhere else today." And I mean that. Today was a good day.

I'm about to say "see you later" when Elli abruptly wraps her arms around my waist in a hug. I only hesitate for a second before wrapping my arms around her shoulders in return.

When she pulls back slightly and presses her lips softly against my cheek, I swear an electric current shoots down my spine at the contact.

"Goodnight, Elli." I say, stepping back before I do something stupid like kiss her.

"Goodnight, Wes."

Chapter 14

Elli

These past few days have thrown me off-kilter, my emotions-*and hormones-* are all over the place.

Izzy leaving? Sad. Heart wrenching. I'll miss my best friend.

Having my own space completely to myself for the first time in my life? Happy, freeing.

Finally dressing how I want? Invigorating. Even if it is only in the comfort of my apartment. Just lounging around in short shorts and a tank top is cathartic.

I've lived in baggy t-shirts and oversized overalls most of my life, wearing loose swing dresses on occasion because I always felt like my body was bad, that it needed to be hidden. The shame that was ingrained into me since I was a child is something that will take a lot of work. I thought I'd hate having so much of my skin on display, but I feel...free. Beautiful. Powerful.

Wes showing up to take us to the airport, then his proposal and shopping? A pleasant, swoon-worthy surprise.

The sexual tension with Wes being so thick I can cut it with a knife? Confusing. Arousing. I don't think I've ever been so turned on in my *life*. Wes didn't even *do* anything. As soon as he left, I used my fingers to try and relieve the ache between my thighs. It sort of gave me some relief, but I'm not sure what I'm doing so I don't think I had an orgasm.

My date with Matt? Well, I almost forgot about that to be honest.

I thought I was confused before about Wes, but Wednesday just amplified the confusion. I could have sworn he was going to kiss me after he helped me unzip my dress.

What kind of man spends a whole day putting together IKEA furniture, listens to a complete stranger have a breakdown about religious trauma, checks to make sure you get in okay, willingly drives your baby sister to the airport, takes you dress shopping and says "You look ethereal", then basically ghosts you?

Wes Jones, apparently.

Maybe I'm reading into it. I don't know Wes that well, even if we've seen each other and talked to each other pretty much every day for the last five days. Maybe he's just always like this with his friends. Maybe he's just being extra nice to me because I'm new and he feels bad for me.

I sound like a damn high schooler. It's only been three days. He's probably just busy.

Swearing feels good. I've been swearing more in my head and I like how it feels.

I have an hour until my date with Matt, so I can't waste any more time stressing over whatever the hell happened this week.

I ended up buying both dresses I tried on, but I'll be wearing the black one tonight. Good thing too, because if I wear the blue one, all I'll be able to think about all night is Wes's fingers gently brushing against my skin as he undid the knot. How the mere closeness of him made my nipples hard enough to cut through glass. How if I hadn't been wearing panties, I'm sure my thighs would have had arousal dripping down them.

Ah, shit. Now I'm turned on again.

I stand in front of the freezer to cool my heated skin because Matt will be here any minute.

The doorbell rings and when I answer it, Matt is standing there in tailored gray pants and with a white collared shirt and rust blazer. His eyes hungrily rake up and down my body. "Wow, Elli. You look absolutely gorgeous."

I blush, "Thank you, Matt. You look pretty dapper yourself."

Matt drives us into downtown Austin to a high rise building, where a valet takes his car from him-I've never seen a valet service like that in real life. He guides me to a nondescript door where he punches in a code, and it leads us to an elevator that takes us up to the top floor.

"What is this place?" I whisper.

Matt chuckles and wraps his arms around my waist and pulls me into him so my back is to his front. "This is a very exclusive restaurant that overlooks the river and the rest of downtown Austin. It's absolutely stunning. My godfather is friends with the chef."

My family considers The Cheesecake Factory to be a fancy, special occasion restaurant, so I can't even imagine what I'm about to walk into. Does Matt just go to exclusive places for dinner on the regular? Is this a normal first date spot for the wealthy? What if I have to eat snails? There are so many questions I have, but all I can muster is, "But why?"

Before Matt can answer, the elevator doors open and we're greeted by a tall blonde woman who has her hair pulled in a sleek chignon and is wearing a very nice black pantsuit. She gives us a soft smile, "Welcome, Mr. Bailey. Your usual table is ready."

"Thank you Carla." Matt says with a charming grin.

Carla leads us through the low-lit restaurant where people are chatting quietly. People, mostly the men, send Matt nods of acknowledgment and greeting as we pass. I can feel the jealous gaze of some of the women when they notice Matt's arm wrapped around my waist. I feel very out of place in my Forever 21 dress and Target heels amongst designer dresses and shoes. Wes was right though; I do feel more comfortable in the black dress.

When we reach the table, my breath is taken away by the view in front of me.

A gold haze mixes with the light blue sky as the sun sets, reflecting off of the buildings and onto the river, making it look like a river of gold is running through the city. It looks like a painting. It makes me long to see the sun set over the mountains in Utah, the pale purple against the golden sky is unlike anything I've ever seen. Though this is a view I could learn to love.

Matt pulls out my chair before taking the seat opposite me, and we're immediately greeted by Sam, a tall, lanky brunette man dressed all in black, who we learn will be our waiter for this evening. Matt apparently knows Sam well, and they exchange small talk while I glance at the drink menu.

"I don't know if you drink, and if you don't feel comfortable drinking, that's totally fine, but their house champagne is delicious, and goes perfectly with everything on the menu. I'm going to have a glass, if you'd like to have one too." Matt takes my hand and strokes his thumb over my knuckles, giving me a comforting smile.

I quickly weigh the pros and cons of the situation. My mind goes back to Wes, *again,* and I decide I'd rather have my first sip of alcohol with him instead.

"I think I'll just take a glass of water please." I tell Sam with a smile.

"Perfect. The chef has prepared a special tasting menu for you both, as requested by Mr. Bailey. I'll have the appetizers out shortly." Sam gives us a curt nod and strides away.

A special tasting menu? How much did *that* cost him? I knew he was rich, but for a first date, this seems extravagant. He doesn't seem like the type to expect me to put out just because he paid for an elaborate meal, but the thought is still niggling at the back of my mind.

Sam brings us our drinks along with our first course which is broiled oysters in shallot butter. I've never had oysters, so I follow Matt's lead in tipping the shell into my mouth, chewing once or twice, and swallowing. It's velvety and smooth, and it's not an unpleasant taste. I don't think I'd order them again on my own, but it's cool to try.

Conversation with Matt flows easily enough, although most of the conversation is based on the dishes we've been served. There's a total of six courses, and by the time the dessert comes around, I am sufficiently stuffed. I'm more relaxed now that I've been fed and I find I really enjoy Matt's company. He has a very chill vibe about him, and he hasn't pushed me about the champagne at all, which I appreciate.

Dessert is a dark chocolate molten lava cake with hand churned vanilla bean ice cream, and it's the best thing I've ever put in my mouth. The moan I let out after the first bite could be described as nearly pornographic.

"You like it, I'm guessing?" Matt grins.

"I would marry this cake." I deadpan, and Matt lets out a deep belly laugh.

"Well, don't let me get in the way of true love." He's still smiling, but a more serious expression comes over his face as he clears his throat. "Can I ask you something kind of personal?"

I nod, taking another bite of cake then placing my spoon down to give him my full attention.

"I know Mormons have a reputation for getting married young, like, right out of high school sometimes. I guess I'm just wondering why such an amazing woman like you hasn't been snatched up yet?"

I don't know how to answer that. I could say it's because I focused too much on school to have time for relationships, which isn't a total lie. I could say it's because

I never found someone who wanted to marry me, which is partially true. There's a myriad of plausible reasons I could give him, but I go with the one that feels the truest.

"That's true, my best friend growing up got married a year after graduating high school. I spent a lot of my time trying to get my degree, rather than dating, but the truth is I just wasn't good enough for the boys I dated." I raise one shoulder.

Matt's brows furrow, "What do you mean?"

I take a deep breath, "Mormon purity culture is extremely toxic. Some people go as far as to not even kiss until they get married just so they aren't subject to *temptation*. I wasn't 'pure' enough for my first serious boyfriend, even though *he's* the one who instigated a heavy makeout session. He broke up with me two days after, saying I was too much of a temptation to be around. That I was going to be the ruin of his eternal salvation. My second boyfriend wanted a perfect little housewife to pop out a bunch of kids and I didn't want that."

"What a bunch of assholes. It sounds like *they* didn't deserve *you*." Matt reaches across the table and takes my hand, rubbing his thumb over my knuckles. "I'm sorry you experienced that."

"Thank you. Unfortunately, my... *reputation* as an 'impure woman' went around so guys either wanted solely a make out session, or avoided me altogether. It's bullshit because they get to get off, and I'm still a virgin who hasn't had an orgasm." My eyes widen when I realize the word vomit I just spewed, "I'm sorry if that made you uncomfortable. I get a little riled up about the double standards in purity culture."

Matt smiles, squeezing my hand, "It's okay. I'm not uncomfortable. Do you ever want to get married? Have kids?"

A loaded question. Three years ago, I would have given an enthusiastic yes to both questions, but I honestly don't know now. I know I'd be a good mom, but I basically raised my siblings, and I just want to be able to live my life.

"I'm not opposed to marriage, but I'm definitely not going to rush into it. I'm undecided on the kids, but leaning towards no. I raised my siblings while my mom barked orders, and I think I'd like to keep my independence."

Matt lets out a chuckle, "You sound like Wes."

My cheeks flush at the mention of his best friend and I try to laugh it off.

My phone vibrates in my purse and I take a quick look as Matt settles the bill with Sam. My heart flutters when I see Wes's name pop up.

> **Wes:** ur so nwsudiful and i wdsny yo lisd u so bad

I furrow my brows., but decide not to respond right now, that would be rude to Matt.

"Bad text?" Matt asks.

"Uh, just confusing. Wes must have pocket texted me or drunk texted me or something." I say with a shrug.

"Oh. I didn't know you two talked after you first met."

"He helped me unpack Monday, and took us to the airport Wednesday. We've texted occasionally, but I haven't heard from him for a few days." I try to keep the hurt out of my voice.

"Interesting." Matt stands and offers me his hand, "Ready to go, sweetness?"

As I stand, Matt's fingers interlace with mine as he leads me to the elevator, waving goodbye to Carla as we pass.

When we get to my apartment, Matt walks me to the door, pulling me in for a hug.. "I had a really great time tonight, Elli. Thank you for joining me."

"Thank you for inviting me. I had a really good time, too." I bite my lip, wondering if he's going to kiss me. Wondering if I *want* him to kiss me. All the little touches during dinner didn't make my stomach flutter or send sparks of electricity through my veins, but maybe I just need time to be more attracted to him.

Matt moves back slightly so our noses are barely half an inch apart, then leans back in slowly so I have time to move away if I want to. When I don't, he closes the distance between us and our lips meet in a gentle kiss.

It's... nice? I guess. There are no sparks.

When he pulls away, he gives me another quick kiss on the cheek. "Goodnight, Elli."

"Goodnight, Matt."

CHAPTER 15

Wes

The lights are too bright and my head feels like it's being hit repeatedly by a hammer. I remember having two glasses of whiskey to prevent myself from driving over to Elli's and interfering with whatever she was doing with Matt.

Apparently, I had a lot more than two glasses.

I don't usually drink, maybe a beer or two if I'm socializing. My mom dated far too many alcoholic assholes that would get violent when they were drunk, so I vowed never to be like them. I don't want to be addicted to something, either. Because of my mom, addiction runs in my family and I don't want to end up dependent on something to get me through the day.

Plus, my anxiety medications aren't supposed to be taken with alcohol. The last time I was this shitfaced was when I broke up with Shelby.

Lucky for me, drunk Wes is responsible and has a glass of water and some Advil on the nightstand. Unlucky for me, drunk Wes is also a fucking dumbass and drunk texted Elli. After swallowing the pills and gulping the entire glass down, there's a knock at my door. I swear to god if it's Luke asking me for another favor I'm going to have to move.

I'm surprised when I open the door to find not only Robin, but Sean, too, holding bags of greasy breakfast food and coffee.

"Don't you two have church or something?" I grumble as they plop themselves on the couch in the living room.

"Hilarious." Sean retorts, handing me a breakfast sandwich.

"We were worried about you." Robin says sternly.

"Why were you worried about me?"

Robin shoots me with what I call her mom stare, "You called me last night rambling on about Elli. It wasn't at all coherent, so I knew you were shitfaced."

"You haven't had more than a beer or two since-"

"I know." I cut Sean off harshly, not needing another reminder.

"So what happened?" Robin pushes gently.

There's no getting out of talking about this, so might as well just lay it all out there.

"I was only going to have two glasses of whiskey, enough so I couldn't in good conscience drive because I was so close to completely overstepping with Elli yesterday. On Wednesday she had on this dress and, *shit* she looked incredible. The tie got stuck and she- anyway, I couldn't get her out of my head, so two drinks turned into three, which turned into more, I guess, hoping the buzz would help me forget a little bit, but all it did was make me want to be with her *more*. The thought of her out with Matt, him holding her hand, kissing her, making her laugh, or making her cheeks turn that adorable shade of pink when she feels flustered, it was making me crazy. I just needed to forget about it for a while."

I leave out the part where I pretty much ghosted her for the last few days. And the part where every time I think about her budding nipples I feel like a horny teenager.

Sean and Robin exchange a few pointed facial expressions and whispers- apparently they have their own secret language now- while I dig into my sandwich. As much as I hate feeling like a burden because they felt the need to check up on me, I'm really grateful they came over. I haven't checked to see if Elli responded, so while they're discussing, I pull out my phone. There's no message from Elli, but there is one from Matt.

Matt: I think we need to talk, man.

Ah, shit.

Wes: Sure, tell me when and where.

Matt: Can I come to yours? 11?

Wes: See you then.

When I look up from my phone, Sean and Robin are looking at me expectantly. "Uh, Matt's coming over at eleven to talk."

Robin's eyebrows shoot up into her bangs, "About what?"

I shrug, "Didn't say."

"Well," Robin clears her throat, "back to your Elli situation. Why haven't you just asked her out? It's not like her and Matt are exclusive."

"I told myself that if she wanted to date Matt I wouldn't get in the way of that. He asked her out, and she said yes. She doesn't want to go out with me. I'm not going to step on anyone's toes. On top of that, I'm trying to help her step out of her comfort zone and see if she can be happy without her religion. I need to stay in the friend zone and not let my feelings get in the way."

Sean laughs, "Bro, you don't know that she doesn't want to go out with you because you didn't *ask*. Matt asked her out and she said yes, but that doesn't mean she would say no to you. You should have seen the look on her face when she came back into the room and I was in your spot. She looked like someone had kicked a puppy."

"We're circling back to you helping her with her religion thing. To add to Sean's point, when I talked to her outside, she asked if you were my boyfriend. Why would she care if she wasn't interested?" Robin supplies.

Well, I didn't know *that*.

That doesn't change anything.

"I still don't want to ruin my friendship with Matt over a girl."

Robin scoffs "Matt will fall for someone else quickly. You? I've never seen you this hung up on someone. Not even Shelby."

I know she's right. Shelby was manipulative, made me think she was one person when she was someone else. I thought she was the one, but that's just because that's what she wanted me to see. In reality, she was never serious about me. It was all about the allure of dating a musician, a bad boy. She was severely disappointed that I wasn't into drugs or drinking or any "bad" shit. She didn't see me as long term, or someone to have a future with. She made me think she loved me, then she smashed my heart into a billion pieces.

Elli has been nothing but genuine with me. She opened up to me on the third fucking day of knowing her, trusting me with her deepest secret. You can't fake that kind of authenticity, that kind of raw emotion. It feels like she *sees* me. Sees past the hard exterior into my soul. I've never wanted to have someone consume me as much as I want Elli to.

"I can talk to her today if you want, we're having brunch in an hour." Robin interrupts my thoughts.

"Thanks Robs, but I don't want to do the whole 'my friend has a crush on you' thing, you know? We aren't in high school. I want to be her friend, if that's all I'll ever be, then that's fine." It's not fine, it might literally kill me, but maybe if I say it out loud enough times I can manifest being okay with it.

"Of course. Now, elaborate on the religion thing." Robin demands.

"We're taking the next month and I'm going to help her try things she's never tried. We went shopping for some new clothes, we're going to get coffee, and I want to take her out to a club, have her try alcohol for the first time. She's started cursing more, which is cute because she's hesitant to say things out loud. She's never gotten the chance to just live as a normal twenty-four year old so I want to help her."

"You're a good man, Westley Jones. Just make sure your heart is protected, okay?" Robin gives me a smile and shares another secret look with Sean.

They stand to leave, giving me a hug and words of encouragement, letting me know they're here for me whenever. I may be shit at showing it sometimes, but I love them. They're the best friends I could ever ask for. If Robin were straight, or I were gay, I would definitely be dating one of them.

Half an hour later, Matt's knocking on my door. Matt looks put together even in his jeans and t-shirt with his perfectly styled hair. I feel extremely inferior in my raggedy pajama pants and holey band t-shirt- I haven't even been able to shower off the hangover.

"Do you want to sit?" I ask, motioning to the couch as Matt lingers by the door.

"Sure." He makes his way over to the couch and sits.

We sit in an uncomfortable silence for what feels like an hour, but it's probably only ten minutes, before he finally clears his throat and breaks the silence. "Elli said you texted her last night and you seemed drunk."

I nod, unsure of what else to do or say. Where is he going with this?

"Why?"

"Why did I drink, or why did I text Elli?" I don't want to answer either question, but the latter would be easier to explain.

"Both."

Fuck.

I clear my throat, thinking through my answer. Apparently I'm taking too long, because Matt sighs and rubs his hands down his face. "Did you drink because of Elli?"

I nod.

"You like her?"

I nod again, preparing for him to tell me back off, she's his.

"What the hell, Wes? Why didn't you say anything?"

"What was I supposed to say? 'Hey bro, I think I really like Elli, even though it's only been two fucking days, so if you could not use your charm on her, I'd appreciate it.'"

"You could have told me you liked her! I wouldn't have asked her out if I knew that." A beat, then, "Why the hell didn't you ask her out? You had the chance before I did."

I shrug, "I didn't want to make her uncomfortable. Then she met you, and I know you're more her type. You'd be better for her, can offer her more. Then, I heard you ask her out and she said yes and I wasn't about to ruin our friendship over a girl I'd known less than twenty-four hours."

Matt stares at me, mouth agape, and then the fucker *laughs.* "You know? I thought I was her type, too. To be honest, I thought she'd want to be a wife and stay-at-home mom and that was part of why I liked her.

That's a dick thing for me to say, I know. But she told me she probably doesn't want kids."

First, what an ass to assume that about her. Second, I'm also an ass because *I* assumed that about her, too. Third, part of me feels like this is a trap.

"Wes, look. Elli is great. She's pretty, funny, and smart. But I could tell she wasn't as into me as either of us wanted her to be. I'm not going to be upset if you were to ask her out. You've already shown up more for her than I have, and I can tell she was genuinely worried about you last night. So stop putting your feelings behind everyone else's and go get the girl."

"How could you tell she wasn't into you?" I may regret asking that later, but I need to know.

"I uh, could tell when we kissed. I know when a girl is kissing because she's interested and kissing just to kiss. And she spent the ride home worrying about *you*."

"I'm sorry if I ruined your date."

Matt waves me off, "Don't worry about it, man. Elli's cool, but I think we're better off as just friends. You deserve to be happy, Wes. If Elli makes you happy, you need to go for it."

"Thanks, Matt."

"Anytime." Matt gives me a pat on the shoulder before he walks out the door.

Well, now I have no excuse. But I'm not just going to rush over there and ask her out. No, I'm going to show her that I'm worthy of her first. I'm going to keep up my end of the deal and help her.

She's the priority, and the wait will be worth it.

CHAPTER 16

Elli

Wes finally started texting me again on Monday and we have plans to try coffee on Thursday morning, which is tomorrow. I've been sending him pictures of my "immodest" outfits and he always hypes me up with them, and I feel like the weirdness from Saturday is finally dissipating.

Brunch with Robin on Sunday was amazing. I was able to talk about my date with Matt, without feeling like she was judging me or like she was going to go tell him what I said. I think it's the beginning of a beautiful friendship. She's hilarious, and I love how she says whatever is on her mind no matter what.

We've been sending TikToks and memes back and forth and have a girl's night planned for this weekend with Savannah. I'm a little nervous because I want to try alcohol, but it feels like betraying Wes if I don't try it with him, as silly as that sounds.

I'm meeting Matt for lunch today, and I'm going to let him know that I want to be friends because I don't see us going anywhere romantically.

I'm waiting out on the patio of a cute little cafe called Hens and Pigs when Matt shows up wearing tailored gray slacks and a light blue button down that makes his skin look extra tan. He always looks so posh and put together, I feel a little underdressed in my lavender sundress, but then I remember he's a bigwig businessman and I work from home so it makes sense that he's all dressed up.

"Hey gorgeous, how's it going?" Matt asks with a beaming smile as I stand to give him a hug. He places a gentle kiss on my cheek and motions for us to sit down.

"I'm doing alright. How are you?"

"Better now that I'm having lunch with a fucking model." He gives me a rakish wink that makes my face turn pink.

I clear my throat, ready to friend zone him, but our waitress comes over and asks us what we want to order. After Matt orders his chicken bacon ranch wrap and I order my chicken nachos, he looks at me expectantly, motioning for me to continue what I was saying.

"Matt, I think you're a really great guy, and I want to keep being friends, but I don't want to continue a romantic relationship."

Now, this isn't the first time I've had this conversation with a man, and usually I get called a bunch of mean names and labeled a tease, but Matt nods thoughtfully as he takes in my words and then he...

Laughs?

Why is he laughing?

Whatever he sees on my face makes him stop laughing and reach across the table to grab my hand, "Hey, I'm sorry, that wasn't cool of me. I'm not laughing AT you, I swear. I'm laughing because I already had a feeling that's what was going to happen, and I feel the same way. You are gorgeous, funny, smart, and so cool, and I would love to be friends."

"What do you mean you had a feeling this was going to happen?"

Matt clears his throat and rubs the back of his neck, "Well, I um. I could tell you weren't super into the kiss we shared, we have different life aspirations, and the way you talked about Wes was different than how you talked to me, so I figured out you were into him."

Oh god, this is so embarrassing. "I'm so sorry Matt. Ugh. I feel like a total bitch."

"Hey, Elli, no. No, you're not a bitch, I swear. I kind of knew we weren't super compatible when you said you weren't sure if you wanted kids. I'm looking to settle down and start a family, but it seems like you're not quite on the same track, ya know? This is going to make me sound like an asshole, but I thought with you being Mormon and all, you'd be looking to settle down too. I thought it would be cool to give it a chance, but I think we'd be better as friends."

"Thank you. I appreciate your honesty, and for not thinking I'm a bitch. Sorry Matt, I do NOT want to be your little housewife with a gaggle of little hellions."

Matt rolls his eyes but laughs. "It's all good babe. Wes can keep you barefoot and pregnant if you guys decide to have kids."

"HA. Right. Wes isn't interested in me like that."

"You're wrong, but I'll let Wes prove it."

I try not to think about that statement too hard.

We don't talk about Wes the rest of lunch. We just get to know each other as friends.

Whoever Matt ends up with is going to be a very lucky girl.

On Thursday morning, Wes shows up to my apartment with to-go coffee cups in hand.

"I thought we were going out for coffee?" I haven't even put on real clothes yet. I'm still in my light green lounge romper that feels buttery soft. I bought two more in black and gray because they're so comfy.

"I was up and thought it might be easier to have a coffee flight taste test from home. Besides, there are a lot of options and I didn't want you to get overwhelmed." He explains, like that's just something a normal person does for a friend.

"Well, thank you." I glance down at my outfit and cringe. "I should change into something more presentable."

Wes shrugs, "If you want. I think you look great. Comfy."

"If you're sure..."

"It's your house, Elli. You make the calls about what you wear."

We stand there and stare at each other in silence while I debate internally. I really don't want to change, so I shrug and plop down on a barstool.

"Alright coffee connoisseur, what've we got." I gesture to the five cups of coffee on the table.

Wes claps his hands together. "Alright here we go. I've got five options for you, but one of them is my regular order so I'm hoping you don't take a liking to that one." He points to each one as he explains, "I've got an iced white mocha, which is espresso, white chocolate sauce, and milk. Regular black coffee, coffee with cream and sugar, a vanilla latte with oat milk, and a caramel macchiato which is just a fancy upside down espresso drink."

"Which one is your regular order?" I think I know, but I want to make sure.

Wes shakes his head with a smirk, "I'm not telling you until you try them all."

"Fine." I grab the black coffee first, knowing that's probably his go-to order and take a tentative sip. The liquid is bitter and hot and I immediately hate it. I shake my head no, pushing the cup away from me.

"That's gross. No thank you. Next?" Wes slides the coffee with cream and sugar over. It's less bitter, more creamy. Not entirely unpleasant. "Okay, not bad. Can I try the vanilla one next please?"

Wes chuckles and slides it over. It's not my favorite either and my nose scrunches as the taste hits my tongue. "I don't think oat milk is my vibe." I say.

"That's Robs' favorite drink. I don't know how she drinks that stuff, but she does." Wes explains sliding over the caramel macchiato.

This one is okay, caramel isn't my favorite flavor unless it's mixed with chocolate, but it's better than the other ones. I shake my head and slide it back, feeling a little dejected. "I don't know if coffee is for me."

"Try the white mocha and if you don't like that, there are a million other flavors to try. If you don't like coffee, that's okay! At least you tried something new." Wes slides over the iced coffee.

It's bitter at first, but it's creamier than the other ones and once the sweetness of the white chocolate takes over, it's actually pretty good. I take another sip and nod my head. "This is the one. It almost tastes like a milkshake."

Wes beams, "I thought you might like that one the most. You seem to have a sweet tooth. I noticed it when you got the cinnamon pretzels at the mall, then you insisted on getting ice cream after lunch with Izzy and Luke." He grabs the coffee with cream and sugar and takes a large swig.

"I thought you'd like black coffee." I scoff, trying to ignore the way my belly flutters at him admitting to paying attention to my sweet tooth.

"Life's too short to drink plain bean water." Another sip, "Robin said you, her, and Sav are going out tomorrow? Are you excited?"

"Yeah, I'm excited! It'll be good to have some girlfriends again. I was thinking about trying alcohol tomorrow night, but didn't want you to feel like I was betraying you by not having it with you for the first time." I feel a little silly saying it out loud.

"Well, thank you for not wanting to betray me," he smirks, "but don't hold out just because of me. I want you to enjoy yourself."

"Thank you. Do you... have any suggestions for drinks for my first time?"

"Hmmm. Something sweet, something fruity perhaps..." He taps his fingers on the counter while he thinks. Then he snaps his fingers, "A Pina Colada."

"I do love some coconut. In Utah they have these soda shops where they put flavored syrup and coffee creamer in them. My favorite was Dr. Pepper with fresh lime and coconut syrup."

"They put coffee creamer in soda? That's... disgusting." Wes pretends to gag.

"Can't drink coffee, so they've got to use the creamer for other stuff." I shrug, taking another sip of my coffee and frowning when the straw makes that weird sound after you finished your drink and are just sucking on air. "Bummer. That was really good."

"I'm glad you enjoyed it. I hate to cut our activity short, but I've got some errands to run. Have fun tomorrow night, okay?" Wes comes around the counter and wraps me in a big hug. "Keep sending me selfies of your outfits. They're the highlight of my day." He murmurs into my hair.

"Thank you for this morning. I'll be sure to send you my outfit for tomorrow." I say against his chest.

He pulls back and grins down at me. "Good. Have a good day, Elli. I'll talk to you soon."

Then just as quickly as he came, he's gone, and I have to go about my workday like I'm not thinking about Wes.

Friday night is finally here, and I am pumped to have a distraction from my own imagination.

My fingers have been getting well acquainted with my vagina, thanks to the smutty books I've been reading to distract myself from thinking about a tall, dark, handsome musician with tattoos and a biteable neck.

Okay, so it hasn't been the best distraction. I always just end up picturing Wes as the male characters, saying the things they say and doing the things they do.

Tonight I'm going out with Savannah and Robin, so I'm going to try and focus on getting to know them. Maybe I'll let loose and let a guy take me home and make me forget about Wes.

Probably not. I don't want to lose my virginity to a stranger, but I might go for some making out, though. Maybe a little fingering, like in my books. Lots of the main characters get finger-banged in the club bathroom. I'm trying to live life without following the rules I was taught, and that seems like a good first step.

I thought about wearing the blue dress tonight, but then I'd just think of Wes and I don't want to think about Wes. He's made it clear he's not interested romantically and if I think about him too much I'll just get sad. Plus, that dress is a bit fancy for the bar we're going to. I opt for a lavender mini skirt with daisies on it and a white top that crisscrosses every which way and wraps around me. It took me ten minutes to get on, but it makes my boobs look good. I know my feet are going to be killing me if I wear heels, so I throw on some white flatform sandals.

I thought I would feel uncomfortable showing this much of my skin on display, but it's actually very freeing. I've hated my body for so long, and I've been told my whole life that it was bad in one way or another. Wearing this cute skirt makes my butt look good, and my boobs look great in the shirt. I don't feel like a sinner. I feel confident, cute, and ready for a good time.

Robin's text saying they're here comes in right as I'm finishing up my laces. My heart is racing from nerves, anticipation, excitement, I don't know, but I'm eager to see what the night has in store. As promised, Drew is driving, Sav's in the front seat, and Robin is in the back.

"Damn, Elli! You look hot! Are you *sure* you're not into girls?" Robin flutters her lashes playfully.

I blush at the compliment and the implication, but say coyly, "I've never kissed a girl so who's to say."

Robin leans over to me, grabs my face between her hands and gives me a gentle kiss. When she pulls back, she has a smug grin on her face, and she laughs at my stunned expression. "So?"

"Sorry Robin, you're gorgeous, and a good kisser, but I'm as straight as can be." I shrug.

She feigns disappointment, but I know she's just playing around.

"So, how are things with Matt?" Drew asks me, wiggling his eyebrows at me in the rearview mirror.

"We went on a nice date, but we decided we're better off as friends."

"What about Wes?" Sav asks, shooting Robin a look I can't identify.

"What about Wes? We're friends. He was really helpful last week, and he's been helping me figure out how to live a normal life without religion." I shrug, and Robin gives me a grin that looks too forced.

Drew, Sav, and Robin are acting like there's a secret I don't know, and as much as I want to ask, I promised myself I'm not going to worry about Wes tonight, so I just keep quiet.

Drew drops us off at a bar slash club called Midnight Luxuries which, in my opinion, sounds more like a high class escort service, but it looks fun. I told Robin and Sav that I've never had alcohol, but that Wes suggested a Pina Colada, so that's my first drink. It's sweet, and the taste of alcohol is clearly there but it's well hidden by the sweetness of everything else. I've seriously been missing out.

Once we're all done with our first drinks, Sav orders us a round of tequila shots. It's terrible. I almost gag when I lick the salt, then I choke a little when I shoot the tequila because of how strong it is, but I muddle through and bite the lime. My throat burns from the alcohol, and I don't think I like the feeling.

"Nope. I'm not doing that again." I scrunch up my nose and Sav and Robin laugh, but agree not to make me try another one.

A shot, and two drinks later I am feeling fuzzy and warm and giggly and I decide that I can have one more drink.

Unfortunately, my inebriated state isn't stopping me from thinking about Wes. In fact, it's making me think about him *more*. So much in fact, that I interrogate Robin about him. She's a good friend and just tells me he's the best, a real gentleman. I tell her about our dress incident, pouting, "...and I wanted to kiss him sooooo bad. I touched myself for the first time thinking about Wes's hands. I bet he's really good with his fingers being a guitar player." Really good. Not that I have much experience, but I imagine it would be *amazing*.

Sav and Robin are looking at me with varying levels of disgust, and I assume it's because of mentioning touching myself, but then Robin says, "I don't want to think about Wes's fingers doing anything other than playing guitar." Sav nods in agreement.

Ignoring that, I sigh "I just really, really like him, you know?"

"Yeah babe. I've gathered." Sav deadpans.

"I've never been so turned on by anyone or *anything* really, that I've wanted to touch myself. I don't think I'm very good at it, I don't really know what an orgasm feels like so I-"

Before I can finish my thought, my phone starts vibrating in my purse. "Oh! It's Izzy. I'm going to take this outside." They wave me off as they giggle, and I make my way to the front doors. I step out into the humid night air, wishing it was cooler-it really sucks that it doesn't cool off much in the evenings.

"Izzzzzyyyyyyy!" I answer enthusiastically.

"Hey Els. What are you up to?" Izzy says with a smile in her voice.

"Don't tell mom and dad" I whisper, "but I'm out drinking at a bar with Sav and Robs. Don't you ever try tequila. It's not good." I shudder, remembering the horrific event of the shot.

Izzy busts up laughing, and it's like music to my ears. I miss her so damn much. *Ooo a swear word.*

"I won't tell them, I'll let you get back to your night, but I'm calling you tomorrow so you can fill me in on everything going on. I miss you."

Oh great, now I'm going to cry. "I miss you too, Iz. I have a lot to tell you." I blink rapidly trying to stop the tears from flowing over.

"Love you, Els." I hear her sniffle.

"Love you, Iz." And then she hangs up.

Gently wiping my eyes to make sure my makeup doesn't run, I make my way back into the club. Sav and Robin immediately wrap me in a hug when I get back, no explanation needed.

"No sadness tonight! More drinks!" I declare, slapping my hand on the table before downing my gin and tonic in one go. The tonic water tickles my nose, and the gin burns going down, but I feel even floatier now.

A cute guy, I think his name is Brad? I don't know. He's tall and muscular and blonde and smells like alcohol, but he asked me to dance, and I said yes, determined not to think about Wes. Right as I'm about to walk away after our dance, he grabs my hips and pulls me against him. He leans in to whisper in my ear, and his hot breath makes me shiver, and not in a good way.

"Let's go to a dark corner, yeah? Maybe you can show me what's underneath this tight little skirt."

I shove him back, "Fuck off."

He grabs my wrist before I can get far enough away pushing my hand into his erection, "Don't be a cock-tease. C'mon. I can make you feel so good."

I don't think too much before I knee him in the crotch and shove him back into the crowd of people on the dance floor. I make a beeline for Robin and Sav to tell them what happened, and that I'm ready to leave.

CHAPTER 17

Wes

"What's up Robs?" I can hear the pulsing music from the club, and I'm already grabbing my keys because I know she's going to ask me to come get her.

"You need to come to Midnight Luxuries and get Elli. She hasn't stopped talking about you all night, and there's a beefy gym bro who won't take his hands off of her and I think she would rather be comforted by you than by us or Drew." She sounds surprisingly sober, which is unusual when she goes out, so I know she's being serious.

My heart flutters hearing Elli hasn't stopped talking about me, and then a white hot rage fills me when I remember some asshole has his meaty paws on my girl. I mean Elli.

The fifteen minute drive to the club feels like hours, and as soon as I park at the curb, I see Robs and Sav huddled around Elli outside on a bench.

Elli sees me first and smiles so big her eyes crinkle in the corners. "Wes!" She stands and wraps her arms around my waist. "I had alcohol."

I tentatively wrap my arms around her shoulders, "I can tell. I heard some gym bro tried to get handsy with you."

She leans back so I can see her face. "Yeah, he smelled gross and was really sweaty," she scrunches her nose, "but I kneed him in the balls."

I can't help but chuckle, "Atta girl. C'mon let's get you home." I resist the urge to kiss her forehead.

"What about Robs and Sav?"

"Drew just got here, he'll make sure they get home safely."

She hums some type of acknowledgment, but doesn't let go of my waist. I finally break free, but keep my arm around her back to help guide her to the car.

The car ride to her apartment is quiet, and at first I think she's asleep, but when I turn to check on her, she's staring at me half-lidded and sleepy. I don't want to say anything, not that I would know what to say, because I don't trust that I'll be able to keep my feelings in if I start talking, and I definitely don't want her to be drunk when we talk about that.

Once inside her apartment, I tell her to go change while I set out to get her some type of painkiller and water. I rifle through the kitchen cabinets and find a bottle of Advil, and then I hear a groan coming from the direction of her room.

Then, "Weeeees. Help meeeee."

I take the glass of water and the Advil with me, and I don't know what I'm expecting to find, but it's definitely not Elli tangled up in her shirt. She already has her skirt off, so she's just in a pair of panties.

"Whatcha doin' Elli?" I lean up against the door-frame, trying not to laugh or stare at her bare thighs.

Elli stomps her foot like a toddler throwing a tantrum and grumbles, "I can't get my shirt off. It's too confusing. Help me, please?"

"Alright." I set the water and Advil on her nightstand and go stand behind her, feeling a sense of de javu. This shirt is confusing, but I figure if I pull the big knot in the back, I can unwrap her, like a present. Pushing *that* train of thought out of my head, I succeed in getting the strappy piece of fabric undone.

I assume Elli's going to hold it to her chest until I'm out of the room, but she lets the fabric fall to the ground. I swallow thickly, looking around the room at literally anything other than Elli in only panties. I hear her dresser open and shut, and when she comes back into view she has on the shortest shorts known to man, and a tank top.

"C'mon Elli, we gotta take your makeup off." I say, holding out my hand.

Jess instilled in me the importance of a skincare routine, especially for someone who wears makeup. She taught me how to braid hair when I was younger so I could braid my hair because I didn't ever want to cut it, and the proper way to clean your face so you don't get acne. After seeing the various skincare items Elli has, it's clear this is probably something super important to her.

"Nooooo. I wanna go to bed."

"Uh uh, skin care is important." She reluctantly puts her hand in mine and I drag her to the bathroom.

I sit her down on the toilet and then gather all of the necessary skin care things she says she uses. I crouch between her legs and hold her chin gently with one hand while the other one softly runs the cotton pad over her eyes to remove the makeup there. I clear the little make-up she has off of her face, and then I apply the various serums and creams in the order she tells me to. I make her brush her teeth while I brush her hair and put it in a simple braid, then follow her back to her room.

Elli sits on the edge of the bed while I make her take the painkillers and drink the entire glass of water. Tucking her into bed, I give in to my impulse this time and place a gentle kiss on her forehead.

"Wessss. Stay with me." She pleads, and *god* do I want to.

"Not tonight, baby. I want you to remember the first time I'm in your bed. Sweet dreams, sweet girl." I whisper against her hairline. The nickname slips out involuntarily, but she doesn't seem to notice. Maybe she won't remember it in the morning.

"Night Wes. Thank you. You're the best." She mumbles as her eyelids grow heavier.

I wait until her breathing becomes heavy so I know she's fast asleep, before I leave to refill the glass of water. I leave her a note next to it with instructions for the morning so her hangover isn't terrible, then I head back to my apartment.

Once I'm home, I decide it's time to put my plan into action. I know I said I would wait until this month is over, but I don't think I can anymore.

I want to be the one she dances with in the club. I want to hold her all night so I know she's breathing and to make sure she doesn't have bad dreams. I want to be there the morning after she gets plastered to make her coffee and take her to get a greasy breakfast.

I want her to be mine.

Chapter 18

Elli

As soon as I open my eyes I regret it. The light is too bright, my head is pounding, and my body feels like I've been run over by a tractor.

I'm never drinking again.

I notice a glass of water and some Advil on my night-stand with a note.

It's not my handwriting. It could be Robin's or Savannah's, but that doesn't seem right either.

I check my phone and see that it's just past eight. I feel sweaty and gross, and decide that a shower is in order, especially if someone is coming over with breakfast.

Stripping my clothes, I realize I'm not in my contraption of a shirt anymore, and I don't know how I got out of it. I look in the mirror, expecting to find a mess of makeup and wild hair, but my face is bare and my hair is in a loose braid.

I don't remember taking my makeup off or braiding my hair.

Standing under the hot water helps ease the tension in my body, which helps lessen my headache some, and now that I'm more awake, the memories of last night hit me like a truck.

Robin kissing me on the way to the club, the delicious pina coladas that I apparently had too many of, the tequila- *gag*- dancing with that stranger, him trying to get handsy, kneeing him in the balls and then leaving with Wes.

Wes.

Wes brought me home. He helped me take off that awful shirt and he did my skincare routine for me, brushed and braided my hair. He tucked me into bed. He must have written the note, placed the Advil, and then left.

I think I remember asking him to stay. Would he have stayed if I did? Why didn't Drew bring me home? Did *I* call Wes?

My headache starts getting worse with all of the questions, but I'm not going to figure anything out in the shower, so I hop out and wrap the towel around my body. I towel dry my hair, apply my skincare, and moisturize my body before slipping on my pink satin robe.

Izzy calls me on my way to the kitchen, her chipper voice is a lot on a normal day, but hungover it's amplified tenfold.

"You alive, Els?" She's mocking me.

I answer with a groan, "Barely. Don't drink, Iz. I feel like I got hit by a- FUCK." The doorbell rings and scares the shit out of me and I almost drop my phone.

"I think it's pronounced 'truck' Els Bells." Izzy chides.

"Oh shush. Someone's at the door, hold on." I leave the phone on and at my side while I open the door to find Robin and Sav standing on the other side holding bags of food and to-go cups of what I'm assuming is coffee.

"Good morning! We brought breakfast and coffee!" Robin says, looking much more alive than I feel.

I bring the phone up to my ear and motion the girls inside. "Sorry Iz. Robin and Savannah just came over with breakfast. Can I call you when they leave?"

"As long as you tell me everything in explicit detail!"

"Deal. Love you Iz."

"Love you too. Bye!"

I hang up as I walk over to the kitchen island and stand on the opposite side of it from Sav and Robs, who are both sitting with enigmatic smiles.

"Good morning...Why don't you two look hungover?" I ask.

"We have a higher tolerance than you do, babe. Plus, we have routines to prevent hangovers. Stick with us, and we'll teach you our ways." Sav says, taking a bite of her breakfast sandwich.

"We brought you bacon, egg, and cheese on a croissant, and an iced white mocha with an extra shot. I hope that's okay?" Robin says while sliding over the sandwich and a cup.

"That sounds fucking delightful. Thank you. But how did you know my coffee order?" I take a long sip of the coffee, almost moaning at the taste. Then, I take a bite of the croissant sandwich and groan. "This is really good." I say impolitely around a mouthful.

"A little bird told us what you liked. We planned on coming over this morning to check on you anyway, but *someone* was adamant that we do." Savannah answers.

She doesn't have to say his name for me to know she's talking about Wes. My stomach flutters, and it has nothing to do with the hangover this time. It has everything to do with how thoughtful Wes is.

We eat in silence until we've all finished our sandwiches and most of our drinks. I take our trash and throw it away, then stand back at the counter while they just stare at me.

"Sooooo," Robin starts, "did you have fun last night?"

I narrow my eyes at her, "Yes... Why?"

Robs shrugs. "Just wanted to make sure you were okay after that douchebag and the drinking. We had a lot of fun with you, and we want to hang out more."

Sav nods in agreement, then clears her throat. "We also wanted to make sure you got home okay and that Wes took care of you. Which, it looks like he did."

"Yes, he took great care of me. He removed my makeup and braided my hair for me. Got me medicine and water. He even..." I trail off, my cheeks burning as I decide if I want to share the shirt thing, in the end I tell them anyway. "He helped me take off that contraption of a shirt I decided to wear. Then I guess he left. Why did he come get me, anyway?"

Robin and Savannah have a silent conversation that I wish I could be part of full of eyebrow raises, head shakes, nods, and random hand gestures. Finally, they both look at me and Robin explains.

"You kept talking about Wes last night after a few drinks." My cheeks heat again in embarrassment. "And after the incident with the dudebro, I figured you'd appreciate Wes taking you home."

Sav jumps in. "Plus, and I love him with all my heart, Drew's not the most... sensitive or caring with new people. He would have just dropped you off and let you fend for yourself. We wanted someone to make sure you got in okay and we knew Wes would do that without overstepping any boundaries."

"He was a perfect gentleman." I assure them.

"Good. Well. He has a show on Wednesday night, and we all try to go and support him." Sav says.

"Oh well that should be fun. I hope you guys have fun-"

Robin interrupts me, "Nope. You're coming with us. We will pick you up at six on Wednesday."

"Wouldn't Wes have invited me himself if he wanted me to come?"

"Nah." She waves me off like it's no big deal. "You're part of the group now. This is what we do."

Tears burn behind my eyes at how easily they have accepted me into their group. I've never had friends like this.

"Well okay. That sounds fun."

"Great! Now get dressed. We're going shopping." Robin claps her hands together then pushes me towards my room.

"Shopping? For what?" I spin to face her and she has a mischievous glint in her hazel eyes.

"You may have rambled about not having a lot of... success... with orgasms. We're going toy shopping." She wiggles her eyebrows suggestively. "And then outfit shopping for Wes's performance. But that's not the most important part of today's journey."

I look at Savannah, like she'll agree that this is crazy, but she just shrugs. "Yep. Sorry babe, as a feminist, I can't in good conscience let you continue to struggle with self-pleasure. Orgasms are a healthy, natural part of life and you deserve them."

"Um. Okay. I'll go get dressed then, I guess."

Forty minutes later, we're standing in front of a store called The Velvet Taco, which apparently is a euphemism for a vagina. I've heard a vagina called a lot of things, but never a velvet taco.

On the way here, Savannah and Robin gave me a rundown of their favorite toys, and how some toys are better solo, and some are better with partners. I swear my cheeks have never been redder. Having people so openly talk about sex and masturbation is new, and feels taboo because of the way I grew up.

The most I was told was "Never touch yourself. Never let anyone else touch you. Not until you're married. Then you are to please your husband and make babies."

There were never really any safe sex talks, discussions about pleasure, or anything like that.

I've done some of my own research, but the internet can only teach you so much. Reading the spicy romance novels has helped me figure out a little bit, and the rest has been self-exploration.

I've considered buying a toy, but the options are so overwhelming and I got so flustered I closed the tab and haven't looked back.

Robin leads our little trio into the store and directly to the vibrator section. Sav and Robs decided a vibrating rabbit, or a suction toy would be the best toy for a beginner. I have no idea what either of those things is, so I follow them obediently while they point out all of the different options.

I know this is a *sex toy* shop, but *holy shit* there are a lot of toys. There's all different sizes and shapes of penises that look both lifelike and fake. There's one as thick and long as my arm! Who's using that????

There's a section for dildos that are "fantasy" shapes. A tentacle, alien fingers, a unicorn horn, a penis that has a bulbous part towards the base that they call a "knot."

There's a whole section for anal play toys and I cannot fathom how anyone fits *those* in *there*.

We've seen sex machines, sex swings, bondage kits.

There are so many vibrators to choose from, too, my poor, sheltered brain is overwhelmed.

"Alrighty Elli. I think this one is perfect for your first toy. You can use it just on your clit, or insert it vaginally, too, and this little part will vibrate against your clit. The stimulation in both areas will bring you *a lot* of pleasure." Robin explains, holding out a pink silicone toy that has a longer part that I assume goes inside, and a shorter arm that I assume will vibrate against my clit while the other part is inside me.

That thing is supposed to go inside me?

Good grief. At least it's not monstrous.

"Sure. Okay. That sounds good." I squeak, cursing my voice for sounding as overwhelmed as I feel.

Robin and Savannah offer me some sympathetic smiles, and Robs wraps me in a hug. "I know this is overwhelming. We're obviously not going to force you to buy a toy, but I do think this is a good step in unlearning the purity culture bullshit spewed to us through our lives."

She's right, and I know she's right. And this is a good first step in taking back control of my body. It's hard to unlearn twenty-four years' worth of shame in an hour, but I can take this slow. I can buy the toy, but I don't have to use it, right?

I take a deep breath. "You're right. It's time to take control over my body instead of letting religion define who I am." I grab the plastic package holding the toy, "Let's do this."

Savannah pumps her fist, "Girl power! You're going to be so glad you did this. I promise."

They suggested buying some lube to make sure things are comfortable with the toy, so after buying the lube and the toy, we head down the road to a boutique that carries plus size and straight size clothes.

While Robs is thin and I'm plus size, Sav is somewhere in between so this store is perfect for each of us to find outfits in.

While we peruse the selections, I learn more about the girls and the rest of the group. I learn that Robin is the social media manager for an art gallery in San Antonio, and she just got asked to head the opening of a new exhibit that opens in August. Savannah is a Spanish teacher at the local high school, which she says is weird because she feels like she just graduated herself.

Apparently everyone in their little friend group, other than Sean, went to University of Texas at San Antonio, and that's where Robin met Matt in one of her business classes.

Sean joined the Army right out of high school and was deployed to Afghanistan shortly after finishing tech school. That was apparently the last deployment the US made to Afghanistan, but it really messed Sean up. He didn't reenlist when his contract was up, wanting to be home more. When he left the Army, he came out as gay, but hasn't had any serious relationships that anyone knows of.

Drew is a cyber security analyst, and works for the government in some capacity. He and Sav have been dating for four years and she's expecting a ring anytime.

The day flies by, and I end up with a really cute outfit for Wes's show, and the feeling that I'm exactly where I need to be.

CHAPTER 19

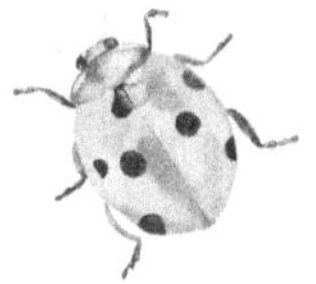

Wes

T he next few days, I bury myself in writing. It's like Elli smashed through my writer's block with a thousand pound wrecking ball, and the music won't stop flowing now. I have four new songs completely composed, and lyrics to a few more scribbled across notebooks, napkins, and the shower walls. Yes, shower walls, because inspiration strikes at the most inconvenient times so I've learned to keep a dry erase marker in my bathroom.

I feel bad because I've only been sending Elli one word answers to her texts, but I'm trying to keep my focus. Robin texted me on Sunday and told me all about their girls' day on Saturday. Where they went, and what they bought, and if I stop to let myself think about Elli with a new vibrator, my mind isn't going to focus on the music.

It's Tuesday, the day before the show. The day before my grand plan to confess my feelings for this girl and win her over.

Hopefully.

Did I have a panic attack yesterday when I thought about what would happen if she rejected me?

Yes.

Did it make me want to finish a bottle of whiskey just to stop the panic?

Yes.

Did I do that?

No. *Go me!*

I'm not going to use alcohol to numb my feelings. In fact, I poured the rest of the whiskey down the drain so I couldn't.

I want to look my best for the show tomorrow, so it's time for my semi-annual hair cut with Jess. I've been seeing her since she got her license, and I don't trust anyone else with my hair. Her shop is just down the street from my apartment, nestled between a quaint little flower shop and a barbershop. It's small, just Jess and another stylist, and that suits me just fine.

The bell above the door jingles as I walk in, and I hear Jess shout "Be right with you!" From somewhere in the back.

I look around, taking in the pale pink walls, floral furniture, and gold accents. I look so out of place here in my dark jeans, black shirt, and tattoos, it's actually kind of funny.

"Westley Jones as I live and breathe! How the hell are you?" Jess exclaims, enveloping me in a tight hug. She smells like hairspray and hair products, but it's a comforting, familiar scent that I love that's so *her*.

"I'm doing good Jess, thanks. How are things with you?"

"Good, good. Come sit in my chair so I can interrogate you about your life." She says dragging me to her station. She plops me down in the chair, ties the cape around my front and starts running her fingers through my hair. "God, I wish I had your hair. I get so jealous every time you come in. What are we thinking today?"

"You flatter me Jess. Just a trim I think. I have a show tomorrow night. A big one. I want to look my best."

"Ooo. A big one, eh? What's so important about this one?"

"Well, you know..." I trail off, unsure how to explain that I'm confessing my feelings for a girl I've only known for a few weeks.

"Come on rockstar, let's get you washed up and then you can tell me all about this girl that's got you twitterpated." Jess says with a firm pat on the shoulder.

"I never said it was about a girl." I grumble.

"Didn't have to, I've been around long enough to know that love struck look in a young fella's eyes. This girl has got you all tied up in knots kid. Not to mention, I've seen you when you're in love."

"Yeah. I guess she does." But I don't like that Jess is comparing Elli to Shelby. The way I'm feeling is completely different. Shelby was a soul-sucking leech that didn't care about anyone but herself, and Elli is...

Elli is the warmth of hot cocoa on a chilly winter day. Seeping into your soul and warming you from the inside out until you're all cozy and content. She's so selfless she moved across multiple state lines just so her sister could visit her boyfriend more. She's strong, thoughtful, and beautiful. She's funny as hell when she's not all up in her head and worried about what she's going to say.

Jess wets my hair, then lathers up shampoo that smells like tea tree and matcha before gently massaging my scalp. It feels so good I feel like I'm going to cry. This is the best part of getting a haircut. Next, she applies a conditioner that smells the same as the shampoo and gently rinses it before wrapping my hair in a towel and leading me back to the chair.

"Now, spill. I'm assuming this girl is Izzy's sister? Luke said you kind of liked her, but she's dating Matt? I need the details kid."

I roll my eyes, of course Luke couldn't keep his mouth shut. But this is Jess. the closest person to a mom I have.

"Her name is Elli. Matt did take her on a date, but they both decided that they'd be better off as friends. She..." I take a deep breath, trying to find the right words to describe Elli to someone who's never met her. "She's like taking a big breath of air after coming up from underwater. I didn't even know I was holding my breath until she brought me back to the surface, you know?

"I thought I loved Shelby. But I think it was just me feeling like I could offer something to someone. Shelby never loved me, obviously. I don't know if Elli could love me, since I don't have a lot to offer, but I'm determined to at least try. I don't know if I can say I'm in love with her yet, but I'm pretty dang close to it. I was in such a bad writer's block I couldn't even pick up my notebook for months. Elli came in and bulldozed the wall I've spent the last two years building, and now it's like there's songs flowing through my fingertips. She's the first girl I've been interested in since Shelby. I just hope I'm good enough for her."

Jess spins me so I'm looking at her, a look of determination on her face. "You listen to me, Westley Ray Jones. You are not unlovable because of the trauma you went through. If Elli can't see that then that is her loss. You have so much to give, Wes. So much love in your heart, and if she's smart she'll see that and she won't be able to stop herself from falling for you. I'm glad to hear your writer's block is gone. Your songs are beautiful. You don't even know how proud of you I am for what you've accomplished so far. Your mom and grandma would be so proud of you, too."

"Damn it, Jess. I wanted to get a haircut, not cry."

"Well that's too bad, kid." She sasses with tears falling down her own face. She swipes them away quickly, back to business. "Okay. Now, tell me about your important show tomorrow while I finish this trim."

So I do.

When she's worked her hair magic, I walk out of there feeling more confident than I have in a long time. And not just because of my haircut.

CHAPTER 20

Elli

I don't know why I'm nervous, *I'm* not the one that's performing tonight.

Matt insisted I come, refusing all of my half-assed excuses and picking me up to make sure I didn't bail.

I want to see Wes perform more than anything, but we've barely spoken since Friday and I don't know if he even wants me to be here.

Instead of bailing, I put on the outfit I bought on Saturday with Robin and Savannah. The denim skirt makes my butt look really good, if I do say so myself. I've paired it with a blue ditsy floral spaghetti strap tank top that gives a hint of cleavage, and some brown strappy sandals. It may be simple, but I love it. It's different from what I would normally wear, but I feel good in it, and I need confidence tonight.

"What if he doesn't want me here, Matt? He didn't even mention it to me." I sound pathetic, even to myself.

Matt gives me a sympathetic look as we park in the parking lot behind the bar. "Elli, trust me, please? Wes wants you here."

"Okay, I trust you."

Robin and Sean are waiting at the front entrance of The Voiceless Piano, the bar where Wes is performing.

"Hey, guys! Sav and Drew are saving us a seat inside. Wes is on in ten minutes, so we can get drinks and settle in before he starts." Robin says as she intertwines our fingers and pulls me in with her into the bar.

The bar isn't what I expected. I don't know what I was thinking, probably something small and intimate, but this place is pretty big. It's got an industrial vibe to it. The walls are all light gray with a big mural of a piano behind the raised platform of the stage. The floors are epoxy and the bar is a big cement slab that spans the length of the entire place. Liquor bottles line shelves upon shelves behind the bar on shelves that look like exposed pipe.

The bar is filled almost to capacity, we have to weave through the sea of people until we find Sav and Drew nuzzling into each other at a table twenty feet from the stage-right in the eyeline of the performer.

Matt offers to get everyone drinks, and as much as I want something to give me a buzz, my stomach is already in knots and alcohol would probably make me feel worse, so I opt for a Shirley Temple.

"Are you ready for Wes's performance, Elli?" Drew wiggles his eyebrows at me, and Robin shoots him a glare.

"I mean, yeah. I've seen some of his stuff on Instagram, but it'll be good to see him live."

"He was really excited for this show, said it'll be one of the most important ones yet." Sean adds.

Matt returns with our drinks before I can ask him to elaborate, taking the empty seat next to me as the lights flash twice, indicating the show is about to start. As the lights in the bar dim and the ones facing the stage turn brighter, my nerves grow. The knot in my stomach turns into butterflies as Wes steps on stage like he owns it, looking like a fucking wet dream.

He's wearing his usual black jeans and black boots, but instead of a t-shirt he's wearing a light gray button-up shirt with the top three buttons undone, and the sleeves rolled up to his elbows. He has half of his hair pulled into a ponytail, the other half hanging down over his shoulders.

He sits on the stool in front of the microphone and leans forward to say, "Hey guys, I'm Wes Jones. Thanks for coming out tonight." Earning him a round of applause. He clears his throat as the applause dies down and the first strum of his guitar reverberates through the room, causing goosebumps to rise on my skin.

Before I know it, he's sung at least four songs and the ice in my completely untouched Shirley Temple is almost completely melted, condensation dripping down the sides. It's like his tenor voice is magic, putting me in a trance. I'm only brought out of trance because Wes starts talking again.

"This last song is a new one, the first one I wrote after a stint of writer's block. It's really special to me, and for a special girl, who helped me get out of my rut." I feel Matt squeeze my shoulder, and I look around the table to see excited, knowing looks pass through the rest of the group.

What is going on?

The melody is soft and beautiful and he locks eyes on
me as he begins to sing.

My palms start to get sweaty
My cheeks begin to heat
I'm always thinking of you
Even when I sleep
There's only one balm for this illness,
The honey from your lips
Hold my hand now darlin'
We both know what this is

Can we stay in bed forever?
Will you kiss me back to health?
Catch this lovebug with me,
I don't want anyone else

You've been on my mind now,
Every minute of every day
My heart keeps beating faster
So baby, what do you say?

Can we stay in bed forever?
Will you kiss me back to health?
Catch this lovebug with me,
I don't want anyone else
You say you're immune, but
I don't think that's true, and
I don't think it's too soon, so
Say you feel it too
I can feel your palms get sweaty
I can see the way your cheeks heat

Say you think about me,
Even when you sleep
We'll stay in bed forever
Kiss until we're cured
We've got the love bug baby
I hope they never find the cure

I'm frozen. Completely unable to do anything as applause and cheers sound around me.

The fact that this tattooed, pierced, long haired, cinnamon roll of a man wrote a soft, romantic love song *for me*? Makes me feel so many things.

First, it makes my heart burst, it feels like it's literally going to beat out of my chest in equal parts anticipation, joy, and anxiety. Second, it makes me laugh remembering the night that inspired this song. Third, it makes me *extremely* aroused. I've been trying to subtly squeeze my thighs together the entire time he's been on stage because watching his fingers move across the fretboard and his forearms flex with movement? *Uggggh.*

Panty melting.

What a combo to feel so fucking aroused and so touched you're almost in tears.

"What did you think of the song, Elli?" Matt says, bringing my attention to him as Wes says some final thank yous and exits the stage.

"I loved it. Did you guys know? That he wrote a song for me?" I look around the table, and everyone nods enthusiastically.

"Well, you must be the lucky lady Westley wrote that song about." Says an older woman, who looks vaguely familiar. She has curly brown hair streaked with gray and pinned back to one side, and brown eyes.

"I-I guess so?"

"Sorry, how rude of me. I'm Jess. Luke's mom, Wes's...aunt?" She says, extending her hand.

"Oh! Hi, I'm Elli. Izzy's sister." I shake her hand and she gives me a small smile.

"Izzy's good for Luke. I'm glad they found each other. Thank you for all you've done to help them."

I wave her off, "Oh it's no problem. Luke's good for Izzy, too. He's good to her."

"I'm glad to hear that. Well, have a good rest of your night, maybe you can come to dinner sometime and we can get to know each other better?"

"I'd love that, Jess. Thank you. You have a good night as well." I say.

"Meeting the parents already, Elli?" Robin teases, nudging my shoulder.

I roll my eyes, "No. I do think it's good that I've finally met Luke's mom though! She seems nice."

"She's the best." Wes's voice says from behind me.

"Wes! You were amazing!" I squeal, throwing my arms around his neck before I can overthink it. "I thought your Instagram reels were good, but they don't even compare to live."

His strong arms wrap around my waist with no hesitation and he squeezes me before pulling back to give me a panty melting smirk. "You been stalking me, Elli?"

My cheeks flush in embarrassment, but Wes just chuckles and squeezes my hip. He leans in so his lips nearly brush my ear. "Let me say goodbye to these knuckleheads and then I'm taking you home. Deal?

I think we have some very important things to talk about."

I shiver, and nod my head in agreement. I think he's going to step away from me to say goodbye, but he keeps a hand on my hip as he fist bumps and hugs everyone else, accepting their praise and compliments, before saying goodbye.

Robin and Sav give me hugs goodbye, and Robin whispers "good luck" to me before she pulls away.

Wes grabs my hand and gently guides me to the back door of the bar and out the door into the humid Texas summer air. As soon as the door shuts behind us, giving us privacy, I pull him to a stop so he's facing me. "Wes. Was that song really about me?"

He steps forward, closing the distance between us so our chests are touching and I have to tilt my head up to look him in the eye. "Yes, Elli. I've spent the last four days writing songs about you. That one was just the one I wrote first."

"Did you... did you mean it?" I whisper.

Wes tucks a strand of hair behind my ear, leaving his warm palm on my cheek, his thumb brushing back and forth gently. "You have no idea how much I meant every fucking word Elli. You're like the first flower of spring breaking through the snow. It's like my heart was barely beating until I met you and you brought me back to life."

My lips part with a gasp, unsure what to say to that. He stares at me a little longer, leans in and kisses me on the forehead. Then pulls away, intertwining our fingers again, and leading me to his car.

He opens the passenger side door for me, but before I can get in, he leans forward and says, "I will kiss you Elli. But not until I know for sure where you stand. So we're going to go to your place and talk, but know that I'll be thinking about your lips and what they'll feel like the entire time."

Another shiver works its way down my spine before I get in the car and he closes the door.

It's like the sweet, shy, quiet Wes I know is meshing with this dominating, confident Wes that knows what he wants.

I just can't believe he wants *me*.

CHAPTER 21

Wes

Tonight has already gone better than I had planned. Elli didn't run off screaming after my set, and she met Jess! Which should feel scary but doesn't. I hope they get to know each other better soon. I know they'll be great friends. Jess's approval means a lot to me, and she seems to like Elli already so that's a plus.

The energy of the crowd is always intoxicating, the rush of performing is always incredible, but tonight it felt amplified. Having Elli in my direct line of sight all night was both a curse and a blessing. She's a walking wet dream in her outfit. I wanted to push her up against the wall outside of the bar, kiss her until her lips were swollen, and slide my hands up her skirt to see what kind of panties she's wearing.

But that will have to wait. I'm not going to do anything other than hold her hand until I know where she stands. Although I think I have a pretty good idea already.

She stares out the window most of the ride to her apartment, her thumb absently rubbing my hand, clearly overthinking if the shake in her leg is any indication.

When we finally get to her apartment, I make her stay put so I can open the door for her, and then walk next to her up to her front door. Once we're inside, she looks even more nervous.

"Um, can I get you anything to drink or eat? I think I have some lemonade or Dr. Pepper, some chips..." She trails off when she watches me go over to the couch, sit down, and pat the cushion next to me. I watch her throat move on a swallow and see her exhale before she pads over to the couch and sits on the opposite side, so there's a cushion between us.

"Baby, there's too much room between us. I promise I'm not going to bite. Yet." I tease. Her cheeks flush and she slides over so our thighs are touching like they have so many times before. Only this time, I'm not too chickenshit to rest my hand on her thigh.

"So," she whispers, then says louder, "So what do you want to talk about?"

"Well, I think I've made how I feel about you pretty clear tonight. And although I think I have an idea of how you feel about me, I would like to be sure before I do anything that could get my heart broken."

She bites her lip, fiddling with the ring on her thumb, and I can feel the anxiety of trying to find the right thing to say coming off of her in waves. I reach my hand up and tilt her chin to look at me, pulling her lip out from between her teeth.

"Elliana Monson, you have turned my world upside down. It's been over two years since I've felt even a speck of interest in someone. Shelby, my ex, hurt me badly. She wanted the novelty of dating a 'bad boy' and was cheating on me with everyone with a pulse and a dick. She could see my talent and wanted to be with me in case I got famous. But then I caught her with a guy from her work when I went to surprise her and she told me she was only with me as a way to 'pass the time.'" I swallow down the anger that still rises when I think about her, and continue.

"She told me I was trash, bound to be a drug addict like my whore mom. She said any fame I got would fizzle out before it even begins, and the only way I would find love is to buy it. No one wants to settle with someone so fucked up, who can't even offer a stable financial future. I didn't even have any family that loved me, so how could I expect anyone else to?"

Elli's face morphs into one of anger, "Well she's wrong."

I shrug, "Maybe she's not, though. My mom died of an overdose. She only stayed with her asshole ex because he was giving her drugs. It's in my blood to be an addict. That's why I rarely drink. I don't have any family other than Jess and Luke, and now the group, I guess. I'm a fucking music teacher instead of a famous rockstar. I don't have much to offer you, Elli."

"That's such bullshit, Wes. Shelby is full of shit. You are the most selfless, kind, beautiful human I've ever met. I'm so sorry about your mom. I can't even imagine the pain you have endured, but instead of letting it isolate you from everyone, you've *found* a family. And they're as lucky to have you as you are to have them. How many other people would agree to go on a random blind date with a stranger so his little brother could see his long-distance girlfriend? Who then sets up a TV for said stranger and sits through a trashy teen romcom? Who spends their days off helping said stranger unpack and listen to the sob story of a sheltered religious girl? Who shows up with their little brother to take his girlfriend to the airport? Who takes a girl dress shopping for a date with another man? Who shows up with five different types of coffee so someone can taste a variety for the first time? Who takes home a drunk girl from a club, takes off her makeup, and makes sure she's safely in bed?"

She takes a big breath, turning so her body is facing mine, and grabs my face in both hands. "Who writes a love song about one obscure conversation, melting the heart of the girl they wrote it for? When I look at you, I don't see a 'bad boy' who's unlovable, or someone who's just to pass the time. I see a strong, talented, confident, *tender* man who has tattoos, piercings, and long hair and who is sexy as hell. I see someone who is worth all the love in the world."

Tears spring to my eyes, and I barely even register that she called me sexy. I'll have to revisit it later.

"Thank you Elli." The tears are falling freely down my cheeks. She pulls me over to her so I'm almost laying on top of her, my head nestled in the crook of her neck with her arms bound tightly around my neck. I inhale her vanilla and coconut scent and feel at peace.

I lean up on an arm and look into her eyes, and she gives me a small smile. "You're welcome Wes. In case it wasn't obvious, I have a big ol' crush on you. I have since the day we met, and it's only grown since."

Although it's what I was hoping for, it still makes my heartbeat rapidly in my chest. I lean forward and place a kiss on her forehead, and her shoulders slump in disappointment.

"Elli, Elli, Elli," I tsk, "I'm going to do this right. Let me take you on a date on Saturday." It's not a question, though it may sound like one. I would back off if she said no, but I really hope she doesn't.

"Hmmm. Let me make sure Matt and I don't have one scheduled first." She teases.

"You're a little brat, you know that?" I say playfully as I begin to tickle her, her giggles are like music to my ears. I'll never get tired of hearing them.

"Okay, okay! I'm sorry! It was a joke! Mercy!" She squeals.

I finally ease up on my tickling only to pin her arms above her head. Her eyes flash with lust. *Interesting.* Something to visit again later. I run my nose along her jaw, her hairline, her neck, addicted to the sweet scent of her. "You better be sorry. I don't like sharing, Elli."

A shiver runs up her spine and her skin prickles with goosebumps, her pupils dilating. "I don't like sharing either." She whispers.

God damn. I like the possessive edge to her voice.

"Good, then we're in agreement. Saturday?" I sit up, pulling her with me so we're facing each other again.

"Saturday sounds perfect." Elli bites her lip again, then looks at me. "Are you going to kiss me now, Wes?"

"Do you want me to kiss you, baby?" I ask, already leaning in.

She nods, but I tsk, sliding a hand up her soft cheek to cradle her face. "Words, Elli."

"Yes. *Please.*"

I slide the hand on her cheek up and thread it through her hair, angling her head the way I want it, whispering "Finally." against her lips. Then I plant my mouth on hers, and I swear to God fireworks explode around us. Electricity shoots through my veins and I know for a fact that I will never get tired of kissing her.

I tentatively trace my tongue along her bottom lip and she eagerly lets me in, our tongues gently dancing together like we've done this a thousand times.

When we finally separate, she whimpers, which makes me groan. I want to hear that sound over and over again. Preferably when she's naked and writhing beneath me.

Not yet.

"That was…" She trails off.

"The best first kiss of my life." I finish for her. I want to say that it's my last first kiss, but I don't want to be too much, too soon.

She nods, touching her fingers to her lips like she's trying to keep my kiss there.

I stand, grateful my dark jeans hide the raging boner I've got like a fucking horny teenager. *Getting hard after one kiss? Seriously?*

Elli stands with me and I walk to the door, turning around to stand in the doorway. "I'll pick you up at nine on Saturday. Don't eat breakfast, there's somewhere I want to take you. Dress comfy."

"I can't wait." Elli says leaning up on her tiptoes to kiss my cheek. "Goodnight, Wes. I'll see you Saturday."

"Goodnight, pretty girl. I'll be counting down the minutes."

Chapter 22

Elli

I can barely sleep Friday night, I'm so excited to see Wes. We've been texting pretty much all day every day since Wednesday night, sending memes, TikToks, Reels, and he sends voice memos of songs he's working on. At night, he'll call me to ask me about my day. When we hang up, I literally kick my feet and giggle in pure delight. Not to mention, my vibrator has gotten a *lot* of use lately.

That kiss Wednesday seemed to flip a switch in my brain from "horny sometimes" to "horny all the time" because I have to use it every time we hang up the phone. After the first time using my vibrator, it's been easier to reach an orgasm with the toy. Much better than my fingers, for sure.

Saturday morning, I get up and Izzy calls me while I'm getting ready.

"Good morning sister dearest." I sing-song.

"Um. Hi? Why are you so chipper at eight on a Saturday morning?" Izzy asks, sleep still in her voice.

"I have a date. Why are you up so early? It's seven in Utah." I ask.

"A date?! I thought you and Matt were just staying friends."

"We are, I uhh, I'm going on a date with Wes, actually."

"WHAT?!" Izzy screeches. "Why is this the first I'm hearing about it? Where is he taking you? What changed?"

"Well, I don't know where he's taking me. He's surprising me. Nothing's changed other than the fact that we finally realized we liked each other. He wrote me a song and performed it on Wednesday and then-"

"He wrote you a song?" Izzy coos, "Luke's never written me a song. What the heck?"

"Luke isn't a writer, Iz. He's a performer. But I'm sure if you asked, he'd write you one." I'm sure he would, and he would make a big show of performing it, too.

"Yeah. You're right. Anyway, I just wanted to call you and let you know that Spencer got his mission call, he's going to Sao Paulo, Brazil. He leaves August seventeenth. Mom and dad expect you to be here for his farewell. I just thought I'd call you before Mom does so you can be warned."

Part of me feels a pang of sadness that my family didn't even think to call me for his mission call opening. I'm sure it was a big, flashy party and not a single person let me know.

Another part of me rolls my eyes. *Ooo Brazil. How original.* I swear everyone from my graduating class went to Brazil or Germany on their mission. "Thanks for the heads up. I can probably swing coming to Utah. Do you think I could bring Wes?"

There's a long pause before Izzy responds. "Is that... I mean, is it serious already? Do you think that's a good idea?"

"I think it will be serious by then. That's just over a month. I know he doesn't look like the typical guys I've dated, but he's special, Iz. I'd feel more comfortable coming back with him."

"You know I support you Els. But just know that Mom and Dad won't be happy, and they for sure won't let him stay at the house."

"That's fine. We'd probably get a hotel room anyway. Or see if Hannah has a spare room." I haven't chatted with Hannah in a while, but we were always close as kids. She got married pretty much right out of high school and started her master's around the same time, so we occasionally got lunch when classes allowed.

"You didn't hear?"

"Didn't hear what?"

"Hannah and Liam are getting a divorce."

"WHAT? When? Do you know why?" Why didn't Hannah tell me? I mean, I guess we aren't super close anymore, not like we were when we were kids, but still. How did I have no idea she was divorcing her husband?

"All I know is she moved in with Aunt Shelly two weeks ago and the divorce is still being finalized. No one's said why."

"That's so weird. Well, I guess I won't ask her for a place to stay. I've got to get dressed, Wes will be here soon."

"Yeah, I have to get to the school to start painting sets anyway. Mandatory stagecraft hours or no credit for the musical this term. Love you bunches Els. Have fun on your daaaate." She says.

"Love you too Izzy bee. I intend to."

"I want to know all the deets later! How good of a kisser he is, and if he's good with his hands since he plays the guitar."

"Izzy!" I chastise.

"You know you were thinking it too! Love you, bye!" And then the line goes dead, the little butthead.

I double check my subtle make up in the mirror, and make sure my ponytail is secure. Deciding it looks good, I head back to my room and try to decide if I want to put on the new pink lacy thong and matching balconette bra I got. I don't know what Wes has planned, or if he even wants to have sex yet, but... it can't hurt to wear something sexy, right?

Slipping those on, I opt for some light blue linen shorts and a white, flowy tank top with little beads on the high neckline. I'm just lacing up my black converse when the doorbell rings. Butterflies erupt in my belly when I open the door to find Wes, looking more casual than I've ever seen him. He's wearing black chino shorts, which show off the ink on his legs, a tight white t-shirt that enhances the ink on his arms, and his hair is pulled back in a low bun.

"Good morning, beautiful." He says, leaning in to give me a kiss on the cheek. "Ready to go?"

"Hi handsome. Let me grab my purse, then I'm all yours." I step to the kitchen to grab my purse off of the counter, then walk out the door.

As I'm putting the key in to lock the door, Wes steps up behind me and whispers in my ear, "I like the thought of you being mine, Elliana."

My breath hitches, and when I turn around there's a heat in his eyes that makes me want to squirm.

"Let's get this show on the road, baby. I have big plans for us today and we need to fuel up." He grabs my hand and leads me to his car. He opens the door for me, but before I get in he grabs me by the waist and plants a dizzying kiss on my lips.

"I was going to wait to do that until after but I've been thinking about your lips non-stop for three days. I needed a fix." He says with a wink before helping me into the car, buckling my seat belt for me, and closing the door.

Once again, I'm speechless. *How does he keep doing that?*

Wes has the radio playing on a low volume as we drive through San Marcos, his hand on my thigh the whole time. We make casual conversation during the ten minute drive, and when we stop, I see we're parked in front of a quaint little diner type restaurant called Ernie's.

"This place looks so cute and cozy!" I say as Wes opens the car door for me.

He places a hand on the small of my back as he guides me to the front door, "This is a hidden gem in San Marcos. It's housed many late night study sessions for me and Robs, and it's the best place to have breakfast after a long night out."

Wes opens the door for me and motions for me to go ahead of him, and I gasp as I take in the retro-eclectic atmosphere of the place.

The diner's walls are painted a light pink, the turquoise booth seats look worn and well used, but extremely comfortable, and the checkered floor is scuffed from so many feet on it, but it's clean and well kept. All along the walls are a hodgepodge of different celebrities. Major league baseball players, football stars, singers, actors, and actresses. I notice a photo of a familiar dark haired man with a guitar, standing in the middle of two older people. Wes sees it catch my eye and he blushes.

"That's from my first paid gig. Claudia wanted to make sure she had a signed picture for when I got famous." He explains. He motions to an empty booth, "Let's have some breakfast, yeah?"

I nod, following his lead. I take one side of the booth, and instead of him taking the other side like I thought, he joins me on one side. I glance over the menu, and am about to ask what I should order when the woman from the photograph comes over with a carafe of coffee.

"Well, look who it is! This isn't your usual breakfast date. Where's Red?" Claudia asks.

"Claudia, this is Elli. Elli, this is Claudia. Ernie's wife, and the maker of the best coffee on this side of Texas." Wes stands to give Claudia a hug, and I offer her a hand.

"Nice to meet you Claudia. I've heard excellent things about this place. Everything looks so good on the menu I can't decide what I want to order."

Claudia's hands are wrinkly and calloused as she grips mine in both of hers. Damn, she's strong for an older lady. "Well, Elli. It's nice to meet you. Wes doesn't bring very many people around here, so you must be one special lady."

Wes tosses an arm behind me and looks at me with a smile so bright it rivals the sun. "She's the most special."

Wes and Claudia catch up on what Wes has been up to, and he tells her about his newfound inspiration, the new songs he's written, and she makes him promise to send her the audio files when they're done so she can "give her stamp of approval."

"Alright kids. Wes, I'm assuming you want the usual?" She asks, and Wes nods. "What about you Miss Elli?"

Wes leans in, "Can I order for you?"

"I trust you." I say, handing over my menu.

Wes gives me a devastating smile, then turns back to whisper something to Claudia. Claudia hums in approval, and then leaves to go put our order in.

"She's super sweet, Wes. I can see why you like coming here." I say once Claudia is behind the counter and out of earshot.

"She's the best. My grandma used to bring me here every Sunday morning, since her and Claudia were such good friends. When I needed a babysitter, Claudia would step up when Jess couldn't watch me. She put me to work wrapping silverware when I was about ten and when I was thirteen, she promoted me to busboy. I worked here every weekend I could to save up for a guitar. It's because of them I was able to afford one and start writing my own songs." Wes says as he doctors up our coffees.

"That's amazing, Wes. I'm glad you had someone like that in your life." I say, laying my hand on his forearm.

"Me too. Probably would have turned into a big troublemaker if I didn't have Claudia and Ernie threatening my behind on a weekly basis." He says with a chuckle. "I don't know if I added enough sugar. Sorry there's no white chocolate here." He slides a white mug my way.

I take a sip of the steaming liquid. It's a bit bitter, so I grab another sugar packet and stir it in. I take another sip, "Ah. That's better. Not bad. I'll have to work on expanding my tastebuds."

He takes a large gulp of his and I watch his Adam's apple bob with the swallow.

Wow, I didn't know swallowing could be sexy.

Oblivious to my blooming arousal, Wes says "Claudia's is good. It's some of the only kind I can drink black. They import their beans from Guatemala."

I scrunch my nose, wondering how anyone could drink it without a cup of sugar, and Wes laughs at my face.

"Have I ever told you how cute your nose is?" Wes asks, tracing the appendage lightly with his finger.

"I don't think anyone has." I answer honestly.

"Well, baby, I think your nose is fucking adorable."

"Thank you." I say, my cheeks heating at the compliment.

Wes boops it gently and then plants a gentle kiss on the tip. "I'll compliment you all day every day. Any chance I get."

CHAPTER 23

Wes

My heart is beating so fast while we wait for our food.

Elli is the only other girl besides Shelby (and of course Robin) that I've ever brought here. I love Claudia and I love Ernie, but no one else was ever serious enough to deal with the inevitable interrogation from them.

Shelby *despised* this place. She said it was ugly and dirty and "too old" for her liking. She said the food was too greasy and that I was probably just trying to make her fat by bringing her here. So when I decided to bring Elli here, I was nervous as fuck. What if she thought the same thing? What if she didn't like it? What if she thought it was weird that I was friends with Claudia and Ernie?

I should have known that Elli wouldn't judge this place or me. I see the way she's enthralled by the smorgasbord of famous people, the eclectic decorations, and the homey atmosphere of the place.

Claudia sets down my usual biscuits and gravy with eggs, and sets a plate of homestyle fried potatoes with a side of homemade ranch for dipping, bacon, and a stack of buttermilk pancakes in front of Elli. "Here you go kids. I have regular maple syrup, but I brought out our famous pecan syrup for you too. We also have fresh strawberry syrup made from Poteet strawberries if you're interested in that. Let me know if I can get anything else for you kids."

"Thanks Claudia. This looks great." Ellis says, grabbing the carafe of pecan syrup.

I watch as Elli meticulously pours the syrup on one section of the pancakes, cuts into the stack with her fork, and takes a bite. Her eyes close and the sweetest little moan sounds from the back of her throat.

"Wes, oh my. This is so good." She moans again.

Well, now my dick's half-mast.

"Claudia's pancakes are the best. I'm not usually a sweet breakfast guy, but even I have to have a pancake fix every once in a while. Try the potatoes in the ranch. They're to die for." I take a bite of my own biscuits and gravy and watch as she does what I say.

"Fuck. Me." Elli groans, taking another bite of potatoes.

Absolutely, baby. You just name the time and place. Hell, I'll take you into the bathroom and do just that.

"Good?" I ask, and Elli nods enthusiastically, shoveling food into her mouth in a way that might be considered impolite. I find it endearing. It means she's comfortable around me, that she likes the food, and that she's not concerned about being judged.

"This is honestly the best breakfast I've had in, I don't know, ever. Thank you for bringing me here, Wes." She says, a drop of syrup dripping down her chin. Before I can think, I bring my thumb up to the sticky drop of liquid and wipe it off, but instead of bringing it to my mouth like I was planning, Elli turns her head and licks it off of my thumb.

I stare, dumbfounded and turned the fuck on. "Sorry. Did you want to try some?" She asks with a flirty smirk.

Instead of answering, I lean in and gently swipe my tongue over her lips. I hum in approval, and relish in her little gasp of surprise.

"Just a taste for now." I wink, and watch her face turn that shade of pink that drives me crazy. "Ready for part two of our date?" I ask, standing and placing two twenties on the table. Claudia hates that I pay for my meals, but I'm not going to let her feed me for free.

"I thought this was the date?" She asks as she stands and I interlace our fingers.

"This is just part one, baby." I walk toward the front door, but pause when I hear Claudia call my name.

"Westley Jones you better bring that young lady back here sometime soon, okay? Come during the lunch lull so Ernie can meet her too! Or for family breakfast!"

"Yes ma'am." I say, tipping my head in agreement, then rushing out of there before she can scold me for paying for our food.

I open Elli's door and help her get in, then round my side and turn the car on so we aren't burning up. "Alright baby. The next place I want to take you involves a bit of walking. Are you good with that?"

Elli nods enthusiastically and I grin, butterflies swarming my stomach as I start the familiar drive to another place I haven't brought anyone, not even Robin. The drive to the little trail is about twenty minutes, and we sit in a comfortable silence, our hands still inter-locked, the radio playing a soft mix of Indie bands I love.

When we get to the little path that will lead to where I want us to go, I stop the car, tell Elli to stay put, and head to the trunk to grab the backpack, blanket, and my guitar. Once everything is situated on my person, I open Elli's door and grab her hand and lead her down the tree covered trail. It's about half a mile to our destination.

Chapter 24

Elli

The only sounds as we walk are the cicadas, the birds, and the rustle of leaves as we walk down the trail. Sometimes Wes will break the silence to ask if I'm okay, but other than that, we walk in comfortable silence for about ten minutes.

"Where are you taking me?" I ask quietly, not wanting to disturb the peacefulness of the moment.

"This is my quiet place. My mom used to bring me here when I was really little, before she started dating the asshole she was with when I was nine. She taught me to skip rocks here, and she would tell me stories about magical beings in the trees." Wes says wistfully. "I remember one of the last times we came here, she told me a story about special water fairies that could tell you if someone was your fated match."

"How could they tell?" I ask, intrigued.

"Well, according to my mom, they could tell by the person's aura. How they matched and whatnot. The fairies would only tell you the answer if you and your love skipped rocks at the same time. The rocks have to skip exactly seven times and sink together. If they do, then they're your soulmate. If not, then they're not. I ate it up as a kid, already planning on bringing someone here to test that out." He frowns a little. "When she started dating Keith, the asshole, we stopped coming here. When I could drive, I figured out how to get here myself, but I've never brought anyone with me. It's just been a place to clear my head, you know? Reconnect with nature and whatnot."

"That's a beautiful story. I'm sorry you couldn't come back for a while. That sounds…" I trail off as Wes stops in front of a small pond surrounded by trees and rocks. The land around the pond is packed dirt sprinkled with sparse grass and I can hear a stream nearby that probably brings water into the pond. It's breathtaking and I can see why Wes comes here. It's almost like another world.

"Wow, Wes. This place is breathtaking. It's almost magical." I say, spinning to face him.

Wes has laid the blanket out, and from the backpack has set out a few water bottles for us. He looks up at me and smiles, "You being here makes it even more breath-taking."

I'm glad my cheeks are red from walking in the heat, because they're aflame with a blush from his compliment. I nod toward his guitar, "Are you going to sing me another song?"

"I thought I would. Run some of my lyrics by you and see what you think. If that's okay?" He looks almost shy as he says it.

"I would love that. But you also have to teach me how to skip rocks later. I've never done that before."

"Deal." He pats the blanket next to him, and I sit cross-legged facing him while he tunes his guitar.

"Okay," he says on an exhale, "this song is still a work in progress, because I was focused on fine tuning 'Love Bug' for Wednesday night, so bear with me."

My stomach flutters thinking about Wednesday and all that's happened in the last three days. It's crazy to go from thinking he only saw me as a friend to being on a date with him in such a short time. I'm so happy that things worked the way they did.

Wes starts strumming his guitar in a rhythmic beat, a little peppier than the slow melody of "Love Bug," and when he starts to sing, I get literal chills. He gets so lost in the lyrics, it's like nothing else exists.

Then during the bridge, he looks up and stares direct-ly into my soul, like I'm the only thing that exists in his world. It makes me nervous, but also makes me swoon.

Who am I kidding? It also makes me horny as hell because being the center of this man's world? His choco-late brown eyes boring into mine like he owns me? It's the hottest thing I've ever experienced. Not to mention his finger skills. The way they dance across the strings like it's second nature?

So. Damn. Sexy.

When he's done, he sets the guitar down and asks me, "So? What did you think?"

"I think... I think that was probably the hottest expe-rience of my life." The words just come out, no filter to be seen. But I don't take the words back because it's also the truth.

Wes gently sets his guitar down, leaning back on his hands and tilting his head to assess me. "The hottest experience of your life, eh? Well that bar is low, baby. I'm sure I can do better."

Feeling a little bold, I retort, "Oh yeah? I'd love to see you try."

In a flash of tattoos and dark hair, I'm covered by Wes's body, his knee wedged between my open thighs, my wrists pulled above my head and held there by one of his large hands. He runs his nose along my jaw, and brings his lips close to my ear.

"Do you know how crazy you make me, Elli? Moaning at breakfast over food instead of me, watching your luscious ass in those little shorts, the way they hug your thighs?" Wes groans, "Do you know how many times I've stroked my cock to the thought of you in that tiny little dress I helped you out of?"

"How many?" I whisper. This is a side of Wes that I haven't seen. He's so... commanding. His words are so filthy. It's *so* hot.

"Too many to count, baby. Not to mention, the absolute rage I felt when I heard about that douchebag's hands on you at the club. I had no right to be that jealous, but I was fuming. I don't want anyone else's hands near your body."

"No one else, Wes. You already know I'm a... I've never had sex. I only want you." And that's the truth. I was only a virgin because my religion practically demanded it. I was only waiting until marriage because that's what I thought needed to happen, but when Packer ended things and I realized I could have sex with whoever I wanted, I just... didn't. I was still too scared to commit such a "sin." Now that I've explored my body and have gotten comfortable "sinning" I'm ready to take the next step.

Ready to take the next step with *Wes.*

And apparently he's ready for me too, if the hard thing poking into my thigh is any indication.

"I'm glad to hear that." Wes kisses the tip of my nose and sits back on his heels, rubbing a hand down his face. "I'm sorry I got carried away just now. I'm not going to do anything in the middle of nature, where anyone could come across us. When we're together for the first time, we're going to take our time, Elli. Not because I don't think you can handle it, but because it's what you deserve."

I have a bit of whiplash from the change in mood so suddenly, but I can tell Wes needs the space and the reassurance that I'm okay.

"Never apologize for being you, Wes. You're never going to be too much for me. I appreciate that you want to take things slow." I reach up to his face and pull him down for what's supposed to be a quick peck, but turns into a slow, leisurely makeout session.

When we finally come up for air, Wes groans, then gives me another peck on the lips before standing and holding his hand out for me. "Come on, baby. Let's skip some rocks."

I grin as he helps me up. He guides me through the process of which rocks are the best for skipping, and which ones will just sink. He teaches me the right wrist flicking technique, and after a few practice rounds, I'm feeling pretty confident.

"How about we skip these last rocks together and see who makes it furthest?" I suggest.

"You're on." We stand side by side, and Wes counts down from three.

When he hits "one" we toss our rocks and watch them sync up and skip one, two, three, four, five, six, seven times.

And sink to the bottom together.

Wes's breath hitches, and I know he's thinking it too.

Maybe the fairies are real, after all.

CHAPTER 25

Wes

I'm not a religious man. I don't believe in some Sky Daddy who controls the universe or anything like that. I'm not sure I believe in fate or karma, but even I have to admit the seven skips and sinking thing was such a specific, unlikely thing to happen. I don't believe in fairies, but it's almost like a sign from the universe that Elli and I are meant to be, despite all of our differences.

After skipping rocks, we lay on the blanket and just talked about everything. Conversation comes so easily with her, it's almost scary.

Elli told me more about growing up in Utah, how the winters were brutal but the spring and fall were gorgeous. How she never really felt like she fit in as a teenager, and was only doing things to please her parents. She wanted to be a chef, but that wasn't considered a "good mom career" so she decided to go into human resources. She was going to go to culinary school, but her parents refused to let her live at home if she didn't pick a better career choice. I know my childhood was bad, but Elli's was rough in a different way. I always knew who I wanted to be and the expectations for my future may have been low, but I always had support in some form whether it be Jess, or Grandma, or Claudia and Ernie. Even now, I have Robin, Matt, Sean, Drew, Sav, and the kids that support me.

Elli only has Izzy.

And now me.

I tell her about the first time I ever played in front of an audience at our high school talent show. I was so nervous I threw up backstage. In the end I think I did a pretty good job, though.

I lean in to kiss Elli, right as her stomach grumbles and ruins the romantic moment. She blushes in embarrassment, but I laugh it off and offer to stop and grab food on the way to her apartment. She refuses my offer and says she'd really like to cook for me instead.

I'm not going to turn down a homemade meal, so I agree.

She doesn't let me help her with dinner, but I watch as she easily maneuvers around the kitchen. She seems at home there, and it's mesmerizing to watch her chop things and cut vegetables so quickly.

When the chicken is cooked, and the noodles are done, she combines the sauce, the chicken, and the noodles all together with a bit of pasta water and puts them on a plate with a slice of french bread slathered in butter.

My mouth waters as she sets the plate in front of me, then joins me at the counter on the other barstool.

I take a bite, and it's so good I have to refrain from shoveling everything into my mouth like a rabid bear.

"Elli. This is fucking amazing. I have to have the recipe."

"Thank you. I um, I don't have a recipe." She says shyly, shrugging. "I just make it up as I go, usually. I had asparagus and mushrooms that needed to be used."

Damn. This girl just gets more and more impressive.

After eating the rest of my food, plus another serving, I help Elli clean the dishes.

It's such a tedious, domestic task, but it's so fun with her. I flick soap at her and she retaliates by whipping me with the dish towel, all with a beaming grin on her face.

Once those are done, I'm prepared to say goodnight, but she asks if she can talk to me about something. She's twisting her thumb ring around her finger like she does when she's nervous, so now I'm nervous.

We sit on the couch, facing each other, and Elli takes a big breath before she says. "I have something to ask you, and I'm not sure if it's too soon since today was our first official date, or if it'll scare you away, but-"

I gently shush her by putting my finger to her lips, "Just ask me Elli. It's going to take a lot to scare me away."

She takes a deep breath, then, fiddling with my rings instead of hers -which I find fucking adorable- she says, "My little brother, Spencer got his mission call. I'll explain more about what that is in a minute, but it's a whole big thing. My parents are going to call me, probably tomorrow, and ask me if I can come out for it. I really don't want to go alone, so I was hoping that maybe... *you* would want to come with me? It's not until August, so that's, what? A month? You can say no, obviously. I just... would really like you to be there with me."

Meeting the parents of the person you're dating is scary enough, but meeting Elli's parents? That's extremely terrifying. I'm the polar opposite of the other guys she's dated. Not to mention, I'm not religious at all. Will they hate me? Will they think I've corrupted their good little girl?

Elli must sense my hesitation because she gently squeezes my hands and looks directly into my eyes. "I know it's soon. I know you're probably scared to meet my parents, hell, *I'm* scared to see my parents. But their opinion of you doesn't matter to me, Wes. I've been happier than I've ever been since moving here. *You* make me happy. You also give me strength. And I'll need that to face them. Like I said, you can absolutely say no. I won't be upset at you at all. But... if things do get more serious with us, you'll have to meet them eventually, right? I figured ripping off the band aid might be the best scenario."

I pull her closer so she's straddling my lap, and I frame her beautiful face with my hands. "It would be an honor to go with you, Elli. I am super worried that your parents are going to, I don't know, deny me entry to their house because I look like a devil worshiper, but I want to go. I want to see where you grew up. And being stuck with you in the car for twenty hours doesn't seem like the worst fate in the world."

She playfully swats my chest, then leans in and gives me a searing kiss. "Thank you Wes. I don't think you realize what this means to me."

"Anything for you, baby."

The words *I love you* are right on the tip of my tongue. But we literally just had our first date. There's no way I'm going to say that right now. Even if I feel like it's true.

God, that's crazy, right? I've barely known her for a month. How can I be in love with her already? I've only been in love once, but it didn't feel anything like this.

"Alright, explain what a mission is. I need to be prepared." I say in faux seriousness.

Elli rolls her eyes, "I don't think anyone who hasn't grown up Mormon can be prepared. But, here goes. You know how some people go on 'mission trips' to Haiti or Guatemala to help build houses?" I nod. "Well it's kind of like that, but not. Once a boy turns eighteen he can submit papers to go on a two year long proselytizing mission. They don't get to choose where they go, and they don't get to leave early unless it's for an extreme medical emergency. They get transferred to different areas every eight weeks on their mission, but they stay in the general vicinity of a certain city. For example, Spencer is going to Sao Paulo, Brazil and will have to learn Portuguese. He doesn't know Portuguese, so when he goes to the MTC- missionary training center- he'll be immersed in that language so he can speak with the people."

"That sounds kind of cool, to learn a language like that, that fast. You said when boys turn eighteen. What about girls?"

"Girls can't go until they're nineteen, and they only go for eighteen months. It's not a requirement for them to go because their job is to get married and pop out babies."

"That's ridiculous."

"Yeah, it is. Also, missionaries have a strict dress code, strict media restrictions, and strict schedules to follow. In certain places they don't have to wear the white dress shirts and suits, but for the most part, that's their attire. They just changed the rules for girls in some areas so they can wear pants instead of skirts or dresses all the time, but for the most part, they have to be in dresses or skirts."

"That seems extremely uncomfortable. I can't imagine having to wear a skirt in below freezing weather, or a suit in the humid summer heat. What about things like transportation and stuff?"

"Oh, in some areas they get cars. Other areas, they get bikes or they just have to walk. In other countries I guess you can use public transportation if you want, but I don't know a whole lot about that. I know in our area, if the missionaries needed a ride, they could call on a ward member. But there always had to be two people in the car so my dad would always make me go with him. This isn't relevant but to stop their companions from masturbating, a lot of the boys have to stand outside of the bathroom door while the other showered, and some mission presidents even required them to sing hymns in the shower to prove they weren't." She shrugs, like it's such a normal thing to do.

What the hell? What kind of Kool-Aid are the Mormons drinking? After what she told me in her room the day we unpacked, and now this? I'm more confused than ever. I'm convinced this is a cult.

"So, what should I expect for this big farewell thing for Spencer?" I ask, just so I can make sure I'm prepared.

She sighs, "Well, we'll have to go to sacrament meeting-sorry about that. It's an hour-long meeting where they sing, they listen to people talk-Spencer is giving his 'farewell speech', and they take the sacrament. You and

I aren't worthy to take the sacrament so that'll be a fun topic of conversation with the ballsy family members. They'll know why you can't take it, no offense."

"None taken." I have no issues with how I look. "Will I have to wear a suit? Because I don't think I own one." I'd buy one, just for her, if she asked me to.

She gives me a soft smile and runs her hand down my chest, "No, babe. You don't have to wear a suit. Just a button up shirt and pants with no holes in them. I'll be in a dress, though."

Babe. Babe. Babe. She called me babe.

"After sacrament meeting, people, mostly family or Spencer's friends, will come to our house for food and to say goodbye. There will be a *lot* of people because my mom has eight siblings and my dad has five and Spencer is a popular dude. Luckily it's summer so they'll most likely have it in the backyard. Be prepared to get asked a million times about your tattoos. If they hurt, what they mean, why you got them. Also, people will make passive aggressive comments about your hair and your piercings. I'll try to keep you away from those people but sometimes I don't know who's going to say what, you know? Just know that I think you're damn sexy just how you are and I wouldn't change a thing about you." She punctuates that with a slow, tantalizing kiss on my lips.

"You think I'm sexy?" I say against her mouth, my dick starting to stand at attention with her delicious body pressed against it.

"Yes, babe. The sexiest man I've ever seen." Another drugging kiss. "Well maybe the second sexiest. Have you *seen* Sebastian Stan?"

I narrow my eyes at her, and start tickling her sides. She squeals, trying to fight back, but I pin her to the couch and continue while she giggles. "Take it back!" I say as I continue my onslaught of tickles.

"Fine! Uncle! You're way hotter than Sebatian Stan." She says breathily. Her cheeks are flushed from laughing, and now I have her pinned beneath me.

I lean down, centimeters from her lips and say "I'm not a self-conscious man, baby, but I do want to be the only man on your mind. Especially when I have you pinned beneath me."

"You're the only man on my mind all the time, Wes."

"Good. You're the only woman on mine, Elli." I drop my body so my dick is level with her clothing covered pussy, and roll my hips the tiniest little bit. Her eyes widen as her breath hitches. I see the desire in her eyes and I so badly want to rip off these cute little shorts and absolutely devour her. I want to make her see stars. I want to claim her.

But I won't today. Not until I'm certain she's ready.

But that doesn't mean we can't have a little fun.

I lean down and whisper in her ear, "Has anyone ever made you come, Elli?"

She shakes her head. "Just me. And my vibrator."

Well fuck me, that's hot.

"Can I touch you, baby?" I ask, skimming my hands down her sides, staying clear of her glorious tits just in case she's not ready for that.

She nods, sits up, and takes off her cute tank top, revealing a white lace bra that barely conceals her pert, rosy nipples. I wasn't expecting that, so I just stare at her dumb struck.

She's so fucking beautiful, maybe I do believe in a God. Only an all-powerful being could create something so heavenly, so gorgeous, that I want to fall to my knees and worship her.

I must have been staring too long because she starts to put her shirt back on. "Don't." I say in a husky whisper. I look into her eyes, "Don't cover yourself back up, please. You're stunning, Elli."

The blush I love so much trails all the way down her chest. "You can touch me, Wes. I want you to touch me." She whispers.

I trace the cups of the bra over the swell of her breast, the skin smooth as silk, before I follow the trail of a lace flower around her budding nipple. She hisses, arching her chest into my touch so I continue, gently circling it with my pointer finger before taking it between my thumb and pointer finger and giving it a light pinch.

Elli's answering moan is the sweetest music I've ever heard in my life. I want to record it, play it on a loop all day every day.

I sit her up so I can remove her bra fully, and when her breasts fall free, I nearly come in my pants. Sure, I saw a glimpse of how delicious they were when I helped her out of that contraption shirt, but I tried to keep my eyes averted for her modesty.

Now? I'm ravenous. They're the perfect handful, the perfect weight to squeeze in my palm. I bring my mouth down to her right nipple and circle the bud with my tongue, and her hands find the back of my head. I squeeze her left tit while I lick and suck on her right one, pulling more and more moans from her that are trying to make me feral.

"Wes, I want more. Please." She begs.

I switch to sucking and nibbling her left nipple while playing with her right with my fingers, and roll my hips so my cock rubs against her pussy. Even though we're both still clothed down there, I can feel the heat radiating from her.

I pop off her nipple to look up at her. "Where's your vibrator, Elli?"

"It's in my nightstand drawer..." She looks confused, but I stand and dart to her bedroom.

I grab the pink rabbit from her drawer, and stalk back into the living room, my eyes glued to my girl and the way she's sprawled on the couch, still half dressed.

I kneel in front of her and snap the band of her shorts. "Can I take these off too?"

At her nod, I gently slide them down her legs, discarding the linen shorts somewhere across the floor. It leaves her in a lace thong that matches the lace of her bra, and I look up at her with a smug grin.

"Elli, Elli, Elli. Were you hoping I'd take off your clothes and see you in this sexy as hell set?"

"Yes." She says shyly, and I watch the blush I love so much spread down her neck.

"Hmm. And were you hoping I'd take off this flimsy little thong and take a look at this pretty pink pussy?"

"I was hoping you'd do more than look." Elli says cautiously, like it's a shameful thing to want.

I never want her to think anything about her is shameful. Her desires, her dreams, her body, her sexuality.

Instead of responding verbally, I pull the thong off of her and discard it across the room with her shorts, then use my thumbs to spread her bare pussy lips and admire the way they glisten with her arousal.

"I never want you to feel ashamed for telling me what you want, Elli. But let me tell you what's going to happen tonight, okay?" I say, removing my hands from her.

She whimpers at the loss, but nods.

"I'm going to use this little pink vibrator on this little pink pussy, and you're going to come from that while I play with these perfect nipples, okay?"

"But-"

"That's the deal, baby. Or I can just leave and you can do it yourself. What would you like?"

Her blue eyes bore into mine and she pleads, "Please make me come, Wes."

Pleased with her response, I turn on the vibrator and put it to her clit, causing her to jolt and arch upwards. She moans my name, making my cock even harder in my shorts. God, I want to take it out and stroke it to the sight of her. It wouldn't take me long to come. Especially with the way she's writhing right now.

"Wes, fuck, I'm so close. Please" She lifts her hips higher to hump harder against the vibrator, so I bring my mouth down and swirl my tongue around her nipple and turn the vibrations up higher.

"That's it, baby. Take what you need." I switch nipples, using my free hand to pluck at the one I was previously latched to.

It doesn't take more than a minute of my ministrations before Elli's thighs clamp my hand and she moans my name loudly while she comes.

Fuck me. I can feel my cock leaking in my shorts.

I turn the vibrator off and she releases me from the vice grip that is her thighs, and when I pull the toy away, it's glistening with her release. I'm so tempted to stick it in my mouth just to get a taste of her, but I refrain.

I'll taste her soon.

As Elli catches her breath, I make my way to the bathroom and wash the toy, then take it back to her nightstand.

When I come back, Elli's looking at me with a sleepy smile.

"That was... incredible, Wes."

"Yeah it was, Elli. Watching you come may be my new favorite hobby." I kiss her forehead. "I don't want to leave, but it's been a long day and you need some rest. Let me help you get tucked into bed."

She nods, and stands. I watch her go through her nightly routine, removing her makeup, brushing her teeth, putting her hair into a loose bun with a satin scrunchie, and doing her skincare routine. It makes me smile, remembering her drunkenly telling me what products to use in what order.

When she's all dressed in a pink satin pajama set, I help her into bed, plug in her phone, and give her a gentle kiss goodnight.

As I'm about to walk out of her bedroom door, she calls my name. "Thank you for today. It was the best day I've had in a really long time."

"You're so welcome Elli. Thank you for coming with me. Get some sleep. I'll talk to you tomorrow."

"Goodnight Wes."

"Goodnight, baby."

I make sure to lock her door on my way out, and I drive home with the biggest smile on my face.

I'm one hundred percent in love with Elliana Monson.

CHAPTER 26

Elli

Waking up to a text from Wes after having the best orgasm, best first date, best day ever makes me giggle and kick my feet. I feel like I'm floating as I go through my morning routine and get ready for the day.

I'm in the middle of making breakfast when my mom calls on Facetime. I check what I'm wearing, and when I realize I'm in a tiny crop top that shows the hickey Wes gave me last night, I hurry and throw on a t-shirt before answering.

I paste on a smile. "Hey, Mom."

"Elliana." She says curtly. "We haven't heard from you in a while."

Well, the phone works both ways as you always say.

"Sorry, I've been super busy with work and settling in. Izzy's called me a few times. She said Spence got his mission call to Brazil. That's exciting."

Mom's eyes glow with warmth for her favorite son. I know it, she knows it, everyone knows Spencer is her favorite. Her golden child. Her voice is much warmer now that I've brought him up. "Yes, we're so proud of him and his decision to serve. That's actually why I'm calling you. I wanted to see if you were going to make it out for his farewell? You know he's your first sibling to go on a mission. It would look bad if you were to miss it."

Wow. Two minutes in and she's already guilt-tripping me. Splendid. I just manage to stop my eyes from rolling while I respond.

"Yes, I planned on coming. I'm going to be bringing..." A friend? My boyfriend? What do I call Wes? "Wes. Someone I've gotten close to while I've been here."

Mom's eyebrow raises, and she doesn't look pleased. "I hope you won't be bringing your *friend* to stay here while you're here. You know we don't have the extra room."

"I know, Mom. I figured we'd just stay at a hotel."

"*We?* Is this Wes a boy or a girl?"

"He's a boy. I'm not just going to abandon him to stay alone while I stay at your house."

That's the first time I haven't called my childhood house "home." It's a stark realization that I don't consider it home anymore. Did it ever feel like home?

"Elliana," she sighs, disappointment evident in her tone. "You know what people will say if they realize you're shacking up with a man when you're unmarried. Besides, what will Packer think?"

"Packer lost the right to think anything about me when he broke up with me and married someone else two months later." I grit out. How dare she bring up my ex of almost a year right now? He's *married* and expecting a fucking child last I heard.

"Well what about your sister? What kind of example are you setting for her?" Mom presses.

"Izzy is almost an adult, Mom. She's not going to base her choices on anyone but herself and you know it. I understand this is probably going to disappoint you and dad, but I'm an adult too. And I've made my decisions. I lo-I like Wes a lot. He's been nothing but kind to me. If you don't want him there, then that's fine but I'd rather you say that then try to guilt me into not bringing him."

The thought of facing my family without Wes there makes me want to throw up. I know I shouldn't be so dependent on someone, and I know Izzy has my back, but I've never done well with family gatherings. The thought of having to sit through another one alone...

Mom sighs again, clearly frustrated and angry. "Fine. Bring Wes. But don't tell anyone you're staying in a hotel alone with him. You're right about me and your father being disappointed in you, Elliana. We raised you better than this. Have you even been going to church since you moved?"

"No. I haven't."

"So you just want to tear apart our eternal family? That's what you want? Do you hate us that much?" Tears start welling in her eyes. Of course, the only emotional reaction would be about her precious eternal family. A show of compliance, not love.

"It's not about you. Or dad. Or anyone but me. I don't believe in the church anymore. I haven't for a while."

"Well. I'm glad to know I raised such a selfish child. I have to go, I have church meetings to attend. I'll see you in August."

And then she hangs up.

Frustrated tears well in my eyes and spill over even as I try to blink them away. I hate when she does the passive aggressive "I'm such a bad mom" thing. It's not fair for her to turn my choices against me like that. Needing some comfort, I do the only thing I can think of.

I text Wes.

> **Elli:** Morning, handsome. I wish I woke up next to you. Any chance you're free today? I could use a distraction.

His response is almost immediate.

> **Wes:** I'm on my way with comfort food and movies, baby. Any special requests?

> **Elli:** Just you <3

I can't believe how lucky I am to have such an amazing human on my side. Fuck what my mom and anyone else thinks of Wes. I love him. I can't believe I almost let that slip out on the phone with my mom.

I love Wes.

The thought terrifies me. But I think about my sad love life.

I think about Brigham and his manipulation and how he blamed me for being a horny creep.

I think about my relationship with Packer. I thought I was in love with him, I thought we would get married.

But he was always pushing me to lose weight. Saying he just "wanted a healthy girlfriend" even though I have no cause for any health concerns.

He was rarely affectionate with me in public, like he was ashamed of me.

When he broke up with me and told me it was because he wasn't ready to be in such a committed relationship, I got it. I thought that made sense. He wanted to date around or whatever.

Turns out, he was just passing the time until a girl he met on his mission moved to Utah for school. He was waiting for this freshly eighteen year old girl. They got married two months after he broke up with me. And now she's pregnant and tied to him forever.

I really dodged a bullet there.

Then I think about Wes.

How he helped Luke out in a time of need.

How he was such a gentleman to me, a total stranger.

How he was attentive and engaging on that awkward blind date.

How he opened up to me about his grandma and mom.

How he let Matt take me on a date because he didn't want to step on anyone's toes.

How he wrote a love song based on a fleeting conversation, for me.

How he always seems to want to be close to me, no matter who's around.

How hungry his eyes got when they saw me naked last night...

My thighs clench automatically just thinking about it. Last night was so hot, so eye opening.

I want more.

But I'm also terrified because I felt his erection. It was pretty thick. And hard. Bigger than my vibrator.

Sex is natural. It'll fit.

There's a knock on my door, and glance down and realize I never changed out of my lounge shorts and the t-shirt I put on to talk to my mom. I debate taking it off, but I'm only wearing a thin crop top underneath and, despite how much I want him, I'm not trying to get in his pants right this second.

Maybe later though...

CHAPTER 27

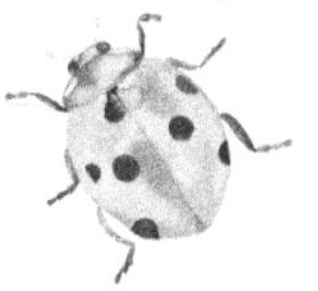

W as I waiting around by my phone for Elli to text me this morning?

No.

Okay, fine.

Yes.

But I had some serious regrets about not being able to wake up next to her this morning and I missed her.

Sue me.

So when she texted me and asked if I was free, I didn't even question it. I hopped in the car and headed to the donut place halfway between her place and mine. I got a dozen assorted donuts, an iced white mocha, my usual coffee and now I'm here, waiting for her to answer her door.

When she finally does, she takes my breath away. I love Elli in makeup, but I also love seeing her bare face. She's in a purple shirt that has EFY on it, and looks like it's seen better days, and a pair of shorts that should be criminal with how they hug her ass and thighs.

I step in, set the donuts and coffee on the counter, and turn back to her to pull her into a tight hug. I can tell she's been crying by the red rim around her eyes, and my heart aches.

"Hi baby." I whisper, gently kissing her lips.

She offers me a small, sad smile in return. "Hi handsome."

"Do you want to talk about it?"

She nods, and I take her over to the couch sitting back so she can fit between my thighs. I wrap my arms around her chest and hug her.

She takes a few deep breaths and tells me about a conversation she just had with her mom. She tells me about how her mom blames her for "ruining" their eternal family or whatever, and how her mom called her a disappointment.

"She had the audacity to bring up my ex. She was all 'What will Packer think?' of me bringing you to the farewell and sharing a hotel room with you. I told her Packer doesn't get an opinion because he dumped me and married an eighteen year old after."

I stiffen, because that's new information about her ex. I obviously knew he was an idiot for letting a catch like Elli go, and that he got married really quickly after they broke up. But to dump her and then marry an *eighteen year old* two months later is a dick move. Not to mention, creepy as fuck.

"Do you want to talk about your ex? I'm a little confused on how things ended now, but if you don't want to talk about it, it's okay." I say cautiously. I don't want to upset her.

She waves me off. "I'm fine talking about him. He's obviously an asshat. When we started dating, I was already questioning the church but I thought maybe if I could get married to a 'worthy man' my doubts would go away. But I think back on it, Packer was a shitty boyfriend. He always made comments about my weight, would rarely touch me in public, and would never make an effort to make me feel special.

"When he ended things, he told me he just wasn't looking for anything serious. I got that. It made sense. I was hurt, but I understood, ya know? But then I saw he was tagged in a picture on Instagram from a petite blonde girl who looked freshly graduated from high school, saying she can't believe she's marrying the love of her life. So I did some digging and found out he met her on his mission in Nebraska. She was, in fact, freshly graduated from high school and was moving to Utah to go to BYU for college. I assume they'd been talking for months in order for things to move that quickly. Now she's pregnant I guess. Izzy's been keeping tabs on the girl, Tiffany, because she loves drama, but I don't really care anymore."

"How old is Packer?" I ask.

"Twenty-six."

"Her parents let her marry a twenty-six year old right out of high school? Who does that?" I'm appalled. That's weird and disgusting on so many levels.

She shrugs, like this is totally fucking normal. "Lots of people get married right out of high school in Mormonism, especially in Utah. The amount of times growing up I heard 'ooo look at that cute missionary. You know, he's only six years older than you. When you turn eighteen he'll only be twenty-four. Maybe he's your future husband!' is obscene. Mormon women are groomed to be married and have babies at a young age."

I do the math in my head and realize that she was *twelve* when she was told that. "That's..." *disgusting. Creepy. Should be illegal.* "Intense."

The understatement of the century.

Elli's head falls back against my shoulder as she releases a long sigh. "I know. It's gross. I don't think I want kids, but if I did have them, I'd *never* put pressure on them at twelve to think about their future partner that seriously. When I turned fourteen and wasn't 'shedding the adolescent weight' as my mom put it, she started telling me that if I ever wanted a good husband I needed to take better care of myself. It's why I learned to cook, too. To be able to be a good housewife."

"I hate that, Elli. A lot. I'm sorry you went through that. Luckily for you, I also know how to cook so you don't have to worry about being the perfect housewife for me."

Realizing what I just said, I try to back track. "Not that you're my wife, or that I want you to be my wife. I mean we just started dating. House girlfriend? Not that you're my girlfriend because we haven't put labels on anything. God, shut me up now."

When I finish rambling, I realize Elli is shaking.

Oh fuck, I've made her cry.

I'm about to apologize when a giggle comes from her, shocking me into stillness.

Oh so she thinks my rambling is funny.

Once her laughing has died down, she turns to me and gives me a peck on the lips. "Thanks babe. I needed a laugh. And don't worry, I'd love to be your girlfriend." She says with a wink.

"Thank fuck. I was worried I totally screwed that up." I say, pulling her back into my chest. "Now that it's clear you're my girlfriend, what do you say to some donuts, coffee, and good old fashion Mary Kate and Ashley movies?"

"Mary Kate and Ashley movies?"

"Hell yeah! *Passport To Paris, Billboard Dad, It Takes Two?* These are classics, baby."

"I mean, I love those movies too, but I didn't expect *you* to love them. I pictured you as more of a *Lord of the Rings, Fast and The Furious, Bourne Identity* type guy."

"*Lord of the Rings* is my jam on toast, and a total classic, but you said you needed a distraction. Comfort food and silly movies is the best way to be distracted, in my opinion."

"You sure know the way to a girl's heart." She sighs.

"Only heart I want is yours baby."

"Well you've got it, babe."

CHAPTER 28

Elli

I t's been a week since my first date with Wes. And I swear, I fall more in love with him every day.

The last week has been nothing short of magical. Wes and I text every day, and more often than not, he comes over here or I go to his apartment after work and we hang out and watch movies and cook together. There have been a few more orgasms with my vibrator, and even one with his fingers when we were at his place and I didn't have it.

He asked me to masturbate in front of him to show him how I like it, but I still haven't seen his cock. I'm aching for him. I'm this close to getting on my knees and begging for him to fuck me.

We're going out with Sav, Drew, Sean, Matt, and Robin tonight to Midnight Luxuries, and then I'm spending the night at Wes's apartment. Hopefully things can *progress* tonight.

Robin and Sav came over to get ready with me. Drew and Sean are here too, but they're in the living room watching some action movie while we get ready.

"So, Elli," Robin starts, "have you figured out how good Wes is with his fingers yet?" She wiggles her eyebrows at me and I blush.

Sav smacks Robs' shoulder, "Robin! You can't just ask her that! Besides, you're gay. What does it matter to you?"

Robin tsks, "I just want to make sure my old best friend is taking good care of my new best friend. Because if he's not, I'm going to have to give him a stern talking to."

"Yes, his fingers are magical. But I've only experienced his fingers, or he's used my vibrator." I say bashfully.

Both of their mouths drop open at the revelation, but Sav speaks up first. "Please say 'psych' right now. That boy hasn't eaten you like his last meal yet?"

My face burns at her question, and I just shake my head.

"Elli! You two have been eye-fucking since the damn pool party! Why haven't you done anything about it yet?" Robs asks.

I shrug. "He wants to take his time with me? He says he doesn't want me to think he's just after me because he's horny. Which is sweet, but I never thought that. No one writes a love song for someone they just want to fuck. I also think he might be a bit nervous because I'm a virgin."

"I'm not surprised he wants to wait. He's going to split you open like a log honey." Savannah smacks her lips together after blotting her lipstick. She's wearing this hot pink color that looks amazing against her tan skin.

"Savannah!" Robin chastises. "You'll be fine, Elli. I'm sure he'll be nice and gentle with you."

"What do you mean, Sav? How... how will he split me open like a log?" I whisper, just in case Sean and Drew are listening in.

"You haven't seen his cock have you?" Sav asks.

Robin gags, "Sorry. I'm allergic to that word and the appendage. Especially if it belongs to my best friend."

"Robs, you're the one that brought this up!" I point out.

"Anyway," Sav continues, dusting glitter into her cleavage, "Drew used to live with Wes so let's just say he knows what he's packing. He's not *abnormally* thick or long, but he's above average, you know?"

"No, I don't really know. The only penises I have experience with are those of my brothers' and I don't want to think about them in any aspect."

"Grab your vibrator." Sav instructs, so I go over to my nightstand and grab my pink little rabbit friend. Sav holds it up and inspects it before handing it back. "Probably two inches longer than that thing, and much thicker."

My eyes bulge. I had a rough time getting that thing inside me at first. I can't imagine trying to fit Wes inside me now. "You're certain?" I ask.

Sav shrugs, "I haven't seen it for myself, and Drew could be exaggerating, but it's probable." She looks up and must see the horror written on my face. "You'll be fine, Elli. I know you've probably heard before that it might hurt a little at first, but if you're aroused enough, you'll be fine. And there's no shame in needing a little lube, okay? Wes is a good guy. He'll go as slow as you need him to."

I take a deep breath and nod resolutely. Tonight I'm going to lose my virginity to Westley Jones.

Once we're done getting ready, I head into the bathroom with my dress for tonight.

The blue satin dress from a few weeks ago that Wes helped me out of.

The cool fabric feels nice against my heated skin, and I know it'll be good for dancing tonight because it's loose and moveable. I have my hair half up, half down, and the chocolate waves cascade down my back and contrast nicely with my dress and slightly tan skin. The blue makes my eyes pop, and with the black winged eyeliner I added, they look extra blue today. I pair the dress with some black strappy wedges and add my usual gold jewelry.

I'm looking at myself in the mirror when a knock sounds on the bathroom door. I open it up to find Wes standing there, looking delicious in his usual ripped black jeans, combat boots, and a band t-shirt for some band I've never heard of. His eyes roam over my body and I see the moment he recognizes the dress. He steps into the bathroom, crowding me into the counter so our chests are brushing. He brings a hand to rest on my hip, the other cradles my neck and tilts my head back so I can look him in the eye.

"Fuck, baby. That dress... you look incredible. I'm tempted to tell them to go without us just so I can have you all to myself."

"I wouldn't be opposed to that." I say, my voice all breathy. Just being this close to him is getting me all hot and bothered.

Wes leans down and seals our mouths together in a kiss so possessive and hot I almost have to change out of my thong.

"If I thought they'd let us bail, I would. But I'm also looking forward to dancing with you tonight, so come on. Let's get going." He says with a gentle smack to my ass.

I like possessive Wes.

We head to the living room where everyone, including Matt, is waiting for us. After "hellos" we decide that Wes, Robin, Sean and I will ride in Wes's car, and Drew, Sav, and Matt will ride in Matt's.

The drive to the club is thick with tension from Wes, if his tense shoulders and locked jaw are any indication. He keeps a firm hand on my thigh, squeezing it every so often in a possessive gesture, and every time he does, I have to keep myself from squeezing my thighs together to find some relief.

We park on the side of the club and wait for Matt to pull up next to us before we climb out of the cars. Immediately Robin links her arms with me and gives a wistful sigh.

"Remember when I kissed you on the way here last time? Good times."

Shit stirrer.

"What?!" Wes shouts from a step behind us, and my ears burn. I thought Robin would have told him about that!

Robin gives me a subtle nudge and a knowing smirk before she turns to Wes and says "Oops. Sorry Wessy. Did I forget to mention I kissed your girl before you did?"

Wes gently pulls me from Robin and pulls me to his side. He leans in and whispers "I'm going to need more information about that, baby. Because the fact that two of my friends got to kiss those pillowy lips before I did makes me a little upset."

"Robin asked if I was gay, and I said I'd never kissed a girl before so I didn't know, and she just leaned over and planted one on me. It was nothing, Wes. I swear. I don't think she's actually attracted to me, I just think she likes riling you up."

He squeezes my hip, "Yeah, she does like to rile me up. I guess I'm just going to have to keep kissing you until you forget you've ever kissed anyone before me."

"Okay." I sigh, tipping my head to look up at him. He grabs my chin and places a gentle kiss on my lips, lingering for only a second, then pulls away.

"If I do any more than that I'm not going to let you go in the club. I'm going to take you to my place and kiss you until you can't breathe. That would be a shame because I want you to have fun tonight, and I definitely want to watch you sway those hips in that damn dress."

Before I can respond, the bouncer is asking us for our IDs and we're transported to a different atmosphere. The club is just as I remember. Neon lights, thudding music, and a sticky floor.

Matt has snagged us a table in the back corner, and it looks like the others are getting drinks. We join Matt, who's scowling at a girl across the way. She's not facing me, but she's got bright pink hair, is wearing the tiniest leather skirt, fishnets, a hot pink tube top, and black combat boots. She's talking to a group of guys, throwing her hair over her shoulder as she laughs.

I feel Wes stiffen as he follows my gaze to the girl.

"What the hell is she doing here? She knows this is where we come. She hates this place." Wes grumbles to Matt.

"I don't know, man, I'm sorry. If you want to head out, you know we'd all understand."

"Who is she?" I ask, turning to face Wes. His body is tenser than it was in the car, his jaw is so strained I'm worried he's going to cause permanent damage, but this is different than the tension in the car. That was lust. This is pure hatred.

"That's Shelby." Matt answers.

CHAPTER 29

I'm seeing red, and it's not just the flashing lights of the club. I have no feelings other than disgust and hate for Shelby Reynolds, and I never wanted to see her and her lying face again. Especially when I'm trying to have a fun night out with my friends and my girl.

Elli looks murderous as soon as Matt says her name, but when she looks at me she softens and leans closer to me. I inhale her familiar coconut and vanilla smell and feel marginally better. I just hope to God Shelby stays the fuck away from us.

"I can't believe that bitch is here tonight, of all nights." Robin hisses as she brings a tray of drinks. She slides me over my usual on nights like tonight: a good old fashioned root beer, and hands another one to Elli.

I'm surprised to see Elli's not drinking, but I don't want to make her feel weird so I'm not going to ask.

"Elli, wanna do tequila shots?" Sav waggles her eyebrows at my girl, and Elli shudders.

"Absolutely the fuck not, thank you." She faux gags, and everyone chuckles at her.

Tequila. That's probably what made her so wasted that night.

Sav and Robin down their whiskey shots and pull Elli to the dance floor, leaving me with Matt, Sean, and Drew.

Fifteen minutes later, the girls are still swaying on the dance floor to *Wannabe* by the Spice Girls. Elli's hips are calling to me like a siren's song. I'm about to go to her when I feel a tap on my shoulder and I swear the temperature drops thirty degrees because I already know who it is. I can smell the cheap vodka and the cigarettes before I even turn around.

"Well, well, well. If it isn't my songbird." Shelby's voice grates against my every nerve ending.

"I'm not your anything, Shelby." I say, not taking my eyes off my girl.

She scoffs, "Come on, Wes. We both know I'm the best you'll ever have. I'm even willing to take you back, especially after that beautiful song you wrote about the lady bugs or whatever." Her hot pink clawed hand starts tracing a line up my arm, and I grab the hand quickly and shove it off.

I feel Sean, Drew, and Matt eyeing me carefully, gauging if they need to step in. I turn my whole body to Shelby and get a good look at her for the first time in over two years.

She looks worn. Smoking two packs a day will do that to you I guess. The bags under her eyes are purple, even through the caked on makeup she has on.

My tone is harsh as I reply. "First of all, you were far from the best I've ever had. Second, I wouldn't get back together with you if it was the only thing that could save humanity. Third, that song is not for your disgusting ears. It's for my girl, the one who's finally pieced me back together after your claws tore me apart. I never want to see you again, Shelby. Get the fuck out of here and go back to whatever boytoy is currently funding your vices."

Shelby opens her mouth to respond, but a head of chocolate brown waves covers my view.

"Is this your new flavor of the week, Wes? Isn't she a little... *heavy* for your taste? Damn, you've really downgraded. This fat bitch is never going to be able please you-"

"Listen, bitch," Elli interrupts harshly, "I may be fat but that just means there's more of me to love. Sorry, not sorry you let go of the best guy in the world because you were dumb. Never speak to or about Wes again. In fact, don't even look at him because I'm not fucking afraid to fight." Elli's voice is calm as she backs Shelby into the wall.

My dick and heart are so confused because I'm scared for Elli's safety- Shelby's a loose cannon- but it's so damn hot watching her stand up for me.

No one's ever stood up for me like that before, definitely not someone I've dated, and I fall a whole lot more in love with this feisty girl.

Shelby's indifferent mask slips back on and she literally hisses at Elli. "Fuck you." And walks away.

Elli turns to me, her face red, her body vibrating with anger. I pull her into my arms and squeeze her, trying to convey my gratitude and how much I appreciate her.

Robin comes over and claps Elli on the shoulder, laughing. "Damn, Elli. I've never seen anyone put Shelby in her place like that. That made my night."

"You okay, baby?" I whisper against her head.

"I saw her talking to you and saw red, Wes. I'm sorry if I overstepped, but I couldn't bear to see her touching you. I'm okay now, though." She replies, sounding almost embarrassed.

"Baby, you can stand up for me anytime. That was hot as hell." I say, grinding my erection into her soft stomach.

She lets out a little gasp, then with mischief in her eyes says, "Come dance with me?"

I grab her hand, leading her to the dance floor. *Shivers* by Ed Sheeran comes on, and our bodies move as one. I spin and twirl her, moving her against me like we've done this a million times. I'm about to combust in my pants by the time the song ends and I seal our mouths together.

"I know it hasn't been long, but I want to get out of here, Wes." Elli pants against my mouth. "Please."

Who am I to resist?

I give her a nod in agreement, then drag her over to our friends so we can say goodbye. I watch Elli hug Sav and Robin while I give the boys a bro hug, then I'm dragging her back out of the club and to the car.

When we get to my car, before I open her door, I push her body against it with mine and take her mouth like it's the oxygen I breathe. I love the way the softness of her body compliments the hardness of mine, like we're two puzzle pieces fitting together effortlessly.

When I break the kiss to open the door, Elli's face and chest are flushed, her lipstick a little smeared, and she looks absolutely wrecked already.

She's so fucking beautiful.

"Alright baby, let's get you in the car so I can take you to my place." I say, my voice husky with lust.

"Okay." She says shyly, ducking her head into the car and buckling her seatbelt.

When I get in, she's biting her lip, her pupils are dilated, and I can see the pointy peaks of her nipples through the thin material of that goddamn dress. It's nice to know she's as aroused as I am. I wonder if she's wet for me. God, I can't wait to find out.

The whole way home I remind myself she's a virgin and I have to go slow. Some of the things I like in the bedroom might scare her if I'm not careful, so I have to be gentle and take my time with her, even if I want to devour her whole right now.

When we get to my apartment, she starts making herself at home, taking off her shoes and leaving them haphazardly on the floor and grabbing a glass of water from the kitchen. I'm hit with a rush of lust and love and desire so big I can't control myself.

I love seeing her in my space, I love holding her in my arms. I want her to stay here forever.

She goes into the bedroom, where she's left an overnight bag for tonight, and starts taking off her jewelry.

"Wes?" She whispers to me, where I'm standing in the doorway.

"Yes, baby?"

"I need some help out of this dress." She turns to look

at me over her shoulder with hooded eyes.

I stride over to her slowly, stopping behind her so our bodies are inches apart, then undo the knot so the top of the dress is loose.

"Thank you." She whispers, keeping an arm banded around her breasts so the dress doesn't fall.

"You're welcome, baby." I trace circles over her hip with my thumb, then lean into her and whisper in her ear. "Tell me what you want, Elli."

She inhales a shaky breath, then turns to me and drops her arm so the dress falls to her feet, baring her tits and leaving her in only a white lace thong. She looks me dead in the eyes and says confidently, "I want you to fuck me, Wes."

CHAPTER 30

Elli

As soon as I say the words, it's like a switch has been flipped on Wes.

He grabs my face and places his lips on mine, and kisses me like my mouth is the cure for every illness he's ever had.

Our tongues wrestle and he nips at my bottom lip, one arm bands around my waist to pull me closer to him so the rough graphic on his t-shirt rubs against my nipples causing the most delicious sensation, it makes me moan into his mouth.

He pulls back slightly, panting, eyes filled with desire. *Desire for me.*

"I know you said you want me to fuck you, but I want to make sure you're okay with everything I want to do. Can I touch you, Elli? Touch these gorgeous nipples?"

I nod, and his fingers come up to circle around the tight bud and give it a slight pinch.

"What about this delicious ass, hm? Can I touch it?"

I nod again, and he slides another hand down my back and grabs a handful of my asscheek, all while continuing his ministrations on my nipple.

He pulls away and pushes me gently to lay on the bed, removes his shirt and pants, leaving him in only his tight black boxers. His erection is poking up proudly, and I want to feel the weight of it in my hand.

He brings his head down to my right breast, gently kissing the swell of it before laving a tongue across my nipple, then sucking the bud into his mouth. He's done this before, but it's so good every time.

"Wes." I pant, wanting more.

He pulls off with a pop and looks up at me. "Can I touch this pussy, Elli? Can I have a taste? Make you feel good?"

"Yes, please Wes. I'm yours, you can touch me however you want, but please. I need more."

Wes groans, peppering kisses along my sternum, down my soft belly, until he comes to my covered pussy. He gives it a kiss over the fabric before gently peeling it off and tossing it somewhere behind him.

"God, Elli. You're so fucking beautiful everywhere it's not fair." He whispers almost reverently.

I'm about to tell him to hurry the fuck up when he drags his tongue from the bottom of my labia up to my clit in a slow, tantalizing lick. He circles the hardening bud with his tongue, and my back arches off the bed so high he has to place an arm over my hips to hold me down as he continues.

"Wes, oh my god that feels so good." I moan, grabbing the sheets and holding on for dear life.

"Fuck, Elli. You're so wet. You taste so good." He says, then dives back in, eating me out like he's starved.

My orgasm comes over me so fast, so unexpectedly that I can't even warn him. My thighs close around his head as he licks me through it, and if I wasn't in a state of orgasmic heaven, I'd feel bad about possibly crushing his skull.

When I've finally released his head from my thunder thigh prison, he looks up at me, my arousal coating his chin and around his mouth, and he's *smiling.* Smiling and flushed with success.

"I'm new to orgasms, but that was by far the best one I've ever had. Toys don't even compare to that." I say.

"Do you want to stop? We can stop whenever you want to baby, no pressure." He says, laying his head on my thigh.

I sit up, pulling his face towards me to kiss him, but he puts a hand up to stop me. "Most girls don't want to kiss me after I've given them head. They say it's gross. Let me go wash off-"

I cut him off by pulling him to me and kissing him hard. Fuck what other girls think. It's a little strange, tasting myself on him. A little sour, a little tangy, but it's not bad. It's not *gross.*

"I don't want to stop, Wes. I want you to fuck me." I slide a hand down to cup his erection.

"Okay, okay." He leans over to his bedside drawer and opens it up, taking out a brand new pack of condoms. He tears the box open and takes out a foil packet, then maneuvers so he takes off his boxers.

His cock springs free, the tip a little red and angry, and my mouth waters. I've never given a blowjob, but I'm definitely going to try sometime soon.

"Can I feel you, please?" I ask, suddenly a little shy about it.

"Of course, baby. But just know the more you touch me, the less I'll last because I'm already bursting at the seams."

I giggle at his confession, then take him in my hand. The weight is similar to my vibrator, though his skin is smooth and soft. He looks bigger than my vibrator and my stomach clenches with nerves of anticipation. Even though he's not massive, *thank goodness*, I'm still worried it will hurt.

"I'll go slow Elli, I'm going to try and make this as painless as possible for you." Wes says, reading my mind. "Lay back baby, grab a pillow for me?" I hand him a pillow and he puts it under my butt.

Then, he slides the condom over his cock and leans over me, kissing me gently. I feel the tip of him hit my clit and I gasp into his mouth, causing him to smirk.

"I'm going to put the tip in now, okay? You let me know if you need to stop anytime and we will."

"Okay." I agree, and he pushes the tip into my opening. The stretch isn't bad, it's a little painful, but I'm still wet from my orgasm so it's not meeting much resistance.

Wes instructs me to take a deep breath, and when I release it, he slides in a little more, then repeats the process until he's seated all the way inside me. He was met with a little bit of resistance at the very end, it filled me with a burning sensation, but in a pleasurable way.

Now, fully inside me, the fullness and pleasure I feel outweighs any initial pain. I need more. I need him to move. I look up to see Wes's eyes squeezed shut.

"Damn it, Elli. You're so fucking warm. So tight. I don't know how long I'll last." He says through gritted teeth.

"Just move, Wes please. I need you to move."

Wes curses again, then starts at an agonizingly slow pace. I don't know if he's going slow because of me or because he's trying to hold off on his own orgasm, but I need more.

"Faster, please!" I practically sob.

"Fuck, are you sure?"

"Yes!"

Wes picks up speed, his mouth latching to my nipple, gently nibbling and sucking on it.

The onslaught of pleasure brings me so close to an orgasm so fast that I feel like I'm getting whiplash.

"Elli, baby, please tell me you're close."

"I'm close!"

Wes stops biting my nipples to bring two fingers to my clit where he pushes down hard and I detonate.

Colorful spots dot my vision as my whole body tenses and shakes and the most overwhelming pleasure I've ever had fizzles through my blood and spreads throughout my entire body.

Wes stiffens and slams into me one last time and I feel him pulse his own release into the condom, groaning my name as he comes.

It's the sexiest thing I've ever seen.

"Elli," Wes says breathlessly, "that was..."

"Amazing." I finish for him.

"Yeah, baby. It was amazing. Thank you for trusting me."

"Thank you for making it amazing. I love... that you were my first. You made it special, made *me* feel special."

If Wes notices my almost slip up, he doesn't say anything and I'm glad. I can't believe I almost just told him I love him while he's still half hard inside of me!

"You are special, baby. Come on, let's go get cleaned up." He places a gentle kiss on my nose, then stands and walks to his bathroom. He's discarded the condom and turned the shower on by the time I join him.

He checks the temperature before guiding me into the tub and underneath the stream of warm water. He gently washes my hair, making sure not to get any shampoo in my eyes, then gently detangles it with a comb he has in the shower before putting conditioner on my ends.

I would be surprised that he knows how to take care of my hair like this if it weren't for his own beautiful hair. He clearly isn't a "3-in-one" type of guy.

I return the favor by washing and conditioning his hair, then we take turns soaping each other's bodies. He's hard again by the time we're done, but he won't let me take care of it for him.

He wraps me up in a fluffy towel when we get out, helps me do my skincare, and then we lay in his bed, naked, with my head on his chest, gently tracing the dark ink etched into his skin.

"I think I want to get a tattoo." I whisper into the darkness.

"Oh yeah? What would you get?" Wes asks, his hands tracing soft lines up and down my back.

"Hmmm. Probably something to do with books, maybe? I don't know. I haven't thought about it."

"Let me know if you want me to get you in touch with my artist. They're really good."

"Thank you." I lean up and kiss him, exhaustion pulling a yawn from me.

"Go to sleep, baby. We have all day tomorrow to talk." He says and kisses my forehead. "Goodnight baby."

"Goodnight Wes." I say, and let the steady beat of his heart lull me to sleep.

CHAPTER 31

Wes

Waking up next to a warm, snuggly Elli may be a new thing, but it's definitely my favorite. Especially since her supple ass is rubbing against my morning wood, and I can feel her pussy radiating heat.

God, last night was *incredible.* I've never had such an intimate, mind-blowing experience, and it's not because I took her virginity, I'm not like that. It's because I've never felt such strong emotions, or so strongly connected to another person.

I meant what I said to Shelby. Elli's taken my battered, shattered, and torn to shreds heart and slowly mended it without even trying.

I wanted so badly to tell her how much I love her last night, but I didn't want her to think it was because of the sex.

I love her selfless attitude, her creative mind, and how easily she can make me smile. I love the way her nose crinkles when she doesn't like something, and how sweet treats are her downfall. I love how non-judgmental she is- I can't believe I thought the opposite when I first met her- I love that she's silly and sexy at the same time.

I love that I'm hers.

I love that she's mine.

Elli shifts, and I can tell she's felt my hard on, because she grinds herself back against me purposefully this time.

"Good morning, gorgeous. How'd you sleep?" I ask, caressing the soft skin of her belly, pulling her closer to me.

"Morning, handsome. I slept great. What about you?"

"Best sleep I've had in a while. Are you sore, baby?" I trail my fingers down her stomach, stopping at the cropped pubic hair on her mons.

"A little," she answers, "but that doesn't mean I don't want to be more sore."

I hum. "You've been grinding that sweet ass on me all morning. I'd already be inside you right now if I didn't want your explicit consent."

She rolls so she's facing me now, a sleepy smile on her face. "I give you explicit consent to fuck me when I'm sleeping and wake me up with orgasms."

Fuck. Did I just discover Elli's a reverse somnophiliac?

"Well you're awake now so I'll jot that down for next time." I slide a finger through her pussy and find her wet and ready.

"Did you have a sexy dream, Elli?" I tease, gently teasing her wetness around her pussy lips.

She arches into my hand, trying to get more. "Yes, but reality is so much better."

I roll over and grab a condom and slip it on, then swing her leg over my hip and enter her slowly, watching her face for any pain she may try to deny.

Her face contorts, but not in pain, in pleasure. I strum her clit and pick up the pace of my thrusts, pulling moans and groans and little whimpers from her.

It's music to my ears.

I grab her waist and roll so she's straddling me, my cock still inside her, and she freezes.

"Wes, I'm too-"

I cut off her protest with a finger to her lips and a sharp thrust. "Shhh. You're not too anything other than too fucking good, baby. I want you to take your pleasure. Be a good girl and ride my cock, Elliana." I say with a firm grab of her ass.

"Oh my god." She whimpers, but starts gyrating on top of me, doing what I asked, seeking her pleasure.

I know she's inexperienced in this, so I help her bounce up and down on me by holding her hips, then place my thumb on her clit and rub little circles until I feel her clench and pulse around me, telling me she's close.

"That's it, baby, come all over me. I want to feel your pussy squeeze my cock. Milk me dry." I grunt, barely holding on as I feel her hips stutter and she comes.

My orgasm is ripped from me by hers, and I spill into the condom. As we catch our breath, Elli is still on my lap, and I pull her to me chest to chest and it feels like our heartbeats sync into a matching rhythm.

I brush an errant strand of hair away from her face and look into those beautiful blue eyes I love. "Hi baby."

"Hi." She says, kissing me gently on the lips. "That was the best way to wake up ever."

That makes me chuckle. She's too sweet. "Good. That won't be the last time. Now, it's time to get ready. We're going to head to Ernie's to meet Jess and Luke for breakfast."

"We are?! Oh my god, Wes! You didn't tell me that. I didn't pack 'meet the parent' clothes. I only packed 'lazy Sunday' clothes!" She scrambles off of me and into the bathroom where she rapidly brushes her teeth.

I lazily walk in, enjoying the view of her naked form leaning over the sink. If we weren't in a hurry I'd get on my knees behind her and eat her out for breakfast. Instead, I stand by her and relish the domesticity of brushing our teeth together. I love that she's so comfortable with me, that she can do things like this already. Has it really only been a week since we started officially dating? It feels longer, in the best way possible.

Elli meticulously braids her chocolate strands into a cute braid that flows over her left shoulder, then puts on a bit of mascara. As she dresses in cute pink linen overalls with a black tank top underneath, I put on my black basketball shorts and a band t-shirt. Jess and Luke have seen me in all sorts of outfits, so maybe dressing down a little will help Elli feel more comfortable.

"Alright. Let's do this." She says, grabbing her purse and heading for the door once she's tied her black converse on her feet.

I grab her hand and pull her back, "Baby, Luke already likes you, Claudia loves you, and Jess will love you too. You don't need to be nervous. And if they don't like you for some bizarre reason? Then that's their issue. Nothing's going to make me stop loving you."

Elli's eyes widen, and so do mine at my admission.

"You love me?" She whispers quietly, searching my face for a lie.

"I do, Elliana Louise Monson. I love you so much it's insane."

"I love you too, Westley Ray Jones." She declares, and my heart fucking *explodes.*

I kiss her, hard, trying to convey how much it means to me. How much *she* means to me. I will spend the rest of my life making sure she knows just how important she is to me.

"Okay, okay, rockstar. Being late will look bad on me so let's go!" She says through giggles as I pepper her face with kisses.

I love Elli.

And she loves me.

Chapter 32

Elli

*H*e loves me. He loves me. He loves me. He loves me!

I was so pleasantly surprised to hear those words come from Wes this morning, that I momentarily forgot to be nervous to officially meet Jess.

I probably shouldn't be nervous, but Jess is important to Wes and Luke is important to Izzy and Jess is important to Wes and Luke so impressing her is important. This could be Izzy's future mother-in-law!

Wes and I walk hand in hand to Ernie's, which is just a few blocks from his apartment, making tentative plans for our road trip to Utah in three weeks.

Hot steamy, hotel sex with Wes.

Fuck. Probably shouldn't walk around turned on when I'm meeting important people, but it's like Wes unlocked something in me. A piece of me that has been kept in a steel box, locked away never to be used.

Now that it's out, it's like all I can think about is the next time I can get Wes naked. I still need to ask him to teach me to give him a blowjob.

"Will you teach me how to give a blowjob?" I ask, deciding to just go for it.

Wes stops, looks at me with a shocked expression, and says "Jesus Christ, Elli. You can't just ask me that when we're supposed to be meeting my pseudo mom and brother for breakfast! Do you want me to walk around with a hard-on all morning?"

I shrug, "Sorry not sorry babe. I didn't want to forget to ask again."

Wes scrubs a hand down his face. "Damn it. Yes, I'll teach you how to give me a blowjob. But can we talk about this after, please?"

We've stopped in front of Ernie's, so I go up on my tiptoes and give him a kiss on the cheek. "Of course."

The bell above the door chimes as we walk in, and I see a familiar mop of curly brown hair sitting across from the woman I met at the bar, and they're both talking to Claudia and an older man with a mustache and bald head, who I assume is Ernie.

"Westley, my boy! So good to see you!" The man says in a thick southern accent, ambling over to Wes to wrap him in a big hug. He turns his attention to me, "This must be the lovely Elli I've heard so much about. I'm Ernest Johnson Cahill, pleasure to meet you, m'lady." He grabs my hand and gives it a peck, his mustache tickling the back of my hand.

"Nice to meet you too, Mr. Cahill." I say, feeling like I should curtsy.

Ernie waves a hand "Call me Ernie, please, darlin. C'mon, let's get to eatin."

We follow Ernie over to a table covered in a family style spread of breakfast foods. Waffles, pancakes, biscuits, gravy, potatoes, eggs, fruit, bacon, and sausage are arranged in the middle while everyone has empty plates to load up on what they want.

Claudia pulls me and Wes in for hugs when we get to the table, and Luke gives me a fist bump. Jess stands and comes over and gives me a hug too, which surprises me since I've only met her once.

Ernie instructs everyone to dig in, and we do. It's strange to not start a meal with so many people without saying a prayer, which I didn't realize was so ingrained into my psyche.

I load up with a waffle, bacon, those delicious potatoes, and some strawberries. Wes goes for his biscuits and gravy and eggs. We sit around the table, Wes to my left, Ernie to my right at the head of the table, Claudia across from me, Jess next to her, and Luke at the other end of the table.

There's pleasant chatter, everyone catching up with what's been going on in their lives. I keep quiet, since I'm the newbie and I don't really want to insert myself. When the topic of jobs comes up, Jess looks at me.

"So, Elli, what do you do?" She asks.

"I'm in Human Resources. I work at a law firm that has offices in a few different states and I handle the job postings, initial interviews and all the new hire paperwork for them, among other various human resource things.."

"Oh! Isn't that interesting. How did you get into that?" Claudia chimes in.

"Well, I've always wanted to travel, and I knew that I'd likely be able to be hired as a remote worker with a job like that. The classes in college were easy, so it was kind of just the most sensible choice." I shrug. I know it sounds kind of lame. I didn't have a passionate calling towards anything besides cooking. "Plus, the gossip I get to hear is top tier because it doesn't involve me."

That has everyone chuckling, and I feel giddy at being able to make these people laugh.

Once everyone has had their fill of such a delicious breakfast, everyone breaks up into little groups to get the tasks done. Apparently this is something they do once a month, so they're all familiar with the way things are run.

"Luke the duke, Wes the mess, you're on dish duty with me today." Ernie says, ruffling Luke's hair.

Jess pulls me aside and asks if I'll help her make sure all the ketchup bottles are filled, and I agree, although I'm a little nervous to be away from Wes.

We work silently together before Jess clears her throat and I look up at her. "So," she starts, "I think you're really good for Wes. I haven't seen him this happy and inspired in a long, long time."

I nod, not sure where she's going with this, but not wanting to say anything.

"I assume he's told you all about that bitch of an ex of his?" I nod, and she continues. "He's had a hard life, Elli. People were very cruel to that little boy and he didn't have a lot of people in his corner. Lord knows I tried to talk Teresa into leaving Keith and going to rehab so many times I sounded like a broken record, but she just wouldn't listen. It was either put up with her shit and be able to keep an eye on Wes or have her cut me off and not be able to protect him from what I could.

"He's a great man, and I don't want to see him heart-broken again. I know you were raised Mormon, and I know they have a lot of rules and standards that my boys don't exactly meet. I just want to make sure you're not just doing this to have a rebellious phase or something. Same with Izzy. My Luke's my life. I know he'll experience heartbreak, but he's so caught up in your sister that I don't know what it'd do to him if they broke up."

I should be offended by what she's saying, implying Izzy and I are just having a "rebellious phase." But it's a valid concern from a mom and a caregiver that I can't seem to be too upset.

"I understand your concerns, Jess. And I admire your protectiveness over not only Luke, but Wes, too. I love Wes. He's the best thing that's ever happened to me. I've left being Mormon behind, for various reasons, and he's helped me learn to be who I am without it. As for Izzy, well, she's a stubborn soul. She's doing her own research about the church to see if it's something she wants to stay in, but I can tell you she loves your son. That girl could charm the scales off of a crocodile if she wanted to, but she's been completely faithful to Luke this last year. I would know, since I shared a room with her and heard *way* too many things I shouldn't have." I shudder thinking about all the cringy things I had to experience.

Jess nods in agreement, "Yeah. They're pretty gross in love, aren't they? I usually put headphones in when they're talking so I don't gag."

I laugh, the tension in Jess's shoulders easing having gotten that off her chest. I'm glad I could put her mind at ease with not only Wes, but Luke too.

"Well Elli, we do pizza nights once a month with just Wes, Luke, and I where we catch up on things we don't want Claudia and Ernie to know, so I'll have to get your favorite pizza toppings before our next one. Welcome to our mixed up little family." She pulls me in for a hug, and tears spring to my eyes at the gesture.

Sure, my mother used to hug me, but it was all surface level. It was never a comforting embrace where you feel safe and protected like Jess's hug is.

Even if my family doesn't really want anything to do with me, I've found my own little family instead. One where I don't have to hide parts of myself for their approval.

CHAPTER 33

Wes

Seeing Jess hug Elli, and having everyone important in my life accept and welcome her with open arms makes my heart want to burst out of my fucking chest.

I know I need to stop comparing my relationship with Elli to my relationship with Shelby but the difference is night and day and I want to kick myself for ever wasting my time with a girl like Shelby.

Not that I ever imagined I'd have a girl like Elli.

Who would have thought that the sweet, good, Mormon girl would end up with a ruffian like me?

Jess comes into the kitchen where I'm drying the dishes, a smile on her face. She sidles up to me, nudging me with her hip.

"She's a good one, Wes. I can see why you've fallen so fast for her."

"Thanks Jess. I would've kept seeing her even if you didn't like her, but knowing you do makes it better." I say.

Jess puts her hand on my arm to stop my drying, and I look over and meet her gaze, which is a little glassy.

"Your grams and your mom would love her. She would have Joyce wrapped around her finger in an instant and if things ever ended, you know she'd bug you about Elli for the rest of her days." I laugh at that. It's true, Grams was a hardass about me keeping good things in my life, and Elli is the best thing.

Jess clears her throat, then continues. "I was a little harsh with her back there, because I needed to know she wasn't going to just play around with your heart. She didn't even flinch. She reassured me that her intentions with you are pure, and that she loves you."

My heart can't take any more bursting or it's just going to stop beating all together. I know Elli said she loved me earlier, but to hear her admit it to someone else makes me want to rip her away from everyone and show her just how much that means to me.

"I love her too, in case that wasn't glaringly obvious." I mumble.

Jess pats me lovingly, but condescendingly on the back, "I know you do. I could see it when you got your haircut. I could feel it in the song you wrote for her. You're not subtle, son."

I roll my eyes which makes her laugh.

"Now I know you don't want to spend all day surrounded by us since you're deep in the honeymoon phase. Go. Take your girl home and... ugh I don't want to know what you do but just go be together."

I lean over and give Jess a kiss on the cheek. "Thanks Jess. We'll be over for pizza on Friday. Love you!"

"Love you too!" She shouts back as I speed walk through the kitchen doors and make a beeline for Elli, who's laughing with Claudia and Ernie about something.

God, I love her laugh. Her smile. I love that she's so effortlessly integrated into my family.

Elli turns her head and our eyes meet, and the amount of love I see there nearly brings me to my knees.

"Hi babe. How did the dishes go?" She asks.

"Good, uh, they're done. We have that thing we need to get to, so we should probably get going."

Her brow creases like it does when she's confused, but she must decide not to question it because she looks at Ernie and Claudia. "Thank you so much for breakfast. It's been wonderful getting to know you. I'll have Wes reach out to you about dinner and we can finish talking about this."

Elli, Claudia, and Ernie stand and they exchange embraces.

"Don't be a stranger Miss Elli. It was lovely to meet you." Ernie says, giving her a big ol' kiss on the cheek.

"Watch it, old man. That's my girl. And *your* girl is right there!" I say in jest.

"No one's stealing your girl, and no way in hell I'm letting go of mine." Ernie says playfully, nuzzling into Claudia's neck.

"Alright you two. Get goin'." Claudia says as she waves us out the door.

I grab Elli's hand and instead of leisurely walking back to our- woah, I mean- *my* apartment, I drag her to the alley between the diner and the Japanese place next door.

"Wes, what are we-"

I cut Elli off by pushing her up against the brick wall and ravaging her mouth. She immediately matches my energy and wraps her arms around my neck as I press my body against hers. My dick goes from limp to hard as steel in a millisecond as our tongues clash and her fingers dig into my shoulders.

I tear our lips apart and kiss down her throat, biting where her neck and her shoulder meet, and immediately soothing the bite with my tongue.

The noise she makes when that happens almost makes me come in my pants.

"Wes," she pants, "w-we can't have sex in the alley."

"I don't know if I can make it back to my place, Elli." I say as I grab her ass, grinding my erection into her.

"But-"

"AHHH. My eyes!" A voice yells down the alley.

Elli and I abruptly turn to see Luke holding to garbage bags, trying to cover his eyes.

"Get a room, you two! My God! I'm going to have to bleach my eyeballs." He screeches.

"Sorry, Luke." Elli squeaks, pulling me out of the alley and down the road.

I can't help but laugh, because we weren't even doing anything that inappropriate. In hindsight I should have thought about people bringing the trash out, but I was too focused on the goddess that I call mine to worry about anyone else.

Elli slows her pace once we're halfway to my apartment, then stops completely and laughs so hard tears are forming in her eyes.

"Why are you laughing so hard?" I ask, laughing with her.

"Do you know the shit I had to sit through when I shared a room with Izzy? Luke watching us make out is *nothing* compared to the cringy shit I had to hear from them. I felt bad at first that Luke had to see that, but now I don't. That was just payback for making me sit through almost a year of their ickiness."

"Good. Now that your guilt is out of the way, can we *please* get back to my apartment? Even being caught didn't dampen how much I want you. Right. Fucking. Now." I growl the last three words.

Elli's eyes meet mine, full of lust and love and desire and then she nods.

CHAPTER 34

Elli

As soon as the door to Wes's apartment is shut, he unties the knot on my overalls and they fall down my legs. Then he's tearing off my tank top and I'm left in just a black thong.

"Elli," Wes growls, eyes locked on my heaving chest, "You aren't wearing a fucking bra?"

I shake my head as Wes pushes me back onto the couch.

I watch as he tears off his clothes like they're offending him. His dick springs free and he gives it two languid pumps.

"If I had known the only thing between me and these gorgeous breasts was that tiny tank top, I wouldn't have been able to focus on anything else at breakfast."

My voice comes out as a husky whisper as I say, "Then it's a good thing I didn't tell you, huh?"

Wes's grin isn't a sweet, loving smile, oh no, it's almost feral. "Oh, baby. You're sassy today. We haven't had much of a chance to talk about our bedroom preferences, but I like things a little... rougher."

What does that mean?

He must sense my hesitance because he gently strokes my cheek, "Nothing too bad, baby, and I'd never do anything you didn't want. So if you tell me 'no' or 'stop' I will stop what I'm doing immediately, okay?"

I nod.

"Words, please, Elli."

"I understand." I whisper.

"Good girl."

Oh god. Is he like the main characters in the spicy books I read? I've always been curious about the kinkier side of sex, but I'd never even had vanilla sex so how was I supposed to know anything about my kinks?

"You said you wanted to know how to give a blow job?" Wes asks, coming to stand directly in front of me so his cock bobs in my face.

I nod, then remember he wants me to use my words. "Ye-yes."

"Good. That's what we're going to do right now. Stand up please."

I stand, and he takes my seat on the couch.

"Now, kneel between my legs baby."

I slowly lower down to my knees, keeping my hands to myself and waiting for his next instruction.

"Do you want to lick my cock, Elli? Want to taste how badly I want you?" I watch as a little bit of liquid pools at the head.

"I would like that a lot." I say, mesmerized and a little afraid. What if I'm bad at this and he doesn't want to hurt my feelings so he just doesn't say anything? What if I hurt him?

"Go ahead, baby. Touch it. Kiss it. Lick it. Get familiar with it." He says, removing his own hands so I can take over.

I tentatively reach out with my pointer finger and run it up the length of him. He hisses at the contact, and I begin to pull away, but he grabs my wrist gently and guides my hand to the base.

I hold him there, then lean forward and lick the bead of liquid off. It's a little salty, but not entirely unpleasant. The head of his dick is soft against my tongue, so I decide to lick from where my hand is to the tip to see if he's soft everywhere.

Wes moans, and I see his fists clench in my periphery. "That feels so good, Elli. Now, if you're feeling up for it, you can put me in your mouth. Just try to avoid using your teeth."

I pause, trying to figure out how to do that. I try to put my lips over my teeth and slowly take him into my mouth. The weight of him is heavy and pleasant on my tongue. I'm glad he's not monstrously girthy or I don't think I'd be able to get more than the head past my mouth. I push him in, in, in, until I feel the tip of him at the back of my throat and his pubic hair is right in front of my nose.

"Christ- baby- oh *god*." Wes moans. "How aren't you gagging?"

I pull off of him, using my spit to stroke him slowly. "I don't have a gag reflex."

"Dear god." He curses, framing my face with his hands. "That is... information. Okay. So you can keep going, or if you want to stop, we can go get a condom and I can fuck that sweet pussy. What would you like to do?"

Instead of answering him verbally, I take him back into my mouth, getting a few more curse words from him. I start to bob my head up and down slowly, but the more he moans, the faster I go because I want to watch him fall apart for me.

Because of me.

"Elli, Elli, Elli" He chants, "I'm going to come so if you don't want to swallow, pull off in the next three seconds."

I don't think I'm ready to swallow yet, so I pull off and stroke him fast and watch in fascination as white ropes shoot out of him and onto my hand and his stomach.

Wes slumps back into the couch, breathing hard, and I go into the bathroom and get a wet washcloth to wipe him up with.

"I said I'd never be addicted to something, but I think I might just be addicted to you, baby." He says, still breathing heavily.

I smile, my heart warming at his admission, then go back to the bathroom and discard the washcloth.

"I was supposed to be giving you pleasure, to show you how much I appreciate you after this morning." He grumbles when I return.

I grin, "Sorry babe. You can give me a few orgasms to make up for it if you want, but I quite enjoyed watching you lose it for me. I like knowing I have that effect on you."

"I love you, Elli."

"I love you too, Wes."

"Now, come ride my face so I can show you how much I appreciate you." He says as he lays back on the couch.

Chapter 35

Wes

Elli's sexual appetite has been insatiable this week, and I am here for it. I love how comfortable she is with sex now, and how unafraid to ask questions she is. There have been times when I'll say a position I want to try, but she doesn't understand so she'll Google it, blush, then immediately ask to try it.

We were able to have a better conversation about our preferences in the bedroom, which has been fun exploring since Elli's not quite sure what hers are.

I was able to explain that I like being in charge in the bedroom. I like having control over my partner's pleasure, and I enjoy tying them up on occasion.

Elli likes relinquishing control for the most part, and I've noticed how much she enjoys being praised.

I wouldn't say we're in a dom/sub relationship because that's not really my thing. I'm not huge into BDSM or the kink community, despite what most people assume. But I enjoy more than just vanilla sex.

We experimented with some spanking the other day. I was buried deep inside her from behind and asked her if she'd be open to trying it. She said yes, so I gave that juicy ass a nice smack and her pussy clenched so hard I almost lost it.

So I'd say spanking is a yes.

As is hair pulling, orgasm denial, and being restrained.

I'm truly living my best life right now with the girl of my dreams.

It's Friday night, which means it's pizza night at Jess's house, and as much as I want to stay at home and continue figuring out Elli's bedroom preferences, we can't.

Pizza night started when I was in college. It was Jess's way of checking up on me and making sure that I was surviving, without being overbearing and pushy about it.

We pull up in front of Jess's little two bedroom bungalow that she's lived in for the last ten years. When she took me in, she and Luke shared the primary bedroom so I could have my own space, and I'll forever be grateful for that.

Elli looks cute as ever in a green sundress covered in daisies, her hair in a messy bun on top of her head.

I know for a fact she's not wearing a bra underneath and I have to avert my eyes every time I find myself looking at her boobs to see if her nipples are hard.

Jess opens the door for us before we even get to the door, ushering us inside where she wraps Elli in a big hug, then does the same for me.

"It's so good to see you guys. Luke's just gone to get the pizza so we can gossip about him while he's gone." She wiggles her eyebrows, and Elli giggles.

"I love your house, Jess. It's beautiful." Elli says, her eyes roaming over the yellow painted walls covered in mismatched frames that are filled with pictures of mostly Luke.

"Thank you Elli. Luke thinks I'm a hoarder, but I like my things, you know?"

"My parents only have family pictures on the walls, and a picture of the Provo temple. I think they might have a picture of Jesus now, too. But other than that the walls in our house were bare and beige or gray. We weren't even allowed to paint our room." Elli says as she stops in front of an older picture.

I know which picture it is, because it's one of my favorites. It's a picture of Jess in a hospital bed holding a newborn Luke. Next to her on the bed is seven year old me grinning at the camera with a missing front tooth. My mom is on the other side of the bed, beaming at her best friend.

"Is this your mom?" Elli whispers.

"Yeah. That was the day after Luke was born. Grams took the picture."

"She's beautiful, Wes."

"Come look at this one. It's my favorite picture of her. I have it in my nightstand drawer at home." I say as I gently lead her to the living room where a five by seven picture frame holds a picture of my mom and me at the pond. Mom is in denim overalls with her dark hair clipped up, but a few errant strands are framing her face. Her eyes, so similar to mine, are clear, and her smile is brilliant, and she looks happy and healthy. My hair is cropped short and I'm wearing a blue bucket hat. Instead of looking at the camera, I'm looking up at my mom in adoration.

"I was eight, when this picture was taken. This was about a year before she met Keith and started doing drugs again. This is how I remember her." Usually when I talk about Mom, it makes me want to cry. I don't like talking about the bad things, but Elli makes me feel safe. I know she'd never judge me for crying, or for my past, so talking to her is much easier.

"I think it's great that you have a picture of her to remember her that way." Elli says, wrapping her arms around my waist.

"Thanks baby. Over here," I guide her over to a picture frame of some high schoolers at a school dance, "this is Jess and Kenny, and my mom and dad at their senior prom. This was two years before I was conceived. Dad joined the Army right out of high school, but he and mom got married on one of his breaks. I was conceived shortly after they made it official. Dad was deployed again when I was three, and died in combat. I don't really remember him much."

Elli goes to say something, but Luke bursts through the door declaring dinner time so I give her a kiss on the forehead, silently letting her know that I'm okay and we can talk about it later.

"Alright kids. Luke's got his usual everything pizza, Wes, I've got your pineapple and ham with onion, Elli's alfredo sauce with mushroom, pepper, and bacon, and my anchovy." We all pretend to gag at Jess's pizza order and she rolls her eyes. "I've also got cheesy breadsticks with ranch and marinara, and I made caramel chip cookies for dessert."

Elli sits down and while we all immediately dig in, she folds her arms.

"You okay, Elli?" Jess asks.

Elli's face turns red, "Yeah. Sorry. I'm just used to having to say a prayer before eating at family dinner. Force of habit I guess." She reaches for her pizza and places two slices on her plate.

"Habits are tough to break. No worries sweetheart." Jess says reassuringly. "So, update time. Wes! You're first."

"Alrighty. Ummm. I sent some of my new songs to some record labels, but I haven't heard anything back yet. I did have Keely and the Kissers comment on one of my reels raving over the song so that was cool. That reel has over three hundred thousand views, which is wild to me. I still plan on teaching at Jude this school year. Elli and I are going to Utah in three weeks for her brother's farewell thingy so that'll be fun. Yeah. That's about it." I take a big bite of my pizza and look at Luke.

Luke shuffles in his seat, "I was able to fix the old ham radio I found at the thrift store so it's functional now. I've been doing online classes to try and graduate early. Work's been good. No one's drowned so I call that a win. Izzy and I still plan on going to college together and I'm very upset no one is letting me go to Utah with them." He says pointedly while looking between me and Jess.

Jess rolls her eyes, "You start school that week and I'm not letting you miss it. Sorry, bub. Glad to hear no one's drowned. Wes, that's cool about Keely and the Kissers. I don't know who they are, but it sounds like they're a big deal. My update I guess is that the salon is booked to capacity for the next three months and I might consider hiring another person to rent out the other booth, or maybe an assistant for the shop. It would be nice not to have to do things myself. Elli! What are your updates?"

"Oh, um. Let's see. On Sunday I was talking to Claudia and Ernie, and they're wanting to start hiring some more staff, possibly another chef and a manager so they can start to think about retiring. I'm going to help them figure out the proper paperwork and help them with the hiring process. I'd be more than happy to help you out too if you'd like. I know it can be overwhelming posting job applications and vetting new hires." Elli beams at Jess.

"I'll keep that in mind, thanks Elli. That's really sweet of you to help out Claudia and Ernie too. Lord knows they need to retire soon. Neither of them can keep working twelve hour days."

"Of course! I'm glad to help them. It's a shame for me, but amazing for you that you're booked out. I was hoping to make an appointment to add some highlights to my hair, and I'm in desperate need of a trim. Do you have anyone else you recommend?" Elli asks, taking another bite of her pizza.

"I think I can squeeze you in. The salon isn't open on Sundays at all so I'd be more than happy to have you in on Sunday. How does that sound?" Jess says with a wink.

"Oh! That would be amazing, Jess. Thank you so much. I've never had my hair colored so I didn't want to find a random person and risk it being bad."

"Jess will take excellent care of your hair. She's been doing mine forever and look how fantastic it is." I say, flipping my hair over one shoulder, causing Elli to giggle.

The rest of the dinner is filled with easy conversation, reminding me how much I miss seeing Jess and Luke all the time. Elli's like the missing piece of the puzzle to this little family, and it warms my heart.

Before we head back to Elli's place, I head to the restroom and when I pull my phone out of my pocket, I see I have a direct message from Keely and the Kissers.

> **Keely:** Hey, Wes! This is Keely from Keely and the Kissers. We have been non-stop watching your reels. Your new song "Love Bug" is AMAZEBALLS. We're going on a North America Tour beginning in January of next year and we'd love for you to be our opening act. Send us over your email so our manager, Misha can send you the tour dates and the pay and whatnot. We'd really love to work with you.

Oh my god.

OH MY GOD?!

Keely and the Kissers wants *me* to go on tour?

I respond immediately.

> **Wes:** Hey! Thank you so much! I'm honored to be considered for this opportunity. My email is <u>wesjonesmusic@mail.com</u>. I look forward to hearing from you!

Wait till I tell Jess and Luke and Elli- wait. A tour of North America. That's usually, what, six months? Could I go that long without seeing Elli? We *just* started dating. And yeah, it's still five months away. Our relationship could survive.

But do I want to be away from her that long?

I don't think so.

Maybe I'll just decline.

But I don't want to do that, either. This is a dream come true.

I leave the bathroom and decide not to say anything until I have all the information. They could be paying me so little that it wouldn't be worth it to go.

We go through the rest of the night as we usually do when we get back to Elli's. We shower together and get a little handsy, then watch *Zombieland* and Elli falls asleep halfway through so I carry her to bed. When I plug my phone into the charger, I see an email from Keelys manager.

I quickly scroll through and see the tour is eight months long, and they're going to pay me my yearly salary from the school, plus all the lodging is taken care of.

It's a damn good deal.

But eight months away from Elli? I don't know...

I decide I'll talk to Elli about it and see what she wants me to do. Except she'll want me to go because this is my dream. She's so selfless that she'd tell me to pursue my dream even if it means leaving her for a while.

I have a fitful sleep that night, anxiety weighing heavy in my chest as I consider all the possibilities.

My dream career, or my dream girl?

Why can't I have both?

CHAPTER 36

Elli

The hotel has been booked, the sightseeing planned, and the playlist curated.

One week until we go back to hell-I mean Utah.

Don't get me wrong, Utah is beautiful. Majestic mountains, stunning lakes, vibrant red rocks, and beautiful snow in the winter.

It's the people and the culture that makes Utah suck.

Not to mention they keep developing the beautiful land to build megamansions, and shopping centers.

Even the state prison got moved from Draper to Salt Lake City and they plan on turning the land the old facilities were on into a little city complete with shops, restaurants, and cookie cutter houses.

My cousin Hannah's family lives in Syracuse, a little further north than Provo, and it used to be a farmland area, but now it's been urbanized. They put in subdivision after subdivision, multiple golf courses, and even a highway straight through the city.

Don't even get me started on all the temples the church has built. There are fifteen in Utah, two in Provo alone. They purposefully build them so you can see them from the major freeway and highways that run through the state. "A beacon of hope." They say.

It's honestly a bit of an eyesore in some places.

But what do I know about land development?

I'm nervous to go back home, even though it's only been two months. I feel like a completely different person than I was in June, and I don't want to backslide on my progress.

I know my mom is going to throw an absolute fit when she meets Wes, and then I'll become the topic of the family gossip.

There will be questions about if Wes is converting, or if I've "strayed from the straight and narrow path." I'll be told that I'm ruining my chance at a spot in the Celestial Kingdom. They'll say they're going to pray for me and put my name in the temple, even if I tell them not to.

I don't want their prayers.

I want to live my life free of guilt and the weight of everyone else's expectations.

"Hey baby, you okay?" Wes asks, nudging my knee with his. I'm working from his place today. He's been a little weird lately, like he has something he wants to say to me but won't, so I'm hoping the more I'm around him the more likely he is to get whatever's on his chest, off of it.

"Yeah, sorry. Just stressing about our trip. I don't know why I thought bringing you into that chaos was a good idea. They're going to be so mean to you. I don't even know why I'm bothering going back." I slump back, abandoning the task I wasn't even paying attention to.

Wes grabs my laptop and sets it aside, then brings my feet to his lap and starts to massage them. I love it when he does this.

"Let's walk through it together. You're going because you love Spencer, and you want him to know he's supported. I'm going because you love me, and you want me to meet some important people in your life. Right?"

I nod. He's right. I want him to meet my siblings and Hannah. If I thought Emma, the third part of our cousin trio, would be there, I'd love for him to meet her too, but she rarely comes back to Utah anymore.

I don't blame her one bit for that. Her family is crazier than mine.

"I'm used to people being judgy and rude to me for my looks, baby. I've done the therapy, and I'm secure in who I am. Some judgmental family members aren't going to change the way I feel about myself, or you."

"You've been to therapy?" How did I not know that?

"Yeah." He shrugs, "After Keith, my mom, my grams, and Shelby, I decided if I ever wanted to be happy I needed to work through the trauma of everything. Jess found me someone and I spent the better part of a year bawling my eyes out and working through the junk. It sometimes still gets me, the trauma. And the anxiety gets really bad sometimes, but it's pretty controllable with medication. I'm a lot better at coping with things now. Instead of never trying to tell you how I felt because I thought I wasn't worthy, I just took a little longer with it. I was terrified that you'd reject me, but the possibility of you wanting me back outweighed my self-esteem issues and doubts. And it was so worth it in the end." He finishes with a dramatic wink.

"Wow. I never thought about that. I'm glad you were able to work through things. And I'm glad you made a move, because saying yes to you was the easiest thing I've ever done." I lean up and give him a gentle kiss on the lips.

"Have you ever considered therapy for your trauma?" He asks.

"I don't have trauma, so no."

He gives me a disbelieving look. "Elli. You grew up in a high demand religion where your every thought and action was dictated by men or your mother. You were parentified as a child, and your two serious relationships belittled you and made you think there was something wrong with *you*. That's a lot to go through, baby."

Well when you put it that way...

"You're right. I probably do need therapy. I remember growing up, if I was depressed or anxious, I was told that I needed to be reading my scriptures and praying more. So I just ignored it and 'tried harder' to be more spiritual."

Wes pulls me into his lap and starts running his fingers up and down my spine. I used to worry I would crush him if I did this, but I've learned not to protest because Wes loves the weight of me on him.

"You have gone through a lot, baby. And I'm proud of you for breaking free. You deserve to feel at peace for your decisions, and I'll support you anyway I can."

"Thank you. That means a lot." I turn my head and kiss him, trying to show all of my appreciation in the kiss. It's slow, languid, sensual. And I can tell he's holding back because we just had a vulnerable moment and he doesn't want to push me.

"Okay baby. You have an hour left of work, then I'll help you take your mind off of everything for a little bit. But you're not getting paid to fuck me, so back to it." He says with a pinch on my butt.

I slide off of him and resume my task for the next hour, and as soon as the clock hits three and I close my laptop, he's kneeling in front of me, spreading my legs.

He taps my thigh, and I raise my butt so he can take off my lounge shorts. He groans when he finds me bare beneath them.

"All day you've been without panties? Naughty." He tsks.

"I was in a rush to get over here last night and forgot to pack some." I explain as his thumbs spread my pussy lips.

"Oh I'm not complaining one bit. As far as I'm concerned, you don't need to wear anything around me." He smirks, then kisses up my thighs, nibbling gently on the dimpled skin.

"Good-oh fuck-good to know." The last word comes out as a moan as his tongue circles my clit. Guess we're not playing around today.

As he continues his ministrations on my clit, one of his fingers circles my entrance and slowly pushes inside me. Then another follows.

He crooks it just right, putting pressure on my g-spot and then picks up the pace with his tongue and his fingers until an orgasm crashes over me so suddenly, but he doesn't stop his relentless pace.

"Wes, stop, I think I need to pee." I panic.

But he doesn't stop, and then another, stronger orgasm creeps up. My entire body tingles with the pending release and I explode. Literally.

Liquid gushes out of me and all over Wes's chest as I scream his name. My body feels like jello as he slowly pulls his fingers from me. He stands and removes his t-shirt and uses it to wipe his face.

"What the hell was that?" I ask.

"That was you squirting, baby. I've been wanting to see if you can for a while and *damn* is it hot." He says with a cheshire cat smile.

Huh. I didn't know my body could do that.

I watch Wes roll the condom on his cock and sit on the couch before bringing over to straddle him. I sink down slowly until our laps are flush, then I roll my hips and he groans.

"I'm never going to get enough of this tight pussy baby. You feel so good. Ride me Elli." Wes says with a smack to my ass.

I pick up my pace, riding him fast and hard, just how he likes it, and he meets me thrust for thrust. Just when I think he's about to come, he stops me by gripping my hips and not letting me move again.

He picks me up, my legs instinctively wrapping around his lean waist, and he carries me to the bedroom where he tosses me on the bed and I bounce.

He hovers over me, kissing me greedily as he teases the tip of his cock against my sensitive clit. "Someday, when you're ready, I'm going to fuck you bare Elli. Really claim you. Watch my cum drip out of you and down your thighs."

My pussy clenches around nothing at his words. I'm on birth control, obviously I haven't been with anyone, and I trust Wes, but I don't think I'm ready for that yet. Luckily I know that he'll wait until I'm ready.

"I want that too, someday." I whisper.

Wes gives me a tender smile that quickly vanishes as he throws one leg over his shoulder and enters me again roughly.

Yessss. This position is one of my favorites. The way he's angled means his thigh rubs against my clit while he hits deep inside me.

"You better come fast for me baby because I'm going to." He says through gritted teeth. "Milk my cock, Elli. Take my pleasure because it's yours. Only yours. Fuck, I love you."

His words are my undoing and clench around him, doing exactly as he asked and milking him. "I love you Wes!" I moan as pleasure runs through my entire body.

Wes stills and I feel him pulse inside me, filling the condom with his release as he moans my name.

"Hey, I'm yours too, you know." I say as he pulls out of me, rolling to the side to discard the condom.

He smiles and pulls me closer to him so I can lay on his chest. "I know, baby. And I'm so grateful."

"You know we still have to eat dinner right?" I say after a moment of silence.

"I know, but let me just hold you a little while longer."

CHAPTER 37

Wes

I know I'm a shit boyfriend for not telling Elli about the tour yet, but I'm still weighing the pros and cons.

Keely's manager said I had until September to make an official decision, but that they wanted to know what I was leaning towards so they could find another opener if they needed to.

I want to go so badly.

If I were single, I'd say yes in a heartbeat. I think Elli would want me to go too, but I don't think my needy ass can be away from her that long. I asked Misha if partners were allowed on the tour, and he said yes, so now I'm just working up the courage to ask Elli to pack up her life and follow me around like a groupie. She already packed up and left the life she was familiar with, it feels selfish to ask her to do that again six months later.

Plus, I don't know if her job would allow that.

So I'm meeting Robin for breakfast so I can work this through.

Elli is finalizing some last minute work stuff before we leave for Utah tomorrow, so now seems like the perfect chance to get a pep talk from my best friend.

I didn't want Claudia and Ernie to overhear us and spill the beans to everyone else so we're at a different breakfast spot called Eggz.

Robin is sitting at a table scrolling away when I walk through the door, but she looks up and waves me over with a big smile.

God, I've missed her.

I didn't mean to focus solely on Elli, but it kind of happened that way. I need to make sure I'm better at giving attention to the rest of my friends because they're just as important.

Robin stands and meets me for a hug as I make it to the table. "I've missed you loverboy!"

"Missed you too, Red." I murmur against her head.

"Just so you don't freak out, we all forgive you for being in an Elli bubble. We're just glad you're safe and happy. We knew you'd reach out eventually and feel really bad so I'm telling you to not feel guilt. Got it?" She pokes my chest to emphasize her point.

"I got it. Thanks Robs. And to be fair, I've been hanging out with Jess, Luke, Claudia and Ernie. Jess even did Elli's hair." and it looks so good. She cut it to just below her shoulder and added some caramel highlights, so it's like looking at a decadent piece of chocolate filled with caramel.

Good thing it's still long enough to pull.

"I saw that on her insta story. It looks good. And you both seem happy. That's all we want for you." Robin gives me a smirk, "Now, I would normally ask how she is in bed, but I respect Elli's privacy too much. So you can keep the dirty details to yourself."

I roll my eyes, "Gee, thanks."

We order our food and coffee, and then catch up on our lives over the last two weeks. Robin's been busy, too, with the gallery opening in San Antonio. I'm sad we'll miss it, since this is Robin's first time heading up an opening, but it's happening this weekend and we'll be gone. I promised her we'd come back and come take a look to support her.

Apparently, one of the artists that's showcasing their work has been non-stop flirting with Robin, and they've been texting off and on about non-work related things and they asked her to go out for drinks after the opening.

"I promised I'd never date artists because they're usually so pretentious, but I don't know. Maybe it'll just be a quick hookup, but they're *really* hot. So that wouldn't be the worst thing." She explains.

I know Robs has been burned by relationships too, so I'm not going to push her to date or not.

"So what do you need to work through?" She asks as the waitress brings over our food.

"Why do you assume I need to work through something?" I defend. I sometimes hate that she can read me so well.

She gives me an exasperated look. "You left your little sex bubble to have breakfast with me so obviously something is bothering you, and I'm assuming it involves Elli or else you'd be talking to her about it."

"Yeah... You're right. So, you know the band Keely and the Kissers?"

She nods enthusiastically. "Yes! I love them! I saw they commented on your insta reel. That's fucking cool!"

"Well... after they commented on that, they DM'd me and asked me to go on tour with them. The tour starts in January and goes for eight months. They'd pay me a year's salary, and all the lodging and transportation is included. It's a sick gig, and I asked if I could bring a partner and they said yes as long as they share my rooms and stuff."

Robin freezes with her breakfast sandwich halfway between her mouth and the plate. Then she drops it and yells. "WHAT?"

"Shhh. Robin. Keep it down please!"

"Sorry," she says quieter. "My best friend just told me he got offered to go on a tour for eight months with a super cool band, I'm freaking out a bit!"

"I know, I know. It's pretty rad."

"So what's the hold up? If Elli can go with you, why aren't you foaming at the mouth to take this opportunity?"

"Elli *just* uprooted her entire life and moved here. I can't ask her to uproot again and follow me around the country for eight months. That's not fair to her."

"Have you asked her to?"

I shake my head.

Robin huffs and mumbles something that sounds like "damn heteros" under her breath.

"Listen, Wes. You can't make that decision for her. Maybe she would hate the idea and you two are apart for a while. Which would suck ass, but you'd work through it. *Or.*"

"*Or,* what?" I prompt.

"Or she agrees to go with you and you spend eight months traveling around with a sick band, playing your music, making industry connections, all with your girl by your side, cheering you on. But you'll never know unless you ask her."

She's right. It's what I've thought too, but hearing someone else say it validates what I was thinking.

"You said 'I love you' yet?" Robin questions.

"Yeah. The morning after the club." I can feel my face turning red. I'm not embarrassed about loving Elli. I *am* embarrassed about not telling Robin immediately.

She rolls her eyes, "Of course you didn't tell me! Rude, Wes. That's rude."

"Sorry."

"I forgive you. But only because I'm so damn proud of you. Even if you choose not to go on this tour, you still got asked. *You* were chosen by a big band to open for their tour! And, you've got one helluva girl at your side. She's the one that inspired the song that they obsessed over. I'd say she's your lucky charm."

"Yeah, you're probably right." I finish off my own breakfast sandwich. "I've got to go talk to my girl. I'll see you when we get back from Utah in a week."

"Have fun! Be safe! Bring me back something cool!"

I wave her off and practically jog to my car, barely managing to go the speed limit as I speed to Elli's apartment. She gave me a key a few days ago so I just let myself in, and I hear her on the phone in her room.

I knock on the door frame quietly, and she looks up from her computer and gives me a small smile and wave.

"No, Mom." She pauses and I can hear her mom's shrill voice talking on the other side. "Do you not want me to come? Because you made it very clear that this was more important than almost anything, and I want to be there to support Spencer."

Another pause to listen to her mom. I can see Elli's hands balled into fists, so I gently sit down next to her on the bed and grab one hand and intertwine it with my own.

"I have no control over Izzy and you know that. Izzy is almost eighteen and can make her own decisions. In fact, I specifically told Izzy that I would not be influencing her about the church either way. So if she wants to leave that's her choice."

Elli's mom is full on screaming at her now, and Elli's starting to cry. Though her voice is calm when she speaks, little drops of sadness fall from her beautiful blue eyes whenever she blinks.

"I'm not canceling my trip. If you don't want to see me then fine, I won't come to the house. But I'm not going to make Spencer think he's unsupported by me. Text me your decision. Goodbye, Mother." Elli says and then hangs up the phone.

The sobs she was holding back come out in full force as she buries her face in my chest. I gently stroke her back, her hair, her arms, waiting for her to cry it all out. I know she'll tell me all about it when she's done.

"Izzy," she hiccups after her sobs stop, "Izzy wants to leave the church. She doesn't believe in it anymore, I guess. And mom thinks I've 'poisoned' her only other daughter against her."

"That's bullshit."

"I kn-know. But my mom thinks that because I left, Izzy's following my example. I *told* Izzy that I wouldn't be persuading her either way. That whatever conclusion she came to had to be made independently. She's texted me a few times to ask me questions and I've given her as neutral an answer as I could. Now mom's saying it's going to affect Gideon and Issac too and it's all my fault."

"Baby, I'm so sorry. I wish I could make some better reassurances but I'm not quite sure how to handle this situation. Just know I'm here for whatever you need. I've met Izzy. That girl is not going to do something she doesn't want to do. I honestly think even if you hadn't left, she would eventually."

Elli sniffles, "Yeah. I think she would have too. Thank you, Wes. I'm sorry if this ruins our trip. I wanted to have a fun time with minimal drama, but it doesn't look like that's going to happen. I understand if you don't want to go now."

I shush her, "I'm not going to let you go alone. I'm excited to see where you grew up. I've got you, Elli."

We lay there quietly while she calms down, then she sits up and sighs. "Sorry, that wasn't how I wanted to greet you. How was breakfast with Robs?"

"It was good. She's been getting flirty with an artist. I told her we'd come visit the gallery once we were back."

Elli's smile is as bright as the sun, "Good for her. I'm excited to see what she's done. Talk about anything else?"

Do I bring this up now?

I feel like I don't want to drop another bomb on her after the ordeal with her mom. I think I'll wait until we get to Utah and have rested after our road trip before asking her.

"Just caught up with each other. Everyone misses us." I say instead.

"I miss them too. We need to hang out with them again when we get back. Ooo, maybe an 'end of summer' pool party? Do you think Matt would be up for that?"

"That sounds good baby. I'll ask him. Now, what do we need to do to get ready for tomorrow?" I ask, trying to get off the topic of parties and the group. I know Elli gets distracted by tasks so hopefully organizing the final details of the trip will help her.

Sure enough, she gets right down to business. We pack up the snacks and drinks into coolers and a box and put them in the back of her car after filling that up with gas so we have a full tank. I'm spending the night here so we can leave at the ass crack of dawn, so our suitcases are waiting by the door so we can pack last minute toiletries.

"I think other than grabbing a coffee before we leave town, we're all set to go." She says as she settles in beside me.

"Are you going to be okay when we get there? We can cancel now if you want." I don't care if we'd lose money. Her wellbeing is more important.

"I'll be okay. Thank you for being worried. I love you, Wes."

"I love you too, Elli."

And with that, we turn off the light to get some zzz's in before our long ass car ride.

CHAPTER 38

Elli

The next morning at the ass crack of dawn, we load up the rest of our luggage, lock up my apartment and head out. We stop at the Espresso Express for coffee before making the eleven hour journey to today's destination: Albuquerque, New Mexico.

We don't talk a lot, I'm still raw from my conversation with my mom yesterday, and Wes seems nervous even if he's saying he's not.

My phone pings three hours into our journey and I see it's a text from my mom.

Mom: Spencer wants you to be there at his luncheon. We'll see you on Sunday.

I huff out a disbelieving laugh, and Wes looks over from the driver's side with a questioning look on his face.

"Mom just texted me that she'll see me Sunday because Spencer wants me there." I lean my head back against the headrest and take a deep breath. "It's like she doesn't even care, or realize how hurtful she was yesterday."

Wes's hand that's sitting on my thigh squeezes gently. "I'm sorry baby. At least Spencer wants you there, right?"

"Yeah..." I trail off, thinking now about Wes and how he's acting. "Are you okay? You seem a bit off. If you're nervous, I get it, and I'd like to talk through your anxieties."

Wes takes a long, deep breath before squeezing my thigh again. "I have some... news. That I wanted to talk to you about yesterday, but then things happened with your mom and I didn't want to make things worse..."

Oh god, please don't be breaking up with me when we're a fourth of the way through our long ass road trip.

But that wouldn't make sense. Why would he still come if he was breaking up with me?

"Okay..." I say, trying to still my racing heart.

"Have you ever heard of the band Keely and the Kissers?" Wes asks.

"I think I've heard one or two of their songs."

"They're getting really popular. So popular that they're going on tour next year, starting in January. And they've asked me to go. With them. On the tour."

My chest aches with pride and a bit of anxiety at the revelation. I'm speechless.

My boyfriend is going on *tour?*

My boyfriend is going on tour?

My boyfriend is going on *tour!*

"Wes, oh my *god*. That is amazing!" I grab his hand from my thigh and shake our arms in a cheer, but when I look over at him, he's only got a half smile on his face. Like he's trying not to be too happy about this *life changing* news. "Why don't you seem excited?"

"The tour is eight months long. We *just* started dating and I don't want to leave you for eight months. I mean, I asked the manager if you could... come along, and he said yes as long as we share a room, but you can't just uproot your life *again* so soon after you uprooted it once and-"

"Are you *serious* right now?" I practically scream at him. Oh, I'm so mad. How *dare* he decide that I don't want to go on a freaking *tour* with my musician boyfriend!

"Well, yeah." He says, looking rightfully chastised. "I didn't... I don't want to put you through more stuff..."

"Ask me, Wes. Ask me what I want to do, because you haven't, and there's no way you could know my answer without asking me." I say, firmly but gently.

But he doesn't, right away.

We sit in agonizing silence for another ten minutes -that feels like a fucking hour- before we come across a little Valero gas station and Wes pulls in and parks.

Wes takes a deep breath, as if steeling himself for battle before he turns to me and grabs both of my hands in his, resting them on the center console. His calloused thumbs rub soothing circles on my palms, his teeth gnawing at his bottom lip in worry.

"I'm sorry I assumed what you'd want to do, baby. I've lost so many people in my life, and I want to keep the ones I care about closest, but sometimes that means I avoid hard things in order to keep them around. I've also never really had to think about how my choices would affect anyone else, you know? Not for a really long time. But I think about how things would affect *you* all the time. And the thought of being away from you for *any* period of time, let alone eight fucking months?" He shakes his head. "That would feel like pulling my heart directly out of my chest. The thought of *ever* causing you pain makes me physically ill. I'd sooner cut off my thumbs and never play guitar again than cause you any sort of pain or discomfort. If you want to come with me, I would be honored. But if you don't want to spend eight months on a tour bus and in hotel rooms, I understand."

My eyes are misty now at his admission. I don't think I've ever had someone so fiercely protective of me. Someone who *actually* considers what *I* would feel.

"I've always wanted to travel. The furthest I've been from Provo, other than Texas, is Zion's National Park, and that's only a four hour drive. My job allows me to work from anywhere, so it's not in jeopardy. I would love nothing more than to go on tour with you, Wes. It's not even a question. I'm sorry you've been battling with yourself for so long over this. Next time, just ask me." I squeeze his hands in mine.

"You're serious? You'll come with me?" He asks, hopefully.

"I just said I would, you silly goose."

Wes tries to pull me over the center console so he can kiss me, but I get stuck part way so instead of a heartfelt, passionate kiss, we're awkwardly craning our necks to reach each other's lips. We both break out into a fit of laughter and I can only imagine how ridiculous we must look like to outsiders.

Not that anyone is really out there to see us awkwardly smooch in a Valero parking lot.

"Let's get through this trip and we can figure it all out. Together. Okay?" I say, wiping the errant tear that fell during our laughing.

"Okay." Wes agrees.

Wes peels out of the parking lot of the gas station and we continue our journey, our fingers interlocked and the music at a soft volume.

"I'm going to need to have t-shirts made so everyone knows you're taken." I murmur. "Girls - and guys - will be throwing themselves at you constantly! How will I compete?"

"I'll get your name tattooed on my forehead if you ask me to, baby, but just know that it's your face I'll seek out in every crowd." He gives me a rakish smirk, "and no matter how many panties get thrown up on the stage, it's only yours I'll want to own."

I roll my eyes and smack his chest playfully. "You can keep a pair in your pocket for every show. A good luck charm."

"You said it, so now it's gotta happen."

CHAPTER 39

We make good time and arrive in Albuquerque at five o'clock, just in time for us to check in at the hotel and get dinner that doesn't come from a drive thru or a gas station.

We decide to walk to a little pizza shop about two blocks from our hotel so we can stretch our legs and eat something that doesn't come out of a bag.

I'm still floating from Elli saying she'll come on tour with me. I still feel bad that she's going to have to uproot again, and there's a little nasty voice in the back of my head saying that she'd be better off staying in San Marcos and figuring out her life, but the voice telling me this is where my dreams start to come true is louder than that one.

I always dreamed of touring and playing music for a living, but I'd never pictured someone standing next to me. I figured I'd be a bachelor for life, maybe fuck a few fans when the need arose.

Picturing Elli standing off stage, watching me in my element and cheering me on, just to go home with her and bury myself inside that sweet pussy night after night?

I'm hard just thinking about it, which is inconvenient since this is a family establishment.

I shut down my naughty fantasy and look at Elli, who's picking at her mushroom and bacon pizza anxiously. A little frown is present on her beautiful face and now I'm wondering if she's as excited as I am about the tour, or if she just said yes because she didn't want to disappoint me.

Then I remember where we're headed and realize I'm being selfish only thinking about the tour when we're about to go to her own personal version of hell.

I reach across the table and gently stroke the back of her hand, offering her a small smile. "Hey pretty girl. You want to tell me what's going on in that beautiful head of yours?"

Her stunning blues meet mine and she sighs heavily, like the weight of the world is on her shoulders. "I'm nervous about you meeting my family." She shakes her head, like that wasn't what she meant to say. "Not because you're *you*, but because they're *them*. You know?"

Not really, no. But it's kind of reassuring that she's not worried about *me*. "I'm not sure I do know what you mean. Can you walk me through it?"

"I've already told you that they're... *a lot*. And there's so many of them that it gets overwhelming for *me* and I've been around it my entire life. I don't want you to get overwhelmed by it or decide you don't want to be with me anymore because one of them says something offensive- and they will, because they suck." She takes another deep breath, squeezes my hand, and stares at me so intensely I get chills.

"I've never loved anyone the way I love you. I don't think what I've experienced before *was* love, to be honest. And the thought of my family ruining things makes me want to turn around and go home."

I don't miss the way she refers to San Marcos as "home" now, and it makes my heart stutter. I already know she loves me, but every time she says it out loud, it's like someone shoots liquid happiness directly into my bloodstream. I don't know how else to prove to her that I'm not going anywhere without her right by my side, but I sure as hell am going to try. I'll spend the rest of my life showing her just how much I love her.

"Elli, I promise you, there's nothing they can say that will make me not want to be with you, okay? You're it for me, baby. There's no one else after you. Hell, I think I've been waiting my whole life for you. People have said shitty things to and about me my whole life. I'm not going to let anyone come between us. I promise."

Elli studies me for a minute, searching for any sign that I'm lying. I know she won't find any, and she doesn't, so she leans over the table and gives me a gentle kiss.

"Thank you, Wes. Let's finish up and go back to the hotel. I'm beat, and we need our rest for the drive tomorrow."

Once we've finished our pizza and make it back to the hotel, Elli says she's going to go shower, so I sit on the bed and scroll through my phone. I text Robs and Jess to let them know we're halfway to Utah and made it safely to Albuquerque.

I hear the shower turn on, and as much as I try to distract myself from the thoughts of a naked Elli getting all wet and soapy, my mind wanders. We've showered together a few times when we've had sleepovers, and the feeling of her heavy, soapy tits rubbing against my skin is one of the best feelings in the world.

I'm hard as stone now, but I don't know if Elli's wanting anything other than some cuddles tonight, and no way in hell would I ever push her.

But I am only a human and when my girl is naked in the shower, I want to sneak a peek.

I make my way to the bathroom, where the door is cracked open just a bit, and open it even more, slowly. When I peek my head in, the mirror is fogged, but it reflects the outline of my girl's luscious body through the sheer shower curtain.

"Are you joining me, or are you going to be a peeping Tom?" Elli's voice startles me out of said peeping.

I strip so fast that if it were an Olympic sport, I'd take gold.

I step in, and Elli's standing there rinsing out her hair with her eyes closed. When she opens them again, there's no denying the arousal she's feeling. Her beautiful blue irises are almost completely covered by her pupil.

I step toward her and crowd her into the shower wall, soaking myself in the process. "You been waiting for me, baby?" My voice is husky with arousal.

She nods, then runs a hand down my chest slowly, inching her way toward my already hard cock. When she finds me standing at attention, her soft fingers gently tickle up and down my length and it bobs in anticipation, but she pulls her hand back.

"Were you touching yourself out there?" She whispers.

"No." I reply.

"Why not?"

"Because I'd rather bury myself in you than come in my own hand. But if you weren't up for sex, I'd have just suffered through until I was calm again because the only way I'll seek my pleasure is if I get to give you pleasure as well."

"Well we can't have you suffering." She says breathily, then slides down the wall and lands on her knees in front of me.

She takes me in her hot, wet mouth, and fucking *moans*. Elli may have never given head until me, but it seems like she enjoys it as much as I do now. I watch as her hand disappears underneath her and then she sucks me in *hard*.

"Baby, are you touching yourself while you suck my cock?" I grit out, trying not to come right then at the sight of her owning her pleasure.

She looks up at me through her lashes and nods as best she can.

"Fuck me that's sexy as hell baby. Is your pretty little clit nice and hard for me?"

She nods again.

I let her bob along my cock a few more times before I step back. I don't want to come in her mouth right now.

"Stand up, Elli. Let me feel how wet sucking my cock made you."

She obeys and I trail a finger down her wet body until I can run it through her soaked pussy. She lets out a moan as I pump my finger inside, then add another, curling them so I can hit her g-spot while I strum her clit. She was already close so it doesn't surprise me when she tenses and clenches around my fingers and comes only a few moments later.

"Goddamn, baby. I need in this pussy, like, yest- *damn it.*" I curse, realizing I didn't bring a condom into the bathroom.

"What's wrong?" She pants, still coming down from her orgasm.

"I didn't bring a condom into the bathroom. I thought we'd just shower, I wasn't expecting a little vixen to try and jump my bones." I tease, giving her a wink.

She bites her bottom lip in contemplation, and then she takes my cock in her hand again. "I had an IUD put in before I moved. And obviously, I've never been with anyone else. I want you to fuck me bare, Wes. Please."

"Are you sure, Elli? Because we can dry off and go fuck on the bed with a con-"

She cuts me off by kissing me. Hard. Then turns around and settles her hands on the wall of the shower. "Fuck me, Wes. Please."

Goddamn this girl is going to kill me.

The trust she just placed in me doesn't go unappreciated. I would never fuck her bare if I had been with *anyone* in the last three months unless I was tested and came back clean. But as it stands, I haven't been with anyone in almost two years, so I know I'm clean. And I always wore a condom with Shelby because I think some part of me always knew she was fucking around.

I step up behind Elli and notch the head of my cock at her entrance and slowly push inside, letting out a string of curses.

Using a condom hasn't bothered me in the past, but that must've been because I'd never had Elli's pussy wrapped around me before.

"I can't be slow and soft right now baby. I'm going to come embarrassingly fast and I need you to come before I do. So play with that clit and come."

Elli does as she's told, bringing one hand down to rub circles on her clit as I pound into her hard and fast. The minute I feel her clench around me and moan my name, I'm off like a rocket, coming harder than I ever have before.

"Fuck, Elli! I love you so goddamn much." I pant, planting kisses along her shoulder and back.

She turns around and gives me a sleepy smile. "I love you too, Wes."

I place a kiss on her forehead, "Let's get cleaned up and then we can go to sleep."

CHAPTER 40

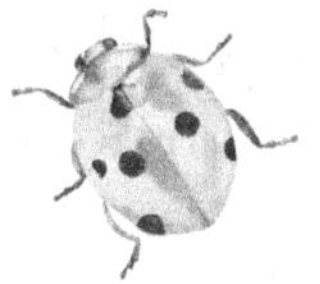

Elli

After a long day of driving, we finally pull up to the Holiday Inn in Provo, right as the sun is setting behind Utah Lake.

I'm not going to lie, I miss the mountains. We drove through Moab on our way in, and I missed seeing the famous red rocks, the majestic mountains, and the beautiful lake that is too contaminated to swim in.

Utah is beautiful, but the air pollution is not.

Wes commented on the beauty of everything we drove past, looking out his window like he was on a tour instead of just passing through. I tried to explain everything to him, since he's never traveled outside of Texas, but there's a lot to take in if you're seeing Utah for the first time.

We have tomorrow to sight see my home town, then Sunday is Spencer's farewell.

I'm excited to show Wes some of my favorite spots.

I will say, it's super weird to see the temples and churches everywhere I look again, even if it's only been a few months. Growing up, it was normal to see at least three temples if you were driving an hour in either direction, and churches are more common than McDonalds.

In Texas, I haven't seen any.

I didn't realize how guilty seeing them made me feel until we drove past the Provo City Center temple and my gut twisted a little because I've never been inside for anything other than baptisms for the dead. I never got my endowment, and I never will. I'll never be sealed.

"You okay, baby?" Wes asks as he comes back from getting our room key.

"Hm? Yeah. Just processing." I say, shutting off the engine and stepping out of the car to grab our bags.

"Want to process with me?" He asks, studying my face.

"Yeah," I look around and see a crowd of people, "but let's get into the room first."

Wes nods, then grabs his duffle bag and slings it over his shoulder. He takes my rolling case in the other hand and I put my backpack on, and he grabs my hand and we walk to the elevators inside and ride the three floors up to our room.

We settle our stuff on chairs, and then Wes sits on the bed and pats the spot next to him.

I settle down next to him and he pulls my feet onto his lap and, despite my protests that my feet are gross, takes off my shoes and socks and starts massaging my feet.

"Alright baby. Let's process. Tell me what's on your mind?" He asks.

"So, you know how we drove down Center Street and I pointed out the temple?"

He nods.

"When I saw it, I felt a little guilty, and I realized I haven't felt guilty since moving to San Marcos, really."

"Guilty about what?"

"Well, temples are like, *super* important in Mormon theology. When you're twelve, you can get a temple recommend and go do baptisms for the dead." Wes looks confused, so I explain, "It's when you find people who have already died and haven't been baptized and then you act as a proxy for them so they can be baptized and their soul is saved or whatever." He nods his head, but I know it's still confusing because even though I grew up doing it, I still don't fully understand everything that goes into it.

"Anyway," I continue, "when I decided to leave the church, I realized there are some things that I'll never be able to do. Like getting endowed to wear garments, or be sealed to my future spouse."

"What do those things mean?"

What *do* they mean?

They mean different things for different people. An active member will feel differently about them than I do.

The temple ceremonies are kept secret "because they're sacred" or at least, that's what they want you to believe. So because I've never been in an endowment or sealing, I have no clue what they entail. I only know what goes into baptisms for the dead because I actually participated in those.

"All I know is an endowment means you make special promises, get a specific blessing, and then you wear garments for the rest of your life, because the garments have special symbols on them that represent the promises you make. People usually only get endowed to go on missions or because they're getting married. Occasionally, someone will be endowed because they're older and just want to be, but that's kind of rare, I think. A sealing is usually a wedding. It *seals* two people, or a family together so when someone dies, they're still together after death. Instead of standing in front of people with a priest, you go to the temple to a special room and do the same things as a wedding, I guess? I don't know. I've never been to one of those either because you have to be endowed to be able to go. In some cases, if a family adopts a child or their family converts later in life, they'll be sealed when the kids are older.

"If I had married Packer or Brigham, we would have been sealed together on our wedding day, and then any kids we had would have been 'born in the covenant' so we wouldn't have had to be sealed to them because they were born already sealed to us. Does that make sense?"

Wes looks at me like I'm speaking a totally different language, but nods slowly. "Kind of, I guess. So, when we get married, we won't be together after we die?"

My heart flutters when he says *when* we get married. Not *if*. We haven't discussed that far into the future, and I don't want to dwell on that right now, so I put a mental pin in that topic of conversation.

"That's why usual vows say 'as long as you both shall live' or 'till death do you part.' The verbiage in Mormonism says 'for eternity' and that's what makes them different from anyone else. They promise you'll be with your family forever, and who wouldn't want that?"

It's one of the things that kept me in longer than I would have been. When I thought I wanted kids and a husband, I wanted to be worthy of them for eternity, so I did what I was supposed to.

"Thinking about it now, it's a really good manipulation tactic. That's one thing my family will say about me. I won't be with my hypothetical kids for eternity. I'm ruining my parent's 'eternal family.'"

"That's so fucked up. I'm sorry you had to go through that." He pauses, searching my face for something, though I'm not sure what. "Is that... something you still want? To be sealed to someone for eternity?"

I think about it for a second before I answer.

"I honestly don't know what happens when we die," I say carefully, "but I like to think that a true, pure love doesn't end in death. That somehow our spirits will be connected forever."

Wes puts his forehead on mine and stares so intensely into my eyes, I think he can see directly into my soul.

"Our love *will* last forever, Elli. Somehow, out of eight point one billion people, we found each other. Somehow, your heart led you to my little corner of Texas and we ended up on the most awkward first blind date on earth. Our hearts have been intertwined since the minute I saw you walk out of your apartment. And even when our hearts stop beating, they'll still be intertwined."

My eyes fill with tears at his vow, and I believe him with my entire being. If he asked me to marry him right now, I would in a heartbeat because he's right. Our hearts, our souls, they're intertwined. He's embedded himself so deeply into my very being that I don't think I'd be able to get him out.

"I love you so much, Westley Ray Jones."

"I love you too, Elliana Louise Monson."

Our lips, drawn together like magnets, meeting in an unhurried kiss so full of love and passion it takes my breath away.

Wes pulls me on top of him, tangling his fingers into my braided hair and angling me to deepen the kiss, slipping his tongue in my mouth. I can feel him hardening underneath me, but he seems like he's in no hurry to fix his problem.

He pulls back, framing my face with both hands, "Thank you for opening up to me, Elli. Your trust isn't something I take for granted."

"Thank you for letting me be me."

"I wouldn't want you to be anyone else, baby."

"I wouldn't want you to be anyone else either." I whisper, and he answers with a wicked grin.

"No? You wouldn't want to role play, baby?"

"Hmmmm. I don't know. Who would we be role-playing as?"

Wes rolls us until he's hovering over me, his dark hair acting as a curtain around my face, and kisses a path up my neck to my ear where he whispers, "You can be my number one fan. You won a contest for a night with your favorite artist."

A nip to my earlobe.

"You're so *excited* to spend time with me. I get *excited* the minute I see you walk through my dressing room door, because who would have thought the fan that won a night with me would be *so fucking pretty*?" He growls, trailing more kisses along my jawline, down to my chest.

"What would you do?" I whisper, arching my back to offer him access to my breasts.

He doesn't take the bait though, and instead continues his path up the other side of my jaw.

"I would play it cool. We'd chat about music, or you. You'd sit next to me on the couch, acting all shy and timid, but I'd see in your beautiful sapphire eyes just how badly you want me. I'd watch you squeeze these delicious thighs together" he squeezes my right thigh, "to try and get some relief, but it wouldn't be enough, would it?"

I shake my head, already lost in the fantasy.

"No, it wouldn't be enough. I'd subtly scoot closer to you, waiting for the right opportunity to ask you if I can kiss you." He places the quickest kiss on my lips. "Would you say yes, Elli?"

"Yes. Please." I whine, and am rewarded with a drugging kiss, like it really is our first time.

"We'd make out for a minute, and I'd pull you on to my lap so you can *feel* how badly I want you." He slowly grinds his covered cock into my covered pussy, pulling a desperate moan from my throat. "Then, I'd ask if I can see those beautiful tits."

I take initiative and sit up slightly and pull my oversized t-shirt off, grateful I didn't put a bra on today because Wes lets out a groan that can only be described as appreciative, before he takes one in his hand and squeezes it.

"Fuck baby, they're so beautiful. They fit so nicely in my hand. Can I suck on them? Please?"

I almost ask him why he's asking, then I remember we're supposed to be in a fantasy where we haven't done this before, so I nod enthusiastically.

Wes brings his head down and circles my left nipple with the tip of his tongue, before gently biting it. He moves over to the right and does the same thing, all while slowly grinding into me.

"Wes."

"Yeah, baby?" He says around my nipple in his mouth.

"I need more." I plead.

He pulls off my nipple with a *pop*. "Yeah? Does my number one fan need my mouth on her pretty little cunt?"

"Please."

"Well since you asked so nicely." He smirks, then shuffles down until his face is directly in front of my pussy.

He slowly pulls my running shorts and panties down my legs, tossing them somewhere behind him.

"Fuuuck. Your poor pussy's weeping for me baby. Who made her so wet?" He asks, tracing a single finger on the outside of my labia, but never making contact where I need him.

"You did!" I moan.

"Hmmm. That's right. Your favorite artist made this pussy wet. Anyone else make you this wet?"

"No one else. Only you. Please!"

"That's right," he growls and licks me from my asshole to my clit, "only I can make you this wet. This pussy's mine now. Got it?"

"But-but you're on tour-" I say, trying to play into the imaginary scenario. My mind is already jumbled from being so turned on I can't think straight.

He gives my pussy a light slap. "I don't care if I'm on tour. This pussy's mine. Made for my tongue to lick.

Made for my fingers to fuck. Made for my cock to fill up."

I moan, unable to think of anything else to say.

"Say it, Elli. Say you're mine, or I'm going to leave you wet and dripping and you can watch me spill my come onto those tits instead."

"I'm yours, Wes! My pussy, my body, my heart, it's all yours! I need more, please-"

I can't even finish my sentence because Wes dives in and eats my pussy like it holds the answers to the universe.

He licks, sucks, and nibbles my clit and my lips so thoroughly I feel like I'm going to combust if I don't come soon. Just when I'm about to beg for more, he slips his middle and ring finger inside, pumping them at just the right speed that I orgasm instantly, releasing a rush of liquid that he laps up like it's water.

"Fuck yes baby. That was so hot. You gonna let your favorite musician fuck this pussy?"

"Yes, need your cock so bad." I whimper, sitting up to pull his shirt off.

He undoes his belt as I pull off his shirt, and his chin is still glistening with my arousal. I pull him down on top of me and pull his mouth to mine, tasting myself and moaning against him.

"Shit, I don't have a condom." He says, pouting.

Right. Role play.

"I'm clean and on birth control." I say with my best flirtatious smirk.

He rocks his hips and runs his cock through my soaking entrance, the tip nudging my swollen clit.

"That's dangerous for someone famous like me. What if you're trying to trap me with a baby?"

"I would nev-" I begin to protest, but he doesn't let me finish because he pushes himself inside me to the hilt in one motion.

"Guess that's a risk I'll have to take. Fuck me, your pussy fits me like a glove. You really were made for me." He groans, fucking me in slow strokes.

I wrap my legs around his lean waist to urge him to go faster. He takes both of my hands in one of his and pins them above my head, balancing on one hand as he starts to speed up.

"Fuck I don't think I'll ever be able to fuck another pussy again. Guess you're just going to have to come on tour with me." He teases.

"I guess so. Fuck, Wes I'm close." I moan.

"Come for me, baby. Clench that pussy around my cock and come for me." He speeds up, hitting my g-spot with every thrust and then I'm coming. I come so hard my vision goes a little blurry and all I can do is babble his name over and over again.

Wes moans out an extended "Elli" and I feel him pulse inside me as he fills me with his cum.

Once he's caught his breath, he places a gentle kiss on my nose and releases my wrists. He stands, presumably to go to the bathroom to grab something to clean up, but he pauses and looks directly at my vagina.

"What?" I question, sitting up on my elbows.

He rubs his jaw, "I didn't think I had a breeding kink, but watching my cum drip out of you is making me ready for round two."

My eyes widen, "I don't think I want kids, Wes so if that's something you want we need to figure that out-"

"No, no, shh baby, shh. A breeding kink doesn't mean I want to knock you up. It just means I like seeing my cum drip from you. It satiates an animalistic desire to make you mine." He says, easing my worries.

"Oh. Okay. Good. Well, I like feeling you fill me up. So maybe I have one too."

He chuckles while he goes to grab a washcloth to clean me up. Once he's done, he goes back to the bathroom to clean himself up and I get dressed again and sit on the end of the bed.

When he walks back out of the bathroom, he has his boxers on. While he gets dressed himself, he asks, "Was that okay? I wasn't too much, right?"

"No, it was perfect. I didn't think roleplay could be like that, but it was really hot." I say honestly.

"Good. Because I think that's something we'll do again on tour."

"I'd love that."

"Me too. Now let's go eat. Fucking my number one fan took a lot of energy."

CHAPTER 41

Wes

Yesterday, Elli showed me all around her favorite parts of Provo/Orem. She drove me past her alma mater, Utah Valley University and pointed out her favorite lunch and study spots. We drove all around Provo where she showed me her old elementary, middle, and high schools, and where she would hang out with her friends after school.

She took me to Deseret Industries, the Mormon-owned thrift store, and I found a vintage Dolly Parton record from 1973 still in amazing condition. The best part? It was only a dollar!

A DOLLAR!

I also found some sick band t-shirts that were only three bucks each. I can see why the thrift store is so popular, since everything there is so cheap.

She explained that the big white "Y" on the mountain represents Brigham Young University and that it's tradition for freshmen to hike up the mountain and light it up at the beginning of the school year.

Elli told me the story of how a few years back, a group of people, both students and not, hiked up to the Y and lit it up with rainbow lights. BYU apparently freaked out and denied any involvement in the act. They said it was not authorized or sanctioned by the school, and any students involved were punished.

That's some bullshit if you ask me. Who wouldn't want to see the mountain lit

Today is Spencer's farewell. We haven't seen anyone from her family yet, and Elli is buzzing with anxious energy as she gets ready. I haven't seen her in a dress like this, it's much more...modest than what she usually wears.

It's a pale pink dress that goes down to her calves, and the sleeves puff a bit and go all the way to her elbows. It's a V-neck, but a higher v, and has a white polka dot pattern and buttons all the way down the front. She's paired it with brown flats, and has pinned her hair into a bun. She's got on gold hoops, and is currently trying to fasten a necklace around her pretty neck, but her hands are shaking so bad she can't get it to clasp.

"Let me help you, baby." I say gently, standing behind her and taking the necklace from her. I get it fastened, then run my hands down her arms and wrap my arms around her waist from behind. "You look beautiful." I say, making eye contact with her in the mirror.

"Thank you." she sighs, leaning into me. "This is how I used to dress all the time. I haven't put on this dress in months. It's weird. Like I'm playing dress up as someone else."

"I can see how it would feel that way. Are you going to be okay today?"

"Yeah. I'm excited to see my siblings, and hopefully Hannah will be here. We better get going before we're late, my mom will have a fit." She sighs, turning to give me a peck on the cheek.

I'm not satisfied with that, so I pull her back and devour her mouth. I can feel some of the tension leave her as we kiss and it makes me feel like maybe I can actually help her through this.

"Say the word any time today, baby, and I'll get you out of there, okay? I love you."

She nods, then turns to walk away. I give that juicy ass a spank and she yelps in surprise but I'm not sorry.

"C'mon baby. We're going to be late." I tease and she rolls her eyes at me.

I can't even count how many identical churches we've passed in the ten minute drive from the hotel, but every time I thought we had arrived, she just drove right past our destination.

When we park, I watch men in suits and women in dresses enter into the red brick buildings, and I glance down at my black chinos and gray button up and feel a little underdressed.

"Elli? Am I underdressed? Everyone here looks like they're going to a job interview or a funeral."

Elli chuckles and shakes her head. "No babe. You're dressed just fine. Besides, it won't be your clothes that draw attention."

I roll my eyes this time. I can see how a tattooed, pierced, long-haired guy would stand out in this crowd. Not like I haven't stood out my whole life, but here, it's *very* obvious.

We walk into a lobby type area and Elli leads me through big double doors into a room filled with benches and uncomfortable looking metal chairs. I see they've opened up an accordion door type thing and filled what looks to be a big gym area with the chairs.

Up in front, where all the benches are facing, there's a big podium with a microphone, a row of benches, an organ, and a piano. Behind those, are more chairs that look like a choir should be sitting there.

Huh, maybe the music'll be good.

Off to the side of the podium is a table covered in a white cloth that looks suspiciously like a body is laying underneath the sheets.

"Um, Elli?" I whisper in her ear.

"Hm?"

"Why does it look like there's a body up there?" I subtly tilt my head towards the table so as not to draw attention.

"Oh, that's the sacrament. It purposefully looks like a body so you can imagine it's the body of Christ."

I don't even know what to say to that so I just nod in agreement.

All the walls in this room are white. Now that I think about it, all the walls in the lobby area are white, too. Except for the bottom half, which is covered in rough looking carpet type material. Even the benches are covered in carpet.

Carpet floors. Carpet benches. Carpet walls.

Interesting design choice.

Elli leads me to one of the side benches where a blonde woman and a bald man are standing with a younger guy in a suit. The woman turns around and I recognize her instantly from Elli's instagram as Louise Monson.

Elli's mom.

The young man in the suit sees Elli first and gives her a head nod, like he's too good to talk to her. That must be Spencer. I can see the resemblance. He has the same dark hair, same nose shape, and the same blue eyes, though his are duller than Elli's.

Elli's mom and dad turn around to see who Spencer is acknowledging and their eyes immediately lock onto our interlocked hands. I watch Louise's face morph from one of disgust to politely impassive in a way that has to be practiced.

"Elliana. So glad you could make it." She says with a fake smile, pulling Elli into a stiff, awkward hug.

"Good to see you, Elli." Her dad says, patting her heartily on the back. "You must be Wes. I'm Kent."

I take his outstretched hand, shaking it firmly. "Nice to meet you Mr. Monson. You as well Mrs. Monson." After I let go of Kent's hand, I offer my hand to Louise and she looks at it like I'm going to give her a disease.

Eventually she takes it lightly in her hand and shakes it once, muttering a "You too."

Louise turns back to Elli and gestures towards three big benches, "We've saved these three benches for the family. Sit on the end of this one." It's not a request, but a demand. I'm immediately in defense mode, ready to defend my lady.

"Sure." Elli tugs me along and lets me sit on the outer edge. She sits beside me, her knee bouncing anxiously.

I place a hand on her knee and rub little circles, hoping to soothe her, but she only offers me a polite, forced smile in return.

Ten minutes later, our bench is filled with people. Izzy was able to sneak over to sit by us before her mom got upset, and that's given me a bit of comfort to know Elli won't be sitting by someone who's going to be rude.

I've been introduced as Elli's boyfriend to seven aunts, six uncles, and at least ten cousins. But those are just the ones who have come to say hi to Elli. She really wasn't lying about having a big family. They've given me looks that range from disgust and fear, to curiosity.

Just as the organ starts to play a soft melody, Elli nudges my arm. "There's Hannah," She nods toward a woman two rows behind us," she's in the black dress and has blonde hair. We'll have to go say hi after."

"Sounds good, baby." I reply.

A middle-aged white man with a bald head stands at the podium and introduces himself as Brother Casey, the first counselor of the ward welcoming all the visitors. His eyes snag on me and he visibly flinches before he continues and avoids looking in my direction the rest of the time.

I lean over to Elli and whisper, "Who's brother is he? Are the three white men up there all related?"

Elli covers her mouth to hide her laughter, and leans over to say, "No, that's how they refer to people who don't have higher titles. Like, I was Sister Monson when I was called on."

Brother Casey gives the agenda for the meeting, and then everyone opens the green books scattered throughout. Elli and Izzy share one, and I lean over to read the chords and the lyrics.

They're singing an upbeat hymn called *Called to Serve*. I assume it has something to do with missions. It honestly sounds a bit like a battle song. The congregation, as they call it, overpowers the organ in sound as people shout the hymn.

Immediately after the song ends, a petite blonde woman who looks to be about twenty-seven, holding an infant on her hip, steps up to the podium and offers what they call an opening prayer.

I lean over and whisper in Elli's ear, "Is it a rule you have to be blonde?"

Elli just shakes her head and tries to contain her laughter again.

Once the woman is done praying, the brother dude gets up again and calls a bunch of names and gives them jobs like "relief society second counselor" or "elder's quorum president." I make a mental note to ask Elli what those mean later.

When he concludes his business, there's another song. This one is monotone and boring, titled *As Now We Take the Sacrament*.

As the people sing, I watch the three young boys around Luke's age sitting at the table that looks like it has a body on it, unfold some of the sheets and begin... tearing up bread? I can't fully see from here, but that's what it looks like.

When the song is done, one of the boys disappears behind the table and a voice begins reading a prayer that talks about the bread being the body of Jesus.

Okay so that's really fucking weird.

But then again, Catholics do something similar, right?

Then a parade of eight boys go up to the three sitting at the bench, take a tray of bread from them, then begin passing it out. One stands at one end of a bench, one at the other, and they trade off directions of the bread passing.

I watch the tray come down our row, and I lean into Elli and ask, "Am I supposed to eat the bread?"

She subtly shakes her head no, and murmurs "We aren't allowed to."

It must be because we aren't "worthy," like she was talking about earlier.

Imagine, not being worthy to eat *bread.*

I grab the tray when Elli passes it to me and hand it over with a smile. The kid looks at the tattoos showing on my forearms and snatches the tray up and steps away quickly.

Once everyone has had the bread, the boys sit back down, another guy disappears behind the table, and he reads another prayer that's essentially the same, but talks about the water being the blood of Jesus.

What the hell kind of sick shit is this?

When they start the passing of the water the same way they did the bread, I lean over to Elli. "I thought his blood was supposed to be wine."

"That's the Catholics."

"Seems like they're doing it better, then." I mutter, and Izzy must've overheard because I see her shoulders shaking with laughter. I look over and catch Louise's eye and if looks could kill, I'd be dead right now.

I pass along the water tray, which honestly just looks like little shot glasses of vodka, and the kid scurries along.

Once everyone's got the water, the boys sit back down and then Brother Casey comes back to announce the speakers. They're sitting up on a row of seats in front of the piano.

The first speaker looks to be an eight year old child who gives a short talk about how one time she was really sick with a fever, but her daddy gave her a blessing and it broke a few hours later and she was all better.

It was cute, but from a logical standpoint, the fever broke by itself. It wasn't because of the blessing.

The next speaker is a (shocker) blonde lady who says she was asked to talk about faith. She gives definitions of faith and examples from their scriptures, and then gives examples from her personal life. She tells a story about how she was pregnant with her *sixth* child and there were so many complications during the birth that no one was sure either of them were going to make it. How she had "faith" in the blessing her husband gave her, and even though she couldn't have any more kids because of how badly that birth went, she was grateful for God in saving her and her baby's life.

This is what I don't get. *Obviously,* I'm glad that she and her baby are alive. But giving credit to some invisible being rather than the doctors and nurses who probably busted their asses to save her and her baby? That's fucked up.

Her husband is the third speaker, and he talks about how he had faith he would get his wife to say "yes" to a date with him. He asked her *four* times and she kept turning him down. He says he's grateful God was able to help her see that they were obviously meant to be.

That sounds a lot like her just being tired of his persistence, but whatever.

Spencer's the last speaker. He talks about how he's going to need faith to get through two years in a country where he doesn't speak the language, and he doesn't know anyone. He talks about how there's been a big change happening in his family and he has faith that if he keeps doing what he's "supposed" to be doing, his family will be together forever.

I feel Elli tense when he talks about their family. I assume he's talking about her leaving the church, and it breaks my heart for both of them. My heart breaks for Elli because she shouldn't be ridiculed for trying to find her own happiness. My heart breaks for Spencer because he shouldn't feel like he's the one that has to "be good" in order to bring Elli back.

There's yet *another* song when Spencer's done, this one is about loving to see the temples. It's not in their green book, everyone just either has it memorized or they read it off the program given out in the beginning. The song, if you listen to the lyrics, is creepy as hell with everyone singing it like this.

There's *another* prayer after the song, but this time by another middle aged white man with thick graying hair.

When he's done, the congregation murmurs and rises, and Elli pulls me out the door quickly and to her car, ignoring the people trying to get her attention.

As soon as we're in the car, I see the tears threatening to spill over her lashes. I cup her face and pull her into my chest as best as I can, and I let her sob.

"What can I do, baby? How can I make it better?" I ask, my thumb wiping away tears as fast as they can.

"Let's just," she hiccups, "get this luncheon over with so we can be alone. Okay? I just need you by my side today."

"You've got me baby. I promise. I'm right here."

We wait another beat until most of her tears are gone, then she pulls the mirror down and blots at her eyes.

"Okay. Let's get to my mom's house." she sighs.

"Tell me the directions." I say, buckling my seatbelt and pulling out of the parking lot. "And while we drive you can explain what the hell a relief society and elders quorum is. *And* why do all the women look the same? And please explain why the fuck the sacrament cups look like little shot glasses?! I thought we were at a rager getting tequila shots!"

My questions do the trick in making her laugh, the sound soothing my anxious nerves.

The drive doesn't take long, so she only gets to explain that the Mormon gene pool is pretty small because everyone marries other Mormons, so a lot of them look similar.

"Well I'm glad to see you don't look like a carbon copy of everyone there."

"Thanks Wes. And thank you for coming, again. Are you ready for this crazy shitshow?"

"Baby, I was born ready. Let's do this thing." I say getting out of the car, rounding to her side, and opening it for her.

I pull her into me for a tight hug before I give her a rated-PG kiss that will hopefully calm her nerves.

"I needed that." She whispers.

"Me too."

CHAPTER 42

Elli

I didn't think that being in a church and having to sit
through a sacrament meeting would be so hard, but
it was.

The only saving grace was Wes's confused questioning, which made me see things in a different light.

Sacrament meeting is fucking weird.

I was doing relatively okay, then Spencer started talking about the "trials" our family was going through, and
I knew he was talking about me and Izzy. Izzy looked
like she was about to stand and leave when he brought it
up. I had clasped her hand to remind her she's not alone.
He's not talking *just* about her. Though I'm sure she's
received many lectures from both him and our mother
lately.

I couldn't be in there any longer, so as soon as the
"amen" was uttered, we were gone.

Now, walking up the walkway of my childhood home,
I feel like I'm going to throw up.

The yellow painted, two story farmhouse hasn't
changed much in the last three months, let alone the

last three years. The front door is still a bright teal that matches the curtains in the front room window. The porch covers the whole front of the house, save for the garage, and above the porch are three windows.

We walk inside and I instruct Wes to remove his shoes. He's not wearing his usual combat boots or Vans today, and it's throwing me off. He has on actual dress shoes, and it's honestly really hot to see him all dressed up.

To our right is the front room which houses a leather couch, a "hot chocolate table" as my family calls it, since Mormons don't drink coffee, and two leather wingback chairs. This is where we would have family meetings, family scripture study, and where the family's assigned visitors from the church would chat with us.

Down the hall we step into the open concept, eat-in kitchen, and the family room. The family room opens right up into the kitchen so there's enough space to host big family gatherings like the one happening today. There's a kitchen island that's currently housing three crock pots full of food for the luncheon.

My mom insisted on having a bright white kitchen, even with so many kids. The cabinets are white with stainless steel hardware, there's stainless steel appliances, and the countertops are white and gray granite.

I personally don't think it matches the exterior of the house, but I no longer live here so it's no longer a relevant opinion.

The living room and kitchen is all light gray oak hardwood flooring.

Wes whistles when he sees the kitchen for the first time. "Dang Elli, this place is nice."

I'm about to protest and say it's not *that* nice, as I've been taught to do, but I just give him a small smile and say, "Thanks. I wish I could take credit for it, but my mother has full ownership over every decoration and design in this house."

"She sure takes the phrase 'go big or go home' seriously."

"You could say that. If you want to have a seat, I'm going to make sure the veggies are already cut."

"No way I'm leaving your side, baby. I'll help." Wes says, heading to the big basin sink to wash his hands.

I stand there and blink, a little taken aback by his willingness to help, though it shouldn't surprise me anymore. I'm just so used to seeing my uncles and father sitting back and letting the women do the work.

After Wes washes his hands, I wash mine, and I rummage through the fridge to find the fresh vegetables for the relish tray.

In a normal situation, I wouldn't have just come into my mother's house and started cutting up random shit I found in the fridge, but I already know as soon as they get here, she's going to be barking orders at me to help her get stuff ready.

There *is* a chance she'll be pissed that I already got started, but this isn't my first rodeo. The same things happen at every farewell luncheon, every baptism luncheon, every homecoming luncheon.

You get the idea.

The base of the luncheon is pulled pork sandwiches, a relish tray, chips, some type of Jell-O salad, and then cookies. It looks like there's probably some little smokie sausages in one crock pot, and the pulled pork is in the other two. Someone's already dropped off a rainbow Jell-O salad, and there's fresh fruit on a tray with a yogurt dipping sauce sitting in the fridge.

As Wes and I cut vegetables, he asks me more questions about sacrament meeting. I try to explain as best as I can, but I've been trying not to use the cookie cutter answers I've been taught my whole life to give.

So when Wes asks me why there were so many prayers, I explain that Mormons believe to start a meeting and feel the spirit, you need to say a prayer. Each part of the sacrament gets its own prayer, and then to close out the meeting and kind of "cement" the spiritual feelings from the speakers, you have to have a closing prayer. But the closing prayer *cannot* be said by a woman for some reason.

"I noticed that there was hardly any woman participation. Is that normal?" He questions.

"Oh, yeah. Women aren't allowed to have the priesthood, and only priesthood holders can do the blessing of the sacrament or hold a position in the bishopric."

"So the literal children passing the sacrament have the priesthood?"

"Yep." I say, shrugging. "When boys are twelve, they get the Aaronic priesthood and are ordained as a 'Deacon'. At fourteen they become 'Teachers' and at sixteen they become 'Priests.' Before you can go through the temple as a man, you have to get the Melchizedek priesthood. Melchizedek priesthood also allows them to bless babies and baptize others. If they get called to be bishop, or have a high position in the church they become a High Priest."

"That's definitely some cult shit, Elli."

I can't help but laugh at that. He's totally right, it does sound like a cult. I'm about to respond when the garage door opens and my mom bustles in, tossing her church bag on the counter. My dad and siblings follow in after and Izzy immediately goes to wash her hands. She looks like she's just barely stopped crying and I'm itching to go talk to her.

Spencer, Gideon, and Issac plop down on the couch and start scrolling on their phones and Wes looks at me with a puzzled expression. I subtly shake my head, because if he says anything about it my mom will chew his head clean off his body.

"Elli chop vegetables." My mom barks.

"Already done, covered, and put back in the fridge." I say mildly. "What else can I do?"

My mom stomps over to the fridge to make sure I cut them properly, but she must notice that the pickles are missing because she snaps, "You forgot the pickles!"

"I looked in the pantry and the fridge and there weren't any." I say as calmly as I can.

"Shelly's bringing them."

"Then I'll cut them when Shelly's here." I say, barely containing my eye roll. How am I supposed to cut imaginary pickles?

There really isn't much else to do until more people show up, so I silently back up so I'm out of her way so she can bang around the kitchen angrily. I bump into a warm body and I already know it's Wes.

He places a hand on my hip and squeezes gently, assuring me he's got me.

"Gid, Issac, Spence. This is my boyfriend Wes. Wes, this is Spencer, Gideon, and Issac."

"Nice to meet you fellas." Wes says politely, but none of them even spare him a second glance.

I look at Wes and mouth *I'm sorry* because my brothers are fucking rude. Wes just shakes his head and mouths *all good.*

Izzy rushes past me, sniffling and heads to her room and Wes nudges me to follow her. I don't want to leave him alone, so I drag him down the hall and up the stairs with me.

The door to my old bedroom is slightly ajar, and I hear Izzy sniffling harder as I approach. I knock lightly before pushing open the door to find her on the floor with her knees brought up to her chest and her head resting on her arms.

"Iz, what's going on?" I whisper, letting go of Wes's hand and sitting next to my sister.

Wes waits in the doorway, taking in everything about the space. Izzy's completely taken over the space as her own in the last few months, you'd hardly even know I used to live here. Her hot pink blankets are all thrown around the room, clothes are littering the floor, the desk she uses as a vanity is covered in beauty products and hair styling tools.

"She-she just said something that hurt my feelings. That's all. I'm exhausted from theater camp this week, and I'm just overly emotional." Izzy says, swatting at the tears falling down and streaking her meticulously applied contour.

Wes steps over to the desk, grabs a box of tissues, and hands it to me silently and I mouth *thank you,* and get a wink in return.

"What did she say?" I ask, hoping Izzy will open up about it. I don't want her to go through this alone.

"She told me she wishes I was a boy. Her sons haven't broken her heart and torn apart the family like her 'spoiled' daughters have." Izzy uses air quotes around the word spoiled, because we both know we aren't.

My heart aches for Izzy. I wish I could do something about it. I can't say anything to my mom, or I risk her taking out her anger on Izzy when I leave. I can't steal Izzy away, as much as I want to.

"I'm so sorry Iz. That was really unfair of her to say." I say, rubbing up and down her arm.

Izzy sighs, then looks over to me. "I wish you didn't have such a cool life so I could just come live with you the rest of the school year. I know it's only a year until I'm gone, but I don't want to walk on eggshells around her."

"I don't blame you. I wish there was a way I could help. Why did you tell mom you wanted to leave the church knowing you had to stay with her for another year?"

"She was trying to talk me into getting my patriarchal blessing. I didn't want to go see that old geezer and have him put his hands on my head for that long so I said no. She wanted a good reason why I wouldn't do it, so I told her I no longer believe that the church is true. She was *livid* Els. I have never seen her so angry. So she asked if it had anything to do with our little trip to Texas, if *you* influenced me to leave, and I told her no, I swear. I told her you wouldn't say anything about the church to me, just that you were done with it. I guess she thinks I'll just blindly follow you. But I did my own research, I swear. I spent an entire night going down a rabbit hole on TikTok and checking the facts."

"I believe you Iz. I know how overwhelming all the information can be. I'm sorry you've had to go through this alone. If I'd been here, or stayed close by-"

"No." Izzy cuts me off. "I have watched you *flourish* in Texas, Els. I've never seen you as happy as you are there, especially now that you have a hunk of man meat on your arm."

"Don't make me tell Luke you said that." Wes teases with a wink.

"Oh please." Izzy rolls her eyes. "He knows you're hot. But he also knows my love and loyalty are his. Anyway, I don't want you to blame yourself. I should have just kept my mouth shut and gone through the motions until I moved out. That's on me. All I need from you is someone to call and cry to on occasion."

"You've got me, baby sis. I promise. I'll answer whenever I can." I pull her into a hug, just as we hear the front door open and a million different chattering voices fill the living room. "Alright. Now it's time to put on our fake smiles and get through this luncheon. I need your help keeping the aunts away from Wes."

"You've got it, boss. Operation keep Wes sane is a go." Izzy salutes me, and we both break out in a fit of giggles.

CHAPTER 43

Wes

When we walk downstairs after Izzy and Elli's heart-to-heart, it looks like the entirety of the congregation is packed into the living room. Izzy's down the stairs first, followed by Elli, and then me, and Elli freezes at the bottom so I end up bumping into her back.

She turns to me with her eyes as wide as saucers. "Oh my god," she whispers. "Packer and his wife are here. She's the blonde in the blue dress who is *obviously* pregnant."

I glance around and spot a guy around our age with brown hair expertly gelled in the front, a clean shaven face, and a snazzy gray suit with his arm around a younger blonde in a blue maxi dress with a baby bump.

Damn, she looks like she's Izzy's age. But from what Elli told me, Packer's bride is only a year older than Izzy so that makes sense.

"Why would he be here?" I ask.

"My mother." Elli seethes. "She must get a kick out of making me miserable." Elli takes a deep breath, then when she releases it, she plasters on a fake smile. "Let's get this over with."

She grabs my hand and we slowly make our way to the edge of the room and grab empty chairs by the back door. The girl Elli pointed out at the church- Hannah, I think- sits down next to Elli and they hug.

"Hannah, this is my boyfriend Wes. Wes, this is my cousin Hannah." Elli says, now with a genuine smile.

I stick my hand out to Hannah, who's looking a little confused, but she grabs it anyway and says, "Nice to meet you. So, um, how did you guys meet?"

I smile, "Izzy's boyfriend is like a little brother to me, and he asked me to go on a blind date with Elli so he and Izzy could go on a date. I knew after that date I wanted her. It took us a minute to get the timing right, but now we're here."

"That's beautiful." Hannah says, looking a little melancholy about it.

"Izzy told me you were living with your parents again..." Elli says carefully. "If you don't want to talk about what happened with Liam, totally understandable. Just know I'm here, and I won't judge you."

Hannah gives Elli an appreciative smile, then looks around to see if anyone is listening to our conversation. "We're in the process of a divorce. I had a few miscarriages and he said he realized he didn't want kids. Which is fine, but I thought we were on the same page, you know? He also told me he... wasn't attracted to me anymore. He said he misses the way my body looked when we first got married."

What a fucking asshat!

I am totally devoted to Elli, but I can appreciate that Hannah is beautiful. She's curvy, like her cousin, has stunning hazel eyes and naturally pouty lips. Her hair is long and golden blonde, and she seems extremely sweet.

"Well, Hannah, I don't know your ex but I'd guess he was an absolute idiot. You are beautiful, and anyone who can't see that is probably looking through distorted glasses." I say quietly so only she and Elli can hear.

Hannah blushes, "Thanks, Wes. That's nice of you to say."

Elli places a hand on Hannah's knee, "Wes doesn't say things just to say things. He truly means what he says, and he's right. Liam is an idiot. Of course your body doesn't look the same as it did when you were eighteen! It's been eight years. Your body is going to change and that's okay. I'm sorry about the miscarriages. That must have been awful."

Eighteen?! That's so young!

"Thanks Elli. I'm glad you've found someone like Wes." Hannah looks at me, "You seem like a really great guy. Treat my cousin right, okay?"

I squeeze Elli's shoulder, "I plan on it."

Elli looks at me with a beaming smile, and looks like she's about to say something when a loud whistle comes from the center of the room.

"Alright," Elli's dad starts, "thank you all for coming to see Spencer off. We're so proud of him and his decision to serve the Lord. The food is ready to be eaten, so we're going to have a blessing before we line up and dig in." Then he bows his head, as does everyone else, and says *another* prayer.

Once the "amen" is mumbled by everyone else in the room, all the moms line up with their kids and get them settled with food, and then everyone else joins in.

Once Elli and I have gotten our food, Elli leads me out the back door and to the backyard patio where there are a few tables and chairs set up. Hannah follows us out and joins us at a table and we chat about our lives while we eat.

"Have you heard anything from Emma lately?" Elli asks Hannah during a lull in the conversation.

Hannah nods, "Yeah, we text every so often. She called me when she saw me change my name back on Facebook and we talked for a while. She's thriving in California. She's got a bunch of tattoos, even pierced her nose. I'm happy for her. I know her mom is *pissed* that she hasn't made an effort to come home, but who can blame her? With the way her family treated her? I wouldn't want to come home either."

Elli turns to me, "Emma's older brother died by suicide seven years ago, and after that, a lot of her siblings started treating her like she was a nuisance instead of part of the family. She ended up moving out to California with her best friend Jordan and their family."

I nod, almost positive there's more to that story, but I won't be asking about it right now.

Hannah perks up and leans over the table conspiratorially, "Did you hear that Uncle John and Aunt Pam sold their house and moved to a farm outside of Independence?"

"Missouri?" Elli clarifies.

Hannah nods. "Yeah. According to my mom, they've joined a different sect of Mormonism and John's like *super* important in the organization."

Elli gapes at Hannah's gossip, "No shit." She winces, "Sorry."

Hannah waves her off, "No worries. It's not like I haven't heard worse."

"Why did they move all the way to Missouri?" I interject.

"Oh, that's where Mormons believe the Garden of Eden is." Elli explains.

"Are you serious? They think that it was in *Independence, Missouri*? Why would it be there?

Elli and Hannah shrug in unison.

"All I know is that a lot of people are moving there because they think the Second Coming is happening soon and that's apparently the place to be when it happens." Hannah explains.

"Someone should warn the residents of the city." Elli says, making Hannah and I laugh.

"What's so funny over here?" Someone asks, and I look up to see a middle aged couple. The woman looks similar to Elli's dad, Kent. They have similar nose shapes and similar eyes. This must be one of his many sisters-her family tree is bigger than a live oak. Next to her is a tall gangly man with only a thin ring of gray hair around his otherwise bald head.

"Hey Aunt Shelly, Uncle Mitch." Elli says. "This is my boyfriend, Wes. Wes, these are Hannah's parents, Shelly and Mitch."

"Nice to meet you, sir, ma'am." I say politely with a head nod, since I'm too far away to shake hands.

"What on earth would make you want to pierce your nose?" Mitch asks me, glaring at the offending piercing.

"Dad!" Hannah chastises, looking embarrassed.

"No, it's okay Hannah. It was an impulsive decision I made as an eighteen year old, and I've just never taken it out."

Mitch grunts in response, then sits down on one side of Hannah and Shelly sits on the other side.

"Did your tattoos hurt?" Shelly asks, delicately slicing a piece of strawberry with her fork.

"The ones on my ribs hurt much worse than the ones on my arms." I say honestly.

Shelly's eyes widen, then she just nods and continues to pick at her food.

"What do you do for a living? I can't imagine many jobs would want to hire someone who looks like you." Mitch says bluntly.

"Dad! Please! That was so rude!" Hannah whisper-yells.

I grin, liking that Hannah feels the need to stick up for me. "I'm actually a music teacher at a private school. They don't care about the tattoos as long as there's no gang, drug, or alcohol paraphernalia, or any naked bodies visible."

"Wes is also a talented musician. He actually just got offered a spot on tour with a popular band." Elli chimes in, and my heart grows three sizes at the pride in her voice.

"Well, isn't that lovely." Shelly says.

"That's super cool, Wes. Which band?" Hannah asks.

"Keely and the Kissers."

"Oh! I love them! I saw they were going on tour, and I was thinking about buying tickets since they'll be stopping in Salt Lake. Now I'll for sure have to come!" Hannah says excitedly.

"I'll see what I can do about getting you free tickets. You're family, after all."

"That would be amazing." Hannah turns to Elli, "If he's stopping in San Diego, make sure to tell Emma. I'm sure she'd love to come see him perform. Maybe you can fly out and see the show with her!"

Elli looks a little sheepish as she replies, "I'm actually going to be joining him on the tour. My job allows me to work from anywhere, so I'm going to follow him around and be his own personal groupie. So I'll be at the show in Salt Lake and be able to keep you company."

"Elliana," Shelly gasps, "a musical tour is no place for a young lady. What does your mother think about this?"

"Mom doesn't know yet. And I'm an adult who can make my own decision, Aunt Shelly. I don't need anyone's permission." Elli looks to the back door. "It looks like Izzy needs some help with something. Come help, Wes?"

I nod, then look at Shelly and Mitch. "It was nice to meet you two. Hannah, I'm looking forward to getting to know you better."

Hannah offers me a small, apologetic smile and a nod while her parents glare at me disapprovingly.

Elli leads me into the house, Izzy nowhere to be found, and takes me back up the stairs to Izzy's bedroom. I got a good look at it when we were here earlier, but I didn't get much of a chance to ask questions about things.

Elli doesn't close the door, which must be a habit from her childhood, but plops down on the bed and groans.

"I'm so sorry, Wes. I thought Shelly of all people would be cool around you. She's always seemed the least crazy. Guess I was wrong."

"It's okay baby, nothing I couldn't handle." I pause to look at some pictures on the wall, "This was your room too, right?" I ask.

"Yeah, why?"

"There doesn't seem to be much *you* in here. It seems mostly Izzy."

"Well, you've met Izzy. She's got a big personality." Elli sighs, coming to stand next to me and look at the pictures. "I never really had anything other than these pictures of my siblings and I. I used to keep everything important to me under my bed, and even then, it wasn't a lot of things."

I hum in acknowledgement.

"Elliana!" Elli's mom's voice cuts through the silence from down the hall. "I need your help cutting the cake!"

Elli huffs and rolls her eyes. "Coming, Mom." Then she says quietly, "Come on. One more hour and then we can go back to the hotel, okay? I need to get out of this dress ASAP."

"I can definitely help you out with that." I purr in her ear and watch as a shiver runs down her spine.

"I don't doubt it." She trails a hand down my chest seductively, then leads me out of the room and back to the kitchen.

I stand out of the way while Elli helps Louise cut a big chocolate cake. Louise complains that Elli's cutting the pieces too big, then too small when Elli tries to correct the error and I'm half a second from stepping in.

"Elli, go get the ice cream from the garage." Louise barks.

"I've got it." I say, already headed to the door.

"No-" Louise starts, but gets distracted by someone else coming to talk to her.

I walk through the kitchen to the garage and decide which of the *three* freezers to check first. The first one doesn't have the ice cream, so I open the second and find a big gallon container of vanilla.

Bingo.

CHAPTER 44

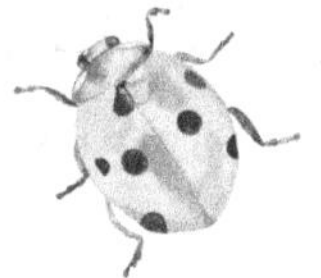

Elli

I go to follow Wes out into the garage because he's going to have to look through all three freezers to find the ice cream, and I don't want him to be gone that long. My mom's being extra bitchy today because of the stress of the luncheon, and I just want to get out of her.

"Elli, I need you to go get the extra plastic spoons from the storage closet." Mom instructs and I sigh and turn the opposite way to go to the storage closet down the hall by the bathroom.

Why she keeps them here instead of in the garage like a normal person, I'll never know.

I can hear footsteps following behind me, and I assume it's just someone wanting to use the restroom, so I step out of the way quickly, but the body follows me. I turn around and see Packer looking smugly at me, and I resist the urge to punch him in his face.

"What are you even doing here, Packer?" I ask, rummaging through the boxes of plastic utensils. *Where are the damn spoons?!*

"Your mom invited me. Said she wanted my opinion on your new boyfriend. She's concerned about you, Elli. And so am I." He *almost* sounds sincere.

I finally find the box of spoons and rip it from the closet, turning to face my ex. "Your opinion of Wes means about as much to me as a bug on the bottom of a shoe. You lost the right to be concerned when you broke up with me."

"Come on, Elli. You know as well as I do we never would have worked out in the long run. You would have hated to be a stay at home mom, and that's what I wanted. Besides, when she turned eighteen and messaged me that she was moving here for school, I knew she was who I was meant to be with. When you know you know."

"So you wasted both of our time knowing I wasn't what you wanted? Was I just a place holder or something?" I want to scream.

Packer shrugs, "Well, yeah. I guess. Tiff *wants* to stay home and raise our kids. She's more... open to criticism too. Plus, she's not too bad on the eyes, am I right? She'll bounce back fast from having the baby." He nudges my shoulder, like I'm in on the joke.

I swear to god I'm going to puke. "That... is disgusting. I'm so glad your child bride makes you happy. Thank goodness I'm not stuck with a pig like you."

"She's nineteen! Not a child." He defends.

"She still has *teen* in her age, Packer. That's weird."

He scoffs, "Well at least she's pleasing to look at. Not some freak covered in tattoos and piercings like your *boyfriend*." He uses a mocking tone when he says "boyfriend," and any patience I may have had evaporates.

"I'm not doing this with you. Best of luck with your teen wife. Goodbye, Packer." I say as I walk away. I can't deal with him right now, or ever. I can't believe I *ever* thought about marrying him.

What a dodged bullet.

I take the spoons back to my mom, and look around for Wes, who's currently talking to one of my little cousins, Kamber. She's five, and looks like she's asking him about his tattoos. I see her parents are watching him like at any minute he's going to pull out a tattoo gun and put an "I heart mom" tattoo on her arm.

But Wes looks like a big cuddly dog with her, smiling and nodding, answering all of her questions enthusiastically. Kamber pets his hair and then pets hers, showing off her braid. She asks him something and he nods enthusiastically and sits directly on the floor. Kamber goes to stand behind him and starts to braid his hair, though not very well.

I walk over and squat down to her level. "Whatcha doin' Kamber?"

"Bwaiding Wes's hair." She says seriously, her tongue poking out in concentration.

"It looks really good, have you been practicing?" I ask.

"Yes. Mommy lets me pwactice on her hair sometimes. I'm still wowking on it." She turns her big brown eyes on me and asks, "Can you bwaid?"

"I sure can. I braid my hair all the time. Would you like some help?"

"Yes!"

"Okay. Why don't you go ask Izzy for a hair tie and I'll get started on this."

She nods and jumps up, running over to Izzy and asking for a hair tie.

When she comes back, I'm already halfway done. I've played with Wes's hair before, but I'm always amazed at how soft and thick it is. Kamber asks if she can put the hair tie in at the end, and I say yes.

"Wow Elli. You're weally good at bwaiding!"

"Do you think I look as pretty as you do, Kamber?" Wes asks.

Kamber giggles, "Boys can't look pwetty. They look handsome."

"I think anyone can look pretty. Besides, I have such looong hair, I think the only way to describe it is pretty!" Wes says, flipping the braid over his shoulder.

"Then yes. You look pwetty."

"Thank you, Kamber."

"Okay, Kamber. It's time to go potty so we can go home." Her mom, Katelynn, says with a forced smile to me and Wes.

"Bye Elli! Bye Wes! Thanks fow letting me play with your hair!" Kamber waves at us as she says goodbye. We hear her tell her mom that she wants tattoos like Wes when she's older, but she wants pink ones.

Oops. Sorry, not sorry, Katelynn.

"You okay?" I whisper to Wes after I help him stand from the floor.

"Yeah, are you?"

"I had a run in with Packer, but I'll tell you about that in a minute. Let's go say goodbye then we can go back to the hotel."

"Okay, my love." The term of endearment soothes my frayed nerves and makes me feel all warm and gooey inside.

We make our rounds of awkward goodbyes, leaving only my mom and brother.

Mom pulls me in for a fake hug, but whispers "I expect you and Wes over for dinner tomorrow so we can get to know him properly."

I nod, "Okay. We'll see you at four."

She nods, then goes back to chatting with someone else.

I walk over to Spence and give him an awkward smile, "I'm headed out. But we'll be here for dinner tomorrow so we'll see you then."

"Sounds good. Bye." He says coldly, not bothering to even hug me.

Ouch.

I grab Wes's hand, we put on our shoes, and then we head to my car. As soon as we pull away from the curb, Wes's hand is on my thigh, squeezing gently. I know he's waiting for me to tell him what happened with Packer.

"Packer cornered me in the hallway at my mom's while you were getting ice cream." I sigh, still disgusted by what he told me.

"He didn't hurt you, did he?" Wes asks.

"No, not at all. He just said he was 'concerned' about me. I guess my mom invited him to 'scope' you out, which is fucking weird. But then he told me that we wouldn't have worked out because I wasn't a 'trainable' wife."

"Ew. What the fuck? Is he serious?"

"Unfortunately. He also implied that I was too fat to bounce back from having a baby. It was all just very gross and misogynistic. I feel bad for Tiffany, to be quite honest. But I'm *so* glad I didn't marry him."

"Poor Tiffany. Poor *you* for dealing with him for six months. And fuck him for implying anything about your body. Your body is so fucking beautiful, if I were a sculptor I'd never stop sculpting you. Your body would live in museums forever."

"That was very poetic, and very sweet, Wes. Thank you. You make me feel good in my body."

Wes grabs my hand and brings the back to his lips and gives it a tender kiss, making butterflies erupt in my stomach.

God, will this man ever stop having that effect on me? Probably not.

"My mom also expects us to go over for dinner tomorrow. I'm sorry, I can tell her 'no' if you want, but she literally demanded it from me."

"Nah, it's okay. Free food is free food, right? I'll be fine. How bad can it be?"

Yeah, how bad can it be?

CHAPTER 45

Wes

We spend the morning and early afternoon of the next day in the hotel room, since Elli has to get some work done.

She stops working at three so she can get ready to go, stating she can't show up to her parents' house in booty shorts and a tank top.

I think she looks hot as fuck, but I also see where she's coming from.

She changes into some denim overalls with a cropped black t-shirt underneath, so the sides of her belly show when she raises her arms. Her hair is down in waves from the braid she's had it in all night, and she slips on some flip flops.

God, she's so pretty.

I'm in some gray chino shorts and a plain black t-shirt. I slip on my Vans and then we're headed out to what I'm sure will be an interesting dinner.

When we get there, Louise is bustling around the kitchen while Kent sits in the recliner, typing away on his laptop. The twins' shouts can be heard from their rooms and it sounds like they're playing some type of video game. Izzy and Spencer are nowhere to be found, but I'm sure they'll make an appearance eventually.

"Hi dad." Elli says as she walks past her dad, and Kent looks up from his laptop and gives her a wave.

"Hey mom, how can I help?" Elli asks from the opposite side of the island.

"Oh no need to help. I've been doing it all by myself all day. No need to inconvenience anyone now." Louise grumbles as she chops lettuce and puts it into a bowl.

"If you insist. I'm going to give Wes a tour of the house since we didn't get to yesterday."

"Fine. Dinner will be ready in fifteen minutes." She looks directly at me, "No funny business under my roof."

"Yes, ma'am." I agree. But I'm tempted to pull Elli into the bathroom and finger fuck her just to spite her mother.

"This is obviously the kitchen and the family room. You saw the garage."

I noticed how stark white and clean everything was yesterday, but with so many bodies in here, it brought life to the space. Now, I look around and see there's one family picture hanging above the couch on one wall, a picture of Jesus and a picture of a temple on another, and then the TV. It looks like a museum almost with how white the walls are.

Elli leads me to the stairwell and points down the short hallway. "Down there is my parents' room, my dad's office, and a bathroom."

We head up the stairs, and at the top we come across three doors. I know the far right one leads to Izzy's room, and the door is currently closed so Izzy must be in there. The door next to that one is dark, and the door on the far left is where the sounds of the twins talking is coming from.

"Izzy's room, Spencer's, and the twins' room." Elli points to each door. "The bathroom is down around that corner."

"Wait, you all share a bathroom?"

"Unfortunately. Why do you think all of Izzy's beauty products are piled on her desk? She doesn't trust the twins not to mess around with them, and there's no way she'd be quick enough for everyone to use the bathroom in the morning. I used to get ready in my room too, because there's no way I was going to get in trouble for not sharing."

"That makes sense. Why didn't anyone use the bathroom downstairs?"

"That's only for guests." Izzy answers, coming out of her room.

"So, no one else can use it? Why not just clean it before guests come and use it in the meantime?" I ask.

Izzy shrugs. "Mom doesn't want to be embarrassed by having a dirty bathroom, or dirty *house* for that matter. So she made it off limits."

Weird. But okay.

"Can you come help me pick a first day of school outfit, Els?" Izzy asks.

Elli agrees and we make our way to the bedroom. I wait in the doorway again, not wanting to intrude on the space. I turn around and look at the hallway and think about how different this place is compared to my childhood apartment.

Elli's childhood home is clean and spacious. Although it does seem more clinical than warm and inviting, it feels safer than where I was raised.

I don't remember much about where I lived before I was nine, but the apartments I was in from ages nine to thirteen were always dirty and run down. The wallpaper would be peeling and it would smell like cigarettes no matter how much we tried to air them out.

Elli's mom probably always has food in the pantry and fridge and cooks homemade meals, where mine would usually get me a happy meal or something off the dollar menu, or would microwave a frozen TV dinner.

My mom tried her best, until Keith got her back on drugs. I don't ever remember having an actual bed frame, but I had a clean mattress on the floor and that was good enough for me. When Keith would get mad, he would take away the sheets and blankets from my bed and make me sleep without them.

My clothes always smelled like they needed to be washed because I didn't have a dresser, just a laundry basket to keep them in. Keith wasn't supposed to smoke in the apartment, but he would anyway.

Elli grew up in a palace compared to me, and it makes me wonder how I can give her a future she deserves.

"Hey," Elli says quietly, pulling me from my wandering thoughts. "Where did you go just now?"

"Oh, just thinking about how differently we grew up. You were raised in the equivalent of a palace compared to my living situations. It's just interesting, you know?" I shrug.

Elli goes to reply, but her mom shouts that dinner is ready. Elli gives me an apologetic look and a kiss on the cheek. "Let's go eat. We'll talk about this later, okay?"

I nod, and walk down the stairs and to the dining area, where Kent is seated at the head of the table. Spencer is to Kent's right, the twins next to him, Izzy is opposite Spencer, and she motions for me to take the middle seat next to her, and Elli takes the next seat, leaving the other end of the table open for Louise.

Louise sets down a ceramic dish of steaming mashed potatoes and takes her seat, and then everyone bows their head and Kent says a prayer.

They pass each dish to the right, starting with Kent and working around the table so Izzy is the last to get food.

"This looks really great, Mrs. Monson." I say looking at the spread of some type of thin, fried chicken, potatoes, gravy, green beans, a salad, and rolls.

"Thank you. It's a German dish, schnitzel." She says curtly.

We dish our food and eat it in relative silence, which is hard for me because usually family dinners with Jess and Luke or my friends are loud and full of chatter and laughter.

Izzy, bless her sweet, chattery soul, fills the awkward silence by giving us a plot summary of the musical she's in this year. I've never heard of *The Drowsy Chaperone,* but it sounds like an interesting musical. I guess Izzy isn't a lead in this one, but she's a crucial background character who gets to dance a lot, which she seems happy with.

The conversation shifts to Spencer leaving, and he grunts one word answers at Elli every time she asks him something. I watch her try to physically shrink every time she speaks, and I hate it. She's nothing like the confident woman I've seen her blossom into over these last few months, and it's making me want to flip this fucking table.

"Elli, Kent, come with me to the garage for dessert." Louise says curtly with a pointed look at her husband.

Elli gives my thigh a squeeze under the table, along with a small, sad smile, but obediently rises and follows her parents to the garage.

"So, Wes, are you excited for your tour?" Izzy asks, turning her attention to me.

"Yeah, I'm really excited. I'm hoping to get a record deal out of it."

"You're going on tour? Like as a rockstar?" Gideon asks, looking a little dumbfounded. This is the first time he's spoken since I've been here.

I chuckle, "Kind of. I don't play rock music, though."

"That's cool!" Gideon says, nudging Issac who nods his head in agreement.

Spencer scoffs and rolls his eyes, pushing his green beans around his plate.

I choose to ignore that.

"Elli must be excited to finally get to travel. I know she's been wanting to see a bunch of different places." Izzy interjects.

"Yeah, she seems excited. I'm glad she's able to come with me. I just hope she doesn't get sick of me since we'll be sharing a space for eight months."

Izzy beams, "I can guarantee she won't be sick of you."

"Thanks, Iz." I playfully ruffle her hair and she glares at me, but it holds no weight so we both just burst out laughing.

Spencer scoffs, again, and I look over to see him giving me a look so cold I'm surprised I'm not frozen.

"Would you like to say something, Spencer?" I ask calmly. I don't want to have to fight Elli's brother today.

"Elli's lost her mind, is all. She's not living her life the way we were taught. Going on a tour, sharing a bed with a man who's not her husband? That's a one way ticket to the Telestial Kingdom."

"Spencer." Izzy warns, but I place a hand on her shoulder to convey that I've got this.

"It's okay Izzy. Let him get it out so it's not eating away at him."

Spencer sits up straighter, like he's preparing for a battle.

"I just think," he starts, "that Elli's going through a rebellious phase. I think she saw *you* with your demonic tattoos and facial piercings and thought 'Wow, he'd really make my parents mad. I should date him. Get it out of my system.' but eventually she's going to want to come back. She's going to realize how empty her life is without the church and she's going to dump you because you can't give her what she needs. You can't give her an eternal family and eternal salvation. The sooner she realizes that, the sooner she realizes *you* aren't good enough, the better. She needs stability. She needs a real man who will provide for her and take care of her. A musician can't give her that. *You* cannot give her that."

My heart is pounding so hard in my chest it feels like it's going to beat directly out of me. How the fuck does this nineteen year old know exactly what buttons to push? How does he know every single one of my insecurities?

"I think you're wrong." I say, my voice coming out much stronger than I feel. "And Elli's an adult who can make her own decisions. Now, if you'll excuse me, I think I'll go see if they need any help with the dessert."

I stand, and Izzy gives me a half-hearted smile that makes me feel a bit better because at least I know she's on mine and Elli's side.

Fuck what Spencer thinks. He's so caught up in the religious bullshit that's been fed to him that he can't see that his sister is happier now than she probably ever was living here.

I go to open the garage door, and realize it's cracked a bit. I can hear hushed, but harsh voices coming from inside.

"...not going to provide for you! He's not good enough, Elli. He's a delinquent. Probably a drug user. What's stopping him from leaving you for the next best thing when he goes on tour? Packer did that. What's stopping Wes? He'll just break your heart." Louise's voice rings out clearly through the garage.

"I love him, Mom. I'm not going to sit here and listen to you-" Elli starts, but she's cut off by her mother.

"What you're feeling is lust, not love! We raised you to make good choices. Going on tour with a-uh-uh junkie sinner like him isn't a good choice. Stop thinking with your body and start thinking with your brain."

I rear back as if I've been smacked, the word "junkie" triggering my fight or flight response. I'd heard it all my life from Keith. From the kids at school. From other adults who didn't even know me.

Your whore mother is nothing but a useless junkie.

The junkie's kid.

You'll grow up to be a junkie loser just like your useless mom.

I'm so lost in my thoughts I only catch the tail end of what Elli says.

"...you're right. But I get to make my own decisions."

"If you don't end things with that boy, you'll no longer be welcome in this family. I think it's best if you leave. I don't even recognize you anymore." Louise spits.

I take that as my queue to walk away so they don't know I'm eavesdropping. I rush to the bathroom down the hall and lock myself inside, willing the tears threatening to spill to stay in.

What if they're right? What if Elli is just going through a rebellious phase? What if I'm not good enough for her? I can't give her a big house with a yard. I know she says she doesn't want kids, but what if she's only saying that because she doesn't want them with *me*?

I'm the one that convinced her to take a step away from the religion she grew up in. I'm the one who's convinced her to "sin" and try the things she never would have in the first place.

Maybe I am all wrong for her.

CHAPTER 46

Elli

I walk out of the garage and look at the table to find Wes gone.

"He's in the bathroom." Izzy says softly.

"Thanks. Um, we have to get going. But I'll call you later, okay?" I say to her, and she gives me a sad nod.

"Love you sissy." She stands and gives me a strangling hug.

And now I know something is really wrong because she only calls me "sissy" when things are bad.

"Love you too Iz." I whisper to her, squeezing her back. She sits back down and I look at Spencer, who's sitting with his arms folded and a scowl on his face. "Bye Spencer."

He looks at me and shakes his head. "I hope you make smarter choices, Elli."

Ouch.

"Right." I say, and Wes comes out of the bathroom looking a little paler than usual.

"Are we leaving?" He asks once he sees me.

I just nod, and I watch his shoulders sag in relief. Something bad happened. I'm assuming Spencer said something stupid and cruel and now Wes can't wait to get out of here.

We slip on our shoes and Izzy walks us out the door. She waits until we pull away before going back inside, and my heart pangs a little bit because my seventeen year old sister is the only person in my family who's supportive of me right now.

The drive to the hotel is quiet, and the silence makes me replay what happened in the garage over and over.

I already know what's going to happen before the garage door is even open. This is going to be some lecture where my mom berates me and my dad stands there sentry to butt in if I say something my mom doesn't like.

"Elliana Louise, why did I hear from Shelly of all people that you're uprooting your life and going on tour with him?" She spits the word "him" like it leaves a bad taste in her mouth. "What about your job? What about your future?"

"I'm not uprooting my life." I argue, "I'm not quitting my job. I'll still have it, I'll just be working from the road."

"What kind of life is that? How are you going to settle down and raise a family when you're in a different city night after night?"

"I don't want to raise a family, Mom. Having kids isn't something I've ever wanted." I feel a little bit of pressure lift off my chest, now that I've gotten that off of it. I don't have to pretend it's my goal anymore. Now they know.

My mom looks like I've just told her I'm going to join the circus. "I can't believe you're being so selfish right now.

What about grandkids, hm? What about our family? You're just going to throw it all away for some deviant?"

I don't hold back my eyeroll this time, which makes my dad speak up. "Watch your attitude young lady." He grunts.

"I'm happy. *For the first time in my life, I'm actually living for me, and not for you or the church. A church I no longer believe in. You have four other kids who can give you grandkids if that's what they want, but I don't want kids. I don't understand why my choices are so important to you when they don't affect you directly."*

"They do *affect me!" My mother hisses. "You not having my grandkids affects me. You not joining our family for eternity in the Celestial Kingdom affects all of us! And now Izzy's going to go and leave another empty chair at our eternal table."*

"No, Mom. I'm an adult and my 'eternal salvation' is my own to determine. You don't get a say in my future anymore. Only I do." I say, surprised that my voice isn't shaking from anxiety.

"Wes is who you're choosing? A devil worshiping sinner who's mutilated his body? A musician is not going to provide for you! He's not good enough, Elli. He's a delinquent. Probably a drug user. What's stopping him from leaving you for the next best thing when he goes on tour? Packer did that. What's stopping Wes? He'll just break your heart."

Okay, ouch.

"I love him, Mom. I'm not going to sit here and listen to you-" I start, but she interrupts me.

"What you're feeling is lust, not love! We raised you to make good choices. Going on tour with a-uh-uh junkie

sinner like him isn't a good choice. Stop thinking with your body and start thinking with your brain."

I straighten my shoulders, no longer attempting to shrink down to the size they want me to be. "Wes is the best man I've ever met. He is kind, gentle, patient, and so unbelievably talented. Not to mention he's made me happier in the last few months than I've ever been in my entire life. I choose him, and the life he can give me, even though it's not the one you say I should want. I'm not going to let you spit vitriol about him when you don't know him. I know you want to think you're right. But I get to make my own decisions."

"If you don't end things with that boy, you'll no longer be welcome in this family. I think it's best if you leave. I don't even recognize you anymore." My mom hisses at me before turning around and dismissing me.

I can't believe my own mother doesn't want me to be happy.

Actually, scratch that. I *can* believe it, but I don't *want* to believe it.

Wes clears his throat, bringing me back from my memory and I realize we've pulled into the hotel parking lot.

"Do you want to take a walk?" I ask, not wanting to sit in this silence in the hotel room. I want to ask him what happened while I was gone.

"Sure." He says almost robotically.

We get out and start walking down the street, but he doesn't hold my hand like normal.

Fuck. Something's really wrong.

"Did something happen when I stepped out?" I ask quietly.

"Spencer just needed to get some things off his chest."

"Oh." That's cryptic. "Are you okay?"

"I'm fine, Elli. Are you okay?" he asks, finally looking over at me.

I try not to overthink the fact that he called me "Elli" and not "baby" like he usually does. I just nod my head. "My mom just had some things to say, mean things, about you and my choices. I told her I don't care about what she thinks. My choices are my choices and I want to be with you. Then she said she didn't recognize me anymore and told me to leave."

I don't even realize I'm crying until the rough, calloused pad of Wes's thumb brushes away the offending tear. I thought I could be strong and not let what my parents said affect me, but I guess that's not the case.

Even as an adult, I still want their approval. But I guess now, I want my own approval more than I want theirs. I want to be happy. And sometimes being happy means disappointing people.

"I'm so sorry, Elli." Wes says, his voice pained as he brings me in for a hug.

I place my face in his chest and sob, right there in the middle of the sidewalk, in front of a plant store. I don't know what Wes is sorry for, but I know he's sincere in his sorrow.

I breathe in the familiar scent of him that I've come to love. He smells like home. He smells like new beginnings and happiness, and I hope he never changes body washes.

I look up at him, probably looking like a racoon with my mascara smeared under my eyes, and give him a small smile.

"I love you." I whisper.

He gives me a smile that doesn't reach his eyes. "I love you, too."

CHAPTER 47

Wes

The heavy weight of the last two hours is sitting like a lead ball in my stomach. I keep wondering why she didn't tell me that her mom told her to break up with me. Is it because she's going to do it? The anticipation and anxiety over if she is is making me spiral a little bit.

I think we're both hungry after not being able to eat much at dinner, but neither of us wants to break the silence that we've been uncomfortably sitting in for the last half an hour. It's like we're both waiting for the other to end things and save ourselves the misery of an extended break up.

I clear my throat, "Are you hungry?"

"A little. Do you want me to go grab some burgers or something?" She's been picking apart a thread that's frayed on the hotel's comforter.

"I can go grab some. You want your usual?"

She nods, and I grab the keys. As I'm about to head out the door, she calls my name. I stop and turn around to look at her, and my heart cracks right in two at the tears in her eyes and the dejected look on her face.

"My mom told me I had to break up with you or else I'm no longer part of the family." She swallows, swiping at the tears on her face.

I brace myself for the impact of her next words.

"I'm going to need some time, and a lot of patience to work through this."

"I understand. When we get back, I'll make sure to tell Robin and Savannah that we're not together anymore, but that you guys still need to be friends. I'll make sure Jess knows it's not your fault and-"

"What are you talking about?" She cuts me off.

"Well, we're breaking up, aren't we? I don't want people to blame you, or for you to lose the friends you've made since moving to San Marcos."

"Do you *want* to break up?"

"Hell no, but I understand that your family is important to you. We just started dating, so I understand you'd want to choose them over me."

"You think that little of me? That I'd let this end us?" The hurt on her face is breaking my heart even more.

"No, but I-"

"I think you should go get the food now." Her voice is robotic now. Void of any emotion, and I can't help but think I totally missed something in this conversation.

With a hesitant nod, I slowly walk out of the hotel room, shaking my head.

I replay the conversation on the drive, trying to follow the maps.

"I'm going to need some time, and a lot of patience to work through this."

I'm stopped at a red light, still processing the conversation when Robin calls me. She starts talking immediately with a harsh "Did you fix it?"

"What do you mean? What the hell is going on?" I ask.

"Elli just called me and told me she was going to need a girls' night as soon as we could. But then she started sobbing and saying if Sav and I didn't want to hang out with her now that you two were *broken up* that she understood. She said you ended things while she was in the middle of trying to work through what happened at family dinner. Care to tell me your side of the story?"

"Her brother and mom said some shit to and about me while we were there for dinner yesterday. They were saying I'm just a phase for her. That I can't provide for her. I'm not good enough. Her mom said I was a junkie and that Elli would be disowned if she didn't break up with me." I explain, knowing I won't have to elaborate too much.

"Elli's mom sounds like a bitch. So does her brother. I'm glad her and Izzy turned out to be decent."

"Yeah, somehow the bitchiness gene skipped them." I smile, remembering how Izzy tried to stick up for me. How Elli *did* stick up for me.

"So why the hell would you want to end things with her, then?"

"Robs, you should have seen the house she grew up in. It was *huge!* Palatial compared to the shitholes I grew up in. She's used to having the picture-perfect house, the big family. How am I supposed to give her that? How am I supposed to give her the life she deserves?"

Robin pauses for a second before quietly asking, "What about the life she *desires?* Elli's told you before she doesn't want the white picket fence and two point five kids. She just wants to be with you."

"Her mom also said I would leave her for the next best thing. I don't ever want Elli to feel insecure about me leaving her. I'd never do that."

"You're so dumb sometimes, I swear." Robin mumbles. "Elli is choosing *you.* Elli was trying to tell you she needed time to process the fact that her mother is going to cut her off to be with you. She needs you right now, and you're being dumb because you're scared. Which is understandable, but I swear to god Westley, if you don't fix this, I will castrate you."

"I'll fix it, I promise." I am dumb. I should have listened more to Elli. I shouldn't have let my insecurities get the better of me. What Louise and Spencer said hurt a lot, but I can get past it. Elli's losing her family for being with me.

The realization sinks in that this amazing, kind, funny, beautiful woman is choosing *me* over her blood relatives.

I grab the burgers, fries, and the cookie dough shake I know she'll want and speed back to the hotel on a mission to make it clear to her that I'm an idiot and I'm sorry. That I'm hers and she's mine.

I just hope she hasn't given up on me yet.

CHAPTER 48

Elli

What's left of my heart is beating faster than a hummingbird's as I wait for Wes to get back. I'm still processing the fact that he thinks I'd choose my mom over him.

I know some people say "blood is thicker than water" but the blood that I share with my mom is so toxic that it's tainting the first good thing I've ever had for myself.

I would never choose someone who thinks Wes is unworthy, dirty, a loser, or a junkie. I would never choose someone who thinks his dreams are silly and achievable.

But he didn't give me a chance to tell him that.

Instead, he jumped to conclusions. Conclusions that hurt both of us.

He's been gone for about thirty minutes, and the longer he's gone, the more my anxiety about the situation grows. I don't know how I'm supposed to share a bed and spend two days in a car with the love of my life who no longer wants to be with me.

I hear the *beep* of the door unlocking and Wes comes in holding a brown bag with grease stains on it, and two cups. He sets the things down on the little desk in the corner of our room, then digs through the bags and brings me my burger, fries, a container of fry sauce, a container of ranch, and a cup with a partially melted cookie dough shake.

I didn't ask for a shake, and I never mentioned the fact that I wanted fry sauce. It's a Utah thing, so most places outside of the state don't have fry sauce. I usually just settle for ranch instead. I unwrap my burger and go to open the bun to take off the onions and tomatoes, but Wes interrupts.

"I ordered yours without onions and tomatoes. I also added an extra slice of cheese, and extra pickles because I know you like them on your burgers."

My lip wobbles and I try to stop it by taking a bite of my burger. We've only been dating for a little over a month, and he's already memorized my burger order? We've only had burgers twice together. He even remembered how I like my fries and what my favorite shake is.

The bed dips and Wes's calloused fingers swipe away the few tears that escaped. "Why are you crying? Did I get your order wrong? I'm sorry, I'll go back and get a different one if you want."

That just makes me cry harder. I set the burger down on the paper and turn to look at him.

"The burger is perfect. The shake is perfect. The fry sauce is perfect."

His brows furrow, "Then why are you crying?"

"Because!" I throw my hands up in exasperation. "Because you want to break up! How am I supposed to date anyone else after you've treated me like a damn queen the entire time we've been together? How am I supposed to move on from the love of my life, especially when you're going to become a big star, and you'll be everywhere."

"I don't want to break up." He whispers, looking a little sheepish.

"What?"

He grabs my hands and stares into my eyes deeply. "I don't want to break up. I was an idiot who got scared and I thought *you* were breaking up with *me*. But let me be clear about something: I'm yours. You're mine. Can you forgive me for trying to sabotage this? Because I don't think my heart can handle not being with you. You're the air I breathe, my heartbeat, the blood that flows through my veins." He says, placing my hand on his heart so I can feel the rhythmic beat. "I don't want to live without you. Without you, there's no music. No sunshine."

My lip wobbles and now I'm crying because I'm relieved. "I wasn't trying to break up with you. You're the best thing that's ever happened to me. If my mom can't see that, then that's her issue. It's not going to be easy to deal with the fact that Izzy's the only family I've got now, unless Spencer or the twins come around, so I'll need some time to work through that. But I never, not for one second, considered ending things with you."

"I'm with you every step of the way, baby. I love you, Elliana Louise Monson."

"I love you too, Westley Ray Jones."

Then, Wes kisses me. My burger and fries forgotten in favor of making up for the last few hours.

Chapter 49

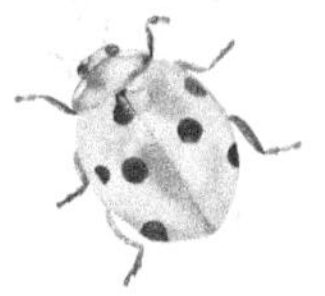

Wes

Before we leave Utah the next morning, Elli asks to make a stop at her parents' house so she can tell them her decision.

I'm nervous for her, but I support her one hundred percent.

We pull up in front of Elli's childhood home at seven in the morning so she can talk to both of her parents before her dad leaves for work. We make our way up the steps and Elli rings the doorbell, my hand firmly in her grasp.

Louise answers the door, the fake smile on her face falling as soon as she sees who it is. "What are you doing here? Have you come to apologize?"

"I came here to talk to you and dad." Elli's voice doesn't waver, even in the presence of her mom, and I give her hand a gentle squeeze to remind her I'm here with her.

Louise steps aside and motions for us to come in. "Kent! Elliana is here and wants to speak to us." She shouts down the hall that leads to Kent's office.

Kent appears moments later and stands behind Louise with his arms crossed expectantly.

Elli straightens her spine before she starts. "I came to tell you that I'm not breaking up with Wes. I'm not going to let you manipulate my life anymore, and I'm not going to let you push me around like a puppet. You said I wouldn't be allowed to be part of this family anymore if I stayed with Wes, so I guess you've lost a daughter. I know you've never been proud of me, and you've never loved me the way a mother should love her child. I came to say goodbye, and to say that if you ever treat Izzy the way you've treated me, you can expect to lose your other daughter, too."

"You ungrateful brat. I gave you everything you ever needed or wanted as a child, and this is how you repay me? What will the ward think? What will your aunts and uncles think?" Louise hisses at Elli.

"You never gave Elli love. And that's what she needed the most. Your ward, your family? They'll think whatever you choose to tell them, and I'm sure you'll paint yourself as the victim. You should be proud of the woman Elli is." I say, wanting to prove to not only them, but myself, that I'm worthy of Elli's love. She deserves someone who will stand up for her.

"She'll come crawling back when the novelty of you wears off. Or you leave her for a skinner, prettier version." Louise looks at me with so much hate, you'd think I murdered her entire family.

"Don't talk to him like that." Elli snaps. Then she turns to me. "I've said what I want to say. Let's go. We have a long journey *home.*" She emphasizes the word home, and that warms my heart.

With that, we walk out the front door. Louise sputters about us regretting this and how Elli is ungrateful, but Elli tunes them out as we make our way to the car. I open the door for her, but before she gets in, she grabs me by the back of my neck and kisses me passionately.

I don't even hesitate to meet her passion, making a show of grabbing her voluptuous ass. I know she's just proving a point to her parents, but damn it, I'm hard for her already.

When we break apart, Louise and Kent are standing on the porch with red faces. Louise's from anger, Kent's from embarrassment, probably.

"Goodbye, Louise." Elli says, getting in the car.

I wave to them, earning a death glare from Louise, but she can't bring my mood down right now.

I've got my dream girl, my dream job, and the only thing missing is being home and not in the car.

The rest of our two-day journey is filled with plans for the tour.

Since my lease is up in October, I'm going to sell most of my furniture and move the rest of my stuff into Elli's apartment. Elli's going to ask Luke if she can pay him to come check on the apartment every once in a while.

Elli's job will still be full-time, but since the concerts are mostly at night, she's going to work away at her computer during the day and be backstage or front row for me every night.

The thought of spending every single day with her makes me want to move in right now, but I think it'll be good to wait another month and a half.

Probably.

Elli's already got plans for t-shirts with "I'm with Wes" and "I'm with Elli" printed on them so people know we're together.

I'm considering buying a ring. So when she's not wearing the shirt, people know she's mine.

That's crazy though... right? Wanting to get engaged so soon? We haven't really talked about marriage yet. She only said she didn't want kids, not that she didn't want to get married.

Visions of a small, intimate ceremony with just our closest friends and family pop into my mind. Elli, walking down a flower lined path in a stunning white dress- or whatever color she wants- she could walk down the aisle in white overalls for all I fucking care.

We'd stand before an officiant, someone *not* religious, and make promises to love each other forever, before she'd slip a band on my finger, and I'd slip one onto hers.

Then we'd have a fucking party. We'd have drinks and dancing, and I'd definitely write a song for the occasion about how much I love her. Jess would cry, Izzy would probably be the maid of honor and give a ridiculous speech.

It would be the best day ever.

"Hey, where'd you go just now?" Elli pokes my shoulder, bringing me out of my daydream.

"Just thinking about the future." I say, bringing our intertwined hands to my mouth and placing a gentle kiss on her ring finger.

"Hmmm. Must've been a good thought." She teases.

"The best." I say with a beaming smile.

She rolls her eyes, then launches back into planning mode, writing down questions for me to ask Misha on her phone, like what the laundry situation is. Will food be provided for us, or do we need to plan our own meals?

She wants to know if I'll be paid up front, or if it will be a monthly thing.

I'm extra glad she's coming with me now because I never would have thought to ask things like this. Not that I *need* her to help me run my life, obviously, but she's much more detail oriented than I am.

After a full day of driving, we've finally made it back to San Marcos. As soon as we pull up in front of Elli's apartment building, Robin gets out of her car and angrily stomps over to us.

"What the *hell* is happening with you two? One minute I'm talking to Wes about what an idiot he'd be to let you go, then you take the phone from me, and then it's radio silence!" She turns to me, "Do I need to kick your ass for breaking up with her or not?"

Elli and I start laughing, which only frustrates Robin more.

"Don't worry, Robs. We're not broken up." Elli says, wrapping her arms around my waist and looking up at me.

I'm sure I look like a lovesick idiot staring back at my girl, but I can't help it. The last two days have been such a rollercoaster, and I'm just glad I didn't lose her for good.

"Good." Robin sniffs. "I'd hate to have to choose Elli over you."

My jaw drops in mock offense, "You'd choose a girl you just met over your best friend of seven years?"

Robs shrugs, "Of course. Hoes before bros. Chicks before dicks. All that feminist stuff."

I look at Elli with a *can you believe this?* expression and she just laughs.

"You always pick chicks before dicks, Robs. So I don't know if it's a feminist thing or a gay thing." Elli teases.

"Probably a little bit of both. Anyway, I've been sitting here for two hours waiting for you to get back and I have a hot date with the hottie from the gallery." Robin gives Elli a hug, and then me.

When she hugs me she whispers, "I'm proud of you." and it makes me want to tear up. I haven't heard that a lot in my life.

"Thanks Robs." I say back.

"Have fun on your date." Elli says, wiggling her eyebrows.

Robin blushes as she gets into her car.

We wave her off, then get Elli's luggage from the trunk, and I walk her into her apartment.

Elli sighs, like being here is a weight lifted from her shoulders, and I can relate to the feeling.

Utah has beautiful scenery, but if all Mormons are like Elli's family, I don't think I could be surrounded by them twenty-four-seven.

My heart aches a little every time I think about how strained the relationship between Elli and her parents now, but I just have to keep reminding myself that she's an adult. She makes her own choices. If she doesn't want to have a relationship with her parents, that's something I'm going to have to be okay with and help her through.

"Well I'd better get going, I'm beat." I say through a yawn.

Elli pushes her bottom lip out in an adorable little pout. "Noooo." She whines. "It's late, why don't you stay? Then we can both go over to your place tomorrow to unpack."

"Baby, aren't you sick of being around me? We've been together non-stop for almost a week." I tuck an errant piece of strand behind her ear.

"I'm never going to be sick of being around you." She says sweetly. "Besides, we're going to be together nonstop for eight months. Are *you* sick of *me*?"

I pull her body flush with mine, "Never. I'll never get tired of you."

Her answering smile could light up an entire city.

"Good! So it's settled. You're staying here. Let's go shower." She chirps, dragging me into the bathroom.

"Yes ma'am."

CHAPTER 50

Elli

I t's been two weeks since the whole debacle in Utah, and I haven't heard a peep from my parents.

I've talked with Izzy almost every day, whether through texts or Facetime. She says no one's even mentioned my name. She's tried to bring me up in conversation, but our mom just ignores her and changes the subject.

It's like I never existed to my mother.

I wish I could say I was surprised, but unfortunately, I am not.

Spencer was dropped off at the Missionary Training Center where he'll spend the next six weeks learning to speak Portuguese and get on the "missionary schedule."

I wanted to reach out to him before he left and give him a piece of my mind, but it would have been like talking to a brick wall. If I want to talk to him now, it'd have to be through letters or emails, but this isn't something I want to talk about through letters or email.

Who knows? Maybe his mission will open his mind and he'll be more accepting by the end of it.

There are generally two ways people go after their missions.

One, they're even more engulfed in the idea of the church. They'll go on to have higher up callings in the church, they're more likely to have bigger families, and they'll stay active most likely for the rest of their lives.

The second group, which is about forty percent of returned missionaries, will leave the church. They may leave because of something they experienced, like the corrupt leadership of mission presidents, the unrealistic expectations placed on them, or the mistreatment of missionaries.

Or they could leave because they learned the fallacies in the doctrine. The things that were taught to them for their entire lives are all based on the musings of a pedophilic conman.

Not that everyone believes that, but that's what I think.

I've been tempted to text my mom and apologize, but the overwhelming need to stick to my boundaries and not grovel wins every time. I've always been the one who apologizes, even when she's in the wrong.

I'm not going to let her guilt trip me into being complacent anymore.

On a happier note, Wes signed the contract for the tour last week, and we've been making lists of things we want to do in each city.

We will definitely be trying pizza in both Chicago and New York, and beignets in New Orleans. Wes is excited to hit up the French Quarter and listen to the jazz there. We're going to try and hit a Broadway show while we're in New York too, but we'll see if we have time.

We lucked out by having a bit of a break when we're in Tennessee and plan on spending a night on Music Row, and then hitting up Dollywood because Wes said he's always wanted to go.

I saw we were going to be in San Diego in May, so I messaged Emma on Instagram and asked if she'd like tickets, she said she's not sure what her plans were that far in advance, but if she's available that night she'd love to come. I'm excited that we might be able to hang out again. It's been a while since I've seen her, and it'd be good to catch up. Ideally, all three of us, me, Emma, and Hannah, would all hang out, but I know it's hard to do that when we all live in different states.

I've already set up Hannah with two tickets to the show in Salt Lake, but she protested, saying there's no way she's going to be bringing anyone. I'm keeping the two tickets anyway, because who knows? Maybe she'll meet someone by then.

Wes has been stressing about what to wear during his performances, thinking that his usual band shirts and jeans aren't cool enough, but I told him he could wear a potato sack and a clown mask and people would still fall for him.

He's been holed away in his apartment for four days writing and I'm not going to lie, I miss him. But I understand that he needs some time to let the creative energy flow right now. I'm so freaking proud of him, and I can't wait to see what he comes up with.

We have plans tonight, which I'm currently getting ready for, and I can't wait to see him. I know it's only been four days, but it feels like a lifetime. Wes was so worried that I'd get sick of him while we're on tour, but I'm so excited to spend every day with him.

I'd love to spend the rest of my life with him.

Which is crazy, but what can I say?

I love him. He's my person.

I'm about to head to my room when there's a knock on the door. I look at the clock, realizing I've been so in my head I didn't even realize it was time for Wes to pick me up.

It's weird that he knocked, though, because he has a key. Usually he just lets himself in.

I open the door ready to chastise him for losing his key, but any teasing dies on my tongue when I see the bouquet of sunflowers mixed with pink gerbera daisies, and the man dressed in his usual all black ensemble- black chino pants, black button up with the sleeves rolled to his forearms, black loafers- holding them with a lazy smile.

"I think you're going to need to change, baby. The place we're going to has a dress code and I don't think 'loungewear' is on it. Though it is sexy as hell." Wes drawls.

I roll my eyes, but go up on my tiptoes to kiss his cheek. "Hi handsome. These are gorgeous, thank you."

I take the flowers from him and scurry to the kitchen so I can put them in water.

"You think you can run away from me without a proper kiss, Elli?" Wes teases, following me to the kitchen after shutting the door.

He cages me in by the sink, my back to his front, while I fill the vase with water. He leans down until his lips are at my ear to whisper, "I've gone too long without your lips, baby."

"Just my lips?" I retort.

Wes hums, the vibrations sending a shiver down my spine. "It's too long without *you*."

I turn around once the vase is filled, and tip my head up to look into his coffee colored eyes. "I missed you too. But you know what they say, 'Absence makes the heart grow fonder.'"

Wes tucks a strand of hair behind my ear, "I prefer 'Absence sharpens love, presence strengthens it.' I know we need time apart sometimes, and I got a lot written, but days without you feel like days without sunshine. One is fine, but any more than that and the gloom starts to kick in."

"You're the one who wanted space to write." I say breathily as his thumb strokes gently along my cheekbones.

"I know, but an artist needs their muse to continue making art."

"I'm your muse?" I tease.

"You're my everything." He says solemnly before finally taking my mouth in a kiss.

A kiss so all-consuming a meteor could shoot through the roof and we wouldn't notice.

A kiss full of love, passion, desire, and unspoken promises.

A kiss that's the beginning of something big, but I don't know what.

When Wes pulls away, I feel a little dizzy.

"Well if you're going to kiss me like that after a few days, I'd love to see how you'd kiss me after a week or two." I tease.

"Not happening, baby." Wes says, giving me a quick peck. "Now go get changed. Our reservation is at seven and if I keep kissing you we'll never make it."

I push past him, and he swats my ass playfully which makes me squeal and dart to my room.

Wes said the place has a dress code, but he isn't dressed in black tie attire, so I slip on my light pink skater dress that has a V neckline, spaghetti straps, and flares at my hips into a circle skirt that meets the middle of my thighs. I buckle on my black block wedges and don my usual gold jewelry before coming out to meet Wes.

He looks up from where he's scrolling on his phone and immediately puts it back in his pocket.

"*Goddamn* Elli. You look downright edible. If I didn't have big plans for us tonight, I'd say let's cancel the reservation and stay in instead." He grabs one of my hands and spins me around.

"You look pretty good yourself, Mr. Jones. What big plans do you have for us?"

"That's for me to know, and you to find out later." He places a gentle kiss on my hand. "Let's go, milady. Your chariot awaits."

He leads me out the door, making sure it's locked before we get to the car where he opens my door for me with a little bow - like our blind date.

I don't know what big plans he has for us, but nervous yet excited butterflies erupt in my belly with anticipation of what's to come.

CHAPTER 51

Wes

I feel bad that I lied to Elli about being busy with writing.

While that was *technically* true, I wasn't *just* writing.

I was planning this date and buying jewelry so I can ask her a very important question.

No, not *that* question.

Kind of that question.

I *do* have a ring... but it's not an *engagement* ring.

I also have a necklace.

And I have a matching ring for myself if she says yes.

I hope she says yes.

I made reservations at this restaurant a week ago, and while it is a little bit out of the price range I usually go for, Brenner's is right on the San Antonio Riverwalk and is supposed to be really good.

As we walk along Presa Street to get to the restaurant the sounds of nightlife in the city act as our background. Cars honk at each other, music plays from the different storefronts, and various stages of drunk people meander through the crowd.

Once we're seated at a quiet table by the window that overlooks the river, Elli catches me up on her past few days. She's been working on interviews for some new hires for the law firm, which is one of her favorite things to do, and it sounds like she's excelled at it. The law firm doesn't have a big turnover rate because Elli hires qualified candidates, and the firm makes sure their employees are well taken care of and happy working there.

We talk about how Keely and the Kissers announced me as their opener for the tour and how my follower count on Instagram grew from 10k to 25k in the last week. I've been trying to post more songs, without spoiling my setlist, and the engagement has been crazy. People love Keely and the Kissers, and now apparently, people love me.

The waiter, Lyle, comes to grab our drink order and Elli orders a pear blossom cocktail and I order a cream soda, and grab an order of bacon wrapped shrimp as an appetizer.

There's a live band playing in the corner, so we sit and listen to the music while we wait for our drinks and appetizer, and when that comes out, we order our main dishes. Elli orders the miso glazed sea bass and I order the pan roasted chicken. The waiter tells us that it should be about a twenty minute wait for our food.

I debate if I should just ask her now or if I should wait until dessert like I planned.

I'm just going to do it. I go to grab the jewelry box out of my pocket, but just as I have it in my grasp, the lead singer of the band grabs our attention.

"Well folks, it looks like we have an up-and-coming star here with us tonight. If you're a fan of Keely and the

Kissers then you know all about their new opener, Wes Jones. He's here tonight, maybe we can convince him to come play us a song!"

I shake my head and wave my hands, looking at Elli with an apologetic smile.

"Go, babe. You're famous now. Give the people what they want." Elli says, her eyes twinkling with pride.

Pride for *me*.

"One song, baby. I promise." I scoot out of the booth and give her a quick kiss, a new plan forming in my mind.

I take the guitarist's acoustic guitar and settle on the stool they have in front of the microphone.

"Howdy folks. As he said, I'm Wes Jones. I'm very lucky to have been offered a spot on tour with Keely and the Kissers. But I'm even luckier to be here tonight with a special lady. She's the sunshine that broke through my clouded mind, my love, my muse. This is the song that brought me back from my writer's block, all thanks to her. This is *Love Bug*."

I strum the guitar, the opening cords a familiar vibration under my fingertips. I usually refuse to play on anything but Dolly, but this guitar is nice, so I have no problem getting into the rhythm.

As I sing, the adrenaline of a performance courses through my veins, and I never let my eyes stray from Elli, who's recording on her phone, but her eyes never leave mine.

After I strum the final chord, I let the applause die down before I say a quick thank you to the band and the crowd, and head back to our table. Elli pops up out of her seat and wraps me in a big hug.

"I'm so fucking proud of you, Wes. You never cease to amaze me with your talent. I'm so lucky to be by your side to witness your success, and I can't wait to see you perform night after night." She gushes.

"Thank you, baby. I have something I want to-"

"Your food, sir, miss." Lyle interrupts, looking apologetic.

We sit, this time on the same side of the booth because I want to be as close to Elli as possible.

"What were you saying before Lyle brought our food?" Elli asks, slicing into her sea bass.

"I want to ask you something. Something important."

Elli pauses with the bite to her mouth before she gently sets her utensils down and turns to me, motioning me to continue.

I take a deep breath and pull out the blue pentagon shaped jewelry box and set it on the table, then take out a little black velvet bag and set it next to it. Elli's eyes go wide with shock, surprise, and a little apprehension before she pulls her gaze away to look at me.

"It's not what you're thinking," I say carefully. "Well, kind of." I open the box and reveal two signet rings. A silver one with an "E" and a gold one with a "W."

"This isn't a marriage proposal, since I think that would be a little fast. And, selfishly, I don't want to plan a wedding while we're on tour. But it *is* a promise." I take out the "W" ring and hold it out in front of her.

"This is a placeholder until I can put an engagement ring on your finger and make you mine forever. It's a promise to love you unconditionally. A promise to be by each other's sides through the good, the bad, the ugly, and the beautiful. A promise that you're it for me, Elliana Louise Monson. If you slip this ring on your finger, you're mine. For good. You'll just get an upgrade to a prettier ring later on."

Elli's eyes glisten with unshed tears, before she grabs the "E" ring. "If you wear this it means you're mine, too. No matter how many bras or panties get thrown at you on stage, you come home to me. I'll wear your initial proudly, Westley Ray Jones, because you're it for me too."

I let out the breath I was holding and slip the ring on her left hand, satisfaction and possession filling my soul the way it looks on her finger. She slips the one in her hand on mine. We seal our promises with a kiss before I remember the other gift I have for her.

"This is more a reminder of how we started." I say, slipping out the necklace and holding it up so she can see the gold pendant engraved with a ladybug, but instead of dots on its back it has hearts.

Elli giggles, "It's a love bug!"

I nod, and she turns around so I can clasp the necklace around her neck.

"I love it, Wes. Thank you. You didn't have to spoil me so hard though." She teases.

"I'll always spoil you whenever I can, baby. Now eat your seabass before it gets cold." I give her another quick kiss before we go back to eating our food.

CHAPTER 52

Elli

Today's the day Wes has been anxiously waiting for.

Well, I have too, but not because it's my dream to be touring. My dreams start and end with traveling with Wes and watching his fame grow as more and more people discover his talent.

We had a joint New Years Eve and going away party with all our closest friends and family a few days ago, and it was very bittersweet. I'm excited to follow Wes on this journey, but leaving a group of people who have become family in the last six months is difficult. Everyone has been so supportive and so helpful, it makes my heart burst.

We're standing outside a big black motorhome that will be our main source of travel for the next eight months, suitcases and duffle bags waiting at our feet to be loaded. Wes spent the entire day yesterday showing me different band t-shirts and asking if they were "stage-worthy."

It was utterly adorable, if not exasperating.

He moved in in October, just like we planned, so we had to figure out how to fit both of our wardrobes in the single closet in the main bedroom. I told him he could just fold his band t-shirts and put them in a dresser, and he looked at me like I just told him to cut off his pinky finger.

We ended up getting a clothes rack *just* for his band shirts.

I'm surprised he ended up fitting all of them in his duffle bag.

Wes stands beside me, anxiously tapping his foot on the ground. We haven't met Keely and the rest of the band yet, just their manager, Misha. Misha is an interesting soul. He's probably in his mid to late forties, has long brown hair that he usually has in a braid down his back, one blue eye and one brown eye, which are usually behind big black rimmed glasses, and his outfits are an eclectic mix of various styles.

Today, for example, he's wearing black dress pants, a pink linen shirt that's unbuttoned to the middle of his chest, and black and white checkered vans. He's always adorned in rings and bracelets and usually has a crystal around his neck.

Not exactly what you picture when you picture the manager for a big band.

But he's nice, very smart, and clearly knows what he's doing in the business world, so I guess when you're that good, you get to dress how you want.

"Ah, here's Keely and the band now!" Misha says, tipping his head towards the black SUV pulling into the parking lot.

Wes leans into me and whisper-yells, "Do I look okay? Do you think they'll like me?"

I turn and give him a quick kiss on the lips to calm his nerves, and he instantly releases the tension in his shoulders. "They're going to love you, babe."

"Hey hey hey, you must be Wes and Elli!" Keely says, holding out her hand for us to shake.

Keely's the lead singer, and she writes a majority of the songs for the band. She's got bright blonde hair cut into a stylish bob, big green eyes, and is much taller than me, probably about five foot nine. She has a lip piercing, a slit shaved into her eyebrow, and three nose piercings- a septum and both nostrils. She's got black ink covering both of her arms, hands, and her throat.

"Nice to meet you too. Thank you again for this opportunity." Wes beams as he shakes her hand eagerly.

"Thank *you* for agreeing to come with us. We're all so stoked to have you with us. Let me introduce you to the rest of the gang."

Leah, the bassist, is a black woman with long black box braids that have random splashes of color tied in. She's got so many gold earrings in her ear I don't know how it doesn't hurt.

KC, the drummer, is a non-binary white person and they're covered in colorful tattoos of various landscapes, dinosaurs, and lots of other pictures I can't quite recognize. They've got a buzzcut that's been bleached, then someone put little hearts in purple dye all over their head.

Mikala, the guitarist, looks like an ordinary white girl with her thick brown hair falling in waves across her shoulders, big brown eyes, and lack of tattoos or piercings. Apparently, she and Keely have been dating for the last two years. Something tells me she's not as shy and timid as she comes off right now, and I look forward to getting to see her come out of her shell.

"Elli, I'm so excited to have you with us too. I love when partners get to come along." Keely beams, clapping her hands together excitedly.

"Thanks, I'm glad I could come too. I'm excited to watch Wes live his dream."

"Awww. You two are so fucking cute! Ugh. Babe, why aren't we cute like that." Keely whines, bumping hips with Mikala.

Mikala arches a brow, "Because you're not a sweet docile kitten, you're a feral trash cat, my love."

I giggle at the description, and Keely lets out a loud belly laugh.

"She's right. We started out our relationship at each other's throats. A real enemies to lovers timeline."

"Alright kids," Misha shouts. "It's time to hit the road. First stop is in Dallas and we've got a sound check in t-minus seven hours so it's time to get a move on!"

The band gets on the bus, and I turn to go with them when I catch a tear falling down Wes's cheek.

"What's wrong?" I ask, wiping the tears away.

"I just can't believe this is actually happening. I can't believe this is my life now."

"Well believe it babe, because this is just the beginning."

He looks down at me and the love and adoration I see there makes my heart kick up a notch. I hope he always looks at me like that.

"Thank you for being with me to follow my dreams." He whispers.

"There's nowhere else I'd rather be." I say, meaning it.

He kisses me then, languid and sweet, until Misha calls our names again and tells us we can keep kissing on the bus as long as we're on it.

"I love you, Westley Ray Jones."

"I love you too, Elliana Louise Monson."

Epilogue

Wes

Eight months later...

We've been back in San Marco for two weeks now, and I'm already missing the highs of performing night after night.

The tour was everything I could have dreamed of. I signed a record deal with a record company based in Austin so I can continue to put my music out there as a full time gig.

I now have over half a million followers on Instagram, and Elli forced me to make a TikTok where I have over a million. It's been incredible seeing how far my music reaches, and having mostly positive reactions to it is incredible.

Elli started therapy right before we left for the tour, and she's made so much progress in the last eight months. She's worked through a lot of her religious trauma, the falling out with her parents, and we've done a few couple sessions so I can learn how to best help her when she's having a hard time.

When we stopped in Salt Lake, she was able to spend time with Hannah and they talked about their similar beliefs and some of their familiar traumas, and she did the same with Emma in San Diego. I think it was really healing for her to see she's not alone.

Izzy starts college in two weeks, so she's moved into the tiny one-bedroom apartment Elli and I were sharing, and the lack of space is getting on everyone's nerves, so we've been looking for a new place.

It's not an ideal situation to live with Elli's little sister, especially since we're still in that lovey-dovey honeymoon stage, but I know Elli feels better knowing she can help Izzy while she starts this new life journey.

She'll just have to learn to be quieter when she comes.

We're in downtown San Marcos looking at a quaint three-bedroom apartment that's close to Ernie's and Toasted Bean, and has plenty of space for the three of us. The third bedroom would be set up as an office space for Elli to work and for Izzy to do homework, which would make everyone's lives easier.

The floors are all a dark hardwood and the walls are pristine white. The kitchen has a big island and stainless steel appliances, and the bedrooms are all very spacious. There's two bathrooms, one in the primary bedroom, and one in the hall, which is nice because then we don't have to try and share the bathroom.

"What do you think, Wes? Is this our new home?" Elli says, spinning in a circle in the primary bedroom.

I step towards her and wrap my arms around her waist, pulling her closer to me. "Home is wherever you are, baby. But yeah, I think this place is it. We should really test out how soundproof the walls are though."

Elli smacks my shoulder and tries to get out of my arms, but I pull her in closer and place a kiss on the tip of her nose.

"I think we better sign the lease and put the deposit down soon so no one snatches it up." She starts texting Izzy about the place we found, and that we're going to put a deposit down on it.

"Sounds good, baby. We've got to get to Ernie's for family breakfast though, remember?"

I've been keeping a secret from her.

When we got back to San Marcos, I told Jess that I wanted to propose to Elli, but I needed her help with a ring. She got all teary-eyed and told me she already had the perfect one. She went to her room and came back with a worn, red velvet box and when she opened it up, there was a simple gold band with an oval shaped diamond in the center. I recognized it immediately as my mom's engagement ring. I thought she had sold it when she got back into drugs, but Jess told me my mom made her hold on to it so she couldn't sell it. She wanted me to have it for my future wife.

I had the ring cleaned and resized to fit Elli, and I got it back yesterday. Just in time for family breakfast.

What Elli doesn't know is it won't just be Claudia, Ernie, Luke, Jess, and Izzy, like usual. Matt, Robin, her partner Pine, Savannah, Drew, and Sean will all be there too.

As we head down the street to our favorite little diner, Elli talks about all the furniture we'll need to buy for the new place, and all the ways she'll want to decorate it with Izzy. I'm listening as best as I can, but my heart is thundering in my ears the closer we get.

I don't think she'll say no, but there's that little niggling voice in the back of my head that keeps telling me it's too soon, even though we've been together over a year.

The bell above the door chimes as we enter, and Elli freezes when she sees everyone standing around waiting for us.

"What is everyone doing here?" She mumbles to me, but before I can answer, Robin is squealing and running towards us.

"Oh my god! I'm so excited for you two! Congrats!" Robs rocks Elli back and forth before moving to me.

"How does everyone know about the apartment? We *just* saw it a few minutes ago." Elli's eyebrows furrow as she tries to make sense of Robin's rambling.

"Apartment? I'm talking about-"

"Robs, lovely, come over here and let Elli breathe." Pine says, dragging a reluctant Robin away from Elli.

"What's going on, Wes?" Elli demands.

"I wanted to wait until after breakfast, but since someone is bound to spoil the surprise," I pull a velvet bag out of my pocket and drop to one knee.

Elli gasps.

"Elli, you came into my life like a beacon of light. You quickly smashed every carefully laid brick in the walls around my heart and you are the most important person in my life. You have loved me- flaws and all, and you have shown me what it is to be truly loved. I can't imagine my life without you. I love you endlessly. Almost a year ago, I gave you a ring to wear with my initial so everyone knew you were my girlfriend. I promised I would replace it someday, and I hope to do that today." I open the box and Elli gasps again.

"Elliana Louise Monson, can I put this ring on your finger and call you my fiance? And someday, call you my wife?"

Elli nods her head, rapidly repeating "Yes!" and I slide the ring on her finger, then stand and kiss her like I need it more than I need air to breathe.

Everyone crowds around us in congratulations, and I can't help but tear up at the abundance of love in the air. Everyone important to me that can physically be here is in this room, and I'm so damn lucky.

Who would have thought that the girl I didn't want to go on a date with would end up being my wife?

THE END

Acknowledgements

This book could not have been written without the support from my best friend, my biggest supporter: my husband Janson. Janson has made sure I have ample time for writing, has read every revision, and has answered the question "Do you really think I can do this?" with an enthusiastic "Yes!" more times than I can count. He's been here through the tears of frustration and the tears of happiness, always ready to get me my favorite snacks to celebrate or commiserate.

This series was inspired by my cousins, Megan and Maddy. Completely independently, we somehow found ourselves dismantling the belief systems we were raised in. Without our relationships, and without having them growing up, this series probably wouldn't exist.

My late grandpa always told me my stories were meant to be heard, and even though he probably didn't mean it in the capacity of a spicy romance novel, he still inspired me to write.

A big shout out to my beta readers, Chelsy and Lexi, who gave me amazing feedback to help make this book what it is.

To my ARC Readers, your support brought literal tears to my eyes. Thank you, thank you, THANK YOU for wanting to read my silly little story.

I have to acknowledge the Tumblr and AO3 community. Specifically, Eddie Munson fanfic writers. In the midst of deep postpartum depression, I found comfort in series and one shots written for a fictional character. Those inspired me to start reading romance novels again after not picking up a book for almost ten years. That sparked my own creativity again.

And finally, I have to give a shout out to twenty-three-year-old me. She made one of the hardest decisions ever to leave the church she was raised in and was taught was the only true church on earth. She had no idea that leaving would be the best thing that happened to her and her family.

ABOUT THE AUTHOR

Daisy Wren lives in the Utah Valley with her husband and three kids. When she's not writing her next book, she's reading, cooking, and spending time with her family. Daisy's love of writing has been prominent since childhood, and she's always felt a call to share her stories. A hopeless romantic since she first saw The Phantom of the Opera at age eight, she's been writing her own love stories ever since. Daisy is a former member of a high demand religion and hopes to bring light to the issues of the church she was raised in, while also telling beautiful stories about life after leaving. Please visit her at www.DasiyWren.com, or on social media for updates about upcoming releases and for bonus content!

Tiktok: @daisywrenauthor
Instagram: @daisywrenauthor
Threads: @daisywrenauthor